THE CHILDREN OF SKAAD

Book Two - The Sunstone Saga

Nicolin Odel

CONTENTS

This story includes scenes of.

Abuse

Alcohol

Attempted rape

Blood

Bones

Death

Drugs

Gore

Kidnapping

Murder

Miscarriage

Profanity

Pregnancy

Slavery

Sexual Content

Violence

War

Chapter One

FLEDGLING

"Please! I beg you! Give me more! I must have it!"

"Such a thirsty girl you are, my little fledgling." The man extended his black-gloved hand through the iron bars of the cage. The faint orange glow of a candle cast lines of a shadow upon her hunched figure within.

Grasping the hand, she inhaled the jet-black powder sharply through her nose, out of the outstretched palm. A ripple of pleasure tingled through her head and down her arms, chest, and legs. She felt the sensation reach every nerve of her body. She steadied herself on the cage's bars as the soothing warmth overcame her. A ripple pulsed from her, and every footstep against the stone floor echoed magically within her.

After a moment, she weakly moved to the side, laying her head down, resting on the soft skin of another pale, naked young woman. *Who is this?* The touch of the skin-to-skin sent an electrifying pulse through her once more. Her eyes widened in pleasure for a breath. Yet the other woman lay sprawled out in unconscious, lethargic bliss.

The two young women found themselves in many delicate crimson and violet silk pillows and sheets that made up the berth they now called home. Deep maroon silk curtains draped the sides of the large, circular bird-like cage.

Everything around her was sinking into a faint haze. Her concentration slowly slipped away.

"Be a good little fledgling and sleep now."

She closed her eyes, letting the heavy cloak of enjoyment overcome her as the man's steps faded into the distance.

A rap on the bars brought her to wakefulness.

"Get up!" a stern woman's voice barked.

She groaned and rolled over. The curtains screeched as they were pulled aside, metal scraping on metal. Sunlight flooded the chamber. Her head throbbed painfully as she placed her pale, freckled arm over her eyes to block out the light.

"Both of you! Up!"

More banging on the metal bars.

Ears ringing, she heard the fiddling of lock and key, the squeak of the cage's old hinges as the iron gate was opened.

Someone grabbed her and jostled her to her feet. She wearily opened her eyes, squinting at the bright light. *Where am I?* She watched a man dressed in a plain grey tunic and trousers usher her cellmate out of the cage. Everything came slowly to her, like a fog suffocating her consciousness. She could scarcely tell when she was also involuntarily forced to join them.

Nausea welled in her gut, eyes still not adjusting to the light. She could make out the form of a woman standing before them, clothed in a clean white, almost *blinding* robe.

"Put these on," the woman ordered sternly.

Some rough fabric was thrust into her midsection; she made no effort to grasp it, her hands hanging loose at her sides. The clothes fell to the floor.

A thin whistle sounded through the air.

Then, *pain*. A burning bite on the bare skin of her thigh. It pulled the haze away momentarily, and she could focus on the person before her. The woman was wearing a bright pendant that drew her eye. Silver inlaid with multi-colored gems—*Or are they marbles?*—circling a sizable obsidian stone. There was a flash of movement in the blackness of the stone. The woman's face was stoic, age lines beginning to form. She held a young green willow branch, arms crossed, waiting intently.

"Pick it up," the woman said flatly. Standing tall, back straightened, she had a regal grace about her. Her light brunette hair was tied back in a bun, greying slightly. Her white robes were trimmed in silver.

The girl wavered, nausea overcoming her, and she was near to vomiting at any second. Another swish cut through the air, snapping against her other thigh. She keeled over, the sickness disappearing in pain, onto her hands and knees, looking down at the simple brown robe. Trembling, she grasped the garment. Slowly, *precariously*, she pulled it over her head.

Her counterpart slowly followed her lead. Finally getting a blurred glance at her cellmate, she saw that the young woman had wavy ebony hair reaching down to her buttocks, covering her face and breasts in a mess of tangles.

The cellmate partly bent over to pick up the robe, and a burst of bile spewed from her mouth, soiling the clothing before her.

"Put it on," the white-robed woman ordered.

"But—" the black-haired girl started. Her bright blue eyes looked horrified.

Another swish and crack across the raven-haired girl's shoulder caused a yelp and a whimper. Finally, she stood, dragging the vomit-soaked robe over her head while tears ran down her cheeks.

"Good," the switch-wielding woman said as she approached the young black-haired girl. Grabbing her chin in hand, she examined the girl's face. Her hand traced down the girl's neck and along the shoulder on which she had just inflicted the wound.

Her cellmate flinched.

"Pretty girl. Though you would do well to miss a meal or two. Nevertheless," the woman cleared her throat. "I am Aerie Proctor, Chanel de Montrichard. You will both be under my tutelage for the indefinite future." She turned on her heels. "Follow me," she ordered as she briskly strode away.

She was shoved forward, stumbling and catching herself in time, almost falling onto the flagstone floor. She tried to take in her surroundings. The grey flagstone continued up the walls into a dome-shaped ceiling. Five large window openings leaked sunlight into the chamber, with wooden shutters swung open. As the group approached, massive solid oak double doors loomed.

The Proctor waved a hand, and the doors groaned outward with their weight.

What is this place? How in Teras's name did she do that? Magic? Wait. Who is Teras? Suddenly, something familiar stirred within, and she recollected the earth answering her, that sensation of people's footsteps around her. Streams of sand once dancing at her beck and call. *Who am I?*

She felt the impacts of each footfall of those around her on the cobblestone path they now traversed. The track led them into a sprawling green garden. Bright patches of many-colored flowers scattered over the turf, Large crooked trees, a canopy blooming pink and white. The path continued to the edge of a thick forest as they came to a t-intersection before the dense part of the woods; they turned to the right-hand way.

Her mind was becoming more transparent, yet everything felt distant. *What am I doing here, and where am I from? What is my name?* Other sensations surged through her, pushing the thoughts away. Hunger and thirst. Yet not merely for food and drink.

It was a thirst for the warm, relieving sensation that the black powder maintained. The girl's mouth began to water as she swallowed against the yearning. The need overcame the compelled silence. "When do we get more of that powder?" she asked eagerly. "Is that man dressed in black coming back? Proctor?"

The proctor stopped abruptly and turned her head to eye them before saying, "This is your first and final warning: do not speak until told to do so." The proctor continued forward.

The girl glanced momentarily at the black-haired young woman, her cellmate; their eyes met briefly before they were shoved again and forced to keep walking. The sunlight hurt her eyes. Aching pain began to form behind her right eye as her nausea and vertigo came in waves. The discomfort crept back into her head and neck.

They followed the woman until they found themselves at another structure, almost identical to the one they had recently departed. It was a rounded cylindrical construction with a domed roof similar to a squat grain silo. *Or a bird's cage.* There were no windows on this building, but the same solid double-oaken doors stood tall. Again, the doors swung outward with invisible force at the Proctor's wave of her hand.

The group strode into darkness. Then a flicker of torchlight blinked into existence, then another and another. One by one, a long hallway was illuminated. *This could not fit in the dome structure we had seen from the outside.* The hall stretched on and on. It seemed like an eternity as they walked.

Finally, the smell of something delicious caught her nose. Freshly baked bread, roasted potatoes, garlic, and herbs. They came to a simple door that could easily have been missed on the left side of the hall. The proctor pushed the door open slowly, by hand, for a change.

The smells drifted over the mind-blanked girl. She stared at the simple, long wooden table laden with vitals. Warm bread, smoked ham, juicy sausages, and a massive pot of steaming vegetable stew. She pushed past the Proctor, half expecting a swat of the willow switch, but nothing came. She dug in, and the ebony-haired girl soon joined her, devouring the food.

"One cannot retain information on an empty stomach, I find," she heard the Proctor state behind them.

She ignored the words, focusing on the feast before her, stuffing the salty smoked ham into her mouth.

"Enough. Your bodies will reject the nutrients if you gorge yourselves now."

She continued eating.

A loud *crack* swatted against the table next to her hand.

Still, she continued eating.

This time, the willow switch cut down her shoulder. She arched her back and clenched her teeth, desperately ignoring the pain, deliberately raising some gravy-soaked bread to her mouth. Another wicked burning sensation tore at her back. Her mind became clear and more precise with the pain. She felt something cool begin soaking into the fabric of her back. She took a bowl of stew in her hands, shakily bringing it to her lips, scooping the vegetables into her mouth with her fingers. The taste seemed familiar to her. Another whip cut against her.

"Enough of this; take her away!"

It tastes just like...just like my mother's stew. My mother...Brena!

Hata Vasara, daughter of Brena, and Baal Vasara, weaver of the earth, named the Sunstone by her Shepherd's Eye companions, *screamed*. The ground rippled around her, sending a shockwave in all directions. In terror, the black-haired girl fell from the bench and ducked under the table. The two grey-clad men moved towards her but were knocked off-balance and had to steady themselves on the walls of the small chamber.

The shockwave parted around where the Proctor stood. The stern woman was undaunted as she casually lifted a hand.

Suddenly, Hata could not breathe. She tried to suck air into her lungs, but nothing came as she gasped and pulled at her neck.

The proctor stood tall, staring at her, one hand extended forward.

Black spots formed in Hata's eyes, and then her vision darkened as the two men in grey moved toward her.

Chapter Two

MOTHER

I have never killed a man before, Simon Meridio thought as he knelt, staring down at the dead man dressed in golden armor. *I have never watched life fade from someone's eyes. Never thought that I would be so apathetic about it.* However, there was a slight relief that he had finally avenged his father Yakeb's death. *Yet why do I feel so empty?*

"What have you done?!" a woman shouted at him. With her same soft brown skin, dark eyes, and Xamidian heritage, she was nearly the spitting image of his wife, Saudett, only older.

"Mother? Is it truly you?" Saudett's voice confronted the newcomer.

"Where did he take her!?" another woman cried in despair, her long blonde hair stained dark with blood, draping low around her blackened, gore-soaked armor.

A massive, red-bearded bald man slammed his bloody fist into the rock wall of the cavern, muttering, "Tytär...my daughter."

"What is this? What do you mean, 'mother'?!" Yet another familiar woman called out as she limped into the cave, supported on the shoulder of a hooded Xamidian man. The man dragged a long-curved scimitar in his free hand.

Is that Kiana Ahmadi? I thought she was dead.

Naurr Andiges, Simon's burly Tulu construction foreman, knelt silently nearby, praying.

Chaos. Complete chaos. Everyone yelled back and forth amid the massacred bodies of helpless women, children, and elders. The Hasieran people, the non-combatants, tried to escape into this cave—only to be trapped inside as the Daanav, demons from another Lân, had their fill of them.

This cave that I excavated with my crew of workmen. I was supposed to carve this cave as an escape path for these very people in the event of the Daanav's attack on the valley of Hasiera. The blood of so many innocent people. *On my hands.*

Luckily, Simon's construction workers had ushered many people into the tunnel to the mystical gateway they had found. Then, the men barricaded the entrance behind them. *Thank Hettra for their quick wit.* Simon himself had been exploring the tunnel, unknowing of the attack on Hasiera at the time. He bowed his head in disgrace.

An older man strode calmly past the throng of people and knelt next to Simon, his violet eyes catching Simon's gaze. *Violet irises, like Kiana's.* Those eyes focused on the body of the man at Simon's knees. The one whom Simon had killed with the help of his newfound powers. The body of the First Otsoa of Hasiera. *I do not even know this dead man's proper name.*

"You did this?" Rojas the Keen, Thirteenth Otsoa, the violet-eyed man whispered.

"I did."

"Have you reason?"

"He murdered my father in Dagad. A helpless old engineer. He killed him for no gain but for his own pleasure. I am not apologetic for this killing, and I will accept the consequences."

The man bowed his head slightly; he was perhaps in his sixth decade. "I am grieved to hear this. Gidraltar tended to let his rage overwhelm him."

"Gidraltar?" Simon asked. "That was his name?"

"Yes. Gidraltar Lein. The First Otsoa of Hasiera. He came upon this oasis in the desert as a boy. Gradually, he built it up with the outcasts of the world. It was a place for those who had no home. He took anyone in, from beggars to bandits. Deformed or mutated, the sick and the dying. Dishonored nobles and peasants alike."

"Shall I regret my decision then?" Simon sighed heavily.

"No. We always look forward to the future; that is the Hasieran way. Your act was in answer to what he took against your father. It is done."

Simon exhaled with relief, slouching visibly into a more relaxed state. He had half expected this man to drag a dagger across his throat at any moment.

Those violet eyes studied him as Rojas said, "Hasiera is yours, First Otsoa."

Simon's mouth fell open. "What?!"

Saudett looked into her mother's eyes, and there was no doubt in her mind. She remembered the woman's face. The mother who had disappeared all those years ago, when Saudett was some twelve summers old.

The woman stared back at her, eyes wide in shock.

"Mother? Is it truly you?" Saudett asked in disbelief.

Tears came to her mother's eyes, along with a slow nod.

Kiana Ahmadi appeared just behind her mother. "What is this? What do you mean, 'mother'?"

Saudett heard Kiana's words. But they did not reach either her or her mother.

"I am so, so sorry, my sweet Saudett," her mother said shakily, taking a step toward her. "I know you can never forgive me. Leaving you is the one thing I regret most in this life."

My mother's name? Anora. Yes, Anora Kafilah. That was her name. Saudett thought of the moments from her childhood, those fleeting junctures she had known of her mother. Short visits before the woman would depart again with another caravan to protect. They were always brief, yet, for the most part, she had fond memories of those times her mother was home with her. Anora had put her whole being into those moments. Saudett took a step forward. *My mother.* Those flashes of motherhood strengthened Saudett. Memories of being held in Anora's arms while she told stories of her travels.

"Why? Why did you—" The words caught in Saudett's throat. "Why did you leave me?"

"I had no choice," Anora stammered, taking another step forward. "Please let me explain."

Saudett recalled the nights when her mother gently kissed her forehead and whispered, 'Farewell and fair night, my sweet Saudett.' The times her mother had told her how much she loved her.

Tears rolled down Anora's cheeks.

Saudett's own tears tickled her face. She remembered when they had snuck into the cellar for a late-night bite and into the garden. The sound of hurried fumbling with the lock on the gate at the back of the estate. *My father.* Saudett stopped moving forward and asked, "What happened to Father?"

Anora's face went cold. "He is dead." She paused for a long moment, visibly taking deep breaths. Finally, she whispered, "I killed him."

Saudett stood in shock. She studied the woman before her, trying to picture her father's face. Just the shadow of a figure came to her mind's eye, an abrupt taciturnity and irritation emanating from him. "Why did you kill him?"

"I hated that man. I *loathed* him. He demanded a son and took me from you when he did not receive one. I wanted to stay with you, raise you, and watch you grow. He is the reason I was never there for you."

"For *you* are such a caring and warm-natured mother," Kiana jeered.

Anora turned to look at Kiana. "I am! I care for you, Kiana, but I was hard on you because the Burning Sea is a brutal place to live, and Hasiera needs strong Otsoa. I admit I did not raise you as I would have my first child because I had learned that the world is unforgiving. I did not raise you as I would have in the comforts and safety of Xamid. The situation was drastically different."

"You could have simply spoken to me!" Kiana's voice strained as she pleaded. "You could have talked to me as a mother does to her daughter. About your past, about this woman!" Kiana angrily waved a hand at Saudett. "Your first daughter, whom you so regret leaving, to be replaced by me. The second-hand one. You have told me nothing about who you were before coming to Hasiera or even how you got here!"

Anora looked back and forth between her two daughters, her eyes full of sorrow. "I have made so many mistakes with you both. I am an appalling mother. I did not fight earnestly enough to stay with you, Saudett." Anora paused momentarily, gazing at Saudett, then turned her eyes back to Kiana. "And I let the years of anger grow and took it out on you, Kiana. I don't think I know how to love." She sat down, placing her head in her hands, covering the two grey streaks in her otherwise midnight-black hair.

Saudett could not take it any longer; she closed the distance to her mother. Kneeling down, she wrapped her arms around the woman.

Anora's arms returned the embrace.

"Oh, Mother," Saudett whispered. "I'm truly grateful you are alive." She pressed tighter, letting her tears flow. "I have a mother again! I've missed you so much."

Anora wept, nodding her head into Saudett's shoulder.

Saudett looked up to see Kiana glaring at her, a flash of burning ember in her violet eyes. Saudett did not get on well with Kiana. *Should I ask her to join us? She is my little sister, after all.* She was about to when Kaplan Mir, the Shepherd's Eye soldier who had accompanied them on their journey to find Simon, walked to Kiana's side and put a hand on her shoulder, leaning in and whispering in her ear. Kiana's violet eyes closed as she turned and embraced Kaplan.

After a long moment, Saudett released her embrace on her mother and took in her surroundings. The bloodied cave interior was a whirlwind of emotions. Saudett saw that Brena Vasara was holding her husband Baal's head to her chest while trying to calm him, as he kept repeating, "My Hata, tyttäreni." His dripping fists added to the pools of blood.

"I swear we will find her," Brena's voice turned into a hiss. "*I swear it*, my mountain,"

Their daughter, Hata Vasara, had vanished into thin air when a mysterious black-clad person appeared and grabbed her. A blinding light had blasted the onlookers, and the man and Hata were gone. All this happened after Simon had a sudden burst of magical ability against the man dressed in golden armor.

What is happening? If not for Hata, I would never have come to find this place, to find my husband. A few months back, Simon had been stolen from her when their village, Dagad, was attacked by these nomadic raiders, the Hasieran, on the western edge of the massive desert called the Burning Sea. Saudett had recruited some of her Shepherd's Eye brethren, the military institution of Dagad, along with the Vasara family and their daughter. Hata had been instrumental in finding Simon because she recently discovered that she could manipulate the earth and sense people who strode atop it.

Simon stood up abruptly from where he knelt before the man he had killed: the man Simon had somehow pinned to the earth with an invisible force and poured sand down his throat to watch him die.

What happened to you, Simon? Saudett was shocked he had killed the man in such a manner.

"Come now, everyone. At the very least, let us vacate this chamber; it is no good for anyone's state of mind," Simon stated as he moved toward the cave entrance.

No one protested. Slowly, each person—some weary, some woeful, some with mixed feelings of newfound happiness—moved out of the cave, into the now bright-burning light of mid-morning day, into the tattered and torn oasis gorge, into the former sanctuary encampment, the Valley of Hasiera.

CHAPTER THREE

ROSE

"Wake up, little fledgling. I have something for you that will make all the pain go far, far away."

She blinked her eyes open. Cracks of sunlight filtered through the slightly ajar shutters, piercing into the darkened chamber.

The man in black and gold robes stood at the bars of her cage, his hand outstretched, a wicked grin on his goateed face.

Her eyes widened, and she began to salivate. She scrambled over to the hand and inhaled deeply, feeling the pain drain out of her immediately. She groaned in relief. *Thank the Gods...where am I?* She shook her head, trying to remember. *Why am I here again? I had eaten something.* She couldn't remember anything before waking up in this damned cage. *But why do I care? As long as I get more of that incredible powder.*

The man removed a glove from his hand, his palm caressed her cheek, and one finger touched her temple. "Forget the past, my handsome cardinal."

The questioning thoughts faded away as she basked in the powder's warm sensation. All she felt was the clammy touch of the man's hand on her face.

"Stubborn bitch," Chanel de Montrichard cursed aloud. "Could they not have left this Vouri miner in her god-forsaken cave?"

"The Vouri are a proud people," a man answered.

She turned to see Ebras Corb sauntering down the cobblestone path toward her. The man seemed to know everything that happened in the secluded Convent Enclosure. *How could the bastard have heard that?* "Alpha," Chanel answered, giving him a most sarcastic smile.

"Come now, Proctor, do cheer up. You should have a truly boisterous time breaking this one."

Ha. Shattering a young woman's will. Breaking their identities, molding them into powerful soldiers of servitude. It is never boisterous. On the outside, she grinned devotedly. "I must admit, she will be a challenge. Most give in after the second day."

"This one is exceptionally talented with the earth element. Like the element she is attuned to, so is the will of the Vouri. Solid as stone. I've fogged up her memory as best I could, but please try to stay on task. Her storm will erupt with unfathomable rage if anything reminds her of her past life in these early days. I felt her anger from my tower in Nidhaut, you know." Ebras smiled wickedly. "I came as quickly as I could."

"I'm sure you did." Chanel bit her tongue. *You disgusting bastard of a man. That poor girl.* "At any rate, she will be broken. I've trained countless young ladies to run off in servitude on the front lines for Aurulan. Have I not proven myself yet? She will be ready to join the northern border patrols within a few months."

"Yet how many of those young sorceresses return alive?"

"Only the strongest are worthy of survival and granted the Primus' blessing to become true servants of the Aerie, Alpha Passeriform." She bowed low. "The rest are tools, destroying their enemies at the cost of themselves. It is our path."

The Alpha arched a brow at her. "I suppose you are correct; carry on, then. And just a forewarning, I will be dropping in daily to administer their fetters."

"My thanks to you, Alpha," she said with a bow. "Primus' favor to you."

He nodded, and a bright crack in the air appeared in the center of the intersection. A moment later, the light and the man were gone.

She shivered in disgust. "Sleazy goat fucker," she muttered after Ebras had vanished. Then, Chanel continued walking, taking the left-hand fork in the cobblestone road, away from the prison cell of the young ladies' living quarters. Gone from the Hall of Transition.

She took a vial from her pouch, dabbing a pinch of black powder on her long fingernail. A quick sniff.

She composed herself. When taken in moderation, *grit* benefits one's mental well-being. It helped her unwind, loosening her body and mind. Also, gifting one with a slight boost to magical potency. The doses Ebras gave the girls left them unconscious for the night and feeble-minded well into the next day.

It is a miracle that I can teach them anything as their cravings peak when the afternoon approaches. Eventually, the girls would become more tolerant of the drug and require even more to get any satisfaction from it. *I need to slowly reduce their intake and make them not depend on the grit so much.* Perhaps, even have them give it up by the end of her regimen. It was challenging to do when Ebras goat-fucker was managing it.

Walking briskly into a third cylindrical domed building, she freed the string of her tight necktie, and her robes fell about her feet. The obsidian pendant around her neck felt hot against her chest. It pulsed like a heartbeat. Gingerly stepping on the balls of her feet across the cold cobblestone floor, she crawled into the maroon and violet silk sheets of her bedding and placed the necklace on the bedside table. The massive four-columned bed had the safety of canvas curtains surrounding her. She lay down, breathing slowly. She was still tense and disgusted with what she was forced to do to the girls, day in and day out. *What I am forced to do to all the young women imprisoned at the Convent Enclosure.*

Another fingernail of powder appeared before her. *One more quick sniff won't hurt.* She inhaled sharply. Relief flooded over her, cutting herself loose from the thoughts of her deeds. Finding the need to relax further, her mind wandered to pleasant thoughts and stimulating ideas. The image of one of her handsome orderlies came to mind. *Luftan.* Her hand crept downward. After some *relaxation* time, she finally closed her eyes and slept.

"Hey! Rose!"

Someone shook her by the shoulders.

"Wake up, Rose."

She groaned and opened her eyes; it was dark. Her head was killing her, that pain flashing behind her right eye. She couldn't see anything but felt warm hands on her shoulders.

"Are you awake? Rose?"

"Rose?" She stammered enquiringly.

"Your hair, it's such a brilliant red. So, I decided to call you Rose."

"My name? What was my name again?"

"Hush." The black-haired girl touched a finger to Rose's lips. "Try not to think too hard. We can just call you Rose for now. Here, eat this."

She felt something pressed into her hand. A small loaf of bread. "How did you get this?"

"Never mind that...eat. Recover some strength."

Rose ate quickly, gobbling up the now slightly hardened bread.

"Thank you. Wha—what is your name, for that matter?" One eye squinting with the pain in her head, she studied the raven-haired girl as best she could. She had removed her vomit-stained robe and wrapped herself in a violet silk blanket.

"Joanna, but please, call me Jo."

"You remember your name? I feel like I should know my true name."

"Shush now; don't fret, Rose." Joanna guided her to the pillows, the silk blanket falling from Joanna's shoulders as she did so. She pressed Rose's head to her bare chest and gently stroked the back of Rose's hair. "Let's not talk about the past, which we cannot even recall. I know we are here now and must make the most of it."

Rose basked in the touch and scent of Joanna. She smelled...so soft. "You smell of wild sage and honeysuckle," she murmured.

Joanna's chest lifted Rose's head as she chuckled. "You are quite the romantic."

"Hmm?" Rose muttered, her mouth beginning to salivate again, her nose tickling with anticipation. "When is the black-robed man coming back? I hope he has more of that powder."

Joanna continued stroking Rose's head. "He came and went while you were asleep. He gave me half a powder dose, fondled me for a minute, and departed. Thank Hettra, he did not decide to go further than that."

"Further than..." Rose's head throbbed, and her mind went blank. She gagged and grasped at her head. "Did he do something to me? Why does nothing make any sense?"

"Shush now. Everything will be alright." Joanna drew soothing strokes down Rose's head and down her back.

Rose felt Joanna's arms tighten around her in an embrace. The woman's round, bare, pale white breasts pushed gently into her face. *Am I in the heavens? She is so very comfortable.* She returned the embrace to Joanna's waist, pressing against her. "Thank you," Rose whispered.

Joanna said nothing, calmly rocking Rose in her arms, back and forth.

I hope it never ends.

The shutters slammed open, flooding the chamber with bright morning light.

CHAPTER FOUR

TRUTH

The Valley of Hasiera was broken. The oasis was no longer a haven in the desert. Simon watched as people tried miserably to put the grey and tan canvas tents back together. Broken bamboo poles were piercing through the linen fabrics. The Hasieran hurried about, dragging bodies away, others covering the black stains of the Daanav corpses with sand. Survivors of the ordeal were handing out brown rice and yam curry bowls. Many were wounded, either moaning or unconscious. They were recovering after the battle. More still, dying where they lay, succumbed to their wounds.

A large group had formed a half-circle a few hundred paces from the cave entrance. People filed out behind Simon, the survivors who had taken refuge in the tunnel. The people stood awaiting as Simon and company made their way out. He recognized Mittal Gohra in his nomadic tan robes, which were torn and bloodied. Mittal had recently been promoted to Sixteenth Otsoa after Kiana Amadi had gone missing after a skirmish with the Daanav weeks earlier in the desert.

Simon saw the Seventh Otsoa, Howler Thien, crouched on all fours behind Mittal, fur matted in crusting dried blood—the red blood of their own and the visceral black blood of their enemies, the Daanav. Thien stood slowly, towering over them, as Simon's group approached.

"Builder. What say you? I smell death upon you." Thien's guttural, almost hissing voice was low and menacing. "I can smell undue amounts of death in that cavern you flee from. What say you?"

Rojas answered, "We have much to discuss, Howler Thien. Assemble the remaining Otsoa."

The Otsoa. The leadership of Hasiera. Two dozen men, women, and others oversaw the segmented encampment areas. Their Otsoak, their people, lived in these sections cordoned off by pathways throughout the more extensive valley camp. Each Otsoa, as far as Simon could tell, had a particular specialty, whether in warfare or other administrations.

"Find us a usable pavilion that is still able and large enough for many," Rojas finished.

"Wait!" Thien hissed loudly. "Where is the First? I smell that he entered that cave, yet he is not accompanying you. Explain yourself, Builder!" Thien leaped in front of Simon, fangs bared. "His scent is on you!"

Then, Simon sighed heavily and said flatly into the Volkinn's canine-like breath, "I killed him." *Volkinn?* A hybrid. Part wolf, part human. He could not determine whether Thien was male or female of the species. *That is obviously because the Volkinn species is of hermaphroditic nature. They are of both genders.* Simon blinked. *Skrull's hairy balls, how do I know that?*

Lost in thought, Simon recoiled as Thien threw their head back and let out an ear-shattering howl.

Thien raised their arms to swing them down toward Simon.

"*Lind,*" Simon muttered, clutching the white bone dagger from his belt, the blade that he had taken from the Gate. A bright white light shone in all directions as Thien's heavy blow came down atop a radiant barrier.

Jagged lightning arched up the Volkinn's arms, and they pulled away with a yelp. Reeling back, rubbing their arms where the energy had spread.

The smell of burned hair came to Simon's nostrils.

"What is the meaning of this?" Thien flinched back, questioning hoarsely.

"Howler Thein. Patience. Please. Let us gather, and we shall discuss all the happenings. Let us also eat, rest, and tend to the wounded. You know everyone here is in dire need of it." Rojas's calming words soothed Thien's bristling neck fur.

The light globe slowly faded from around Simon. "Indeed, I will explain everything that happened to me from the moment I entered that cave yesterday evening. I, in turn, need to know what in Skrull's hell happened out here since then."

"Come, the First's pavilion in the camp center has miraculously gone untouched during the clash. It is sizable for all the Otsoa to gather and more," Mittal Gohra said, suspiciously eyeing the newcomers behind Simon. With that, people murmured agreement and began to disperse.

Simon nodded to Mittal and began to follow. He stopped and turned to his wife, Saudett, gesturing her to his side.

She was still walking close to her newfound mother, but she smiled at him and made her way over.

He whispered under his breath as she leaned in close, as everyone was now following Mittal towards the tents.

"Congratulations are in order, my star. You found something else besides your charming, handsome, bygone husband on this journey."

Saudett smiled faintly. "I never could have dreamed she was yet alive. Alive and well. I had put her behind me long ago, thinking she was lost forever."

"Hettra's blessing; it seems some good has come out of all this anguish."

"Do you have any idea of what's going on?" Saudett glanced ahead to the backs of the three Otsoa—Mittal, Rojas, and Thien.

"This man, Rojas, claims I am the new leader of these people."

Her dark eyes widened as she shook her head in disbelief, nose rings jingling. "You? But why?"

"Perhaps, on account of the fact I murdered the First Otsoa. I did not think the Hasieran ranked their leadership by their ability to kill one another."

"What are you going to do? There is much to deal with." Saudett turned to look behind them at the two Vouri, the large man dragging his feet dejectedly. "I owe a debt to those two. I need to aid them in bringing their daughter back."

"Another quest for my adventuring wife?" Simon said mischievously. "Was it not a few weeks ago that we lived a peaceful life?"

"Aye; then you suddenly started spewing water from your mouth in bed," Saudett grinned slightly, but her face soon darkened. "In all seriousness, I owe Hata and her family everything and would not be here without them."

He nodded. "I will help you with that, my dear wife; it's the least I can do. They decided to join you in the foolish recovery of your poor, feeble husband." He smiled wryly, trying to lighten the mood.

She nudged him in the ribs. "Feeble indeed."

"Ouch!" he yelped too loudly as people turned their heads to look at them. "Ahem," Simon straightened up. "Uh, carry on, good people," Simon grumbled with a wave of his hand. As he waved, a translucent shock wave of force shot out of his hand. A few Hasieran walking ahead cried out in fright as they were flung to the ground.

"Oh, Skrull's sodden balls in my mouth!" Simon cursed. "My deepest apologies! I'm still getting the hang of this."

The people stared at him in shock and silence as they returned to their feet shakily. Others murmured at the spectacle. Noticeably, from then on, the crowd gave Simon a much wider birth as they continued into the camp.

"Husband?" Saudett's head tilted in that spousal way when she wanted something from him. "What is this newfound power, and is that trinket the source of it? You haven't taken your hand off it since the wolfman tried to eat you."

"Volkinn, if you will; they are neither he nor she."

"Of course," she said, then paused. "This dagger, then?" She guided Simon back to the topic effortlessly.

Ah yes, my star, she knows me so well. She is used to me getting sidetracked easily. Simon smiled warmly. "Oh, how I missed you so, my love. Yes, this old thing?" He patted the dagger. "I acquired it after a brisk swim through a depthless pool, drowning me in my dreams every time I closed my eyes. Plucked it out of a magical gateway and acquired knowledge that only seems to come to mind when the timing is pertinent."

She took his hand. "Well, it does make me worry a little less about you. I don't have to watch out for you so much if you have some means to defend yourself. Before all this, back in Dagad, I never worried about you. I never thought anything like this would happen. I figured we would continue with our relatively simple life together, you with your engineering and me with the policing of Dagad, working my way up the ranks." She looked down at her belly and guided his hand to touch it. "We were to start our own family there, in Dagad."

"We will still have our family, my star; the situation has just changed," he paused, pondering. "It has changed vastly. *But we*'ll make the best of it. Who knows, maybe even end up back in Dagad after all this?"

"We shall see. It looks like we have a long road ahead of us. And many paths to choose from."

"Indeed. Now, my dear wife, I haven't seen you in months; give your depraved husband another kiss!"

Saudett pulled away playfully, grinning slyly, but quickly leaned up and grabbed his face with both hands, pulling him down.

Qav's luck to be blessed with such a woman. As their lips parted, he trembled as his senses absorbed his wife's smell, taste, and touch. *By Hettra's tits, she is beautiful.* He had not seen her for months and longed to be alone and entangled with her.

He snapped back to reality as the groans of the wounded surrounded him.

Simon surveyed the area as they continued into the center of the valley camp. The stream, the source of the valley's abundance, was drying up. Where water once flowed, pools of muck lay still, and mud now cracked in the hot sunlight. The valley was doomed to die without this source of water. Simon feared that the people here would have to flee; the oasis would soon join the desert of the Burning Sea and become merely another dune in the ocean of sand. He saw the large patches of crops the nomads had grown that would soon wither and die away. The palm trees and bamboo leaves swayed slightly with a warm midday breeze—a sliver of peace in an otherwise painful time.

People watched as they continued through the ravaged encampment; Simon saw the despair on their faces. He sighed. *What have I done? Perhaps I could tamper with the Gate, connect it to another Lân, or something with a water source. But how?* That was how the Daanav made their way here, through the gateway.

He fiddled with the hilt of the white bone dagger. An image of a hand, not his own, resting on the black-green marble of the archway, a flash of light as the portal's surface rippled and changed colors ever so slightly. Simon shook his head. *This knowledge.* Since he had torn the dagger free from that marble stone of the gate and shut the Daanav out of the Earste Lân, his mind had become overfull. As if someone else's memories had suddenly flooded in.

"Simon?" Saudett's voice faded in.

He blinked. "Yes, my dear?"

"We await you."

Saudett was standing at the entrance to the large pavilion, holding the canvas open for him—once home to the First Otsoa of Hasiera, the man Simon had just murdered in cold blood. The leader of these people.

"Quite right." He ducked under the opening. His eyes adjusted to the lower light as gentle rays of sunlight peeked through cracks in the canvas above. Many people were cross-legged around a small fire pit in the center of the circular chamber. Hasierans hurried about, dressing wounds with clean linen bandages; many sat shirtless or in their under-wraps as they were tended to. One such nurse woman of Tulu descent rushed to

Saudett as she noticed them enter. He blinked again, realizing his wife was covered in blood, particularly on her legs.

The woman took a short knife and began cutting Saudett's leggings away.

"Skrull take you, woman," Simon scolded. "This should have been tended to hours ago; you risk infection!"

"I am fine," Saudett answered sternly. "Others need it more than I do."

"My dear wife, let the woman tend to you. I know you are stubborn, but you are no longer alone in that body."

Saudett grunted in reply.

The woman tending her was pulling Saudett's bronze scale skirt off. "Be having a sit down now." The woman pushed Saudett towards the side of the pavilion. "Here."

"Can I sit closer to—" Saudett started.

"Nay," the woman interrupted, having none of it, as she began tending to the wounds.

Saudett met Simon's gaze as he moved to the center of the area to join the Otsoa.

He noticed the two Vouri warriors had seated themselves near Saudett. He shrugged and sat down.

Rojas stood near the firepit, waiting patiently for all to be seated. A woven basket of flatbread was passed around. Rojas spoke once everyone had acquired a piece and had quieted down, silently chewing their bread. "The First Otsoa is dead!"

Chaos erupted in the pavilion:

"How can this be!"

"No! Not the First!"

"We are doomed!"

"Skrull, take us!"

"How did he die?"

Rojas raised his hands, motioning the room to fall silent. The room obeyed.

"The First Otsoa, Gibraltar Lien, murdered the Builder's father during the attack on Dagad. Simon's father did not resist; therefore, the murder was unjust. Simon bested the First in combat when confronted by the First at the end of the battle for Hasiera."

A clamor of shouting ensued:

"Hettra's cunt, he did!"

"The man can barely lift a hammer, let alone a sword!"

"It's not possible."

"Skrull's hell! He must have murdered the First as he was defenseless and weak after the battle!"

"He used magic! You saw how he guarded against the Seventh's attack earlier."

"SILENCE!" Rojas's voice boomed over the course. "Builder, care to defend yourself from these accusations?"

Simon stood nervously and patted his tunic and trousers before clearing his throat, "Ahem. Before I go into why and how I was able to best the First, let me explain exactly what happened from the beginning."

Murmurs from the crowd. Some nodded in agreement, while others scowled, staring fiercely.

"It all started the day you people took me from Dagad. It started with a dream." He left no detail out. He told them of the dream in which he found himself submerged in the underground pool, being pulled by invisible hands, always trying to swim upward and away from the pulling. In the most recent days, he had drowned every time he fell asleep.

"I couldn't handle it any longer," he sighed. "I desperately needed to do something about it, so I took my men into the cave when they should have been working on the escape route. The people who hid there were trapped because of me. They died because I was selfish and needed to purge the dream from my mind."

Murmured whispers rippled through the listeners.

"Thank Hettra, my good men rescued many evacuees in the tunnel. Still, too many helpless people died." *Skrull take me.* He paused as he cursed inwardly. "The children."

A woman wailed near the back of the crowd.

"Finally, we found the source of my dream. My foreman, Naurr Andiges, myself, and one other, Ilan Bronwen. Ilan died finding the chamber with the gateway. Fell from an underground pool suspended in the air and broke his neck; he died showing us the way."

More whispers through the gatherers, thumbs to lips in a gesture of thanks for Ilan's efforts.

"Finally, the dream became a reality. That same pool was here, and I was fully awake. At the end of the underground river that feeds the Valley of Hasiera. Instead of fighting, I let myself be pulled downward, only to breach the pool's surface below me." He told them of the gate affixed to the ceiling of a small chamber underneath the pool and the waters supernaturally flowing out from it and along the cavern's roof.

"The Gate. It was like a storm. One of the hulking Daanav tried to penetrate the barrier, and we saw its form fighting against the storm. I noticed this bone-white dagger jutting from a crack in the Gate's construction. My counterpart here, Naurr, could not see this dagger. Ultimately, I felt I had to pull the blade free. Upon doing this, the gate changed or closed; I am unsure. But I believe this Gate, this doorway, as you can see by the aftermath, was why the Daanav came to the Earste Lân. And closing it seemed to end their drive to destroy us."

"Aye, it was why they so desperately were set on slaughtering all of Hasiera," Kiana Amadi said, her violet eyes fixed on Simon. "I learned that the Daanav use these gates to traverse to other planes and worlds."

"How can you know this, Kiana Ahmadi? Did you speak to the Daanav?" Mittal Gohra rebuked, questioning her.

Kiana turned with a frown to Mittal. "Sixteenth Otsoa, Mittal Gohra! I challenge you for the rite of Sixteenth on the morrow's eve. We shall decide this."

"Mittal Gohra accepts your challenge, Kiana—" Mittal began.

"Why are you doing this?! Surely the Otsoa can be reworked, reorganized!" Simon interrupted. "Why? To risk the lives of two such strong individuals who are needed now more than ever?"

"This is the way of Hasiera, outsider!"

A chorus of agreeing shouts were directed at Simon.

"Peace all." Rojas once more took the floor in mediation. "The Builder is not accustomed to our ways; it will take time for him to learn. To take up the mantle of First."

"First?"

There was another chorus of shouts in disagreement.

"That is our way," others nodded.

"Are we not all outsiders?" Rojas called out. "Barring those born in the valley. You all were taken in from the world outside, under the wing of the founding First Otsoa, Gibraltar Lien. When you had nowhere to go, he took you in. He created the way of Hasiera; he was astute in upholding that path. But circumstance has changed our existence. If we do not change, we will die here and now of infighting, thirst, and starvation. We look not to the path behind us, only forward to the road ahead."

Silence fell on the gathering; then, one-person repeated Rojas's last words after a long pause. "Forward to the road ahead."

"Forward to the road ahead." Simon heard Anora and Kiana say in unison.

"Forward to the road ahead!" The call rippled through the crowd.

Rojas nodded and turned back to Simon. "Continue your story, Builder."

Should not this man, Rojas, be pronounced First Otsoa? Simon took a deep breath. "Ah yes, closing the gate to the Skaad Lân." He tilted his head curiously. *How do I know it is the Skaad Lân.* "Unfortunately, it also shut the way of the valley's only water source. This doesn't make much sense to me, as the Daanav struggled to break through the gate, yet the water was unimpeded. And why were they trying to break through from the other side and yet trying to find it on this side?"

The dagger of my flesh was causing malfunction in the Gate. The Daanav could break through slowly but were cast out into the desert.

Simon blinked heavily. *Dagger of my flesh?*

Everyone stared at him in silence.

"He is telling the truth," Naurr Andiges said.

Simon started; those were the first words from the man's mouth since they had trekked back through the underground tunnel to the cave entrance. Nodding at Naurr, Simon cleared his throat, "Thank you, my good man. At any rate, I need more time to think of a solution to this. Please, all of you, give me time. I will fix this. I will restore the Valley of Hasiera; I swear it on my life."

Some tense shoulders loosened, and more whispers flowed about the low-lit pavilion.

Simon scanned the onlookers; his gaze fleeted over the beautiful Kiana Ahmadi, her violet eyes regarding him steadily. *Gods, she is technically my sister-in-law. Even for the wife and I, with our open-minded relationship, that is a no-go.* He tore his own away from hers.

He then came to his wife, equally beautiful. The two women looked so similar, yet different. Saudett sat rigidly, bandages now wrapped around her wounded legs. When his eyes met hers, she nodded. Relief, comfort, and love churned within his heart. *No, she is far more beautiful.* That steadfast nature and fierce reassurance bolstered his confidence.

"From that point on, we made to leave the Gate behind for the moment and return to the surface. Here, we found disaster. We found the butchered people that I failed to protect. The First arrived soon after and went into a rage." Simon paused; he thought of lying about how he managed to kill the man, but the people had already witnessed his abilities during the confrontation with Howler Thien. He looked for Thien among the people. He found them huddled with others of their kind on one side near the pavilion wall.

"This dagger." He took the blade from his belt and held it high. "This dagger has granted me knowledge. A vast knowledge, almost as if another person's mind has merged with mine. Yet the knowledge comes more naturally when I am not grasping it. It comes to me when I think nothing of it." He paused again. "When the First Otsoa charged at me, I did not think about the magic I used to hold him to the earth; my only thought was vengeance." His voice became lower, *menacing*. Satisfaction poured through him. "Of slowly, *ever* so slowly, pouring sand into his gaping *fucking* mouth, letting him suffocate and *choke* on it."

The chamber burst into turmoil. Simon renewed the barrier of light as the Hasierans rushed him. W, weapons drawn. The lightning arches responded to the blows as blades fell upon the shield. Shooting up weapons and arms, blasting the attackers back. Simon stood, unmoving, unwavering. *So, this is power.* It did not seem to quell the anger and only further outraged the mob. They began throwing their bodies at the barrier. He felt the light quivering with each blow. *It was weakening.*

He heard a bellow.

Saudett, flanked by the two Vouri, battled toward him.

The massive bald man swatted through the crowd with giant fists.

The blonde woman's shield knocked people aside.

On the other side of the pavilion, Kiana Ahmadi and the Shepherd's Eye soldier were pushing through the throng.

Rojas and Saudett's mother drew their blades behind where Simon stood. He expected they would dispatch him as soon as the barrier fell. The magical shield continued to quiver. *It won't last much longer.*

Just as his wife's group and Kiana and her companion reached him, Rojas and Anora surged to his forefront. Their blades landed blows on the attackers, yet no blood was spilled. The two Otsoa were using the flats of their swords, moving swiftly. Simon was mesmerized by the fluid movements, the twirls, and spins as if locked in a mortal dance of death.

Kiana soon joined the two in the dance, her speed blurring, seemingly faster than her father and mother.

Saudett, the two Vouri, and the Shepherd's Eye formed a circle around Simon. The three Hasieran blade dancers held the front line. *The three of Hasiera themselves.* The attack faltered at this. The Hasierans own people were now defending Simon. It soon came to a standstill. Tensions were still high as the small group stared down the warriors of Hasiera.

Howler Thein moved to the forefront of the mob, flanked by a score of their Volkinn brethren. Simon thought the Volkinn would charge them at any moment, the fur around their necks and arms bristling. Yet Thien appeared relaxed, unlike their kin.

"We are all of us conflicted," Thien grumbled. "Builder, you saved us from the Daanav horde. Yet doomed us all to die. You killed our one true leader; you killed him without honor. The one who made Hasiera what it is today. The one who saved me…" Thein paused and gestured to their kin. "Saved us. Many years ago. The one who accepted us for what we are and gave us a home."

"Little was the First's honor as he took my father's head," Simon stated.

Thien nodded. "This is also a truth." They paused momentarily. "The greatest boon for you, Builder, is that Rojas the Keen stands with you. Had he not, I would have eaten of your flesh before night fell on this day."

Simon shivered as Thien's yellow-green canine eyes fixed on him thirstily. He looked at Rojas Ahmadi's stalwart back. "Surely, Rojas is more suitable for the position of First Otsoa? Is he not?"

"He is, or any other Otsoa here present," Thien answered.

"Wonderful!" Simon exclaimed. "Then I relinquish the title."

"You cannot," Rojas snapped.

"Hettra's saggy tits! This is ridiculous! The valley will be dead in a matter of weeks without water. What does it matter who is Otsoa at this point?"

"It is our way," Kiana said. "But again, Simon the Builder speaks the difficult truth. Does our way matter in the face of things to come? Perhaps we must adapt on this day?"

Thien gave a low, gruff grunt, looked from side to side at their flanking Volkinn, and nodded. Their furs slowly receded as they calmed. Thien crouched down and whispered, "We will listen."

The chaos had subsided for the moment as they settled into seated positions once more and began to discuss the fate of the people of Hasiera.

Chapter Five

PRIMUS

The routine began once more. Joanna and Rose were ushered out of the cage, and a new set of clean, simple brown robes was thrust into their arms. They quickly dressed themselves to avoid the stinging willow switch of the Proctor. A brisk walk through the garden, right at the intersection. Into the second domed structure, stop for a quick breakfast. *Breakfast is always cut short.* Continuing through the corridor, a long walk down a seemingly endless hall finally found them at the door to the Chapel of the Primus. To partake of the morning rites.

The chapel was small, with three simple oak hardwood kneeling pews in a semi-circle before an altar. There was no exterior light, only many candles covering the surrounding grey stone walls. Benches facing a golden-silver tabernacle in the icon of the Primus. A golden sun, curved hooked sunbeams wrapping the circumference like a bladed wheel. A silver crescent moon was atop one edge of the sun. A white eye-opening wide between the sun and the moon, partially covered by the crescent. The icon was held aloft by four golden rods atop a simple altar covered in white linen. They would kneel for nearly an hour, reciting the morning rite to the Primus.

Rose knew the ceremony off by heart now. Proctor Chanel de Montrichard began the rite each time, "Repeat after me. I accept the Primus as the creator of all beings. I accept the Primus as the creator of the Earste Lân. The creator of the Households of the Gods and those seated there. I accept the Primus before all other Gods, who are but servants to His will. The Primus is pure and absolute. Pray, I am ever blessed with his favor."

Following this, the Proctor would open a small book and read the day's sermon.

"The Nobleman met the wretched man while upon the road. The man was feeble and disheveled. 'Alms for a poor man, honorable sir?' the miserable man asked, grasping at the Nobleman's robe. The Nobleman sneered in disgust and kicked the wretched man in the stomach. 'Begone, vagabond!' the Nobleman shouted while continuing down the road. The wretched man squealed in pain, calling after the man, 'Heed my words! Your deeds this day shall not be forgotten!'

"Moments later, the Mason came down the road, accompanied by many of his children. 'Alms for a poor man, honorable sir?' The wretched man asked, grasping at the mason's shirt. The Mason laughed. "Look at this poor idler of people's honest work. Earn your alms the truthful way, beggar.' The children began to laugh and push the wretched man. The Mason and the children moved on down the road. The wretched man scowled after them, calling, 'Heed my words! Your deeds this day shall not be forgotten!'

"Then, a Queen and her royal entourage came, riding in jewel-encased carriages with mighty steeds. 'Alms for a poor man, virtuous lady?' The wretched man called out over the throng of people. The entourage ignored the wretched man, yet the Queen heard his cry. Signaling for the escort to halt, she stepped out and down from her private carriage to approach the wretched man. Taking the wretched man's hand in hers, the Queen guided his hands to pull one of many large, jeweled rings from her finger. The Queen did not speak; she returned to the carriage and waved the entourage forward. The wretched man smiled widely after them, calling out, 'Heed my words! Your deeds this day shall not be forgotten!'"

"It came to be that the Nobleman would be dishonored and exiled in years to come. He lost his entire wealth and became a beggar on the streets until his death, which would release him. 'Casio Skrull, repeat this man's life forever in your halls. Grant him suffering and death. Now, and always,' the Primus declared.

"It came to be that the Mason would lose his children, one by one, to sickness, to murder, to misfortune. Lastly, he lost his wife. In his despair, the mason gambled his life savings and, by luck, became wealthy. Yet he was unhappy and finally took his own life, which would release him. 'Met Qav, repeat this man's life forever in your halls. Grant him both fortune and misfortune. Have calamity engulf him. Now, and always,' the Primus declared.

"It came to be that the Queen would reign for hundreds of years, well longer than an average person's life. The Queen was loved by all her people. 'Alexandria Hettra, repeat this woman's life forever in your halls. Grant her all her comforts and desires. Now, and forever,' the Primus declared."

After the reading, there was a time of complete silence, all three women kneeling before the altar. The Proctor knelt in the center of the three pews. This time was meant for personal reflection on the story. Rose found her thoughts focused on the black powder, how long it would be until she saw the black-gloved man again. *How long until I will find pleasure and alleviation once more?* That sensation prickled her mouth and nose as she kneeled, fidgeting with her fingernails.

After an eternity, or so it seemed, the Proctor stood and moved in front of the altar, kissing the open eye, genuflecting, and saying, "Primus favor us." She then moved aside and motioned the two women to follow suit.

Rose watched as Joanna replicated the Proctor's actions. She did not want to do it; she had never heard of a Primus before, an all-knowing creator of the world. *All I remember is waking up in the cage. Why should I care to follow some unknown God's decree?* On the other hand, she did not want to be whipped again or be deprived of the black powder. She kissed the open eye; it was cold and tasted of metal. She knelt and said the words, "Primus favor us."

They followed the Proctor out of the small chapel room. Into the long hallway once more. After a further minute of walking, another door appeared on their right. This door opened into a study room of sorts. Only two plain wooden desks and small chairs were placed in a simple chamber, including a large window on the left-hand side of the room with an ocean view. *Today.* On other days, it would be a vast forest or a mountain range. Other times, a trickling stream or snow-covered garden.

After being seated, the Proctor would pinch them both on the shoulders while standing between them. Here, they would be schooled, learning about everything and anything. Each day was focused on a different subject. For example, today, they were learning which plants in the wild could be used for healing purposes in many regions.

"The ethel leaf plant is jagged-leafed, low-growing, and easily missed," said the Proctor. "An Aurulan native, primarily in the boreal forests stretching leagues in all directions from the capital city of Nidhaut. The grey-blooming creeping myrtle clings to the North Iron Belt cold mountain rock. Or, in warmer climates, the cooling aloe vera plant on the coasts of Xamid and the Isles of Tal'tulu."

Rose's eyes became heavy as the Proctor went on about appropriately mixing and infusing certain magical elements with the plants. They learned which herbs could provide healing properties or boosts in other senses, such as stamina or vision. Rose found herself struggling to retain all the information. Or paying attention, for that matter. Gods, it was dull. After the first hour of listening to the Proctor carry on about the perfect grinding technique for mortar and pestle, her eyes began drooping, her head bobbing, startling herself awake for a moment, then bouncing again.

Pain surged through her ear and cheek. Grasping her face, there was a ringing sound in her ear. She saw the Proctor standing before her with the willow switch, readying for another blow.

"If you fall asleep again," the Proctor said, "you will not find yourself in the comfort of your silk sheets tonight."

Rose glared at the woman, still holding her ear. "Why must I do this? Why am I here?"

"You are here to learn how to control your powers. You must also learn all aspects of society far and wide. You must be educated; you are no longer peasants, fumbling through life, wondering where your next meal will come from. But I warn you that you will go hungry tonight if you keep this up."

Rose glanced at Joanna; their eyes met, Joanna's head tilting slightly as if to say, *stop fighting it.*

"Still, Proctor. How did we get here? Nothing makes sense. I can't remember anything from before waking up here."

After a long moment of the Proctor studying her silently, she said, "Your memory will return. Eventually, I promise. For now, try to cooperate and stay attentive. One day, you may both be magi of the Aerie, advisors to kings and queens in all the lands."

Joanna sat straighter at those words, her blue eyes brightening. "Truly?"

"Undoubtedly."

I don't want to be an adviser, Rose thought. *I merely want to remember who I am.* Her head was beginning to throb again. She closed her right eye, which seemed to lessen the pain somewhat.

"Shall we proceed to practical training now, girls?"

"Uhm, can we have some lunch first?" Rose asked.

"You've already had lunch, for you awoke a quarter past the eleventh hour."

Rose's stomach grumbled.

"Furthermore, it is not good to physically exert oneself after eating. Provisions will be provided afterward. Come now." The Aerie Proctor, Chanel de Montrichard, raised the willow switch menacingly.

The two pupils scrambled out of their chairs and into the hallway.

Chapter Six

UNION

Simon lay on his back, the light beginning to dim through the soft tan canvas above, his wife cradled in the nook of his arm. Their bodies pressed together. Her head lay on his chest and shoulder, one hand gently tracing his bare chest. Her leg draped atop his own. *This is just like the morning of the attack on Dagad.* He took a deep breath of her short, raven-black hair. He released a long, satisfying sigh. "Gods, you smell delectable, my dear."

She tilted her head to look at him slightly, an eyebrow arched suspiciously. "Dear husband, why are you sniffing me?"

"I have longed for months to relish your presence; just let me have this."

With a small grunt, partly a snort, she smiled but said nothing.

Simon rubbed his hand along her back, resting on the cheek of her toned buttocks; he squeezed. "That was a long time coming," he murmured. They had finally had a moment to themselves. It was a quick, passionate moment. They were both exhausted after the events of the last few days and the lengthy discussions of the Otsoa. And still, the Otsoa had not agreed on a solution to their situation.

She groaned quietly in acknowledgment, her eyes now closed.

Rest now, my star. Simon's mind wandered back to the meeting.

"For the time being," Simon reiterated once again, "I would suggest we uproot and take refuge in either Dagad or the outskirts of Xamid."

"The people of Dagad will not take us," Kiana Ahmadi interjected. "We killed many of your kin and stole you away from them."

"We can make them see reason; they will come to understand," Saudett responded promptly to the woman. "We have some reputation in Dagad, after all."

"We are not welcome in the outside world; we are bandits," Someone called from the back of the crowd. "They think *we* are the monsters!"

Grumbles of agreement rippled through the gathering.

"What of the jungles to the south?" Rojas Ahmadi asked. "There would be some semblance of water and food available there."

"It would be a fresh start, that is certain." Mittal Gohra nodded. "Only the clothes on our backs and whatever we can carry."

More muffled agreement.

"The jungle is widely unknown and uninhabited from what I've been taught," Simon pondered aloud. "Though my brief and young geography studies of the Earste Lân were limited."

"It is a dangerous place," Howler Thien hissed. "We have patrolled near the edge. The smell of that place was heinous, surrounding us in a foul rank, a sickness. We did not aim to venture into such a place."

There was a moment of silence, soon accompanied by whispers of apprehension.

"Well," Simon chuckled nervously. "If that isn't in the least bit foreboding,"

"The jungle is a few days to the south," Rojas said. "We should send a small Pack to scout. Investigate the jungle, determine its safety and natural sustenance."

There were nods and murmurs of agreement.

Rojas continued, "It is settled then. We await the Pack's return. Ration what food we have, harvest anything we can before it is lost to drought."

"I would lead the Pack," Kiana said.

"You forget our contest, Kiana Ahmadi," Mittal stated loudly.

"I will finish you and set out within the hour of your defeat."

Mittal furiously sprang to his feet. "You will die on my blade!"

Kiana snorted.

"Arrogance does not befit the dance, daughter," Anora Ahmadi rebuked.

Kiana's glare turned frigidly toward her mother.

Rojas looked at his daughter steadily and smiled warmly. "You are *wounded*, daughter. Your mother will lead the Pack to the south."

"Thien will join you, Third," Howler Thien added ominously.

Anora nodded.

"The seat of Fourth Otsoa is empty, Kiana Ahmadi. Should you not cast your slate there?" A man that Simon did not know spoke up for the first time. He looked like many other plain-dressed nomadic peoples, with dark tan linens nearly black and a covered face.

"The seat is still warm, Ninth," Kiana retorted. "You would dishonor Gaspar Haytham's sacrifice?"

"Lass, you have no patience. You may assume the seat after the month of meditation on Gaspar Haytham's legacy."

Simon tilted his head. *What about the month of meditation for the First?*

"Shalasar speaks true. We must cast our ambitions aside in this dire time," Rojas added.

Kiana visibly withdrew at her father's words and stayed silent.

"First. Would you agree?" Rojas turned to Simon.

"Ahem," Simon coughed. "Yes, yes, of course, have at it. A sound suggestion!" He paused briefly. "A question, if you will, good people?"

Rojas nodded.

"Should this month of meditation not affect the First Otsoa's position?"

"Not when bested in one-on-one combat," Rojas answered. "Hence, my daughter's haste to combat Mittal Gohra and be done with the matter."

"Ah, I see. You are oh so knowledgeable and wise, dear Rojas." Simon shrugged inwardly; *it didn't hurt to try.* "Are you certain you don't want to relieve me of this title, Rojas?"

The room burst into roars of disdain, all concentrated on Simon.

Saudett's faint breathing soothed him. He let the tense minutes of the latter part of the gathering leave his mind. Rojas had once again managed to settle the crowd by dismissing everyone gathered and telling all present to get some much-needed rest. *Blast these people and their troublesome traditions. Rojas should be the First, without a doubt.*

There was another option he had not raised during the meeting. He could attempt to connect the portal to another Lân, a world that could once again supply the valley of Hasiera with life-giving water.

His free hand touched the dagger's hilt laid close by. He was reluctant to remove it from his person at all. Bubbling rage came to him when he thought of someone trying to take it from him. The knowledge this item provided him was extraordinary. Yet he could not control that knowledge coming to him only at certain times.

Truly fascinating. I need to go back to the gate, analyze it, and touch it. Try to sense something through it. Perhaps Simon could steal away tomorrow morning to inspect it for an hour before the turmoil began again. His wife had much-unfinished business here in Hasiera and elsewhere. Her newly-found mother, for one, and this Sunstone girl. *Hata was her name? I am dying to hear that tale.* He let his mind wander but soon eased himself into a deep, *dreamless* sleep.

Kiana Ahmadi lay on her stomach as Kaplan Mir's weight lifted from her. She had hurriedly ushered him back to her tent after the meeting had come to an unsatisfying conclusion. Kaplan Mir intrigued her, from the short story of his upbringing in Al'Jalif to his blunt, no-nonsense perspective. Their place in battle, side by side, the bond strengthening their attraction while fighting for their lives. *Together.* Protecting each other. Passion had overtaken them that night. *By the Primus, he was enthusiastic for his age.* She enjoyed it when a man took the lead like that.

She lay still as Kaplan left the pavilion, watching his muscled bronze back and round, dimpled buttocks disappear through the entrance flaps of the tent into the dark night as her eyes slowly shut. She did not want to move; she lay in euphoria...

...the morning sun began to seep through the canvas.

"The she-wolf is alive?" A clicking reptilian voice broke the silence of dawn. "She was in her death throes long into the night?"

Kiana blinked awake, rubbing her eyes, still half asleep.

Kogs, the small, red-maned lizard man about the size of a child, crouched nearby. He was staring at her intently. His green reptilian eyes occasionally blinked back at her with a silky membrane.

"Kogs? Where have you been?"

"Kogs hide from the she-wolf. Kogs afraid she blames Kogs for the masters' attack."

"Well, you did disappear when we finally arrived at my home. I thought you had betrayed us."

Kaplan groaned and rolled over next to her.

"The she-wolf shows Kogs that the masters lied to us. That they would hurt my precious Gaks. She-wolf promises to help Kogs get home."

Kiana nodded. *Oh, where to even begin? Especially with the current state of the valley.*

"Shall we investigate this gateway that Simon Meridio claims is the key to the Daanav world?" Kaplan grumbled as he pushed himself to a seated position. His solid, curly-haired chest, black with a hint of grey, and those taut arms looked very inviting.

Kiana wanted to leap back into his arms. For a man in his fifth decade, he was in peak condition.

"Otsoa?" Kaplan arched a brow her way.

"Uhm, yes. That is a swell plan. Let's break our fast, then head to the cave," Kiana answered quickly. She leaned over to whisper in Kaplan's ear, "I was hoping to have another go with you this morning."

His eyes twinkled down her body as he examined her longingly. "I am ready." He flung the thin linen sheet away to present his morning glory.

She grinned. "Kogs, can you give us a minute? I have more throes of death to bemoan."

"Why does the she-wolf wail so?" Kogs clicked, tilting his head.

"I'm simply enjoying my man," Kiana laughed and glanced at Kaplan; he did not seem to react to the comment. "Surely you, Kogs, and your mate Gaks enjoy lovemaking?"

"Lovemaking?" Kogs blinked. "You mean laying eggs? But does not matter. Kogs and his Gaks cannot lay eggs. Kogs and his Gaks are both male." Kogs raised the moss and plant-covered skirt that was his only garment. No penis lay beneath. He began to shake his head back and forth, his red-haired mohawk flopping from side to side. After a breath, two white translucent appendages emerged, short and stubby yet disproportionately large compared to his tiny body.

"Oh gods, I see. You can put that away now, Kogs." Kiana's urge to be with Kaplan was waning at the sight of Kogs's appendage.

"Kap-man put his away first!" Kogs hissed back.

"Skrull take me; I will never unsee that," Kaplan sighed, turning his head and sniffing. "I need a bath."

She glanced down to see the moment had passed. "It will be a long time before we have the luxury of a bath once more. Perhaps the jungle to the south will have a stream."

"It must, else it could not strive into such a landscape." He paused and scratched his beard. "On that matter, I agree that we should have led the scouting party."

"We?" Kiana asked, tilting her head. "You would follow me around as a mewling pup?"

"For I am yours."

Kiana's face warmed as she whispered, "And you are mine."

He nodded and looked at her with those dusky, somber brown eyes.

"KAH HA!" Kogs screamed. "You are mates!"

CHAPTER SEVEN

PRACTICE

The blast scorched against the earth wall Rose had summoned in front of herself only seconds before. She was sweating profusely, hands on the ground, holding the earthen barrier vertically with all the resolve she could muster. Even with the wall, the heat of the fire from Joanna's attack blistered around her.

"Prepare for another!" Joanna called out.

Rose ground her teeth while she focused on the wall before her and held onto the image. The second blast sucked the air out of her lungs, the heat surrounding her further. Trying to gasp for air, she desperately tried to keep the wall from falling. She heard a cracking sound as the fire still raged. *The explosion should have stopped by now! It is growing. It is pushing through! The wall is breaking!* One hand still to the ground, she raised her other, and another layer of earth sprang up before her. Rose screamed in agony. Her other hand left the soil. And she *pushed*. Pushed against the flame. Still screaming, the wall surged forward, and the heat dispersed.

"Rose, stop!" Joanna's muffled cry was barely perceptible.

Rose snapped out of it, releasing the attack. The wall fell into a crumble of dust and dirt inches from Joanna's feet.

"Hettra's mercy," Joanna laughed nervously. "I thought I was nearly through that impenetrable defense of yours this time. You proved me wrong yet again."

"Very good, both of you," the Proctor announced, clapping her hands to get their attention. Chanel de Montrichard looked at Joanna. "I suggest refining your blast to a single point against a barrier like this rather than the sphere of flame you used. Imagine the tip of a spear or harpoon boring through the wall."

"Yes, Proctor!" Joanna answered enthusiastically.

The Proctor turned to Rose. "A wall is a simple, versatile tool. It can be stretched wide and tall at the cost of density. It can be concentrated to a point. You could perhaps even form a hardened, deadly projectile by bringing the earth to a single focus point. Perhaps you could make it rotate, maybe cause it to create heat."

Rose frowned. An image of a lanky, stone-like black and molten beast, a single red eye boiling and staring down at her, came to her mind. A vision of the monster being attacked, pelted with hundreds of small projectiles, bursts of black spraying from the creature. The creature stepped forward, *reaching* for her.

Pain shot through Rose's eye, head, and neck. Grasping her head, she keeled over. Nausea gathered in her gut. *I cannot think straight.* Vomit suddenly filled her mouth and splashed onto the ground before her.

"Qav's luck, is it that time already?" the Proctor pondered nonchalantly.

Rose lifted her head slightly; Joanna looked slightly pale and green, one hand on her stomach.

"Come here, the both of you." The Proctor pulled a glass vial from her sleeve. The contents of which were pitch black.

Rose scrambled to her feet and hurried across the brown and yellowing grasses of the stretching plains they found themselves in, as far as the eye could see. The bright sun shone down on them. The only thing out of place was the door standing upright next to the Proctor awaiting them. *This door somehow connects this massive field to the Hall of Transition.* Rose fidgeted with her robe, waiting as the Proctor unstopped the small vial, holding it out to pour some powder. Rose put her hand out so the powder would fall on the top part. She inhaled the meager amount quickly. The headache began to recede nearly instantaneously.

Joanna repeated the action.

"Steady now, girls; this will hold you over before the Alpha administers your evening dose."

The girls nodded in acceptance. Rose's eyes met Joanna's. *Which one of us will have to please the Alpha tonight? Both of us?*

"Off to the dining hall now," the Proctor said.

Through the doorway and back into the long hallway, they quickly found themselves in the familiar chamber with the simple wooden table laden with provisions.

"Enjoy yourselves; I shall return within the hour." The Proctor closed the door behind her, and they heard keys turning in the lock.

"Using our magic is quite enjoyable," Joanna said as she stuffed some bread soaked in a soup of creamy potatoes and mushrooms. "Your powers far surpass my own, Rose."

"Is it so enjoyable?" Rose rebuked. "I would have been scorched to death if my wall had not been held. Your flames are far deadlier than soiling your clothing with a little dirt."

"Your wall would have crushed me, Rose. It was hard as stone."

"Possibly. I doubt it, though. Still, I find no fun in this. Why should I strengthen myself? To what end? Why should I study the outside world, yet I am locked in a cage every night?"

"You remember, the Proctor said they were preparing us to be sorceresses, advisors to kings, magi of the utmost standing. Do you not long for this?"

"No...I do not."

"What do you long for?"

"I long to remember *who* I am. Is this feeling not slowly scraping away at you? This tightness in my chest. How can you not want to know who you were before all this? Jo?"

Jo blushed suddenly and smiled faintly. "I believe that is the first time you have called me *Jo*. Thank you."

Rose unexpectedly felt her face redden as well. "Oh, um, is that okay? That is what you wanted?"

"Yes," Jo nodded. "This name is the only thing I hold onto from the past. This was my name before the cage. Something in me knew that. Yet I remember nothing else."

"I shall try to say your preferred name more often." Rose smiled at the fair-skinned woman. Her blue eyes, framed with dark lashes and eyebrows, were stunning. Her long black hair was tied in a high ponytail, still hanging halfway down her back. She was shorter than Rose by almost a head's length. *She is pleasing and soft in all the right places*, Rose thought yearningly. Something within her knew that she did not ogle men like this. The plain brown robes were tight and framed the women's hips and breasts like an hourglass.

"Ahem," Jo cleared her throat.

Rose realized she had been staring. *Gods, I'm an idiot.* Heat rose in her cheeks, and she hurriedly looked back to the table and clutched at the nearest food platter. A roast duck leg. She bit into the greasy meat.

"Rose?"

She looked back at Jo, the drumstick in mid-bite.

Jo had a finger to her lips in a shushing motion. "Do not let the Proctor become aware of your attraction to women. It is against the Primus's teachings."

Rose's bashfulness turned into a flare of fury. "Yet another shackle to my existence then! Am I not allowed to be attracted to anyone I want? Or find pleasure in anything other than the Skrull-forsaken powder? Are the Alpha's nightly *visits* aligned with the Primus's will? I won't take this any longer!"

Rose turned to the doorway in a fury. Focusing on the stone and mortar surrounding the wooden door, she reached out a hand and pulled. There was an explosion of dust and the sound of stone crashing down. The door fell forward with the rubble. She began to run, picking her way through the debris, knowing exactly where to step through the wreckage. *I feel it!* Her connection to the earth grew stronger.

"Rose! NO!" Jo's voice disappeared in her wake.

Rose ran out the door, to the right, towards the massive oaken entryway. She heard shouting behind her, yells from men, and Jo's voice. The hallway stretched on endlessly; minutes passed. *Far too many minutes.* She continued. *Where is the entrance? The massive doors?* The hall just kept going and going. The shouts were distant, at least. She stopped and turned to the wall beside her, placing one hand against the smooth quarry stone and closing her eyes. The wall was thick, nearly twenty paces. But she felt it; she felt the wall end and the earth stretching out far beyond it. She opened her eyes and stepped back from the wall.

Then she began to *pull*. Pull away large stones and mortar with her mind and into the hallway. Then, pushing them back down the corridor the way she had come. Shouts were becoming nearer. She kept pulling the stone away, and soon, she had created a new wall out of the debris. She had closed off the direction she had run from. The men had reached the other side, but they could do nothing.

Faintly, she heard Joanna's voice. "Stand aside, please."

The blast shook the hallway. *Jo is trying to melt her way through!* She saw the rock glow in a single place in the center of the rubble.

"Skrull's balls, she learns fast," Rose cursed, then turned and charged forward into her half-completed tunnel; she began to beat the air before her, the stone crushed inwards again and again. There was a sudden explosion of rubble, and suddenly, there was light.

Dim. Twilight. She found herself standing in the forest, the wall of the cylindrical building stretching up behind her. Without a second glance, she sprinted into the woods.

VERMIN

Saudett did not want to stand up. *If I do, I know I'm going to vomit.* She was unsteady and nauseous. Like the contents of her stomach were trying to crawl their way out. Simon entered the tent holding two bowls of warm lentil mince and a small stack of flatbread. She knew the food was good, but she felt like she could smell each individual spice, overpowering her.

"Thank you, husband, dear, but can you just get me something to drink?"

"Of course, my star. Very little water to go around. I can scrounge up some wine or goats' milk, perhaps?"

"The wine sounds splendid."

He set the bowls down gently, taking a piece of bread with him as he left to acquire the beverage. Saudett pushed herself to a seated position but soon crawled for the exit. Once outside in the hot sun, she circled to the side of the tent and heaved.

"Friend Saudett, you are with child?" Brena's voice came to her.

She turned to see Brena and Baal approaching. Baal seemed in slightly higher spirits than the latter day after losing his daughter. His teeth bared in his usual part smile, part snarl. His bald thunderbolt-tattooed head ever glistened in the sun.

"It would seem so," Saudett replied.

"Teras' glory to you and your child. Let them be strong as steel and be a bane to thine enemies," Brena blessed. Her long blonde hair was in a tightly tied thick braid resting down her back. Though her armor was still donned.

Was she looking for a fight? Or they must be thinking of setting out today after Hata. "My friends. We will find Hata. I will honor my debt to you. The blame falls to me, the loss of her."

"Worry not, friend Saudett," Brena reassured. "We are all equals in that right. We have both been shamed for bringing our daughter on this dangerous journey."

"What makes it worse," Saudett sighed. "It was not the Daanav that harmed her, but this mysterious man."

"Auru," Baal growled menacingly.

At that moment, Simon strolled up, walking alongside Saudett's mother, their arms hooked together, chatting idly as they approached.

"That is how I wooed your daughter with my beguiling smile and ridiculous handsomeness," Simon said cheekily. "She fell for me in nary a single rising and fall of the moon."

"I would think my daughter would have greater fortitude than that," Anora answered, half smiling.

"Mother. He greatly exaggerates!" Saudett smiled wryly. "The man stalked me from the shadows of Dagad's streets months before even uttering a word to me."

"Hettra's sagging tits," Simon cried. "Take back your lies, woman!" He was grinning like a mischievous child.

"Did you bring your pregnant wife the drink she begged you for?" Saudett reminded.

"Ah-ha! Yes, yes, of course, my dear. Freshly squeezed goat's milk. It's still warm!"

She took the simple clay bowl from his outstretched hands. It was creamy and tepid; the smell overwhelmed her. She slowly brought the milk to her lips, then shook her head and returned the bowl to Simon, saying, "This won't do."

Simon studied her briefly, then shrugged and quickly downed the contents, giving an audible 't-ah' and wiping away the milk around his lips on his sleeve. "I will find something to better suit your palate," he reassured her. Then, looking around, he acknowledged the two Vouri. "I don't believe we have been formally introduced. Simon Meridio, Meridio Enterprises. Many appreciations are in order." He gave a slight bow with a thumb to his lips in gratitude. "Appreciation for your defense in that heated meeting the other day. And especially for escorting my lovely wife back to me. My deepest regret to you both for the loss of your daughter."

"Friend Saudett, your mate looks weak and puny," Baal grunted pointedly. "He not match friend Saudett's strength. Why walk the mountain with him?"

"I beg your pardon, sir!" Simon coughed abruptly.

"You're right, friend Baal," Saudett chuckled. "But he makes up for it with his witty charm. Though my husband is sometimes so preoccupied with certain thoughts, he is foolish in others."

"I'm standing right here."

"He is rather handsome as well," Brena said, playfully nudging Baal.

Baal grumbled and shrugged.

"At any rate," Simon said. "I was hoping to have a second look at the Gate in the cave. Perhaps I can use it to fix this situation with the water supply for the valley, and then we can get on with finding your daughter."

"Do you think that is possible?" Anora joined in, an eagerness underlying her tone.

"After yesterday," Simon said. "I think anything can be a possibility. I just need time to work it out."

"We go after daughter now," Baal grunted once more.

"We need to find her; the longer we wait..." Brena trailed off.

"Do we even have the slightest idea of where that man took her?" Simon asked.

"Jude Nelon."

They all looked at Anora.

"Jude Nelon?" Saudett questioned.

"It's his name," Anora whispered remorsefully. "We attacked him and his comrades' caravan in the desert. He claimed to be a weary merchant, looking to finally settle down. I was naive. I had too much empathy for him."

"His comrades?" Saudett asked.

"Yes. We have the two tied up near the hills," Anora paused. "Shall we go *speak* with them?"

Saudett nodded.

Baal gave a low growl, and his usually toothy smile faded.

"I will leave you all to that. Let me know what you discover," Simon said. "I will begin investigating that gate."

"Be careful, dear husband. You are not particularly studied in the ways of magic."

"Worry not, my wife. I will be at the pinnacle of Mount Careful." He smiled wryly.

She squinted at him. "The last time you said you were going to be *careful* was after that damned dream;, then you were captured by nomads."

He grinned and turned. One hand clenching the white bone dagger in his belt, the other giving a casual wave as he strode away.

She gazed after her husband, longing not to let him walk away again. *That Skrull-forsaken man!*

"Shall we?" her mother prompted.

Saudett exhaled her frustration. "Lead on, Mother."

"Go ahead; we will hunt down some vittles to break our fast, then join you," Brena stated as Saudett and her mother got underway.

"So, we meet again," Saudett said as she approached the men tied to a livestock picket. The two men sat in the dirt, their hands over their heads, attached to the bamboo pole above them.

The man dressed in the uniform of the Shepherd's Eye soldiers of Dagad cursed as she approached. "Pah! Did you find that fucking bastard of a husband of yours? By Hettra's fucking cunt—"

"Ryon," Saudett interrupted. "What brings you out here? I thought you were ordered to lead a detachment to the North Iron Belt?"

Lieutenant Ryon Laniel began laughing hysterically. "Buah ha ha! I would do anything to be in that position at this very moment. This is *your* Skrull-fucking fault! If not for you, I would be safe, commanding an army, promoted even!"

"That is highly unlikely, and you did not answer my question."

Once dressed in fine green robes and a bright red turban, now tattered, soiled, and faded, the other man looked up at her pleadingly. "Sergeant, please have these savages release us. I can pay you whatever you wish!"

She looked down at the broken men. The green-clad merchant had tried to drug, rape, and sell her into slavery. He would have been successful if not for Baal Vasara's intervention. Lieutenant Ryon Laniel's normally slick-backed blonde hair, was a mess of tangles and dirt. Ryon had hated her from day one of her induction into the Shepherd's Eye. He was once her superior. "Whatever I wish? Why are you here, Ryon? Why are you with this filth who calls himself a merchant?" Saudett nodded toward the short Xamidian man.

"I'm not telling you anything. You can fuck off," Ryon spat once more.

She clenched her fist. Before she could do anything, her mother's strike collided with Ryon's face.

"Speak, wretch!" Anora shouted.

Saudett's brows raised at her mother's brashness.

Ryon spat again, his spit bloodied this time. "Gah, the fucks to you, too!"

"Oh, by the way, Ryon, meet my mother." Saudett smiled at her, and Anora's fist collided with his face again.

He slumped where he sat, his body hanging limp.

"Please! I beg of you! I will cooperate. I'll tell you everything!" the green-clad merchant wailed.

"*You.* You are nothing but a blighted wart on Skrull's cock," Saudett growled as she leered at him. "I never did get your name, *merchant*."

"Yes, yes, of course," the merchant said. "I am Zalias Ershya. Of the Serikat Buruh or Trade Union, as the Auru name it. I have many connections in Xamid and Aurulan that would benefit all parties."

"Aye, your connections to whom you sell off the young?" Saudett snorted in disgust. "Without so much as a second thought. Eh? You fucking snake!"

"Peace! Peace!" Zalias cowered as best he could under the circumstances. "Hettra's mercy upon me! I repent!" He continued muttering prayers, closing his eyes to her rage.

"The gods shall not pardon you!" Saudett screamed in his face. "Look to all those who have suffered because of you!"

Anora gently pulled Saudett away from the two men and whispered, "I think it would benefit us to show some empathy here, or else they'll keep the information we are looking for."

Saudett felt the heat in her neck and face lessen. "This man tried to rape me, Mother."

Anora's face grew sullen. *Cold.* Her hand slowly went to the sword on her belt.

Saudett touched Anora's arm reassuringly and composed herself. "It's alright. *For now.* And you are right, Mother." She looked at her mother's stern expression, a flame forthcoming in those dark brown eyes.

Anora nodded. "Let us give them a moment's respite. Let the thin one awake."

They strolled away from the pair of prisoners.

Once further away, Anora stopped and turned towards Saudett, clasping her hands. "Once we acquire this information from these two, I will immediately set out to the south with the scouts. I long to speak with you more, to get to know you and your husband. I wish to know everything! He was indeed quite charming from my short spell with him."

Saudett shook her head, grinning. "The foolish man has little to hold back his tongue."

"As I met him at the communal pavilion this morning, he addressed me as 'mother.' I was taken aback, and the next thing I knew, we were arm-in-arm. The man didn't stop talking from then. I could barely get a word in."

"Then he was truly and utterly terrified!" Saudett laughed. "He tends to ramble on when nervous."

"Really?" Anora tilted her head. "He seemed so...*natural*. I did not see a hint of disquiet in him."

"Besides building things, his second greatest skill is talking someone's ear off. Yet he still talks himself into a fix more often than not." Saudett smiled weakly. "It is saddening you must leave so soon, as I have just gotten you back."

Her mother stared longingly into her eyes. "Yes, my sweet Saudett, I have so much I want to tell you. Come with me? We can speak on the ride south."

"I—I don't know," Saudett hesitated. "I need to find the girl Hata. I made a promise to her family. I made a promise to her that I would protect her." She lowered her head, guilt welling within her. "I failed. I failed miserably."

"You did the best you could," Anora comforted. "Perhaps I shall let Kiana lead the scouting party in my stead. I wish to make the most of what time I have with you. Make up for all the lost years."

"I would enjoy that. You could perhaps join us in our search for the girl?"

"Your search will lead you far from Hasiera, I'm afraid. My people need me. My partner and daughter."

"*Daughters*," Saudett said faintly.

"Daughters. We had one true rule under the former First Otsoa's reign: nobody was allowed to leave our people once they had come into the fold. I believe that rule has gone to the wind with the current situation."

"Is that a yes?"

"Perhaps. I make no promises. Though your husband, the new First, may be able to help with that."

They made a wide circle back through the wreckage of the camp. The green palms and grasses had begun to yellow and shrivel with the lack of water. Crops of yams and lentils were hastily being harvested by many of the nomadic peoples.

"Unfortunately, your people must uproot themselves and find a new home. The Valley of Hasiera is, or was, truly beautiful and bountiful." The valley's northern side was a wall of rock in which the river flowed out of the cliff face and webbed across the valley. The grassland stretched up the hills to the south.

"Aye, I have spent nearly two decades here. You were quite young when I departed Al'Jalif. Departed it for the last time."

"I need to hear why. What happened with father and you?"

"If I am not to leave with the scouting pack, I will tell you tonight."

"So be it." Saudett nodded. "I look forward to it. In any case, that would make," she paused to ponder. "My sister Kiana nearing her third decade?"

"Indeed; she is in her twenty-third summer."

Same age as Hata. "Roughly twelve years my minor."

"Correct," Anora said. She paused and sighed before saying, "She is strong. She has her mother's rage. Much like yourself, I've noticed." Anora smiled sideways at her.

Saudett chuckled, "My husband would attest that I am quite quick to anger."

"Hmm, fortunately, Kiana also has her father's level head. Her martial ability and leadership surpass mine when she stays calm and true."

Saudett raised her brows. "You have sculpted her into a fine woman."

"And she hates me for it."

They walked in solemn silence for a long while.

"It is so hard not to regret the past," Anora finally said. "Leaving you, treating Kiana like an apparatus, to be shaped and molded into an image I had of myself. Or what I wished that I was. I try to look forward, live in the day, and imagine the future. Yet, I lay awake at night thinking about what could have been."

"We all live with these regrets, Mother. Do you remember the man Ismael Kaur?"

"I do; he was a respectable man and soldier."

"I am responsible for his death. I got him killed in this desert, chasing after you."

There was another long pause.

"Then that is yet another fault for me to bear."

"No, Mother. I did not listen to Ismael's advice; I ran off alone, and he followed me. He saved my life. He gave me his horse as we were attacked by desert wolves."

Something flashed across Anora's expression for a moment.

Saudett continued, "I escaped. He did not." She felt the fury simmering within her at the thought of her reckless stupidity. *Skrull take me. I killed him.*

There were a few moments of silence between them when, finally, Anora spoke up, a slight smile on her lips. "If things hadn't happened like they did, you may have never met your husband."

"Ha," Saudett grunted. "I suppose that is also true."

Her mother put an arm around Saudett's waist and squeezed her close. "We must try to look back at the good. Look at how the fates have bound us. When we were not searching for one another, we still came together. The Primus has blessed us."

"He has."

There was another pause as they continued to stroll through the camp.

"Tell me more of Simon. He is quite pleasant."

"Simon is sincerely the greatest thing the Gods have given me. He is kind and just. Handsome, cunning, and amusing. He has made me a better person as a whole." *I, on the other hand, use people for selfish gain. I used the Vasara family, Kaplan, and Taryn. Now Hata is lost, and Taryn is dead.*

As she continued, she ground her teeth. "Simon's parents shaped him into a spectacular human being. I never had the chance to meet his mother, but I heard many good things about her from Simon and his father, Yakeb." She paused to bring the image of the smiling old man that was Yakeb to her mind. "Simon is the spitting image of his father, down to the smallest of quirks. He is a younger version of that man. It saddens me how it ended between them. Simon told me he had rebuked his father and told him off just before he died. Simon dismissed Yakeb because the old man only wished to help his son with his project, and Simon was sick and tired of it."

"Yet another regret for this family," Anora said.

Saudett smiled slightly at her mother's reference to them as a *family*. A warm sensation grew within as she whispered, "For this family."

"Behold, my husband is speaking with the prisoners."

Looking with alarm, Saudett realized the two prisoners' hands were untied. She followed Anora's gaze; Rojas sat before the two prisoners. All three men had steaming food bowls and were murmuring quietly while eating.

Saudett began rushing over as she was about to reproach Rojas.

Anora grabbed her arm. "Patience, Saudett. I trust in Rojas."

Saudett grunted in answer but slowed; as they closed in on the trio, she could hear them speaking softly.

"It was that magi hunter. He was from the Aerie in Nidhaut and presented the black iron feather of their order," Ryon was babbling. "He came to Dagad nearly a week after the girl had left town."

"Magnus Huntsman of the Aerie," Zalias corrected.

"Aye, that's what I just said." Ryon glared at Zalias. "Said he was looking for the red-headed Vouri girl."

"He threatened us," Zalias mumbled as he shoveled the thick brown curried rice into his mouth. "Stated he would report us to the Aerie for our uncouth business practices if we did not aid him."

Rojas finally asked, "What were these business practices you speak of?"

"The bastards abduct young people to sell them off as slaves," Saudett answered in their place. "And this one," she motioned to Ryon, "iIs a member of the town's watch, the Shepherd's Eye, a protector of the people. He aids this criminal by overlooking his illicit activities."

"My cut was triple that of my monthly coin as a Shepherd," Ryon sneered.

Saudett clenched her fist. *I want to beat the man to death!* "You knew where *and* who Baal got that grit from in the market! You knew and said nothing. We could have unjustly punished Baal and his family as you two crooks made off with his daughter!"

"Aye, he, his daughter, and especially *you* can all be fucked!" Ryon spat, jumped to his feet, and turned, beginning to make a run for it.

Anora had silently moved behind Ryon.

He stopped dead as Anora's tulwar blade leveled at his neck.

"Peace! Calm yourselves now," Rojas said. "If you are cooperative and civilized, I will grant you the freedom to live and roam in the camp as you see fit. For now, I would have one of my people accompany you."

"Hettra's blessing to you, sir," Zalias groveled, motioning for Ryon to sit back down. "We are at your service."

Ryon sneered and sat back down with a huff.

"Can you tell us any more about this Magnus Huntsman?" Rojas asked gently.

Zalias cleared his throat. "Very little; as you know, he has access to the same magic he hunts. He uses the power behind the Aerie for leverage. Also, quite quick with a dagger."

"Not to mention the art of blackmail," Ryon grumbled. "That fucking whoreson pulled us into this mess."

"That's what I just said, you idiot!" Zalias hissed at his companion. "He uses the Aerie for leverage."

Ryon scowled back at the merchant.

"We need to find out more," Saudett muttered.

"Do you not have contacts in Nidhaut, Zalias?" Anora questioned gently. "I can think of a few myself from my days in the caravan, though that was a very long time ago."

Zalias studied them, looking from one to the next, seemingly weighing his options. Finally, he said, "Of course. I have ties in Nidhaut, people who are in the business of *knowing* things. People who can investigate specific individuals."

"Then you will—" Saudett started.

"But!" Zalias raised a finger to silence her. "But...should I aid you, and we come to the conclusion of this matter. You shall let me go free if I discover the girl's whereabouts. Without question."

Heat bristled on Saudett's neck. "You bastard! You sell innocent children into slavery. You do not deserve a second chance!"

"Truly, you are both lucky to be alive," Anora added, glaring at the men menacingly.

"You have my word." Zalias bowed his head. "I will retire from such a business. The risks far outweigh the profit, with so many noses in it."

"Eh? What will I do then?" Ryon probed Zalias.

"You can damn well do as you please; your services are no longer needed."

"What? I?" Ryon leaped to his feet again. "You cock—you fucking shit-stained son of a cock!"

At that exact moment, there was a roar.

"RAH!" Baal Vasara, the massive tattooed Vouri man, came hurling around a tent, charging toward them.

Brena hard on his heels.

Oh, gods, Saudett thought. She moved to cut them off, standing in front of Zalias. "Wait! Baal! Bren—"

Baal, seeing Saudett in his path before Zalias, veered towards Ryon.

Ryon's eyes sunk back into his head, mouth agape, quivering in fear, standing in a daze.

Anora and Rojas moved to block Baal, drawing their weapons.

Brena did not hesitate and attacked Anora, quickly sprinting past her mate Baal. Swords clanged and sparked as the two women met.

Rojas ducked under Baal's left-handed backswing only to take the following right fist in full force in the gut; Rojas was hurled to the side, landing with a grunt and holding his midriff.

Ryon sputtered a few words, waving his hands in front of his face defensively, "I had nothing to do with it!"

Saudett tried to stem her satisfaction as Baal's hands lifted Ryon from the ground by the neck. Ryon's own hands clawed at Baal's massive forearms.

"*Hata*," Baal hissed through clenched teeth; his eyes were bloodshot red, *watering*.

From rage? From sorrow? This is all my fault! Saudett screamed internally.

"Stop," Rojas groaned from the ground.

A clash resounded as Brena's sword deflected Anora's blade. Deftly catching a second blow on her round shield.

Anora danced. Strike after strike rained down. Saudett was in awe of her mother's speed and precision, yet Brena caught each attack.

Brena towered over Anora and had much more reach and strength behind her attacks.

Anora came with a left diagonal cut toward Brena's chest. The Vouri warrior countered, swinging her shield with a left-handed punch. It caught Anora's blade, and to Saudett's awe, the weapon spun upwards out of Anora's grip. Horror-filled Saudett. Brena's next attack would reach her defenseless mother.

A massive arching right-handed swing. In the time of one breath, the broad sword whistled through the air into *nothing*.

Anora spun to her knees, catching her blade as it fell from the sky. Her back to Brena, grasping the hilt with both hands, the tip of her sword aimed backward directly at Brena's exposed midsection.

Saudett's eyes widened. *Brena is about to die.* She began to react all too late, taking a slow step forward.

The blade sunk into the Vouri woman's side.

"I'm sorry," Anora whispered.

With a closed fist around her sword, Brena smiled wickedly and backhanded Anora across the face.

Blood sprayed, spattering into the dirt as Anora fell.

Brena stepped over her, sword lifting to finish the job.

Saudett reached them in time, shielding her mother with her body. "Please! Stop this!" she pleaded, looking up at the tall blonde woman.

Brena slowly lowered her blade, eyeing Saudett, and then sheathed it, putting a hand to her wounded side. "We will have our vengeance on these vermin of the Dagad."

A sound of wet popping and snapping bones came to Saudett's ears. She turned to see Ryon's head lying unnaturally to one side, his neck broken. Baal casually dropped the body and turned towards Zalias, cracking his knuckles and rolling his shoulders menacingly.

Rojas pushed himself to his feet. "Stop! This man will help us in finding your daughter!"

Baal tilted his head, then looked at his mate.

Brena held up a hand to halt Baal and said something in the Vouri language.

"How?" Baal growled.

"Yes, Teras tell, how will this vile scum help us find our Hata?" Brena responded flatly.

"He knows where she has been taken," Saudett beseeched. "He has contacts in the capital city of the Aurulan kingdom. In Nidhaut."

"You speak the truth, friend Saudett?" Baal grumbled.

"Aye. I do."

"Do you give your word, *friend?*" Brena added.

"I give my word. I vow to aid you in bringing your daughter back. I swear I will repay all you have done for me. From all the struggles we have faced to find my husband, Simon. If this man breathes a word of deceit, I will end him myself." She looked down at her mother, still lying in the dirt. "You have my word—"

Anora groaned painfully, and Saudett immediately helped roll her over. To her surprise, her mother was smiling.

With a cough and a grin, Anora said, "It has been long since I was struck. I forgot what it felt like." She touched her jaw gingerly and flinched.

"Ha," Brena answered. "I would be dead if not for my chain mail." The towering Vouri patted her injury. "Barely a flesh wound."

"I have never fought against a Vouri before," Anora said, pulling herself to her feet with Saudett's aid.

"Do not make a habit of it," Saudett chuckled. "I've faced off with my friend Baal here a time or two. It is monumentally taxing."

"It would seem the matter is settled then," Rojas said as he nudged the now limp body of Lieutenant Ryon Laniel with his foot.

"You were right, Zalias," Saudett mumbled. "I suppose his services were no longer needed,"

"The man was a whimpering idiot; he stuck around because he was addicted to grit. In return, he kept the Shepherd's Eye out of my business. And seeing as how my business is now concluded in Dagad, may he forever rest in Skrull's hell, enjoying the god's calloused colossal cock." Zalias strode over and kicked the limp corpse of Ryon.

Saudett smirked; she ultimately agreed with the words Zalias spoke. The Earste Lân was better off without Ryon Laniel, as far as she was concerned. *Once Zalias has fulfilled his use to me...he will meet the same fate.*

"Come, let us find the First Otsoa. We must make ready to depart." Rojas motioned for everyone, including Zalias Ershya, to follow.

Chapter Nine

ASPIRATION

Chanel de Montrichard exhaled heavily. *I only left the two alone for a moment, and the ginger ran off almost immediately.* She rubbed her temples impatiently. "What, Primus tell, were you two discussing that got the lass in such disorder?" Chanel demanded from Joanna.

"Uh, um—" Joanna stuttered.

Chanel lifted her willow switch.

"Alpha!"

Chanel stopped mid-swing. "What?"

"Aye, the girl dreads the Alpha's visit tonight; she hates the abuse. She said she didn't want to do it, screamed, and ran away."

Chanel studied the girl. *She is lying, this Joanna. Why lie to protect the ginger?* Finally, Chanel conceded, "I cannot blame her for that, but some things must be endured." *Skrull, take that man to your hell! If that goat-fucker would not interfere, I could better focus on developing the girls and not have commotions such as this wasting my time.* "Well, she will have to learn the hard way."

"Please, no. I will satisfy the Alpha myself; she is still just a girl at heart."

Chanel arched an eyebrow. "You would sacrifice your grace to protect this woman's virtue? Look around; you are a prisoner here. You should be looking out for none other than yourself."

"I am doing this for *my* own gain." Joanna grinned wickedly. "He is a disgusting man, but if I can be useful to the Alpha, perhaps he will grant me leniency. I'll do anything that needs to be done to find power."

What an ambitious little whore, this Joanna. The thoughts of the Alpha using Chanel the same way when she had first arrived in the Convent Enclosure came back to her like a nightmare. . *Pain.* The black iron bars all around them. Crying and screaming. Chanel forced the thought away. *I have become so numb to it these days. His attention is no longer on me.* "Wise of you to appeal to the Alpha. You will go far in the Aerie, Joanna Ohleoc." *Perhaps this girl could be groomed into my successor.* Take her place, teaching countless young women in statecraft and magic, only to watch them fail or die to the will of the Aerie. *Perhaps I can finally take up a position on the council proper.*

"What about Rose? Are you going to go after her?"

"Hardly, my young pupil," Chanel said, shaking her head. "She won't make it far. Soon enough, she will come slinking back for her nightly dose of grit. You will see." *Not to mention the impenetrable sphere that surrounds the entirety of the Convent Enclosure. None enter or leave here on foot.* The only way in was through the Alpha's teleportation spells. "Let her spend a night sleeping in the cold dirt if she would be so stubborn."

"Will not the Alpha be upset?"

"Perhaps. Should he be, you may have to appease the Alpha's distress, my dear. Add a little something further to tonight's repertoire."

Joanna's lips twitched slightly, but a smile was pasted over it.

What an excellent little liar you are, Joanna. "Be off with you then; back to your chamber."

"Yes, Proctor."

She watched as the girl hurried away, down the path back to her cage. The same cell Chanel herself had awoken in so many years ago.

Rose ran and ran as fast as she could, ducking under low, overgrown branches and through tangles of bushes. Scratching at her face and arms, pulling at her hair. She ran and crashed headlong into solid *nothingness...*

...groaning and rolling onto her stomach, she tenderly touched the massive welt on her forehead. Her skull was throbbing, the mix of a headache and physical pain. She winced and pulled her finger away. Bringing them down her face, she felt crusted, dried blood below her nose, mouth, and across her left cheek. *Dry? How long was I out?* She realized it was dark, and the forest was eerily quiet. Then, another feeling gripped her in urgency. A ravishing need to inhale the black powder into her nostrils, that tingling at the back of her throat. To lay back in bliss and forget about the pain.

She pushed herself to her feet, fumbling forward. *Which direction was it? I had been fleeing when I slammed into something.* Almost as the thought came to her, her outstretched hand gently brushed into a smooth surface. Yet nothing was there. Knocking her fist gently against the invisible barrier created a shimmer faintly, and then it returned to its imperceptible state. Anxiety and panic seized her by the core, an overwhelming feeling of being trapped. *I need to get out!* Slamming both fists against the unseen wall, the shimmer rippling outward. *Hettra's mercy, help me! Please!* She fell to her knees.

A thought came to her. Placing her hand on the ground, she extended her senses. Feeling the land stretching out and underneath...no, the barrier cut through the earth like a knife.

"No!" Rose screamed, slamming her fists against the barrier again while kneeling on the soft forest floor. *I need to get back. Back to my...my what?* She closed her eyes, head thundering and the overwhelming arid feeling of needing the powder in the back of her throat.

A memory materialized before her as if she were really there.

Her mouth was dry; she was walking, the searing sun beating down on her. She watched as her feet fell, sinking slightly into the red-orange sand. She saw other footprints in the sand ahead of her, and following them with her gaze, she found the source. Silhouettes of figures walked ahead of her. A large, broad-shouldered man. A tall, armored woman. A hooded man. A shorter, lithe woman. No details; they were just dark profiles of people.

She opened her eyes to the forest's darkness before her once more. *Who are those people? That desert? It feels so familiar.* The images of the people comforted her. Rose felt a moment of peace, the need for the powder waning. Her nerves calmed, and she decided to sleep in the woods for the night. Seeing no escape, she would rebelliously spend the night here and then make her way back in the morning. *Perhaps a night without the drug will help bring more memories back.* Though she was surprised, nobody had come after her. With the barrier, she imagined the Proctor did not worry significantly about escapees.

Jo would be nestled into the soft silk cushions and sheets at this time, her body huddled against Rose's as they slumbered after the large dose of the black powder. Jo's bare skin against her. *I wish I was back in the cage with Jo; I wish I could have the warmth of the drug.* Instead, she was cold and alone in a silent wood.

"Hettra's tits," she mumbled aloud, breaking the silence. The sound seemed to echo through the trees, louder than she had anticipated. She put her hands to the ground once more and felt for the direction of the trio of cylindrical buildings. The garden path was too distant for her reach. The barrier must encompass quite an area as she had run far. She chose the opposite direction of the invisible field and began to stumble back through the dark.

After what felt like an hour, the tree line broke. The garden path was ahead. Rose hurried to the building they slept in as quietly and quickly as possible. The massive door was ajar. She stepped silently into the room, a brisk draft following her through the doorway. In the darkness, she heard whimpering and crying. She rushed to the cage, pulling the unlocked squeaking gate open. *Was it ever even locked?* She saw Jo curled up in the fetal position, naked. Massive bruises, scratches, and welts were all over her body.

"No, no, Jo..." Rose knelt, gingerly cradling the beaten woman in her arms. "What happened?"

A strained whisper came through Joanna's whimpers, "The...the Alpha. He was *upset* you were not," she paused, gasping for breath, "not here."

"Oh, Gods. I am despicable. I should never have left you, Jo. Joanna. You will never forgive me." Rose could not hold back her tears.

"Hush, Rose. I need to sleep. Please, just keep me warm tonight."

Rose nodded and gently lay beside Joanna after undressing. She wrapped an arm around the young woman's waist. *This is all my fault. I did this to her!* Rose thought ruefully as she pulled a silk blanket over them both.

Joanna's quick, sobbing breaths soon receded into slow breathing.

Rose lifted her head slightly to look at Jo's face. She was fast asleep. Rose whispered, "I'm sorry." Then she laid her head back down and soon fell asleep.

Chapter Ten

REUNION

Marigold groaned as Simon scratched the camel's neck. "Long time no see, my good man. Have you found a young gentleman camel yet to ease your heartache?"

Marigold spit negatively. Or so Simon interpreted it.

"Still not yet? Fear not, Marigold, Simon Meridio is on the case."

The camel blinked unfaithfully at Simon's words, then returned to grazing the drying brown grass.

"You'll need a drink soon, too," Simon muttered as he left Marigold to his devices. *If I can figure out how to do that.* He shook his head. *Right, back to work,* Simon thought as he headed toward the cave in the cliffside. "The early eagle gets the snake, as they say."

Simon's mood darkened as a stench lingered out of the cave. As Simon entered the cavern, he noted it had been cleared of the dead, yet blood still stained the stone walls and ground. To his surprise, Kiana Ahmadi and her companion, the Shepherd's Eye ranger, Kaplan Mir, were just inside. A strange little lizard man perched on Kiana's shoulders.

"My sister...in-law!" Simon exclaimed. "Kiana Ahmadi. Firstly, let me say I truly thought you had died back there in the desert. Your conviction spurred me on to aid your people." He then shook his head shamefully. "Unfortunately, it was not enough."

"I thought the same. I was to die for my people there. But the vile creatures left me alive. As a consequence, they followed me home. Who is at fault that Hasiera was attacked at all?"

"They would have found this place sooner or later," Kaplan Mir reassured.

"Aye, they would have. Still, I hastened the outcome."

"What is it your father, Rojas was saying?" Simon asked. "Look to the future. Don't dwell on regrets."

Kiana and Kaplan glanced at one another as Simon spoke. Kiana's violet eyes flashed.

Hettra's mercy; she looks so much like Saudett. How did I not see it? Put two and two together. She is my sister-in-law, for Skrull's sake! He tried to shake the thought from his mind. *Thank the Primus, nothing had happened between us.*

"It seems to be a recurring point in my life," Kiana answered.

"I regret so, so many things." Simon nodded in consolation. "Ever since this whole ordeal started. The last thing I told my father before he died was to get the fucks away from me." There was a moment of silence before Simon spoke again, eyeing the lizard child...thing. "Ah yes, secondly! What is this strange little snake upon your back, Kiana Ahmadi?"

"This scrawny he-monkey is rude," the lizard man answered, challengingly jumping down from Kiana's shoulders. "Kogs is not snake. Kogs is Kogs!"

"Of course, my mistake, Sir Kogs! How have you found yourself in the company of these fierce warriors?" Simon gestured at Kiana and Kaplan.

"Kogs spy on them for the masters to bring about the destruction of the stupid humans!" Kogs shrieked excitedly. It began cackling evilly and muttering to itself.

"Uh, *alright*. At any rate, my friends," Simon interjected, returning his focus to the two *stupid humans* before him. "What brings you to this place of death?"

"We would like to look at this so-called gate you speak of," Kaplan answered flatly.

"Please join me then." Simon beckoned. "I am looking to further study it myself. Come." With that, he led the way into the tunnel, the trio soon trailing behind him. They walked into the darkness.

"Where did you learn how to do that?" Kaplan's monotone voice rose behind him.

Simon looked down, his eyes widening at the small globe of light that floated and bobbed above his right hand. "Things like this seem to happen without my say in the matter. I don't even think about it like it is an ordinary thing to do," he paused contemplatively. "Fascinating. It's like the habits and natural ticks of another's mind, someone who has long lived with this power and knowledge. And it's just there in the back of my head."

"Well, we hope you can *naturally* save the valley," Kiana answered sarcastically, her gaze burning into his back.

"Indeed," he mumbled. *I honestly have no idea what I am doing.*

"The he-monkey-warlock shall be outdone by the master's cunning!" Kogs chimed in with a cackle.

Simon turned and cautiously eyed the lizard man.

"Just ignore him," Kiana said with a grin. "He often plots our demise. You'll get used to it."

They continued down the tunnel of the once life-giving underground river that supplied the valley. Until they came to a drop. Looking over the edge, they could see a faint white light in a cavern below.

"I forgot about this part," Simon muttered, pausing and eyeballing the others. "*Afléotan!*" he exclaimed in his most wizardly voice.

All three of them began to levitate.

"Follow me, if you will." Simon kicked off the wall and floated out over the open space. He gripped the opposite side and crawled headfirst down the wall using his hands and feet. Kogs shrieked and leaped off Kiana's back, retreating down the tunnel they had just come from. Kiana shrugged and squeezed Kaplan's hand with a moment's hesitation as they drifted in midair. Then, following Simon's lead, they descended into the chamber below. As they reached the ground level and righted themselves, Simon gestured with his hand, and they dropped gently to their feet.

As they approached that gate, a strange voice said, "Yes, very good indeed. I see you have fastened the way to the Skaad Lân, Simon Meridio."

CHAPTER ELEVEN

SUNSTONE

"I accept the Primus as the creator of all beings," they said in unison.

Rose winced as she looked at Joanna's tender shoulders. The woman's bruises had lessened after a handful of days. Rose had obeyed every rule, every order spoken to her since that beating.

"I accept the Primus as the creator of the Earste Lân."

I don't care if he hurts me. I can't put Jo through that again.

"The creator of the Houses of the Gods and those who are seated there."

I'll say the prayers. I'll study fervently. I'll satisfy the Alpha's every need...without question.

"I accept the Primus before all other Gods, who are but servants to His will."

The day after the beating, and every night after, the Alpha assaulted Rose, and she was in constant pain. Physically and mentally violated. During those times, truth be told, the comforting cloak of *grit* shielded her. She took the black powder each night and became nearly unconscious. Oblivious to the Alpha's defilement. Her last sight before succumbing was the Alpha removing a black glove from his hand and placing it on her head. Then blankness. Come morning, she would awaken and feel disgusted at herself. *What is that sick bastard doing to us?*

"The Primus is pure and absolute."

At least as long as the drug coursed through her, she was detached from it. *Numb to it.*

"May I ever be blessed with his favor."

She felt ill. *I always feel ill.* Was it the revulsion thinking about that greased black hair and goatee? His dark, stomach-turning eyes drinking her in. Or was it the withdrawals of the grit? She tuned out the Proctor's voice as the woman said today's reading. *Another reading, most likely about a man doubting the Primus and being cast into Skrull's hell.* As the Proctor finished, they went to the altar to pay their respects. After which, as usual, they made their way to the study.

"Today," the Proctor began, "we learn about the minerals in the Earste Lân, primarily in Aurulan and its bordering nations."

Rose stared at the magical illusion out the single window in the chamber. Today, it was a white peaked mountain range. The grey rock below the peaks was jagged and towering. The illusion changed daily, offering a peaceful and comforting place for learning.

"Take the North Iron belt, for example." The Proctor gestured to the scene around through the window. "Copper, iron, silver, gold, and gemstones. Along with, most importantly of all, *volframi*. A rare ore only mined from the deepest depths of the mountains."

A vision flashed into Rose's mind. A frozen waterfall, a village buried in the side of the mountain. She grimaced, rubbing her forehead. *Why is it so bright in here?*

"These ore and gemstones are infused with magical properties and become one. It can be infused with power and refined into a vessel." The Proctor touched a gem on the pendant that hung about her neck. "After much research, the Aerie could infuse small amounts of the ore and gems with spells."

"Can anyone use these captured spells?" Joanna asked enthusiastically.

"Indeed. The only power one needs to unlock the spell within is a meager amount of blood."

Rose felt an invisible hand cover her mouth from behind. A flash of light. Blinking, she sat still at her small desk, her head thundering. She looked about behind her. The feeling of the hand over her mouth was gone.

"Something the matter, girl?"

"No, Proctor." Rose shook her head. "Uhm, is the North Iron Belt a part of the kingdom of Aurulan?"

"Not quite. It is the northern border of our nation. It is only inhabited by a sparse population of savages."

"Savages?" Rose questioned.

The Proctor peered at her momentarily, then shrugged. "The Vouri. They live and breathe the earth, go so far as to worship a pagan god who would rule rock and stone."

Hata. Rose heard voices whisper in unison. She kept her expression neutral as the images of people's faces filled her mind. Her mother's gentle touch, her father's bear-like smile.

"May the Primus smite down this false god," *Hata Vasara* said quickly.

"Difficult to destroy a figment of a people's mind. It is better to send out pilgrims to the Vouri. Make an offering of everlasting peace from the Primus as long as they name Him the one true God."

"Primus's favor to us all," Joanna and Hata said in union. Hata felt fury boiling within her, but she did not let it escape. *I will hold it in. I will bide my time and will not allow my parents' memory to fade again.* Of everything they had been through. Of Dagad and the Burning Sea. Of Saudett and Kiana. Of the Valley of Hasiera. The Daanav, those strange creatures of the night.

"Well, no one will be making the pilgrimage to the North Iron Belt in these troubled days," the Proctor continued. "The Vouri have been pushed out of their homes in the mountains."

"By what?" Hata asked.

"We are unsure. My station does not permit me with the knowledge of every coming messenger, and the Alpha is not one for sharing." The Proctor's voice was strained.

"My apologies, Proctor," Hata reassured with feigned empathy. "Please continue with the lesson."

"I am suddenly weary," the Proctor exhaled severely. "We shall break for lunch. Meet me in the practical use chamber in two hours." Disappearing through the doorway, the Proctor left the two girls sitting at their desks. As the door closed behind the Proctor, Hata jumped to her feet.

"Jo...I..." Hata's voice broke. "I remember who I am!" she announced the surging feelings. "I remember my parents!" *I remember Saudett.*

Jo's eyes widened in shock; she rushed over to Hata and wrapped her arms around her. "Shush now, Rose. How long have you known? You've been holding this in?"

"Hata."

"Hata?"

"My name is Hata Vasara. I am the Sunstone."

I have taken a significant risk speaking of that girl's people. Skrull's forsaken hell. The girl had spaced out for a moment but had not indicated that her memories had returned. In the rare cases someone's memories did return to them, there was almost always a fallout along with it. Terror, sorrow, and rage were usually accompanied by an arcane outburst. The girl had shown no change in temperament. *Nothing. She is truly gone, now but a husk of her former self.* The same bodily vessel, yet a new mind. *Another fucking pigeon of the Aerie.*

Chanel snorted the grit as she urinated in her chamber pot. She stood, pushing the bedpan with one foot back under the massive bed. Chanel paused momentarily, then took another considerable portion of grit onto her hand and inhaled it. A wave of tension released from her as she crawled into her sheets, sighing heavily and closing her eyes. *Just a moment to myself is all I need.* She fiddled with the vial of grit. Shrugging inwardly, she sat up and poured the remaining contents into her palm. *There is not much left.* She sniffed the powder, making sure not to waste any of it. It was exceptional, clearing her mind with that overwhelming, sustaining feeling.

It had been three hours. The Proctor had yet to return. Joanna and Hata had finished lunch and were now strolling about the gardens in the compound's center.

"It's been a long time, Rose...sorry, I mean Hata," Jo corrected. "Should we go check on her?"

"Keep calling me Rose, please, Jo. I do not want to raise suspicions. I want to keep it secret and figure out how to get out of here."

"I know you want to get back to your family, but at the same time, we are learning many things about the world. About our powers."

"I can learn on my own. I did it before, and I can do it again. I had a good teacher." The image of Saudett's toned bronze skin glistening with sweat came to her mind.

"You knew someone else who could use magic?"

"Well," Hata hesitated. "No."

"Then how could it be more beneficial than this?"

"She did not use magic, but she knew how to fight. She taught me how to cope with the loss of battle. The loss of friends, even family."

Joanna paused, studying Hata momentarily. "What happened to you? Hata Vasara?"

"It's a long story. But yes, I think we should check on the Proctor."

"Perhaps she is entwined with one of the male orderlies?" Jo giggled.

Hata grinned mischievously. "Let's see if we can catch a peek!"

They skittered through the garden, the ever-blooming colorful pedals gently moving with the breeze. They took their time, stopping and chatting about the different flowers and plants. Joanna particularly speculated on which orderly the Proctor would be to bed with.

"They have names?" Hata questioned sardonically.

"Tomas is the shaven-headed one. Marginally smaller of the two, short and stocky-like. Luftan is the taller lad with broad shoulders. You can tell he doesn't miss his eggs during breakfast. I also imagine he enjoys lifting heavy things."

"Shall we make a bet?" Hata giggled.

"Aye, let us."

"I'm going with Luftan. If I'm right, you must deal with the Alpha tonight."

Joanna's expression went solemn. "I thought you would take the brunt of the Alpha's expectations for a while?"

Hata nodded vigorously. "I will...I mean, I have been. I'm sorry, Jo, you're right. I just hoped for a break. I haven't had a night off from him since he beat you. It's been nearly two weeks, I think."

Joanna's blue eyes burned into her.

Was that hatred?

Then the eyes softened, and Jo smiled naturally at her. "You are right. I should be the one to apologize. I—" Jo stammered and turned away from her. "I was scared ever since he—"

"Never mind the bet, Jo. I should never have asked. If I win, I will seek one favor from you later."

Jo smiled meekly, nodding. "I would do the same should I be the victor."

Hata returned the weak smile.

"Shush, we're getting close to the Proctor's silo," Jo whispered.

Hata nodded.

They crept closer, skirting away from the front path and doorway. Opting to approach from the side to look through the large shutters. As they neared the opening, they could hear a muffled noise. The shutter was half-open, and a candle burned low on the chamber's opposite side. The sound became more explicit.

A gurgling noise? Heaving? No. Someone is gasping for air.

A body on the bed was convulsing horrifically.

She is choking to death! Hata pushed with all her might, and the stone and mortar at the base of the shutter crashed inwards. She dashed to the bed.

"Hata! Leave her be!" Joanna called after her.

Hata ignored it. As she reached the bed, the Proctor lay on her back, vomit and foam dripping from her full mouth. Her chest heaved upwards, back arching.

Hata pushed her over onto her side.

The contents of the Proctor's mouth were expelled onto the red silk sheets. The woman's eyes rolled up in her head.

"I need help! Jo!" Hata screamed as she tilted the Proctor further onto her stomach. Bringing a hand down hard on her back.

"How? What do we do?" Joanna said quietly from nearby.

Hata's palm slammed into the Proctor's back again. "I don't know. Do something! Go get Luftan and Tomas!"

Joanna stood there, unmoving.

"Jo, please!" Hata hit the wheezing woman again. "She doesn't deserve to die." Hata's hand came down again firmly.

"GUUUAAH!" The Proctor sucked in a massive breath.

Hata looked down at her.

The Proctor looked back, eyes wide with terror. A hoarse whisper trickle from the woman's wet mouth, "What?" The Proctor's eyes cleared momentarily. "Rose, my lung. I...I think it is torn. It is a labor to breathe."

"Please, Proctor," Hata pleaded. "Tell me what to do." Joanna was nowhere to be seen as she looked about her frantically.

"The lung is filling with blood. We must make a stint. A tube to drain the blood and inflate the lung once more."

Hata's eyes widened. "You are truly amazing, Proctor. How can you stay so level-headed in this situation?"

"Skrull's sack girl, not now. Can you fashion metal to your will?"

"Metal?"

"Are you daft? Yes, *fucking* metal. It is of the earth as much as is the stone you stand on."

Hata blinked. *She's right.*

The Proctor's breathing was shallow and strained. "The braces on the bed frame, copper," the woman rasped hoarsely. It is the weakest of minerals, so it should be simple for you. Create the image of a cylinder in your mind—" the Proctor coughed again, blood dripping out her mouth.

Hata closed her eyes and reached out. The metal braces fastened with black iron nails fought against her will. She focused, bringing the rage inside her to the forefront. There was a creaking sound of wood against metal, and suddenly, a *thud* as the braces popped out of the corner of the wood frame, and the bed fell at an angle.

The Proctor bounced slightly at the impact. "Fucks," she groaned. "Now the tube, hurry!" With a feverish urgency, the Proctor stared at Hata, eyes full of fear.

Hata closed her eyes again, breathing deeply; she imagined the braces becoming flimsy, almost liquid. They turned bright yellow as she formed the two pieces of metal into a long, thin tube. Opening her eyes, the brass tube floated just above her hand. Her hand felt warm. The cylinder was giving off heat.

"Good, good. Now, find a spot between my ribs. Help me get this robe off."

Hata sat the woman up and loosened the tight belt around the woman's waist. She then pulled the white robe up and over her head.

The Proctor took Hata's hand and placed it on her side, both their hands tracing her rib cage until she decided on the right spot. "Here. We need to make an incision first."

"How? With what?"

"I shall handle this part." The Aerie Procter, Chanel de Montrichard, *began to cast a spell.* The shutters flew open as the wind rushed into the room. Gusting to a single point. A thin cyclone formed just above Chanel's hand, spinning rapidly. With a quick flick of the Proctor's wrist, the spinning vortex thinned and pierced her side precisely at the point she had indicated to Hata.

"Now!" the Proctor screamed through clenched teeth.

Hata jabbed the tube through the hole in the Proctor's side, and an orange liquid immediately began to pour out through the thin copper rod. The muck drained onto the bedding. Akin to a river down the mountain, plasma dripped off the edge of the mattress, pooling onto the cold floor.

The Proctor's breathing began normalizing as she started taking deeper breaths slowly, in and out.

Hata sat on the edge of the bed, unsure of what she should be doing now. The Proctor's hand gently touched her forearm.

"Thank you, my girl. You saved my life."

Hata looked into the woman's watering-tired eyes; she saw great sadness there. A great weight weighed down on Chanel de Montrichard. Hata shrugged. "I did what anyone would have."

"Only one with kindness in their heart." Chanel glanced momentarily around the room. "I do not see your counterpart, or my aides, for that matter."

"Jo went to get help."

"Did she?" Chanel grunted. "Come, help prop me up on some pillows. There should be an empty carafe on the dresser there. Yes there. Put it under the stint."

Hata nodded and did so before asking, "Can I get you anything else, Proctor?"

"Hmm, no—no. Can you perhaps stay with me for a moment? Keep me upright. I just need to close my eyes for a moment."

"Yes, Proctor."

"Dear girl, when it is just the two of us, please, you may call me Chanel."

Hata nodded, smiling genuinely. "I will." She paused, studying the woman's expression. *This woman is yearning for affection.* "Chanel."

"Is that my real name?" Chanel mumbled as she fell into sleep.

CHAPTER TWELVE
WAYFARER

Kiana and Kaplan's swords glided from their sheaths as they prepared to attack the grey-cloaked figure.

The figure standing in front of the dim white light of the gateway raised two hands in a passive gesture and then a third from under the heavy grey cloak, palms outfaced. "I mean you no harm, denizens of the Earste Lân."

Simon's eyes widened as the duo stepped forward. "Wait, wait!" he urged his companions. "I was the one who closed this *thing*," he addressed the strange man. "It was connected to the Skaad Lân, you say? What is that? Who are you?"

"Indeed, I am Gaelin Yesnala of the Iban'mael," the figure said as he pulled back the hood covering his facial features. He had light grey skin and snow-white hair tied back; the man's face was smooth and fair, lacking any facial hair.

"And pardon my boldness, what are you?" Simon questioned further.

The man smiled softly, black teeth contrasting with the pale grey face. "As I said, I am of the Iban'mael. I am the last of a dead race of people. Wayfarers of the Lâns. A people once far advanced in the study of the elements."

Simon motioned for his companions to relax; the two warriors' eyes met each other's for a moment before lowering their blades but not sheathing them.

"A dead race? Kiana asked, tilting her head curiously. "What happened to these people of yours? The Iban'mael?"

"Eradicated by the creatures of the Skaad Lân. The creatures of shadow."

"The Daanav, as we call them," Kaplan said matter-of-factly.

"Ah yes, the Xamidian word for *demon*." Gaelin nodded. "That is an apt name for them."

Kaplan let the tip of his scimitar rest on the stone floor as he spoke, "You speak our languages? Are you from this Skaad Lân as well?"

The strange man's eyes moved to each of them steadily. They were inverted. His sclera was pitch black, with a grey iris surrounding a white pupil. "No, not the Skaad Lân. My home was called the Hiel Lân, but the Earste Lân was my assigned Lân to explore, document, and protect, should civilization exist. I have studied it for nearly a millennium. My studies were halted when I learned that these Daanav had conquered the Hiel Lân and were now set on doing the same here."

Simon sat, dumbfounded and enthralled, wanting to soak in the knowledge. Yet as this man spoke, he realized the information was already within himself. As if with every word the man said, Simon remembered it again. *Skrull's hairy balls*, he cursed inwardly as he closed his eyes and rubbed his forehead.

You are the bearer of the arm? Gaelin's voice entered his mind.

Simon's eyes shot open, and he looked up at the man who had not stopped speaking. *I've heard this voice in my mind before...*

"The Wayfarers Gates connect to many other Lâns," Gaelin continued aloud. "We built the Gates in all of our cities and towns. As we could not only travel to other worlds, we could travel quickly amongst our civilization. Our curiosity to explore new Lâns was our undoing. The Daanav used them against us. Pouring through the gates one night in vast hordes, slaughtering everyone. I fear the only survivors were those akin to myself. Those who were gone, exploring other Lâns when the attack happened." As Gaelin spoke, he undid the clasp of his cloak and let it fall to the ground around him, revealing his three arms and the stump of a fourth under his left arm.

You are the bearer of my arm! Gaelin's voice boomed within Simon's head.

"YES!" Simon shouted back. "Is this what you want?!" Simon pulled the dagger from his belt, gripping it in his left hand. The scars of the lightning burn itched along his arm.

Kiana and Kaplan turned to him, tensing unknowingly at his sudden outburst. Puzzled looks on their faces.

"Have you gone mad, Simon?" Kaplan questioned.

"Skrull's cock," Simon groaned. "The man is *speaking* in my head." He waved the dagger around desperately. "This dagger used to be his arm! See there!" Simon pointed with the tip of the blade toward Gaelin's stump.

"Careful with that, *Simon*." That last word echoed once more in Simon's mind. "I have no intention of taking the dagger from you. And you are correct. That tool was once my arm." Gaelin pointed with the second arm on his right side to the stump on his left.

"Why?" Simon pleaded desperately. "What is this?"

"Indeed, the bone of my arm was used to forge that blade, to pass my knowledge to one I chose. To unlock your full potential, Simon Meridio. And as it turns out, to save your world."

Simon shook his head in disbelief. "How do you know my name? By the Primus, this is insane!"

"As I said, I have been studying the Earste Lân for centuries. I have met you before, Simon Meridio, though you were just a babe then."

By the gods, I feel nauseous.

"Yes, I marked you when you were young, should the need arise, and I would be indisposed." Gaelin paused for a long moment, scratching his chin thoughtfully. "I went home. I saw my people's destruction. They were being mutilated and fed upon. Unnatural darkness covered the skies. The enemy did not take long to notice my presence, and I retreated. I came back here. I was a fool; they followed me. I fear I am the reason these abominations of the Skaad Lân now set their sight on the Earste Lân."

"You did this?" Kiana breathed sharply. "Do you know how many of my people have died because of you?!" She took a step toward Gaelin.

"Wait, Otsoa," Kaplan cautioned. "This man has also lost much. You cannot blame him for leading the Daanav here. He was fleeing for his life."

Kiana shot Kaplan a glare, but after a moment, she visibly relaxed; taking a deep breath, she nodded to him.

"Indeed, I was. The creatures of the Skaad Lân have some access to the Wayfarers' Gates; they could simultaneously attack through many of them all at once. In my time here, I have constructed a few other gates around your world and placed them in these remote, hard-to-access locations." He gestured with his lower right hand to the cavern around them. "Remote, but near enough to your different kingdoms to have access."

"You came to this gate when you fled from your Hiel Lân?" Kaplan asked.

"Indeed."

"Then why did the Daanav not attack directly from where we stand?" Kiana urged inquisitively. "Instead, they were spread about the desert?"

"True. Alas, my dear, I'm afraid that is somewhat of a mystery. But I believe it is thanks to the dagger. When I struck it into the gate, it created an unstable portal. The beasts could no longer use the portal directly. If they did so, they would be spat out randomly somewhere in the Lân or sometimes simply disintegrated. I believe this action halted the greater forces the Daanav have at their disposal."

"What does this have to do with me? Why choose me to be the bearer of this bone? Why give me this power?" Simon asked suppliantly, but he knew the answer before Gaelin said a word. An image became present in his mind.

Gaelin burst through the portal, dropping to his hands and knees and vomiting as the memory of thousands of his people lay outstretched before him...dead. A dark cloud over the ruined city. *The abominations slaughtered everyone!* Their torn bodies were a mess of tangled limbs and gore. *They need to die!* Those black-haired beasts pulling, ripping, and eating the flesh of his people. *I will see them all dead. All of them!* Tall buildings crumbled and burned.

He stood just as two of the hounds leaped through the Gate. Gaelin shot one hand out and upward. "*Windan!*" he called as he did so. A blade of air hissed toward one of the creatures. Cleaving the beast in half through the middle of its head and down its body. Black blood sprayed about the small cavern.

The other beast lunged at him. He was too slow; it clamped onto his lower left arm.

"*Strangung!*" Gaelin screamed through the pain. He felt strength swell within his body. Grabbing the hound by the neck, he pulled with all his might. There was a wet burst as he flung the beast against the wall. A cold sensation came to where the beast had bitten him. He looked down at the wounded arm. It was gone. Only blood dripped from torn flesh and stripped bone. His vision began to haze as he peered at the beast he had thrown, the lower half of his arm clenched in its jaws. *Ah, yes, I suppose I did that to myself.* He shook his head, reeling from shock.

He raised his upper right hand, pointing his index finger at the beast. "*Bael cnytells,*" he murmured. A string of white fire shot from his finger.

The creature shrieked in pain as a hole instantly burned through its side. It fell limp, his forearm rolling from its jaws.

I'm losing blood. I must heal the wound and close the Gate before more creatures arrive. "Bael cnytells," he said once more as he burned the remaining bone from his stump, cauterizing the wound. Placing a hand over the charred stump, he spoke another spell. "*Gehae.*" The pain fled as a faint glow of yellow light pulsed from his hand.

A wailing drifted from beyond the Wayfarers Gate.

He gathered his material into a pile. His hand and forearm. The small piece of bone he had burned off. He began the transmutation.

"Besmidian baan, befégan bréostloca!" A hammer of white light appeared in his right upper hand. He swung it downward. The pieces before him began to hum and glow, brighter and brighter.

"Besmidian baan, befégan bréostloca!" The hammer fell once more.

The wailing grew louder, closer this time.

Shards of white spat out about Gaelin as the hammer fell for the third time. "Besmidian baan, befégan bréostloca!" Sparks flew, and a beam of light filled the chamber and shot straight up through an opening in the stone ceiling. He watched as the light turned in the sky and disappeared from his view.

His soul is now connected, he thought as he looked down at the glowing rune-etched dagger made of his own self before him.

A lanky, red-eyed abomination slunk through the gate. Skin crackling, an almost molten being. "You are the last of the arrogant," it hissed. "The last one to satiate us."

Gaelin Yesnala stood tall, holding the dagger in one hand. He answered, "I am not the last. For me and many others, protect all the Lâns. You trespass on the Earste Lân. You trespass on my ward." He rushed the vile beast of Skaad, shouting, "Begone, abomination!"

The monster screeched, seemingly surprised by his attack. Rearing back, it lashed out with extended arms toward him.

Light surrounded Gaelin, the creatures' attacks bouncing off the bright white barrier. He collided with the beast.

It's back toward the Gate; it was forced back. It screamed and clawed and dug at him in fury.

He pushed and glanced the dagger in an upward slice at the being.

It shrieked as the blade sliced through a glowing red eye.

Gaelin pushed on, step by step, driving the creature back through the portal.

Its clawed hands sunk into each side of the black marble archway as he pushed against it. "I have your scent; I will remember this place!"

"*Begone!*" Gaelin boomed as he leaped, plunging the dagger high into the marble archway. It sank deep, cracking the marble about it. White light filled the cracks, magically fusing the blade to the gate. The portal began to flash and thunder, arcs of lightning spreading out from the focal point that was the dagger.

The monster roared as it was partly submerged in the storm. "Tether this Lân for destruction!" It screamed out, and a sudden flash of white light filled Gaelin's eyes. When his vision cleared, the beast was gone. The gate had somehow become inverted, like that of an upside-down doorway. The white light of the gateway had changed to a clouded mass of green and black. Moments later, water began to trickle through the gateway. Defying nature and bubbling along with the stone ceiling upward.

The trickle grew steadily, filling the tunnel Gaelin had taken long hours to carve out. *To hide this place.* He sighed in relief and sat, leaning against a wall. As the storming portal crackled and roiled with the green-black clouds, Gaelin Yesnala closed his eyes. *The boy should be nearly a decade old now.* He opened his eyes again and studied the dagger protruding from the gate. *That should keep them out.* Then he heard another scream, and the silhouette of a hulking figure began pushing up against the crackling portal from the other side. *No, it cannot get through.*

It pushed further and further, lightning flashing and snapping as the image of the beast became solid. Then white light filled Gaelin's vision again, and the creature had vanished.

What happened? Is the portal broken and unstable? Perhaps. He studied the storm for a long while. *Possibly, one by one, the creatures can still get through. They are being spat out across the Earste Lân, no doubt.* He cursed himself and forced himself to his feet.

He thought of the numerous Wayfarers Gates he had created in this world. *I must make haste and close them.* This one was of no use to him now. He gazed upward. "Afléotan," he muttered and drifted upwards toward the unnatural stream of water. He held his breath momentarily, ascending up and out of the water through the small man-sized hole in the ceiling. His feet gently touched down on the rocky surface that surrounded him. The sky shone bright with stars on a beautiful desert night.

Gaelin Yesnala began to walk.

Simon lurched, dizzied by the images, clawing at his hair. "This is too much. Take me to Skrull's fucking hell! I need a drink!" Nausea was twisting within him.

"Oh, you don't want to go there," Gaelin answered nonchalantly. "His Lân is far worse than even the Skaad Lân. But at least your so-called Gods keep to their own Lâns." He paused with an eerie head tilt and smile of black teeth. "For the most part."

"Uh, I think a drink is very much needed indeed," Kiana stammered, eyes wide with disbelief. "Let's make for the surface."

Kaplan nodded but said nothing, never taking his gaze off Gaelin Yesnala. Until the moment Simon fainted.

"Wonderful!" Kiana threw her arms up.

"What have we here?" Gaelin said excitedly.

Kiana watched as the strange man rushed over to a cowing Kogs.

Dragging Simon's limp body, Kaplan and herself unceremoniously dropped him in some shade onto his back.

"Kya!" Kogs cried, hissing and covering his eyes with both hands.

"Is this not a denizen of the Moreas Lân? How has it come to find itself here?" Gaelin leaned over, closely inspecting Kogs, his eyes squinting.

"The Daanav took him from his home," Kiana answered.

Gaelin touched his forehead and sighed heavily, "Another Lân destroyed."

"Perhaps, but they did not kill Kogs but instead were using him as a scout in this world. He believes his mate is alive but held captive."

"My Gaks!" Kogs wailed, his mane rattling. "My poor Gaks!"

Gaelin's hand went from forehead to chin. "Fascinating. They left none alive in the Iiel Lân, and it appeared they would do the same here in the Earste Lân. Why did they not do the same for this one's home." He reached out and gently petted the lizard man's shaking head.

Kogs relaxed and began purring, or what a lizard's equivalent of purring was. Kogs peeked an eye out from under one of his hands. "My home is gloomy, not like this wretched place. Blazing hot light in the sky makes Kogs's skin crusty! Kogs's people are simple. Small. Weak. The masters do not consider us worthy of all-mighty destruction like on the she-wolf's humans."

"Truly fascinating!" Gaelin exclaimed. "There is a thread here we can perhaps take advantage of."

Kiana studied the newcomer.

"Speak your thoughts," Kaplan said in his usual flat manner.

Gaelin looked around the dusty camp.

Kiana followed his gaze; the palm trees and bamboo stalks slowly wilting and browning. The soil kicked up more dust than before.

"This grew into a beautiful oasis," Gaelin observed. "However, I fear it was not part of the natural order. It was due to my interference. This place should be left to return to what it once was."

"This is our home, Gaelin Yesnala," Kiana glared at the man. "I do not know how you can take responsibility for creating it, but it is now ours."

"Ah yes, the water source was a phenomenon created from the broken gate; that water source was not from my home, the Heil Lân. It was from the Skaad Lân, home of these Daanav."

There was a moment of unease, and then they heard a groan. They looked to see Simon rolling onto his side in the shade of a half-collapsed canvas.

"He speaks true," Simon grunted, pushing himself to a seated position. "He somehow created a tether between the Earste, Heil, and Skaad Lâns. He did this when I was just a babe, over three decades ago, perhaps. The Daanav had been slowly penetrating the broken gate, but they were being displaced into the desert. They slowly gathered their forces. The water was from the Skaad Lân."

"And you are suddenly an expert on the matter, Simon Meridio?" Kaplan tilted his head at Simon doubtfully.

Kiana watched Simon, in turn, look to Gaelin.

The strange man had been scratching the little lizard man's head to his enjoyment as he finally stood and stretched his upper arms. "You took the words right out of my mouth, Simon. For they are indeed my own words."

"Skrull's balls," Simon shook his head. "I am never going to get used to that."

Kiana was smiling, refreshed by Simon's humorous antics; *I remember speaking with him daily as he was held captive and escorted to Hasiera. I was growing quite fond of him. Fantasizing about things with him.* That woman of his, Saudett, was not to be taken lightly. She was hot-tempered and quick to action. *That woman? She is my half-sister! What am I thinking?*

"Three-arms! Three-arms missed a spot!" Kogs grabbed Gaelin by the leg, rubbing his head against it.

"Now, now, Kogs. I was about to explain how we may be able to kill two birds with one stone, as the saying goes."

Simon snorted loudly. "I've never heard of such a saying!"

They all eyed Gaelin Yesnala expectantly.

"We can repair this gate, point it toward the Moreas Lân, and find a new water source."

Chapter Thirteen

INFLICT

"Come at me then," the Alpha taunted, gesturing with his gloved hand for the two to commence their attack.

Hata's teeth scraped together as she surged forward. A tidal wave of the earth grew before her, rushing toward the Alpha. She heard an explosion.

Joanna launched overhead, smoke billowing from her hands and feet behind her. Then, Joanna raised both hands above her head mid-air, a flame growing between them.

Hata pushed her wave with effort; it grew, towering over the Alpha. Just as the tide was to reach him, Joanna, now right over the head of the Alpha, launched her sphere of flame downward.

Both the attacks exploded in unison. Earth and flame engulfed the Alpha Passeriform.

Hata shielded her face from debris and heat as Joanna disappeared on the other side of the explosion. Hata squinted as the dust began to clear.

The Alpha stood, dusting off a shoulder casually. "Shall I have a turn?"

Something hit Hata from behind. He had both hands up, one facing Hata, the other Joanna. The next thing she knew, she was hurling through the air toward the Alpha.

Joanna flew toward the Alpha from the other side.

They were aimed to crash together.

I can't move! Teras give me strength! She felt like a giant fist was wrapped around her, her arms stuck to her sides as air buffeted her. She closed her eyes and rapidly formed a wall of soft earth between herself and Joanna.

They collided.

Dirt filled Hata's mouth and nose, but she still painfully crashed into the other woman. Agony coursed through her as she fell back onto the ground, the magical grip releasing her.

The Alpha stood over the two of them. "Is this the best you can do? Is the Proctors' training inadequate? May Skrull forsake that woman, that I even need be here at all."

Hata coughed, spitting out dirt. She tasted the tinge of blood in her mouth.

Joanna groaned and sat up.

"*Pitiful*," The Alpha spat disdainfully. "You will only receive a half dose of grit tonight to be more *present* in fulfilling my desires." The sides of his mouth lifted into a wicked smile.

"I will please you, Alpha!" Hata blurted. "Use me as you wish."

The Alpha arched a brow. "You think I am daft, little fledgling? You have been enthusiastically volunteering since your little escapade into the woods. You think I know not that you are offering yourself to protect this plump little magpie?"

"I—" Hata's words caught in her throat. "*Please*, Alpha. Don't hurt her again." She glanced at Joanna, who sat unmoving, staring ahead blankly.

"Perhaps." The Alpha fiddled with the golden buttons on his black robes. "Shall we play a little game then? Whoever should be the first to land a strike against me shall get a full dose and will watch as the other is used and beaten."

Hata reeled in surprise as Joanna leaped to her feet, intense flames gathering quickly on her fingertips. Ten strings of fire crackled, arched, and weaved through the air toward the Alpha.

He grinned, "You would enjoy watching me beat the little cardinal, wouldn't you? My meaty magpie."

The strings of fire impacted. Small bursts of flame and smoke exploded rapidly, striking the Alpha.

No, Hata realized. *They hit something around him, an invisible shield, just like the one surrounding the convent grounds.* She was shocked that Joanna reacted so swiftly and eagerly to win the Alpha's proposal. *To see me punished.* Hata looked back and forth between Joanna and the Alpha. She was finished being guilt-tripped by Joanna. *That's how it is, then.* Hata turned back to the Alpha. She studied him further as he stood still, grinning wickedly.

Joanna continued her attack, the Alpha not so much as noticing the explosive power impacting him.

Hata saw the glint of gold on the forefront of his robe. *Golden buttons.* She focused on them, imagining the buttons changing into sharp, jagged cones. She made them spin rapidly, *digging* into the Alpha's flesh.

He shrieked in pain. As his gaze met hers, a sudden flash of white energy illuminated his eyes, and his hand raised toward her.

This time, Hata saw the force coming straight at her. Its invisible momentum streaked through the air, leaving a draft in its wake. Hata leaped, using her hand simultaneously to form two earth pillars at her feet to propel her diagonally away from the barrage. She heard the blast hit where she had been standing but a moment before. Tumbling, Hata rolled to her feet as another blast of force shot by her. She ran.

The Alpha's attacks were relentless, one after another. *Teras give me strength!* She could not stop moving as explosions erupted at her feet behind her. She formed a hundred spinning marbles and sent them whistling toward him. *Take that, you bastard!* The hardened beads of earth bounced harmlessly off his unseen shield. His attack paused for a moment. *Am I imagining it, or are his attacks coming less frequently if he is defending?* She continued firing, endlessly pelting him as she ran. She glanced to see Joanna standing, doing purposefully nothing to aid her.

Pain glanced through her. White light burst in her head as something struck her back, knocking her face first into the ground. She looked up to see the Alpha striding toward her, an ugly sneer on his lips.

"You've had your fun, little cardinal—"

Hata's boulder-sized sphere of spinning earth struck from his side. The man went streaking through the air, bouncing across the ground. Though still surrounded by his invisible protection, he looked like a child's wicket ball bouncing through the streets. He exploded into a small hillside.

"Rose, stop!" Joanna screamed. "You will only make him angrier; he will punish us both!"

"Then we should finish him here!" Hata cried in answer. "Help me, Jo!"

Joanna hesitated, looking at the settling dust and debris where the Alpha had landed, then back to Hata. Joanna shook her head, turned, and ran to the doorway back to the Hall of Transition.

A hoarse, malevolent cackle filled the air.

"You are eager, my little cardinal. Indeed, if the magpie had aided you. Perhaps I may have broken a sweat. I now tire of this game." He touched the buttons on his robe and looked down to see blood on his gloves. His eyes seared with rage. "As that magpie said, you will *both* be punished. But for you, for the one who made me *bleed*. I shall return the favor." He walked out of the dust, his eyes aflame with white light.

Chanel was sitting up in bed, pillows propping her up. The sheets had been changed, and the bed corner was fixed back to its original state. Every breath ached in her chest. The tube was still jutting from her side, tender to any movement she made. But she could take full breaths now. The Alpha had sent for Theta Passeriform, master of healing magic, Cygne Caladrius, to see to her.

He had yet to arrive.

I hope those girls are abiding by the Alpha's wishes. If the girls do not try anything brash, they should be fine. I hope they are fine. The bastard Alpha could end their lives in the blink of an eye if he wished. He would test his fledglings occasionally, but he was not supposed to be administering their training.

"Aerie Proctor, Chanel de Montrichard, I presume?" She heard an elderly voice as one of her orderlies pushed open the door to her living quarters. A hunched man with a long, dragging white robe entered the chamber. Leaning on a humble branch, stripped of its bark and etched with small carvings, he hobbled into the room. Luftan, the orderly, hurried in behind him carrying a large brown bag.

"You presume correctly," Chanel whispered hoarsely in answer.

"Well, what in Hettra's name has happened to you, dear lass?" He had a bushy white beard and eyebrows, but his crown was nearly bald, with short white hair wrapping around the back of his head from ear to ear.

"I believe my lung has collapsed, but I was able to inflate it for the most part."

The man leaned in close, inspecting the tube in her side. She was still shirtless as it was too painful and inconvenient to be clothed.

"This is precise work. The incision and this," Cynge paused as he inspected the wound. "What is this cylinder made of? Looks to be brass; surely not designed for medical use?" He sat on the side of the bed and motioned to Luftan to bring the bag over. He quickly pulled a steel tray from the pack, removed other medical instruments and bandages from the bag, and laid them neatly on the tray.

Chanel was surprised he needed *any* instruments at all. "Your magic will not be sufficient for the situation?"

"Oh ho ho. No, no, my dear lass," he chuckled. "My blood magic is decent at accelerating the healing process and many other things, but it cannot close an open wound. It needs a little bit of rudimentary assistance on that front."

Chanel raised her brows, fascinated. She knew some essential wound treatments she tried to pass on to the women who found themselves in the Convent Enclosure. But perhaps she should inquire about having the Theta impart some knowledge to the girls. *I can't believe I have not thought of it before now. I suppose I have never needed it.*

"Shall we get started then? I need to determine where the lung ripped in the first place. We will need to repair that as we remove the tube. You there," he ordered Luftan. "Pick the woman up for a moment."

"Sir," Luftan answered and made his way over to her.

"Gently now," Cygne reassured.

Luftan put an arm under her legs, behind her back, and effortlessly lifted her from the bed.

She felt his solid arms, his scent filling her. It was comforting, gentle, and caring. She looked up at him and caught his eyes.

He quickly looked away, his face pinking slightly.

Ah, well, I am in the nude. Chanel smirked to herself, then winced as the tube moved somewhat.

Cygne Caladrius, to her surprise, ripped the sheets and pillow from the bed and tossed them to the floor. "Alright, lay her back down as close to the edge as possible.

Luftan gently placed her down, leaning close to her as he did so.

Gods, he smells delicious. She breathed him in. Or as much as she could with only *one lung*, she scoffed to herself.

"Now, Chanel," Cygne said. "I will need you to try and turn onto your side with the wound facing upwards. Can you manage that?"

She nodded in response, but it was easier said than done. It was a struggle to move.

Luftan's hands rested gently on her shoulder and hip, pushing her upward.

"Thank you," she whispered.

"Of course, Lady Proctor," Luftan mumbled in response.

"Brilliant! Now, it is time for some magic! May I place my hands on you, Chanel?"

Nice of him to even ask. He is the polar opposite of the Alpha.

"You may, Theta."

The man's hands were warm and soft yet calloused in places. His hand rested on her ribs, one just under her armpit, the other just below her breast. She felt his hands begin to warm further and further. Now hot to the touch, she clenched her teeth. The heat pushed into her chest, into the damaged lung. It suddenly concentrated on one particular spot within her.

Chanel screamed.

"Ah-ha! Found it." Cygne pulled his hands away quickly.

"Skrull take me," she breathed.

"I'm afraid, my dear, I have only found your troubles' source. I will now have to quicken the healing process of the rip inside you, as I have no physical means of stitching it up from out here. You will have to bear with the heat a bit more."

"Do you happen to have any grit?" she groaned.

His eyes narrowed upon her. "I do not believe such a substance to benefit one's health and will not administer such a thing as an anesthetic." He studied her momentarily and spoke sternly, "I have another less harmful substance that will let you rest peacefully. And when you awake, this will all be taken care of."

A few moments later, she was drinking a cold soup of sorts. The cooling effect flowed through her body. Then, drowsiness clouded her mind. "Theta?" she murmured.

"Yes, my dear?"

"You are kind. If only you could take the Alpha's place?" Her voice began to trail off.

"I'm afraid," there was a hesitant chuckle in response, "I do not have the strength to contest."

"Hmm, you...you should teach my girls..." *My girls.* The lights and sounds faded from her mind.

CHAPTER FOURTEEN

VERDICT

The sun was setting as Kiana entered the circle of onlookers. Mittal Gohra stood chatting with a posse of men on the opposite side of the dusty ring. As he noticed her, he said something to the men, who all laughed as he turned to meet her.

"I was beginning to think you would not show, Kiana Ahmadi," Mittal called as he unsheathed his fine tulwar sword. A rope bola was wrapped around one of his hands tightly.

"I was planning on doing drills instead. At least then, I could break a sweat."

She looked back at Kaplan, who nodded at her as a murmur and cheer from the onlookers on her side erupted at the jeer. Opposite, the men shouted insults back.

"You will eat those words, Ahmadi!" Mittal pointed his blade toward her, his face contorted with anger.

Kiana leveled her blade, the other hand out with two fingers directed at her opponent. She *breathed.*

Mittal dashed forward, bola suddenly loose and spinning in his left hand. His blade arching in high on her left.

She parried the blow with a two-handed grip and saw the bola lash out on her right. With a stoop, the bola whizzed through the air above and into the dust beyond, and she countered with a slash at Mittal's exposed legs, low at his ankles.

He leaped back just in time.

Kiana did not let him recover. She skipped two steps and lunged, aiming for his heart.

Barely catching the blow in time, he deflected it upward, and the blade sliced along the top of his shoulder. He sneered and kicked at Kiana's gut.

She caught the leg under her arm and surged forward. Sending the man off balance onto his back with her atop him.

He managed to land a blow with his free hand.

Kiana blocked with her arm, but the force caused her to roll off him. She continued the roll to her feet and spun back.

He began to push himself up as she leveled the blade behind his neck.

"Yield, Mittal Gohra," she panted. "And relinquish your title."

"We do not surrender in Hasiera!" he screamed. "Finish it!"

"Perhaps this *is* a time to change."

He turned to look at her, eyes burning with rage. "You dishonor the First and his teachings. Everything he gave to us."

"The First is dead, and so are his ways. Mittal, I do not want you to die."

Mittal's eyes softened as he sighed, "Fine, have it your way."

She removed the blade. "Very well—"

He lashed out immediately with his own.

Kiana's sword severed his hand.

He screamed, staring at the bloody stump.

The cutting edge of her sword danced and sliced through his neck.

Mittal Gohra's cries of agony went silent.

"Repair the gate!" Simon exclaimed.

"Repair the gate?" Saudett echoed, murmurs of the same question rippled among them.

Everyone had gathered. Saudett surveyed the people seated in the center of the former First Otsoa's pavilion. Simon and herself. Baal and Brena. Rojas and Anora. Kiana and Kaplan. Zalias Ershya. Kogs and now this newcomer from a distant Lân, Gaelin Yesnala. Only this time, there was no crowd of gatherers shouting in protest of every suggestion. It subtly contrasted the previous day's turbulent arguments between the Otsoa and their people.

"Indeed, repair the gate. If we do this, we must weigh the difference between the boons and banes that are to come of it," Gaelin clarified. "Firstly, this is a great opportunity to renew the water source that breathes life into this valley. The Moreas Lân is a giant bog riddled with rivers and swamps. Our little friend here could tell us more."

Kogs was watching some flies buzzing about his head. Suddenly, his tongue shot out almost faster than Saudett could follow. Snapping right back into his mouth. He continued to eye the ceiling, watching for more flies to wander too close.

"Kogs?" Gaelin reiterated.

"Three arms?" Kogs answered.

"Skrull's balls," Simon sighed and muttered. Then, he sat up taller and spoke loudly, "Sir Kogs! What can you tell us about your home? What does it look like? Are there cities or towns?"

"KYAA!" the lizard screeched. "What does the he-monkey-warlock want with poor Kogs?"

"Kogs." Kiana stood and walked over to where the lizard man was seated. She crouched low so her eyes were level with his and said quietly, "We are trying to find out more about your home so we can help you save your mate, Gaks."

Kogs blinked at her momentarily, then began shaking his head. "No, no. The masters are home. They will hurt my poor Gaks if we try to take him."

"I won't let that happen," Kiana reassured him, gently stroking his red mane.

He gave a hissing, clicking purr, "Yes, the she-wolf demon promised to save my Gaks."

"And that is what we will do," Kiana whispered close to the creature's head. "Now tell us about your home."

"Yes, yes. Kogs' grub-farm. A small stick hut near a big river. Kogs and Gaks pile rocks in circles and defecate in the middle of the circle. Thorn beetles gather and lay eggs, grubs grow, and Kogs and Gaks eat grubs. Sometimes, wrap grubs in large flat leaves and bring them to Rawa to trade."

"Rawa is a town?" Anora asked.

Kogs turned to look at the speaker, then turned his head back to Kiana. He tilted it one way, looked at Saudett, and then back at Kiana. Tilted his head to the other side. "Three she-wolf demons look the same?"

"We are..." the words caught in Saudett's throat emotionally. "*Family.*"

Anora smiled genuinely.

Saudett noticed Rojas watching his spouse from the corner of his eye.

Kiana glowered.

"Ahem," Simon cleared his throat. "Let us try and stay on topic, Sir Kogs."

He is trying desperately to get the creature back on track. Remind you of yourself, my love?

"We just make soup; lizard still looks tasty," Baal gave a rumbling chuckle.

Kogs began to hiss in protest, then abruptly stopped, his eyes widening in realization. "Big one *is* funny!"

Smiles and quiet laughter rippled among them.

"Rawa. What is it?' Kaplan questioned impatiently.

The man is not one for merriments, Saudett thought. *What does my sister see in him?*

"Is a large gathering of mud and stick huts. Many Kadal live here. Hmm, Kogs never made grub soup before." The lizard mirrored Gaelin, who was resting a hand on his chin in thought.

"Kogs!" They all cried in unison. All except Gaelin.

It continued for a long time, constantly keeping the creature in check. The group discerned that the Moreas Lân was a vast swamp with large, thick, moss-covered trees protruding from the miry green waters. Creating a canopy that covered the sky. If one ever saw the sky peeking through the overgrowth, it was always a cloudy dark grey overcast. Rain would fall almost daily. The larger body of water was a river that Kogs lived beside. The canopy stretched over to cover most of the wide river. Kogs's people, the Kadal, used the river for transportation and trade. Rafts were made of broken branches or logs carved from the inside to create makeshift canoes.

Kawa was a town of mud-stick and thatch huts gathered on a unique plateau that rose slightly from the swamp. The big river flows through its center. They had also built their homes along the massive tree trunks and the canopy. Rickety vine bridges connected far above the din below. Some of the Kadal had a membrane growing from their wrist to their ankle, allowing them to glide among the trees. There seemed to be many different species of Kadal. There were the larger, stumpy ones, who were still half the size of a full-grown *she-wolf*, as Kogs put it. These were hunters and warriors.

"Would these warriors help us fight the Daanav?" Saudett asked.

"No, no, the Kadal is small and weak compared to the masters," Kogs said, shaking his mane in sorrow. "They kill many, many Kadal."

"Very well," Kaplan stated. "Now that we know the lay of the land, we can send a Pack to scout."

"We must first fix our means into this Lân before we can do anything," Simon answered.

"RAAAH! Enough!" Baal stood with a roar. "We find Hata. We leave now!" He glared fiercely at Saudett. "Farewell, friend."

Brena stood to join him. "Indeed, it is high time. You all seem preoccupied with matters here, and we have our own."

"Please wait!" Saudett stood up quickly. "We haven't had a chance yet to discuss it, but perhaps Gaelin and Simon can help us get closer to Hata's location. You saw how she was taken and vanished in the blink of an eye. And now these gates allow travel between worlds. They must know something that can help us!"

"All you do is talk," Baal growled in frustration. "There is no spine. No result."

"Certainly, I may try to bring some guidance," Gaelin said. "But I am sorry, as I am not privy to the situation; can someone explain what has happened to me?"

"Their daughter was stolen," Anora answered. "A man. He somehow teleported her away during the chaos of the fighting."

"He had some sort of stone or glass bead he had been fiddling with when we met him at the entrance of Hasiera after the battle," Kiana added.

"Gods, you people," Zalias Ershya snorted. "We've been over this. He is a Huntsman of the Aerie. From Nidhaut. No doubt about it."

"Another new face," Simon muttered.

Saudett eyed Zalias. *I have not yet told Simon that the merchant tried to take me.*

"Ah yes, the Council of the Aerie," Gaelin said. "I have dealt with their curious talons grasping at my heels before."

Saudett studied the strange man before asking, "Are they after you, Gaelin?"

"Quite right, they covet all things magical; they monopolize the market in beings of magic powers, as it were. You would rarely find other countries near Aurulan with as many magi as they have all been poached by the Aerie. I have been lucky enough to avoid them so far."

"How do they discover these magi?" Saudett pondered aloud. "How did they find out about Hata?"

"Just so," Gaelin said, scratching his chin and nodding. "I speculate they have a network of spies throughout the countries. They could even have them among the people of Hasiera."

"It is doubtful," Anora said. "Hasiera is far away, and we have kept its location secret."

"How secret is it, truly?" Zalias questioned. "You freely chose to bring me and some of my *goods* back to it."

Anora frowned at Zalias. "We bring people into the fold; we do not let them leave it."

"It would be difficult to send messages from Hasiera by rider or bird," Rojas added. "The ruse would be discovered immediately."

"A lot of good that does us," Kaplan said blatantly. "The man who took Hata knows where Hasiera is. It will be noted. It will be mapped."

There was silence for a moment.

Baal began fiercely fidgeting and pacing around the others seated in a circle.

"Ah yes," Gaelin continued. "You want to travel closer to the kingdom of Aurulan. This can be accomplished with the use of the Wayfarers Gate. I have constructed another such Gate deep in the Tobek woods, a few days from the capital of Nidhaut."

"That is excellent news!" Saudett's eyes widened as she exclaimed. "Baal, Brena, we can cut down our journey by months with this!"

The two Vouri looked at one another, then back to Saudett. Baal gave his toothiest smile, and Brena's face warmed.

"Of course, repairing the gate and deciding where to point it will take another day," Gaelin added. "Another day to align the portal to the Aurulan Gate or the Moreas Lân way. And vice versa. Where do you all wish to go first? To save this young woman abducted by the strongest magi congregation in this Lân? Or to the Daanav-infested Moreas Lân to secure a water source for the people of Hasiera and save my little friend's mate?"

Silence held once more as everyone looked around at each other.

Simon sighed somberly, his gaze meeting Saudett's.

He is afraid yet knows he must take charge. Saudett held his gaze, his eyes glistening in the low light.

He smiled at her and stood taller. "We will accomplish both. First, we will send a party to Aurulan to secure Hata Vasara, the Sunstone. Saudett, Baal, Brena, and whomever else wishes to aid them will depart first. Once that is done, we will point the gate toward the Moreas Lân, and then," he paused for effect, "Hasiera will go to war once more. This time, we will be on the attack against the Daanav. We will secure the other side of the gate in the Moreas Lân and free the Kadal."

Baal grunted in agreement.

Brena, arms crossed in front of her, nodded.

"Well said, First Otsoa," Rojas affirmed.

"So be it," Kaplan added.

"I will go with Saudett," Anora said excitedly. "I am somewhat familiar with Nidhaut, though it was long ago."

Saudett noticed Rojas's face fall momentarily, and then he righted himself, and his usual calmness returned. He said nothing.

"Thank you, Mother." Saudett gave a warm smile to Anora.

"And I am in debt to Kogs and must aid Hasiera. We go to the Moreas Lân," Kiana said, putting a hand on Kaplan's shoulder.

The man gave a slight nod.

"I will organize our people for the excursion into the Moreas Lân," Rojas stated. "Perhaps we should keep our plan to have a Pack scout the jungles to the south. Just in case we cannot secure water from this new Lân." As he said this, he was looking at Anora. Then he spoke again, "Howler Thien will handle the jungle excursion."

Anora touched her husband's arm gently.

"The merchant Zalias Ershya will come with us, as previously discussed," Saudett grumbled, glaring at the bastard. *Skrull forsaken son-of-a…he is more likely to be a hindrance than any good to us.*

Zalias shuddered under her gaze but put his hands together prayerfully, "Hettra's mercy that we will find the innocent young lady."

Saudett snorted.

Baal growled.

"That leaves the newcomer, Gaelin. Along with our First Otsoa," Rojas said. "What will the two of you do?"

Simon looked at Gaelin.

"Indeed, indeed," Gaelin said, nodding. "We must both be present to configure and open the portal. Simon will not be able to go to the first location."

Saudett sucked in a breath in utter shock. *After all this time. The struggle to find him. Traveling across this Skrull desert, fighting the damned creatures. Carrying his child! Why?* "WHY!?" she screamed.

"My star, hear me—" Simon began.

She ran away. Away, out of the pavilion. Out into the dust. She ran away until her legs burned and her feet sunk into deep sand. *Furious.* In agony. She fell to her knees, slamming her fists into the sand.

Chapter Fifteen

CHANEL

Just let me die! A hand gripped Hata's throat and slammed her head back against the iron bars of their cage. Then, the man struck her face. Once. Twice. One of her eyes swelled, and her nose bled. Blood flowed down her face and neck. *I wish I was dead.* A savage kick to her leg made her buckle. The grasp released from around her neck as she fell to the floor. With another kick to her stomach, she curled up in agony.

"Enough. Keep the fledgling cardinal alive."

Hata could barely distinguish the Alpha from inside the cage through swollen eyes and his two new orderlies. It was not their usual caretakers, Luftan and Tomas. Instead, they were two heavy-set men dressed entirely in black.

Joanna was chained to the opposite wall of the cage, her back facing them, a score of bruises and welts covering her. She sagged against her chains. The Alpha had laughed as his men beat and whipped Joanna repeatedly.

"No relief in the grit tonight, my little birds. You will feel this pain for days to come. Your bodies will reject you as they long for more grit in their systems." The Alpha turned and pointed a gloved finger at one of his men. "Watch them. Deprive them of food for a few days. But keep them alive, water on occasion. Keep them in anti-magic chains so they cannot use their powers. They are not to leave this chamber until I return. I have some business to attend to for just over a fortnight." The Alpha crouched in front of Hata, a finger tracing down her neck and shoulder. "Be aware, *my little birds*, we will pick this up right where we left off."

Hata moaned and crawled toward her pillows and sheets.

The massive doors groaned and banged shut as the Alpha left the cage room.

Ebras Corb exited the enclosure, opening and clenching his hands furiously. His fingers were paining from joining in on the beating. His hand trailed to the blood on his chest. *I can't believe that little bitch managed to wound me.* He headed into the garden toward the left-hand building. The Proctor's quarters. He did not make it far as he was met by an elderly man. *Hobbling on his damned stick.* One of the Proctor's orderlies carried a large case behind him.

"A fine night, isn't it, Alpha? Primus's blessing upon you," the Theta Passeriform, Cygne Caladrius, greeted him as he approached, his white robe dragging behind him.

"Fine indeed." Ebras didn't so much as glance at the sky. "Were you able to see to the Proctor's condition?"

"Firstly, the woman has a substance addiction. Frequent use of said substance caused a rip in her right lung. I managed to stitch it up, and she did wonders to drain the lung of nearly two pints of fluid to reinflate it. She is a brilliant woman and magi, undoubtedly. But she must stop using the grit, or it may happen again."

The grit is supposed to be for the containment of new fledglings, not for self-indulgent, Ebras reproached internally. "Very well, I shall have a word with her. Is she conscious?"

"Afraid not; had to put her under for the procedure. Will not wake until the morrow."

Ebras glared; *I will punish that bitch as well. But the bastard king has called on me to attend him. Doesn't he know who is in charge?* He was to accompany the king to the north for a routine inspection and morale improvement. *The king will give the soldiers some Skrull-forsaken speech or another before sending them off to die. Apparently, the presence of the Alpha Passeriform is encouraging for the troops.* "I'll be on my way, then," Ebras sighed. Turning, he began returning to the crossroad in the garden's center. This is where his pylon of travel was anchored to the Convent Enclosure.

"Alpha?" Cygne's elderly voice called after him, following close behind.

Ebras clenched his teeth but turned with a forged smile as they approached the crossroad. "Yes, Theta?"

"The Proctor asked if I could teach her students some basic healing lessons. Care if I go introduce myself this night?" The old man's eyes flicked toward the other building.

"The fledglings are not of your concern; their training is tightly regimented." Ebras waved a hand in dismissal.

"Of course, Alpha," Cygne nodded repeatedly.

"Would you be so kind as to exit the Convent first, Theta?"

Cygne kept nodding as a light crackled into existence in front of him. He turned and took the heavy bag from the struggling orderly. Lifting it effortlessly with one hand over his shoulder.

The orderly's mouth hung open.

"Farewell, Alpha, good night."

Ebras said nothing.

The Theta Passeriform disappeared, as did the crackling light.

Caladrius is a threat to my operations. Perhaps it is time for a little accident to befall the old man.

Chanel de Montrichard awoke in a sweat, her chest burning. But she could breathe deeply once again.

"You're awake! Chan—um, Proctor." Luftan fumbled over to her bedside from a chair he had been seated in nearby.

"I am," she groaned.

"How are you feeling, ma'am?" His young face, ordinarily clean-shaven, had a dark brown stubble beginning to take shape. Making Luftan, a man in his mid-twenties, appear older.

She gazed at him momentarily before mumbling, "You should grow your beard out, Luftan." She reached up and caressed his face.

He blushed. "Ma'am." His eyes danced down her body.

Fucking hells, I am still completely naked. Gods, what is that smell?

As if he had heard her thoughts, he asked, "Shall I draw you a bath, ma'am?"

"Aye, please do, Luftan," *Skrull take me. I must use the chamber pot, but I can't manage alone. I don't want Luftan to see me like this.* "It has been a while," she hesitated. Blushing, she mustered her confidence, straightening her back. "First, if you will help me onto my chamber pot."

He did not miss a beat. He swept Chanel up, holding her in his arms.

She flushed as she wrapped her arms around his neck. *Such strong shoulders.* She wanted to undress him right then and there.

He kneeled beside her as she did her business, still supporting her with his arms and body.

Well, isn't this romantic? Shitting and pissing before this young thing. This handsome, even caring young lad. It's too good to be true.

Luftan helped clean her up, then deposited her on the chair he had been seated in earlier. Then, he began to fetch water to pour into the large wooden tub wrapped in a canvas sheet in the corner. It was an arduous process. There was a well in the garden to fetch water, but the groundwater was cold as ice. Luckily, her bathtub was enchanted to heat the water to just the right temperature.

Thank Qav's luck for the Epsilon's enchantment magics. They were the only enchanter Chanel had any knowledge of. And the Kingdom of Aurulan was fortuitous to have them as part of the council. *'Epsilons Exciting Enchantments,'* they were eager to say. She had only met them once. Her mind drifted to memory as Luftan readied the bath.

Chanel met *them* one day when the Alpha had brought her as a display of his hard work to a celebration of the Aerie. It was a lavish ball, where everyone was dressed in delicate gowns and extravagant uniform suits. The Epsilon was a tall, feminine, unconstrained, and marvelous individual. Though they had been dressed for the occasion, their garb outshone all the others. Chanel remembered their long-sleeved, open violet and white jacket, which only covered their torso's upper half, exposing the mid-drift and chest. They wore no shirt underneath; instead, their flat chest was painted, or perhaps tattooed, with a colorful canvas of swirls and elegant depictions of many birds flying about their skin. A violet skirt hung just below their knees, and massive fluffy white feathers decorated the dress. They sported polished white high-heeled boots below.

"And who do I have the pleasure of meeting on this fine night of celebration?" The Epsilon bowed low as they greeted Chanel. Their voice was low, soothing, and melodious.

Beautiful makeup of greens, violets, golds, silvers, and whites came to fine points around their eyes, mouths, and other regions.

"I am Chanel de Montrichard," she answered formally. "Newly pronounced Proctor in service of the Alpha Passeriform,"

"Another beautiful maiden *lifted* to the Alpha's office," Epsilon said, smiling coyly. Their blonde hair was combed over, hanging to their shoulder on the left, shaved on the right side, and streaked with vibrant violet.

Lifted. Stolen. Enslaved.

"I thank the Primus for bringing me to the Alpha," Chanel answered mechanically. "He rescued me by taking me under his wing."

"Indeed, Primus and all that. Oh!" they exclaimed. "By Skrull's lovely balls, I haven't introduced myself!"

"No introduction needed, Epsilon Passeriform, Rofous Hornero. Master Enchanter."

"Ah, if only my goods could be expressed to the world! I would open a shop! *Epsilon's Exciting Enchantments!* Come one, come all!" They flourished their arms wide. Then, they abruptly spun around, holding the sides of their skirt. "Do you like my dress?"

I like it, but I won't show it. "It is quite...loud."

"It is! I *adore* it, Chanel de Montrichard, the rescued and the *willing!*"

Chanel was about to retort her loyalty again before the Epsilon cut her off.

"Tell me, Chanel de Montrichard," Rofous bit their lip seductively. "What is one thing that would comfort you in your service to the Alpha." They brought a ringed finger of a white and silver stone to their lips. They kissed the ring and stretched out their hand to touch Chanel on the shoulder.

She suddenly wished to tell Rofous everything. *I have devoted myself to the Alpha's bidding only as a need to survive. I only remember waking up in that cage all those years ago with no name. No memories.*

"I want," she began, then saw a dark figure dressed in gold and black striding up behind the Epsilon, and her mind snapped out of the trance. "What I wouldn't give for a hot bath!" she blurted, pasting on a beaming smile.

The Epsilon narrowed their eyes on her, then seemed to sense the presence behind them. "I shall have one sent to your quarters, my dear Chanel de Montrichard; it will always be set to the perfect temperature."

With that, the Epsilon Passeriform gave a sweeping bow and moved on to another partygoer.

"Have a good chat?" Ebras Corb interrogated, leaning sickeningly close to her face.

"The Epsilon was just offering me a gift to welcome me into the service of the Council."

"Indeed. Do act the part and show the Council that I make exceptional magi out of my lost little fledglings."

"At your will, Alpha."

"Yes," he drawled. "At *my* will."

Chanel snapped back to reality as Luftan lifted her from the chair.

"Here we are, ma'am," he gently guided her into the tub. "Do you need help washing?" He asked politely.

"I do. Please get inside the bath with me," she said confidently, but her face burned with anticipation. "It is large enough for both of us. It will be easier for you to clean all my nooks and crannies that way."

"Uh, are you sure?" He looked at her disconcertedly. "I can probably just lean over and wash from here."

She put on her Proctor's voice. "Need I repeat myself."

"Of course not, ma'am." He moved behind her so she could not watch him undress.

Silly boy, we will soon be naked together in the bath. Why hide now? He walked into view but stayed turned away; his pale, round buttocks were dimpled nicely. *Fucks, his muscles have muscles.* Thick-sinewed thighs rippled as he put one foot into the bath, still facing away from her.

"Turn now," Chanel ordered.

He listened.

She admired him as he blushed at her.

Then, suddenly, his bashfulness was gone as he took a step forward. Though his gentleness was still ever-present. His light brown eyes were soft yet dancing with eagerness. His arms, shoulders, and chest were chiseled and inviting. A patch of darker hair gathered on his chest and trailed down to his abdominal arrowhead and more. *He is a man. How long has it been since I was with someone of my own free will?*

She spread her arms, beckoning for him to come to her.

His gaze softened further if it was at all possible.

They embraced.

For a long time, *he simply held her*.

Chanel de Montrichard wept.

Chapter Sixteen

COMPROMISE

"Surely you can handle the portal alone. How else would you have been using it up to this point?" Kaplan asked after Simon's wife had run from the pavilion.

"Quite right," Gaelin answered. "You have a keen mind...sir?"

"Kaplan Mir."

"Sir Mir." Gaelin turned to Simon. "Care to elaborate, Simon?"

Simon sat with his head in his hands. "No," he muttered dejectedly. *They can all go to Skrull's hell. Primus forsake all of them. I simply wanted to go home, be with Saudett, raise our child, and return to work.* Have a steady life once more. He let his hand fall to the dagger on his belt. *And throw this power away?*

"Very well," Gaelin said. "I will explain. Simon could indeed go with his spouse, but it is better to say that he is unable, simply due to the logistics of things. His talent is more suited to our struggle in the Moreas Lân. He will be in charge of constructing defenses around the portal once we open it." Gaelin spoke in a tone as if it were common knowledge. "He must then set into motion routing a nearby water source toward the gate."

"Not to mention his duty as First to stay and protect his people," Rojas added.

"*My* people? My people!" Simon leaped to his feet, shouting madly. "*My people!* The people who abducted me from my true home! From my wife with babe! The fucking bastards who killed my father! Hasiera is *not* my home and *not* my people." He pushed past Rojas. "Fucks to you all."

"Where are you going?" Rojas grabbed and held his arm. "We are not done here."

"Oh, we are done. I'm going to find my wife," Simon seethed as he freed his arm and exited the pavilion. Shadowing his eyes from the bright, burning sunlight of early afternoon. *The oasis is becoming more and more of a desert,* he thought. Dust blew through the drying brown palms and bamboo patches. *These people will soon die of thirst if they do not take some sort of action. By Hettra's mercy, this is a desperate situation.* He wanted nothing more than to go to Saudett and take her home, but he couldn't leave these people here to die. *Yet I cannot be separated from her again.*

He checked the tent they had slept in the night before, but she was not there. Simon continued to the east through the opening in the wall he had built into the devastation of a battlefield. Finally, the sands began to ascend. He spotted the silhouette of a figure moving in the dunes before him.

He soon spied his wife angrily drilling with her spear. Her face was wet with tears. Thrusting the spear forward, twirling it around, kicking backward, another jab followed by a cross-body swing.

The shaft is a natural part of her body. Simon watched for a long moment, taking in her adeptness and feeling her rage.

She stopped abruptly as she noticed him watching her. She glared at him; he could tell her teeth were clenched behind her closed mouth.

"Saudett, my star, I am caught between a hammer and an anvil," he said as he stepped closer. "If I do not help these people, they will die. And the *last* thing I want is to be away from you."

"And I must help Baal and Brena find Hata."

"You speak true."

"Why can't you come with me? There are plenty of capable people here to lead these people. Why does it have to be you?"

"I don't know. Hasiera's foolish traditions have named me First Otsoa simply for killing another man. Hasiera is a relatively young society. The First founded them; his rules should not be set in stone."

"Then come with me," Saudett pleaded.

"I am tasked with building defenses on the other side of the gate to the Moreas Lân. Not to mention, we must try to reroute a river. If I could just see the lay of the land, I could draft a plan and have my good man Naurr carry it out." *Unfair to Naurr; the foreman has been through enough as it is.*

"Yet you are to send us to Aurulan first."

"If we could convince the Vasara family to wait a little longer," Simon breathed. "We could establish the outpost, then send them on their way, and perhaps I could accompany you. Waiting another week or two will take less time than *walking* to Nidhaut."

"There is another thing time has against us. Our child grows," she said, touching her stomach. "I will soon be of little use. I may as well be a sack of stones weighing them down."

"By the Gods!" Simon rebuked. "You should not be swinging that stick around. You should be resting!"

"I am fine, Simon," she glared back.

"Nevertheless."

She tilted her head. "How long has it been since that morning of the attack on Dagad? Nearly three months? I can get another month or two of action before I settle down."

"Skrull's scrotum, woman, you need to be careful. Getting this *Hata* back will be no small feat and will require your martial abilities. You could miscarry if the child is bounced around too much."

"I know!" she cried with tears in her eyes. "I know! What am I to do? Go back on my word?!"

Simon moved close and wrapped his arms around her. "I'm so sorry. I'm sorry we got dragged into this mess. All this saving the world nonsense. We will figure this out without being separated again. I just need some time to think."

"The time for thinking has passed," a voice said from behind.

They turned to see Brena and Baal.

"You stay and help scrawny husband, friend Saudett," Baal stated with his signature grin.

"No, please," Saudett mumbled. "I *need* to save Hata."

"You are with child; you should be with your husband." Brena smiled warmly. "Circumstances change. It is the way of things. We understand. We knew the risks of going on this journey with you and do not regret helping you."

"You are too kind." Saudett's eyes stayed staring at the sand.

"We do have a request." Brena regarded Simon.

"Whatever you wish," Simon blurted. "We are in debt to you."

"Kiana Ahmadi and Kaplan Mir will accompany us in your stead," Brena answered. "I'm afraid this merchant, Zalias, would not last long in our company alone."

"Kiana does want to help her lizard friend, but I think she could be convinced," Simon pondered aloud. "If not, I will abuse my power as First to make it so."

"Lizards could make a good food source for starving people," Baal grunted, looking around the destitute camp.

"Skrull's balls, man." Simon choked.

Baal's teeth gleamed as he grinned at Simon.

Saudett dropped her spear and went to Brena, embracing her. "Skrull take me. A thousand times, you are too fair to me."

Brena touched Saudett's head and gently stroked her hair. "When you have completed your task here, perhaps you can follow us?"

Saudett nodded. "I will try."

"Alright then," Simon chimed in. "Gather what you need. Gaelin and I will begin repairs on the portal soon. Hopefully, we can have you away on the morrow. I will inform the others who are to accompany you."

Brena and Baal departed.

Saudett and Simon began to make their way back to the First's pavilion.

"I am abandoning Hata," Saudett muttered shamefully. "I am worse than scum. This girl. I told this girl that I loved her."

"And did you love her?"

"I don't know. Hata comforted me in my grief. I think perhaps I used her to satisfy and distract myself from losing you and Yakeb."

Simon nodded, his arm around her waist as they walked. "It is understandable."

"I shouldn't have led her on," Saudett said, shaking her head. "As we traveled together, I became frustrated with her. She was still so young and *stubborn*. I took advantage of her. Though, she immediately got on with my younger half-sister, Kiana." Saudett exhaled with exasperation. "Hata, somehow, sees the good in everyone. Her parents raised her well."

"She seems like a fine young woman still finding her way."

"Simon, when this is all over, and we go home with our child, can we stop seeing other people? Make it just the two of us from now on?"

He raised his eyebrows in surprise. Saudett had been enthusiastic and encouraging in all aspects of their open relationship. What had changed? "Of course, if that is what you wish." He leaned over and kissed her head as they walked.

"Is that what *you* wish?" She looked up at him.

"Perhaps. I don't know. As you know, I enjoy being with a man occasionally." Simon smiled wryly. "But it is far from the mind at the moment. When this is all over, and like you said, things have settled down. We will talk about it. And truly, with a newborn babe," he chuckled. "Will we even have time for such fun?"

"Alright," Saudett whispered, then smiled warmly and momentarily tilted her head to rest on his shoulder.

They soon found themselves back at the flaps of the large tent where the meeting was being held.

"My dear," Simon readied himself. "Let's get this over with."

Simon and Saudett, hand in hand, strode into the pavilion.

The room was still in a heated discussion. All except Baal and Brena were present, with the addition of Howler Thien, Naurr Andiges, and a few other Otsoa.

"Attention, everyone," Simon commanded as he joined the group.

All eyes turned to him.

"Change of plans. The Aurulan party members have changed. Saudett will stay with me here. I implore Kiana Ahmadi and Kaplan Mir to accompany the Vouri to Aurulan."

Kiana frowned at Simon and pointed toward the little lizard man sitting in Gaelin's lap. "What of Kogs. I am to abandon him?"

"He seems to be in good hands," Simon stated, nodding at Gaelin. "And we have all the Hasieran focused on ridding the Moreas Lân of the Daanav. We *will* find Sir Kogs's mate."

Kiana looked at Kogs for a long moment, who was not paying any attention to the conversation. She shrugged. "As is your will, First Otsoa."

That was easy. Simon addressed the others, "Would anyone else wish to volunteer to rescue the magi Hata, the Sunstone?"

"Have any of you ever been to Nidhaut before?" Anora enquired. "Other than the slaver, Zalias?"

Silence answered.

"Another reason I should be with them," Saudett muttered beside Simon.

"I have been," said Naurr Andiges. "Though I am thinking that the boss has other things in mind for old Naurr and the boys, eh?"

"I'm afraid," Simon cleared his throat nervously. "I will need you and the men for another little project, my good man."

"So, *when* do we plan to go home? Boss?" Naurr's expression was brooding.

"Let's talk about this later, please," Simon pleaded.

Naurr held Simon's gaze.

He looks so tired, Simon thought. *His son and wife are waiting back in Dagad for him. How many people had to suffer because of the Daanav?*

"Then I will also go, as previously decided. I have experience in that city," Anora said.

Nods and murmurs of agreement.

Anora moved to Saudett's side and said quietly, "Let us go speak. I need to tell you of your father before I leave."

Saudett looked at Simon, and he nodded.

The two women departed.

"As of now, I am retracting the former First's law that nobody may leave Hasiera. Dire times call for dire measures, as they say. Speak with your Otsoak. If anyone is wanting and willing to leave Hasiera and head for civilization, properly outfit them and have them make way as soon as possible."

"You would throw years of our culture into the dust!" Howler Thien growled.

"Years!' Simon cut them off. "Hasiera was founded only two decades ago. It is young and needs to adapt to what is happening. Its culture is still taking shape. It could indeed be a part of the outside world. A stop along the way through this treacherous Burning Sea. A watering hole, a place for trade and merriment. It could grow and flourish. But none of it will matter if we cannot save it!"

Quiet murmurs of agreement ripple through the room.

"There is no place for the Volkinn in the outside world," Howler Thien hissed in frustration.

Simon was finished debating. "Enough! Make ready. On the morrow, we will send the Aurulan band on its way." Simon turned to exit the tent once more.

Come, Gaelin Yesnala, we'd best get started repairing the gate.

The three-armed Iban'mael followed him out, Kogs cradled in one arm.

CHAPTER SEVENTEEN

FLIGHT

Hata felt everything. No grit to dull her agony. Her bleeding wrists were chained to the cage. The pain and hunger tore at her, and what little food was given her was impossible to keep down. She vomited it up almost immediately. Her body constantly shuddered involuntarily, and her head was continually throbbing, feeling each heartbeat explode within. The back of her throat and nose desired the powder, watering with craving. *I cannot do this any longer,* she thought as she looked at the large oak doors to their prison. *I don't want to feel anything anymore. I need more grit.*

Joanna whimpered and moaned on the other side of the cage. Hata could barely move her head to look at the woman, quivering upon her back, her hands stretched out above her, still chained to the cage.

The two men took turns watching them, but they were getting restless. She feared they would soon do more than just beat them. It felt like ages since the Alpha had departed. *Was it days? Or merely hours?*

The cage door rattled as one of the men entered. "Enough of this Booth! He never said we couldn't have any fun now, did he?"

"Nay, he did not, Durant," the fat man said as he stood, stretched. His scraggly ginger-white beard shaking. "Oh, it will be a grand ole time from here on out, my little lassies. Alas, I bet they're dryer than your nan's fanny!" Booth slapped the other man on the back as he chortled. "Eh there, Durant?"

"Fucks to you, Booth, my nan's a saint!" Durant was a younger, heavy-set man with patchy chestnut hair.

"A saint? Never mind that. Look, this one is a giant! It will be like fucking a tree, Durant. Of course, you would be used to that," Booth heckled while picking his fingernails with a dagger.

"What? I ain't fucked no trees, Booth." Durant strode over to Hata and leered down upon her. "More like a bony dead fish, she is," he muttered, kicking Hata in the stomach.

Hata heaved vomit. It was reddened, a blend of blood and mucus.

"Oh, Skrull's warty balls. She done it again. Damn, fuckin' stinks in here. I think they are starting to rot, Booth."

"The boss might not be too happy if they go and die," Booth paused and gave a gapped-toothed grimace. "*Unless* they was trying to escape? Eh there, Durant?"

Durant scratched his patchy chin. "You might be on to something there, Booth."

There was a squeak and groan of wood as the large doors to their chamber opened slowly.

Tomas peaked his head in. His eyes widened in shock. "What are you doing!?" he exclaimed, rushing into the room. "You are killing them!"

"Eh, boy, we're just having some fun," Durant answered impishly.

"The Proctor will not have this!" Tomas moved toward the entrance of their cage. Hata could see anger in the young orderlies' eyes.

"We are acting on the Alpha's orders, *boy*," Booth hissed as he slid behind the young man.

"This is not the Alpha's Convent—" The air was pushed out of Tomas with a guttural grunt as Booth's dagger was jabbed into his back, diagonally into his lung. Tomas's mouth began opening and closing repeatedly, trying to suck in a breath. His eyes extended further with realization and horror. He tried to turn, swinging his arm at the man behind him.

Another dagger plunged into his heart.

Durant pulled the dagger free. Blood spurt from Tomas's chest as he collapsed forward.

The door creaked and groaned once more.

Chanel de Montrichard stood, one arm over Luftan's shoulder as he supported her.

Durant stuttered, "Now, now, Lady Proctor. This is the Alpha's bidding—"

"*Fuck* the Alpha."

Durant's head exploded.

Chanel had poured forth a gale of wind, like a ballista, from her outstretched hand. Swiftly and violently.

The cage behind Durant dented inward.

Gore spattered across the man named Booth. Raising one hand above his head in surrender, Booth bent and placed his dagger on the cobbles. "We didn't mean no harm, Proctor Lady."

The Proctor, Chanel de Montrichard, made a motion with her hand. This time, a wind blade cut horizontally just above the man's head.

His hand lopped off. He screamed. The dagger skittered across the ground as he kicked it in his turmoil, clutching at his wrist.

"Do grab that knife and cut his tongue out, please, Luftan," Chanel respired wearily. "He will have a slow death, but silence his bewailing."

Luftan nodded, but first, he helped Chanel into the cage before moving toward the screaming man.

Hata stared in awe.

"My dear girl," Chanel knelt before her. "I'm so sorry it came to this. Had I been here, none of this would have happened."

"You are here now!" Hata sobbed in relief. "*Chanel*."

"I am," Chanel smiled warmly, touching Hata's cheek. But we are getting out of here. I am finished with the Alpha and his ways."

"Thank you, Chanel. My name is *Hata*. I remembered quite some time ago."

Booth's screaming ended abruptly.

Hata leaned her head to see Luftan with the dagger moving about in the man's mouth, who was now on his back, twitching sporadically.

Chanel looked into Hata's eyes, a glint of satisfaction reflecting in them. Chanel raised her brows, returning to the conversation. "You surprise me, *Hata*. You are strong-willed; I hadn't the slightest idea your memory had returned."

Hata did her best to smile back at the woman. The pain still gushed through her. "The Alpha said he would be gone for a long time. He left these men here to guard us."

"Did he say how long?" Chanel asked urgently.

"Just over a fortnight."

"Good, that will give us time to heal before we move."

"Uhm," Luftan cleared his throat. "Proctor."

"Yes, Luftan?"

"He's holding something. A marble or stone, like the ones around your neck." Luftan bent over and pried a blood-covered marble from the dead Booth's hand.

Chanel squinted and motioned Luftan to bring the object over to them. "Oh gods," Chanel muttered as she inspected the coloring.

It was a pale, tawny, off-white stone.

"What is it?" Hata urged.

Chanel swallowed nervously. "It is a message marble. It is meant to notify the Alpha in case of emergencies."

"What are we going to do?" *The Alpha will punish or kill all of us.* Hata felt a shiver of fear overcome her.

"Luftan, get her free and help her up. We need to go to the pylon in the garden. I have one teleportation stone we can use."

"Yes, ma'am." Luftan promptly acquired keys to the fetters from the dead man and aided Hata to her feet, draping a silk sheet over her as he did so. Then he asked, "What about the other woman?"

Hata looked to where Joanna lay, seemingly unconscious, though she was still whimpering and groaning every so often. Pain washed through Hata's entire body as Luftan moved her out of the cage. "We must help her!" Hata begged.

"I can barely move, girl," Chanel hissed, her face contorted in pain. "Luftan cannot carry you both."

"Joanna," Hata began, but a thought came to her. She thought about how quickly Joanna had leaped at the opportunity to put her before the Alpha's violation. *Even so, I can't just leave her.* Saudett's voice came to her mind.

Do not hesitate, or people will die.

Hata nodded resolutely. "Let's go."

They issued forth into the mid-morning light, hurrying as quickly as they could toward the crossroad in the garden.

The rip in matter appeared before them, and out stepped Ebras Corb, the Alpha Passeriform of the Council of the Aerie.

"What is the meaning of this?!" he shrieked. His eyes were burning with white light.

At that exact moment, Chanel's attack struck him. The winds force thundered into him, his invisible barrier taking the blow yet pushing him back.

"Take this!" Chanel ripped the pendant from her neck, tossing it to Luftan, who caught it deftly.

"What is it?!" Hata screamed.

"The translucent stone, activate it with blood—"

Chanel was suddenly constricted and flung toward the Alpha. His hand was outstretched as if clenching the Proctor.

It is the same attack he used on me. Chanel is going to be caught! Hata focused on the Alpha. Gold still gleaming on his robes. *Arrogant bastard. He hasn't learned his lesson.* This time, she envisioned the buttons into long, jagged, pointed nails. She *hammered* them in.

Chanel crashed into the cobblestones a handful of paces from the Alpha.

He clutched his hands to his chest and hunched over.

Chanel reacted swiftly, raising her hands above her head. Dark clouds suddenly formed, twisting rapidly and snaking toward the ground. The tempest struck Ebras Corb directly, and he was sucked into the maelstrom.

"NOW!" Chanel screamed. "To the crossroads; it is the only place in the convent that you can teleport! Go now! Luftan, take her!"

Hata was pulled along by the young man, closer and closer to the roaring whirlwind.

As Luftan pulled her past the Proctor, hands still reaching the skies, Hata saw a grim look of acceptance in Chanel de Montrichard's eyes. *Acceptance of her death.*

"No! Chanel!" Hata cried. "Come with us!"

Luftan, holding Hata with one arm, fumbled with the medallion that Chanel had tossed to him. His hands were covered in the blood of the dead man, Booth. He pried the creamy marble-free into a sticky, bloody hand using the dagger he had taken. He crouched low, pulling Hata down with him. He rolled the now-coated marble forward.

The fissure of light opened before them. They both looked back at the Proctor of the Convent Enclosure, *Chanel de Montrichard.*

Chanel smiled. And then, her face contorted in anguish as her arms were torn from her body.

Hata shrieked, reaching out toward Chanel de Montrichard.

Luftan pushed Hata through the light. He did not follow her.

Chapter Eighteen

FAITHFUL

Kiana sat outside the tent where her mother and newfound sister, Saudett, had entered. Kiana sat and listened.

"Your father. I killed him," Anora's voice drifted through the thin canvas sheets. "Out of pure hatred, I killed him."

"When? Why?" Kiana heard Saudett ask eagerly.

"Let me tell you."

"Let them through!" A voice shouted down from above.

A portly city guardsman waved the lead wagon forward. "Aye, Company Kafilah is welcome in Nidhaut."

"Primus's blessing to you," Gaddaar Kafilah said with a bow.

"And Hettra's bosoms be soft; I haven't got time for blessings. Move these wagons through quick like," the guardsman ordered, ushering them down a long tunnel under the portcullis.

Anora Kafilah followed her husband, Gaddaar, into the capital of Aurulan, the city of Nidhaut. The train of wagons and pack animals trailing behind them.

As they stepped back into the light of day, immediately upon entering the city, eight massive towers spiraled upward into the sky. Each building was uniquely different. The centermost one, broad at the base, tapered skyward, abruptly changing to a spherical shape. Its stone was of obsidian. Bands of gold weaved through the pitch-black stone, the glimmering gold then spiraling down the column to its base. Another spire was purely white, with jagged angles. And there was yet another that looked nearly tree-like.

Anora was always in awe of these monoliths, fascinated by the talk of council members who resided there. The Council of the Aerie. She had yet to meet one in the hundreds of visits to the country's capital. She wondered if they were but a myth, propaganda to bolster the people's spirits. Yet those towers, some of them seemed to defy logic. She shrugged to herself; *I am no architect.*

"I am speaking to you, woman."

Anora startled. "Yes, dear—"

"Finish handling the details here with our clients," Gaddaar cut her off. "And begin looking for others to return to Xamid."

"Yes—"

"I have much business to attend to." His dark eyes looked everywhere but *at* her. "I expect to be departing no later than the dawn of the day after tomorrow."

"Perhaps the men could take a few more days of rest? We have been on the road for weeks."

Finally, his eyes met hers and ignited in anger. "I did not wed you so I could listen to your prattle. I wed you to bear me sons and obey my orders."

She sunk back. "Yes, my husband."

"Now, *do it.*"

"Of course." She watched as he turned and walked into the crowded streets, his maroon cape of their house waving behind him. Anora sighed heavily. *What business could he possibly have that is all important? By the gods, I should follow him.*

"Lady Kafilah?" a voice with a slight Vouri accent said from behind.

Anora turned to see one of her caravan guardswomen standing behind her.

"You look like you need to know where Lord Kafilah is off to, my Lady?" She was stout, often mistaken for a man; wearing silver banded armor, a soldier's helm, and the maroon linens of Company Kafilah.

"Ovella," Anora answered slowly.

"Speak now before my eyes stop tracking him."

Anora nodded, putting a thumb to her lip in thanks. "Go."

"Lady." The woman trotted off in the direction her husband had gone.

Anora gazed momentarily, watching as Ovella vanished into the streets; she regarded the tall, white-washed homesteads framed with black pine logs. *Very pale and dreary in comparison to the colorful city of Al'Jalif, the Jewel of the East. Where I left my daughter.*

Anora sighed in relief this time. She had an inkling, no, a *need* to see where that bastard of a husband was going. She heard a commotion, looking back at the caravan still trickling through the gates. People were starting to yell with irritation at the slow goings of the many wagons. She briskly marched over and began issuing orders.

Perhaps two bells later, the entire caravan was through the gate, goods were delivered, and payment was received from the body of merchants who had employed them.

"Take rest and drink well," she said to the three dozen or more members of the caravan guard. She handed out a gold piece to each from the wealth she had just acquired. "We meet at this gate at dawn the day after tomorrow."

"We have been walking for over a month, Lady Kafilah. Can ya not give us a longer leave?"

"Yeah! This is horseshit."

There were grumbles and calls of disagreement.

"Lord Kafilah commands it," Anora answered solemnly.

The dissatisfaction quieted a bit. The guards began walking off into town.

"If it weren't for the pay, I'd find a different company to join," one young man mumbled.

"Aye, you're right on that front, laddie."

"The Lady tries to look out for us grunts; she does. She is a kind soul."

"It's that Skrull-damned Lord Kafi..."

The words dissipated as the speakers moved out of earshot.

Anora headed toward the *Marché de la Ville,* a square carved out of the city with storefronts on the buildings bordering the four-sided market. The square's centerpiece was a massive white stone fountain depicting an eagle swooping to clutch a fish in its talons. Avenues of market stalls were neatly organized about the thoroughfare.

Anora made her rounds. It was routine at this point, starting with the more significant buildings and inquiring with the owners if they were planning to send goods soon. If enough were interested, she would organize and pool all interested parties and give them the departure date. For such short notice, few merchants would be inclined to sign up.

She had a half dozen signed as she exited a jewel shop back into the market proper. The sun was beginning to set, and the marketplace was dying down. She took a few steps and then jerked as someone touched her arm.

"Lady Kafilah," Ovella grunted.

"Ovella! You startled me," Anora said, straightening. "What news of my husband's whereabouts?"

Ovella pulled her down a side street away from the bustle of people. "Aye, 'tis not a pleasant report, my Lady. He entered a bawdy house in the back lanes of the *Ville de Voleurs*, southeast side of the city."

"I feared as much. My thanks to you, Ovella," Anora put a hand on Ovella's shoulder. "What was the name of this house?"

"*La Maison du Paon.*"

"I know of it. Would you care to accompany me? I must visit my dear husband."

"No, ma'am, 'tis none of my business what goes on with you and the Lord Kafilah."

"Then why offer to follow him?"

"Know this, Lady; we, the guard of Company Kafilah, are on *your* side. I am simply offering a Teras- willed nudge in the right direction, as it were." A gap-tooth smile obscured by the soldier's helm peaked through.

Anora nodded in response. "My thanks again, Ovella."

Ovella clutched Anora's shoulder. "May Teras' fortitude grant you a steel heart."

Anora gestured in thanks once more as the guardswoman Ovella departed.

Sometime later, Anora had returned to one of two wagons the company kept for personal items. She assumed this place, *La Maison du Paon*, would consist mainly of men gloating over scantily-clad women. She removed her armor and weapons, sliding only a dagger into her sash. She donned a simple tan robe and covered her face with a shawl. *Perhaps I should dress more suggestively to try and blend in?* she pondered, then shrugged. *This will have to do.*

Ville de Voleurs was the seedy underbelly of Nidhaut. The criminal's corner. The streets were not as smooth as on the main streets and upper-class districts of Nidhaut. By contrast, the road here was cracked and missing cobbles, caked with mud and shit, as there was little to no upkeep in this part of town. Beggars and the homeless riddled the district. Darkly-clad figures whispered in shaded alleys, while bulky goons sat and leaned on porches with cudgels at their sides.

Anora looked upward at a jagged, towering turret. It was almost mountain-like, with natural angles of stone jutting forth, like cliffsides, yet ascending unnaturally in a cylindrical column, as if the rock had grown skyward. She could faintly make out the dark shapes of large wings circling at the tower's height. *This is the home of one of the Aerie magi.*

Graffiti was scrawled across the base of the turret:

FUCK THE AERIE

DELTA'S CUNT

LIARS

SKRULL TAKE THE BIRDS

There were poorly scrawled images of genitalia and what she assumed was a carcass of some sort.

Anora continued, avoiding other passersby as much as possible. Finally, she approached a structure that stuck out from all the other downtrodden buildings on the street. This one was well-kept and colorful. Painted a multitude of blues and greens. Bright cerulean lanterns lit the house's exterior, framing an intricately painted sign that read *La Maison du Paon.*

Armed guards stood barring the entrance.

As Anora approached, one of them hailed her, "Step off, tramp, unless you have gold to spend."

Anora casually opened her robe and jiggled a pouch full of coins.

"Ah, head on in then." The guard moved aside.

The faint sounds of carnal pleasure tickled her eardrums as the door opened inward. *So, this is where the bastard spends his time away from his dear wife.* After a short hallway, she moved into a mid-sized antechamber. On her left stood a beautiful dark-skinned Tulu woman with thick dark locks fanning around her upper body. An undergarment that left nothing to Anora's imagination. Beside her was a feminine, pale man who invitingly lounged on a cushioned chair. Third was a tan and muscular man wearing a tight, semi-opaque silk loincloth.

A young man sat behind a quaint desk and greeted her as she entered. As she approached, he stood and adjusted a slimming, fine azure tunic. "My Lady! Welcome to *La Maison du Paon.* My name is Personne. How can we be of service to you?" He gestured to the three figures. "Take your pick."

"In truth, I am not looking for your services—"

"Then see to the door." He sat back down abruptly. "What do we pay those fools outside for," he mumbled, removing a comb from the desk and neatly pulling it through his fair blonde hair. A small mirror sat on the desk before him.

"I'm looking for my husband."

He didn't look up. "We don't kiss and tell here at *La Maison du Paon*. Business is business. Off with you now before I call the guard."

"I beg you; he is a Xamidian man dressed in crimson and armor. He would be difficult to miss."

Personne began applying dark makeup to his eyelids. "Enough, woman; either pay for a whore and be escorted to the back rooms or leave. *Now.*"

Anora eyed the three figures. *Escorted to the back room? Perhaps I can sneak off and investigate while I'm back there.* "Is this all the selection?" she asked curiously.

"Well, well. That is more like it. Your name for the records, Lady?"

"Kafilah."

His grey-green eyes flinched for a moment. "Ask away. What type of selection are you looking for?"

"These three are beautiful, to say the least. But I'm afraid I only have a fancy for men." She pointed to the man standing at the end of the row. "I want him and another who will enjoy him as I watch."

"Make it so," Personne nodded to the drab man.

The man strode over to Anora, slipping her hand into the edge of his silk loincloth, ready to lead her on.

"A moment, Lady Kafilah." Personne stopped them. "We take half the payment up-front."

"And how will you know what my total payment will be? I have not yet used the goods," Anora answered sternly, naturally ready to haggle with this panderer.

"We have a flat rate per body, no time limit. You want two bodies. That comes to fifteen gold per. Oh, and we *graciously* ask that you offer a gratuity to your servers." Personne smiled, waved a hand, then continued powdering his nose and cheeks.

Anora hesitated. *This must be a high-end establishment, for that is expensive.* That was a lot of coins to invest in this little endeavor. *What if he isn't even here?*

Her husband left the financials of the Caravan House to her. He would not even know she had spent it. *He is here. I know it. I questioned where a heavy lump of our income had been going. Now I know.*

"Done," she spilled some coins on the desk before Personne. "Take what is needed."

He looked up at her apprehensively before counting out the coin. "One more thing."

"By the gods, what now?"

"This is a no-weapon establishment. Please leave that lovely knife with me."

She felt her teeth grinding; then, with a smirk, flicked the dagger out, spinning it deftly, and thudded it into the desk.

He didn't even blink. "Very good, be on your way."

Her server escorted her through a doorway just behind the man's desk. The sounds of ecstasy she had heard earlier slowly increased in volume as they approached yet another entrance. Then, the sound peaked as they entered a large room into a massive binge of bodies, sweat, and smells of fornication.

"We could join the pit?" the man escorting her asked.

Most of the people involved in the orgy were of pale Aurulan complexion. The darker tones of the Tulu and Xamidian present contrasted against the rest. Anora was surveying every face, looking for her husband. It did not take long for her to see that Gaddaar was not among them.

"What about those chambers?" she pointed to what looked like booths along the walls, only translucent sheets covering the openings.

"Ah, a private quarter it is, then. You are also looking for another man to join us?"

"Indeed. Can you give me a little tour?" Anora squeezed his *firm* buttocks. *Hettra's tits! That is a fine arse.* She pointed to the second level of curtained chambers above them with her spare hand. "See the sites, as it were? What is on the upper balcony?"

"Upper balcony is for business meetings. Our *servers* provide entertainment for those undertaking long and arduous transactions."

Anora had a strange feeling her husband would be up there. "Well, lead on; let's find another fine young man to join us. Perhaps one slightly on the feminine side would be to your liking?"

He looked at her for the first time and grinned. "It would."

She nodded and let him bring her about the establishment. There was a bar serving drinks and other substances. She witnessed many people snorting a black powder off other people's bodies as their eyes rolled back in their heads.

As they made their way around the lower floor, she glanced into most of the canvased chambers on that floor. Gaddaar was not present in the countless different sexual positions she witnessed. Patron and server alike took no notice of her.

"Please take me to the upper floor. I want to look down on this passionate display of lust."

"As long as we stay out of the meetings."

"Of course, of course."

He led her up a fine wood staircase draped with navy blues, violets, and coral silks. They strode along a banister, looking down at the copulations. Then she heard her husband's voice behind her, gasping and grunting between words.

"Grit? How—how much do you—do you need this time?" His voice broke every so often. She could hear skin slapping against skin.

"As much as that damn caravan of yours can carry, for Skrull's sake," another voice answered.

"Lisak, you know this; we are but the guard. We do not handle...by the gods! Fucks!" Gaddaar groaned as he struggled to speak. "We do not handle the goods. And my cunt of a wife sees to my company's wagons."

"What good is keeping that bitch with you, Gaddaar?"

"It was an arranged marriage; I had no say. The woman only bears me a daughter and insists on staying with it. Not in my house; I will tear her from her child's clutching hands until she bears me a son. Though no matter how often I give it to her, she never comes of babe."

Sick son-of-a-whore! Anora clenched her fists and clenched her jaw.

"Lady, we had best move on; they will accuse us of eavesdropping," her server whispered.

Fucking bastard! she screamed internally, but let herself be led off.

"Shall we choose another now, my Lady?"

"I have something else in mind. What is your name, by the way? I do not think I caught it."

"I am Personne."

She tilted her head. "Personne? Like the man in the lobby?"

He gestured to the others about them. "All *La Maison du Paon* personnel go by that name."

"Oh, I see. What does it mean?"

"It means that we are *nobody*."

Fitting, she thought. "Personne, do you think you and I could act as entertainment for that chamber back there? I need to get inside."

"You wish to encroach on their business?"

"He is my *husband,*" she hissed. "It *is* my business."

He studied her momentarily, then nodded. "As long as you can act the part."

"I'll be fine. I know how to make the whore-fucker finish. No offense."

"None taken. You'd best lose the clothing."

She untied the robe's sash, let it fall to the floor, and removed her linen trousers, shirt, and underwrappings. They were of practical use, not very pleasing. She decided to go in stark naked, only wrapping her head and face so as not to be recognized. Her dark eyes peered through the mask mysteriously.

"You are enticing to witness, my Lady," Personne stated, looking her up and down.

Anora felt her cheeks warm. "Thank you, Personne. I'm sure you tell all your customers that."

"Only the ones I admire." He winked.

"Shall we?"

He led the way back to the chamber her husband's voice had come from. He held the curtain open and ushered Anora inside.

Her husband had a rotund woman sitting on his lap. Bouncing up and down, slapping enthusiastically, as Gaddaar held her enormous breasts in his hands.

"Ah-ha, more entertainment! You may have that sturdy young man there, Lisak," Gaddaar said to the other man in the chamber. "The Xamidian is mine."

A round man, wearing violet and red fabrics, accented with much silver jewelry, sat with a seemingly unconscious man lying before him. Rows of black powder were neatly lined around the unconscious man's genitals. The fat man, Armand, inhaled one of the lines in a quick snort. "Yes! Come here, Personne," the large man warbled. "They sent one of the *good* ones for once. Play with my cock here while I finish this."

Personne did not hesitate and moved to find a seat beside the large man, Armand.

"What are you waiting for, whore? I've had enough of this one," Gaddaar ordered as he pushed the chubby young woman off. She rushed out of the chamber. He bent over and snorted one of the lines of powder on the man sprawled out before them. "Don't make me repeat myself."

The words echoed in Anora's head. *The last thing he had said to our daughter before leaving on this trip.* She clenched her jaw and knelt before her husband. Pulling her mask down, she began to pleasure him. Pleasure him better than she *ever* had before.

"Skrull take me. Keep up with that," Gaddaar gasped and continued his dealings. "As I said, I cannot begin to conceal your *honest* goods as long as my wife is around. She handles all of the logistics. I will say— *fucks*—I will say, she is too quick for her own good. I wished I'd been set up with a daft, fuckable dimwit instead of her. She nearly escaped with her daughter one night. Did I tell you that story, Lisak?'

"Only a thousand times, Gaddaar. You beat her to a pulp for that display of disobedience."

"Fucking hells," Gaddaar snickered. "The bitch never done me as good as this whore!" He looked down at her.

She held his gaze with ferocious intent.

"Skrull's balls, the fire in this one's eyes has me brimming."

"Well, Gaddaar," Lisak said, putting an arm around Personne and leading him down. "Perhaps it's time this lady wife of yours met with a terrible accident on the road?'

"Ha!" he laughed again. "The guard would turn on me. Only a few I pay extra would stay at my side. It would even start a bloodbath."

"It will be an *accident*. Say the word, Gaddaar, and I'll put someone on it."

Gaddaar Kafilah did not hesitate a moment. "*Do it.*"

An image flashed before Anora's eyes. She pictured herself biting down as hard as she could.

Then, Gaddaar's screams of agony as he tumbled backward, clutching his bleeding crotch.

An image of Anora spitting the appendage out of her mouth. Of her straddling him, jabbing both thumbs into his eyes. Whispering as she leaned in close to his ear, "Know this. It was your wife that *fucked* you in the end." She pressed down as hard as possible, digging his eyes out with a sickening pop.

His screeching and babbling incomprehensively a melody to her ears.

An image of her pulling a long, thick pin from her tied-up bun. Stabbing it into Gaddaar's chest. Again and again and again. Blood covering her. She pictured him gurgling and twitching and *dying* beneath her.

Anora returned to reality as he finished with a feeble moan in her mouth. "Now, begone, whore!" Gaddaar waved her out. "Send in another."

She stood, turned, hurried out, and spat.

"You should have done it, Mother. You should have bitten the bastard's cock right off." Kiana heard Saudett's heated voice from inside the tent.

I couldn't agree more, dear sister.

"Perhaps...perhaps I should have," Anora said remorsefully. "Things might have turned out differently if I had. Instead, I bided my time. I waited for an opportunity. That opportunity took place on our return journey through the Burning Sea."

CHAPTER NINETEEN

FRIEND

"We need more bones to repair this thing?" Simon asked suspiciously. *I don't know why I even asked, as I already know the answer.*

"Indeed," Gaelin answered nonchalantly. "Preferably bone from someone still alive, as it is far more potent. Alas, I wouldn't go so far."

Naurr shuffled nervously, shovel in hand. "This is witchcraft. Skrull will be taking us all."

They stood over a mass grave up the hills on the south side of the valley. The sun hanging low in the western sky.

"It leaves a bitter taste in the mouth," Simon agreed, giving his tongue a distasteful click.

Naurr nodded. "We dishonor these people."

"Even so, it is the only way. Please, Mister Andiges, if you will." Gaelin nodded at a mound in the granular earth before them.

With a squeal, Kogs jumped down from Gaelin's shoulders. "Kogs can dig!" He scurried over to the mound, and a mixture of sand and dirt began spraying behind the Kadal lizard man.

"It looks to be you got no need of me then, eh?" Naurr let the shovel fall from his hands.

"Naurr, may I speak to you for a moment?" Simon touched the foreman's back, leading him away from the other two.

"Aye, boss, what do you need now of your faithful servant?"

Simon noted the bitterness behind the words. "Naurr, my good man. Would you like to return to Dagad once this portal is in working order?

"Eh?" Naurr frowned. "What of these fortifications of the lizard lands?"

"I have it under control. You've done enough service for me for a lifetime."

"You are forgetting. I've not been paid a copper in months. What will I bring home to my dear Cena and little Noa?"

Skrull's balls, I hadn't thought of that. "I do owe you much. If only I could have you withdraw from my account with the Freemen."

"Must withdraw in person. No other way around it."

"Qav's coins! Simon cursed. "Blast it all!"

"The darling wife has enough to get along for a while. However, I thought we could divide the team if things returned to normal when we got home. Possibly dividing the finances more evenly?"

"Ah, like a partnership?"

"Aye."

Simon smiled. *Naurr deserves it.* "That sounds excellent, my good man." He held out his hand.

Naurr shook it. "Alright then, I'll stay for now, boss." He smacked Simon's back heartily. "Though all these strange, foul magics are far above me. You just tell me what needs to be built, eh."

"Aye. Thank you, Naurr. You are more than just my employee, you know that? You are a dear friend."

Naurr winked. "I know what you and your *friends* like to do in the bedchamber."

"Oh ho, not that kind of friend, my good man. You know, *regular* friends!"

Naurr smacked his back once more, and Simon winced. The burly Tulu grinned widely. "You the boss. Look at this lizard; here is a pile of bones!" Naurr motioned to the heap of bones ejected behind the little lizard man.

"Good gods! That is enough!" Simon called out, rushing back to the scene.

Gaelin was standing with his hand on his chin, off in thought. He stirred as Simon approached. "Certainly. Oh my, more than enough."

Kogs shook sand and dirt from his mane. "Kogs did good, Three-arms?"

"Oh yes, very astute, my young Kogs." Gaelin scratched behind the lizard man's ear hole.

Rattling purrs emitted from Kogs.

Simon held back a gag as he looked at the pile. "There is still flesh on these bones."

"True, let us get that cleaned up." Gaelin gave an off-handed gesture and muttered, "Bael bescréadian."

The flesh on the bones began to sizzle and burn away. Soon, only blackened bones were left.

"Well then," Simon said with a nod. "Shall we maneuver our catch to the cavern, as they say?"

"Nobody says that, boss."

Gaelin bent and picked out a decent-sized femur. "This should do."

That's it? Simon arched a brow. An image of grinding the bone to dust and mixing it came to him. *Do we need to crush this up and combine it with a bonding agent to solidify the crack in the gate?*

Indeed; the sandstone mixture you used to construct your wall would do nicely, Gaelin answered.

"Are you two going to stand there, staring at each other like lovers?" Naurr interrupted. "Or shall we get on with it, eh?"

Simon sputtered as he realized Gaelin and himself had not been speaking aloud. "Quite right. Lead the way, my good man. Bring a barrel."

Sometime later, Simon watched Naurr stirring the sand, gravel, bone, and water blend as they stood before the Wayfarers Gate to another Lân. A makeshift ladder had been propped up near the side of the gate so the broken fissure could be easily reached.

Simon clambered up as Naurr heaved the barrel up over his head. Simon scooped up the dough-like mixture with a piece of flat wood and spread it over the crack. It was satisfying to see the surface even out nicely.

"Besmiðian ísenbend." Simon scrawled a series of lines over the additive unconsciously and automatically. It glowed suddenly. He covered his eyes. Upon opening them, the mixture was gone. Left in its place was the same green-black marble that made up the rest of the structure.

"Witchcraft," Naurr mumbled.

"Undoubtedly, Mister Andiges, it is not far from that description," Gaelin said with a black-toothed grin. "A charming little concoction, if I do say so."

Simon thought he saw Naurr shudder before asking skeptically, "Anyways, are we ready to align the gate to Aurulan?"

"Indeed," Gaelin answered. "It will only be a second. The party should soon gather to depart."

"Only a second?!" Simon blurted in disbelief.

"Quite right."

"What happened to all the 'taking days to align the gate' nonsense?"

"A trick to get your spouse you ever long for to stay with us, since she is so prominent in your mind."

"Good gods, man. Next time, just tell the truth," Simon rubbed his eyes wearily. "At any rate, once the gate is open, it can stay as such until needed?"

"Of course, but the longer we wait, the thirstier we become."

"It's getting late. We will configure the gate and have the party depart in the morning. My wife is busy catching up with her mother. They *need* that time." Simon felt a tinge of impatience within. *Where did that come from?* He eyed Gaelin readily.

"Naturally, I'll handle this, Simon. You should join your wife," Gaelin answered.

Simon squinted, then shrugged. "As a matter of fact, I think I will."

Gaelin nodded but was preoccupied with studying the gateway.

"Let's head out, Naurr, my good man. Afléotan!" Simon began to drift upward.

"Eh?! No, no, I'll take the ladder." Naurr answered hastily, rushing for the rope and bamboo ladder that descended into the chamber from the tunnel above.

"Have it your way."

"Simon!" Saudett gestured for her husband to sit beside her. "Mother was just getting to the good part. The part about how she killed the Skrull-fucking shit-stain who called himself my father."

Simon's face became awry. "Sheesh, that sounds quite dreadful."

"He was a *dreadful* man," Saudett said, looking at her mother. "You deserved better."

Anora smiled back warmly. "I found better."

"Rojas?" Simon queried expectantly. "He is thoughtful and wise. He should be the First Otsoa."

"Please refrain from saying that aloud any longer, oh son-in-law." Anora's stern gaze made Simon quiet down.

"Oh, um, shall we invite Kiana in? She is sitting outside with an awful aura emanating from her. Even Kaplan is giving her a wide berth."

"Is she?" Anora asked. Then, she said louder, "Kiana is a competent adult who can partake in adult conversations, is she not."

They heard a snort, and after an awkward amount of time, Kiana pushed through the canvas curtains. Not saying a word, she sat, poured some wine for herself, and plucked up a piece of fried flatbread. Her eyes met Saudett's and held them firmly.

Why is she such a wench? Saudett pushed the negative thought away. *Hettra's mercy, she is my sister, and I must try to be civil.* Saudett smiled awkwardly back at Kiana.

Kiana averted her eyes.

"Much better!" Simon exclaimed. "Almost the whole family is here now! Minus your wise husband, dear mother."

"He already knows this story," Anora said.

"Of course. Please, continue said story," Simon expressed as he huddled into Saudett's side.

She took his hand in hers, fingers entwined. *He is so kind, gentle, and loving. He is too good to me, compared to how my father treated my mother.* Saudett thought about Simon romping around with other men and women, as they used to before all these insane things began happening to them. *It was enjoyable, but I want us to be alone now that our baby is coming. I do not want to share him any longer.*

Anora began to tell her story once again.

CHAPTER TWENTY

COMPANY

Anora noted one extra carriage as she counted each as the caravan crept out of the gates of Nidhaut. The carriage was extravagant, with silver and gold bordering the violet and red painted panels, and large transport chests strapped to its roof. *Primus's favor, I guarantee it is the man from the brothel. What was his name? Lisak?* Anora turned to the Vouri woman riding at her side. "Ovella, inquire with my husband about that carriage's intent."

"Right away, Lady," the stout warrior rode toward the front of the caravan.

Extra guardsmen were stationed around the carriage. Eight Company Kafilah soldiers rode in a circle about it. *These must be the ones deep in Gaddaar's purse. Would they bar me, the Lady Kafilah, access?* She pondered this as she spurred her horse toward the carriage.

Her answer came swiftly, for one of the men crossed her path as she approached.

"Hold there, Lady." Anora recognized Vasil, a thin, lithe Auru man. "No one is to enter the carriage."

"I am Lady of House Kafilah. Move aside."

"The Lord Gaddaar's orders, ma'am."

"Our orders are equal in this Company, *soldier.*"

"Lady, if the lord was to accompany you—"

"I do not need the lord to do anything. Move now, or you shall be stripped of rank and pay when we return to Xamid."

Vasil's eyes darkened through his helm. "Aye, Lady, at your will." He reined his horse aside.

Anora got up alongside the lavish carriage and rapped on the shuttered window. No one answered, but she heard shuffling within. She slammed her fist against the door. "Assets check! Open the door, or I will do it myself!"

There was a muffled yelp within. "Shut it, boy," a man's voice hissed.

The shutter creaked open. Lo and behold, Lisak's fat face appeared. *Making deals right under my nose now, Gaddaar?*

"My Lady?" Lisak wheezed. "How can I help you?"

Anora pulled a ledger from her saddle bag. "Your name and what goods you are transporting. This carriage was not on the list."

"I am Jean Alan. I am on my way to visit my dear sister in Al'Jalif, the Jewel of the East. She has gotten herself engaged to a high-born House Lord of Xamid. Would you believe it?"

I don't believe a word out of your mouth. Anora studied his grotesque smile and returned it. "Congratulations, Lord Alan. We shall make a toast at tonight's fireside for your sister's happiness."

"A-ha," he gave a counterfeited cough. "I regretfully will have to decline. I'm feeling under the weather, and all this bumping along is going to my head. I will likely retire early this night, but my thanks to your patronage." Not waiting for an answer, he slammed the shutter closed.

Still, muffled words reached her through the carriage walls. "Where were we, *boy*? Get over here."

She thumped on the door again.

The shutter slid open. "Skrull's hell, woman! What?"

"Goods?" She gestured atop the carriage, waving her ledger.

"Ah! Of course, my many garments and vittles for travel, my Lady." He raised his brow as if to say, *is that enough?*

Holding her rage within, she nodded and left it at that.

The shutter clanked closed once more.

She noticed Ovella riding slightly ahead, waiting for her. Anora urged her steed and moved up to join her. "Does my husband's story match up, I wonder?"

"A lord going to visit his estranged sister?" Ovella asked.

"Indeed," Anora sighed. "A simple cover. But I suppose I would not second-guess it typically."

"By Teras, what are they covering, Lady?"

"*Grit*, I imagine. He could fit a fair amount in those chests atop the carriage. And the man seems to have a slave on board with him."

"Teras's justice grind him to dust! No honest people deal in slaves."

"As is Company Kafilah policy. Though it would seem my husband is turning a blind eye to it."

"Dishonorable. If we were in my homeland, I would challenge the bastard to a fight to the death. The winner takes the throne. Or Company, in this case."

"If only," Anora sighed. "But I fear you would end up with a dead lady, and the lord would then run Company Kafilah how he *truly* wished."

"Give yourself more credit, Lady. I've seen you train with the sword every day since I joined the Company. Do you know how many times I have seen him training?"

"I do not."

"Not a *single* time."

Anora smiled. *I do not need to fear him. Perhaps Ovella is on to something here.* She needed a plan. "Ovella, speak to those you trust. We will confront my husband once we have entered the Burning Sea."

Ovella gave a toothy grin. *Or perhaps a grimace.* "Yes! About damned time!"

The days went swiftly as they made their way through the farmland and deciduous forests of western Aurulan. A noticeable divide in the guard was becoming apparent. Gaddaar and two dozen of the Company would camp around the Armand's lavish carriage. Reveling and drinking late into the night. Gaddaar himself would usually disappear into Armand's transport.

This left Anora and her own guardsmen, mainly consisting of the woman warriors of the Company, to set a perimeter around the other wagons. Taking watches and tending to the needs of the caravan. Most nights, Anora, to her relief, found herself going to sleep alone in the back of the Kafilah personal wagon.

But one night, Gaddaar stumbled drunkenly into the wagon, waking her and demanding to have her. He was already atop her when she sleepily realized what he was doing. "I'll fuck you as often as needed until I have a son! Skrull-damned bitch!" He began pulling her long sleeping blouse up as he tore at her under wraps.

You'll never have me again! She kicked and clawed at his face. Her foot caught him in the stomach and knocked the wind from him.

He gasped.

"Get out!" she screamed.

"You are my property!" he hissed, renewing his attack with clenched fists.

She covered her head as the blows came down upon her while simultaneously trying in vain to push him away with her feet. An impact caught her in the ear, and she reeled.

He took the opportunity to flip her onto her stomach and put his total weight on her, holding one of her arms at a painful angle behind her back.

"No! Stop!" she screamed and struggled with all her might. "Please!" Then she *felt* him.

"Fucking whore. I'll have you whenever I wish—"

His weight abruptly vanished.

"What?" Anora groaned and pushed herself to her knees, then crawled to the doors on the back of the wagon.

Gaddaar lay unconscious outside, Ovella standing over him.

"Shall I finish him off, Lady?"

Oh, how I wish it. "Not yet. My husband's men might cause problems should he suddenly go missing. Drag him to the closest fire and leave him. He will awaken soon enough." Anora winced and touched her head. "Gods, Ovella, thank you."

"My pleasure, Lady." Ovella gave her a toothy grimace. "Returned him the favor, I did."

"Can I ask you another favor?"

"Lady?"

"Stay with me henceforth. There is plenty of room in my wagon."

"Joo, Lady," Ovella said with an empathetic smile. "But no funny business now. I'm only interested in scrawny little men! You know this."

"Ha, yes, I know, Ovella. I could desperately use the company and a friend. We must think about how we deal with Gaddaar and his people."

As she said his name, the man groaned.

"Quickly, take him away."

Ovella nodded and dragged the disgraced Lord Kafilah away.

Anora could live with the fact her husband hated her. She could live with the fact he bedded whores. She could even live with the fact that he forced himself upon her. Their marriage demanded it.

But he has taken my life from me. My daughter, Saudett. Alone at home, being raised by maids. I want my freedom. Even when she was rarely with Saudett, the young child reminded her of him and his abuse. *I wished my life were different. I wish there was someone out there that actually cared about me.* Ovella's snoring was comforting, though loud. *At least he will not be able to surprise me again with both of us here.*

*Do it...*Gaddaar's words echoed in her mind.

They came to Dagad a fortnight after leaving Nidhaut. *Still no attempt on my life,* Anora thought as she strolled the market road in Dagad. Colorful canvas rippled in the breeze above her. *I will simply do my job as always.* Querying with merchants, directing unloads to others.

She noted a surprising amount of building materials were shipped through Company Kafilah to Dagad. The town seemed to have new structures every time they passed through it. One of the older central homesteads was having an additional floor constructed near the market road. Young men hollered at one another as they worked. A little boy on the heels of a handsome man zigzagged through their midst. *If only my daughter could have such a relationship with her own father.* She shook her head. *No. I will never let him. Never.*

Ovella shadowed her as she made the rounds. Anora procured three more wagons full of goods to be sent to Xamid. *That is a decent amount for a town the size of Dagad.* Satisfied with her work, she nudged Ovella. "Everything is in order. We leave on the morrow. Care for a drink?"

"Teras's mountain, I thought you'd never ask! There is only one tavern in town that serves Vouri dark ale."

"Grohl's?"

"Grohl's."

"To Grohl's then."

They set off through the narrow back streets of squat rectangular sandstone buildings. The bar and inn were set aside from the main road that curved through Dagad. Shepherd's Eye soldiers patrolled the streets in pairs. She nodded as a couple walked by. Company Kafilah was highly reputable and in excellent regard with all city-states. *No thanks to my husband. He leaves everything to me.* She was thinking increasingly about poisoning the man and saying he had died of a disease. *Perhaps I could put some bloodroot in his drink? Then I could take over Company Kafilah, rid it of the vermin, and bring my daughter with us.* It would be perfect for teaching Saudett while traveling the Earste Lân. *We could see the world together.*

They entered the tavern at a raucous hour. People were flooding in, as work had finished for the day for the most part.

Anora noted Company Kafilah guardsmen and Shepherd's Eye soldiers strewn among the town patrons.

Ovella pushed her way to the front of the bar to order drinks.

Anora followed in her wake.

The Vouri waved at the young, mustached, broad-shouldered bartender. After an excruciating amount of time, they were both furnished with double flagons of the thick, dark Vouri cream ale. With no seating available, the two women stood near a side wall while they enjoyed the beverages.

"Gotta piss," Ovella grunted and strode off to the latrine.

Anora stood lost in thought, leaning against the wall. *How am I going to do this? I tried taking Saudett and leaving, but he didn't let me.* She had even less freedom when they were home at the walled estate in Al'Jalif. She closed her eyes, dreaming of a new life.

Do it!

She was jerked from thought as a man faltered, stumbling toward her. Cold steel slid into her side. Instinctively, one hand grabbed the man's wrist while the other smashed her tankard into his face.

He let go of the blade and stumbled backward into the crowd. Then, he turned and ran.

The other patrons took no notice in the loud ale house.

Anora took a few steps in pursuit, the knife still embedded in her. *I cannot chase.* She cast about for Ovella in vain, then walked toward the nearest Shepherd's Eye soldier, a middle-aged man with grizzled scars.

The soldier grinned coquettishly at her as she approached.

Anora gestured to the dagger.

His face changed from flirtatiousness to shock.

"HOLD!" he bellowed. The tavern went quiet. "Cad! Renard! Kanti! To me!"

A man near Anora's age, plus two young guards, trotted up, still grasping flagons.

"This woman is wounded; carry her to the barracks," the scarred man ordered. "Be careful now; don't move the weapon until we have her in the infirmary."

"Yes, Captain!" the three answered in unison.

Anora shook her head, "I can still walk."

"You heard her! Escort her at once. The perpetrator may try and finish her off."

"Yes, Captain!"

Anora noticed Company Kafilah guards watching the procession as the four Shepherd's Eye guided her through the throng, the din beginning to rise now that all was in order. Those were Gaddaar's men, she expected, all of them turning a blind eye. Anora's arm dangled over the shoulders of one of the young men.

As the group exited the tavern, the captain spoke up. "Don't worry, lass, we'll get you fixed up quickly."

"My thanks, Captain?" Anora paused, raking her memory for the name of the garrison commander of the Dagad Shepherd's Eye. "Blake, isn't it?"

"Indeed; have we met?"

"No, I am Lady Kafilah of Caravan Company Kafilah. I make it my business to know all relevant parties in all townships we enter."

"Very well. But it seems a less reputable party has a vendetta against you," Blake said, nodding toward Anora's wound.

"I do not know," she lied. *Yes! It is my own husband! Oh, I could ask this soldier for help? He is the town's justice... surely he would help me?* She kept the thoughts to herself as she continued, "Company Kafilah is in good standing with the merchant guilds and all city-states."

"A personal grievance, then?"

"Perhaps, but for the most part, I keep to myself."

"Indeed. Well then, we shall get you patched up. I will return to Grohl's and ask some regulars if they saw or know anything about your attacker."

"My thanks again, Captain Blake."

"Sergeant Dermont, you're in charge. Take good care of her, and have the doctor summoned immediately when you return to barracks."

"Yes, Captain!" the handsome soldier answered with a salute.

He nodded and marched back to the tavern.

"Come on then, Lady Kafilah," said the man, Dermont. Anora had guessed he was in his late twenties or early thirties. "This way."

She followed, watching the man's broad back as he led the way through the back streets. Not ten minutes into their walk, he stopped abruptly.

"Sergeant Dermont?" Anora asked hesitantly.

He turned his head to regard her. He was an attractive man with a slightly olive complexion.

Was he of Auru-Xamid mix? Anora shook away the thoughts. "What is it?"

"It seems like your attackers have not given up." Dermont nodded behind them.

Anora saw two figures approaching from the rear, dressed in dark leather and wearing masks.

"Be a good little lass and *die!*" a voice shouted at their forefront, and two more shadowed figures strolled forward.

"I'll handle these two. Renard, Kanti." He indicated with his head toward the two at their back.

"Yes, Sergeant!"

"I can help," Anora pleaded.

"No." Dermont rebuked, then drew his sword, holding it in both hands. Suddenly, he gave a shout and charged forward. At the same instant, Renard and Kanti did as well.

Anora painfully unsheathed her own curved sword as the soldiers met the assassins. She inched toward the sergeant, who was overwhelming both his adversaries.

The two assassins danced about him cautiously, syncing their attacks with one another.

He needs help! At least the two behind should fare better, as it is one-to-one.

The attackers were dual-wielding a short sword and a dagger in each hand.

As Dermont swung at one, the assassin would parry or dodge, and the other would strike at his side or back. Small slashes of blood were forming already where their blades had reached him.

"It's me you want!" Anora shouted. She stumbled toward the assassin at Dermont's back. The man turned, ducking under her blade as it sped above him.

His dagger reached out.

She ground her teeth through the pain in her side, raising her knee in time to deflect the hand and blade upward. Her sword parried the short sword as it swept in from the other side. Spinning, she planted and released a high sidekick to the assassin's head. He was knocked back, stumbling toward Sergeant Dermont.

Dermont took the opportunity to thrust his sword through the man's back. His blade twisted as he punctured the man's chest.

The other assassin rushed in, raising his blades to strike.

No! He doesn't have time! Anora pulled the dagger from her abdomen and launched it. Blood immediately began gushing from the wound.

The assassin stood, wavering, with the dagger sunk to the handle in his eye. He collapsed onto the dust-packed street.

They heard a cry behind them and turned to look.

Renard lay in a pool of blood, as did one other assassin.

Kanti fought for her life against the last.

Anora, suddenly light-headed, took a step forward. Then, she collapsed.

"By the gods," Simon exclaimed. "First of all, Cad! You met Cad?"

"Oh, you know him?" Anora asked.

"Oh, we know him *quite* well," Simon said as his gaze met Saudett's playfully, and they both grinned mischievously. "Nevertheless, please, your story is oh-so-exciting! Go on, go on!"

"Ha, my son, be patient," Anora chuckled. "As you can see, I survived."

"Skrull's hell, mother, your life was lively," Saudett said. "It was always so dreadfully dull on the road when I was with the caravan."

"As it should be," Anora said with a knowing smile. "The Company's presence alone should be enough to ward off bandits and beast alike."

"At least you *both* had the opportunity to see the world," Kiana muttered.

"Well," Anora answered. "Your own opportunity has come to pass, as you are to chase after the Sunstone."

Kiana shrugged as if it was not a big deal.

"It grows late," Anora added. "Shall we continue this once we are reunited?"

"No, Mother!" Saudett pleaded. "We do not know when that will be."

Simon stretched. "It will be a rough morning, but I agree with my dear wife."

"Then," Anora paused, smiling widely. "We require more wine!"

Chapter Twenty-One

FATHER

The blizzard bit at Hata's face and exposed skin. She had nothing but the thin silk sheet Luftan had covered her with. *Teras, protect me. I am going to freeze to death!* Dread gripped her while she trudged through the knee-deep snow. Step by step, she slogged onward, shivering uncontrollably. She had appeared in the ruins of an old hunting shack; partial stone walls were the only thing left of the building. With no shelter, she decided to move on.

Suddenly, the silhouette of a dark shape was lumbering toward her through the storm. She heard a roar. Her eyes widened in terror. *A mountain bear.* Her body reacted on its own. She plummeted her bare hands into the snow, the silk sheet flying off her with the blizzard's wind.

The bear was nearly upon her.

She formed the jagged tip of a spear of rock in her mind and threw her arms upward. The rock pierced the grey and black fur of the massive bear's neck, its open jaw mere inches from her face. She stumbled backward, falling into the snow as the bear flailed wildly, blood pouring from its neck.

The beast gurgled and wheezed. Finally, the mountain bear slumped onto the thick, jagged rock, dead.

Hata called the image of a knife to mind using more stone. A long, flat, and sharp rock. It protruded from the stalagmite she had just conjured. With a crack, it came off. She immediately began sawing into the dead beast's belly; the hide was thick and difficult to cut and penetrate.

I can't feel my hands, and this is not working. Teras, give me strength, for I am weak. She shook her head, trying to stay conscious. With a scream of exasperation, she lifted her arms skyward. The earth groaned and fractured around her, then lifted, enclosing her and the bear's body in a jagged mountain-like dome. The wind howled above, a small fissure peaking through the upper part of the dome.

It was instant relief from the cutting blizzard wind—though Hata was still kneeling in the snow, leaning against the coarse fur of the bear. She struggled with the stone knife. *Sluggishly, achingly,* she was able to open the bear up. Its guts discharged, staining the snow below it as Hata crawled into the corpse. Hata closed her eyes as exhaustion took her. *Thank Teras, it's so warm.*

"The mountain bear is the chieftain of its territory," Baal said in Vouri. "When a challenger enters its borders, it has no choice but to fight."

"Even if we leave it alone?" Hata asked, looking up at the hulking figure of her father.

"Even so," he grunted. "Look here. It was sharpening its claws on the stone." He pointed at a series of white lines and stone powder on the cliffside. "The mountain bear does not sleep through winter, for it is nearly always winter in the North Iron Belt."

They had traveled for two days and nights, seeking the valuable adversary that was the mountain bear. The North Iron Belt elevated about them, the mountain range that cut the world of the south off from the northern ice flat. Its sprawling peaks grasped unimaginable heights.

"It is close," Her father whispered. They heard muffled rumbles, air expelling from nostrils.

Hata shuddered in terror.

The next moment, a patch of scrawny pines shook and broke as the bear charged through them.

Her father stood tall, pickaxe in hand, giving a bellowing shout at the animal.

It stopped. Then, it stood up on its hind legs and roared a challenge in return.

Baal stepped toward the massive bear.

The bear had darker fur cresting its head and back, fading into a grey, almost white, on its underbelly. Its claws were as long as hunting knives. It shook its head menacingly and burst into a charge once again.

Baal stood unfazed as the beast hurled toward him. Then, unexpectedly, her father twisted around and retreated toward Hata.

The bear bawled a warbling, almost disappointed growl as its challenger became prey.

"NOW, HATA!" Baal bellowed as he dived past her.

Hata lifted the carved wooden pike out of the snow.

The bear surged onto her.

The wooden shaft pierced the silvery fur of the massive bear's chest, its open jaw mere inches from her face. She stumbled backward, falling into the snow as the bear slumped down, blood pouring from its chest. It gurgled and wheezed. Finally, the mountain bear lay still on the thick wooden carved pike. *Dead.*

"Voitoon! You did good, Hata, my daughter! Now, you will learn how to skin such a beast." He rested a large hand on her shoulder, giving her a hearty shake.

Baal showed her where to use the knife to peel the hide away from the carcass. The process was long and arduous, and her father did not help. He simply watched and told her what to do. When she had finally removed the hide and tied it in a bundle, Baal grunted in affirmation as he picked up the body and placed it on a long sled they had brought with them.

"Let's return to Oitilla. Your mother will be pleased. By Teras's strength, we will feast in honor of your first hunt!"

"Thank you, Isä." Hata followed behind as her father pulled the sled effortlessly through the deep mountain snow.

Hata awoke to the smell of animal innards clogging her nostrils. She struggled, pulling herself out of the dead bear. The snow around the carcass inside the dome had lessened around the vicinity of the dead beast. It was still cold to her bare feet but certainly *bearable.* She groaned inwardly. *Skrull take me; that is something my Isä would say.*

She crouched, naked, alone, and covered in drying animal blood and fluids. She did not wait long, as the cold would soon overcome her. She began skinning the bear as her father had taught her so long ago.

Chapter Twenty-Two

PROCTOR

"Close the wounds, Theta!" Ebras shouted at the elderly magi he had summoned to the Convent Enclosure.

"No! Please!" Chanel shrieked in agony. "Let me die, Theta!"

"Why have you done this?" Cygne Caladrius questioned in bewilderment.

"It does not matter!" Ebras hissed. "Do as I say, or you will be next!" *By all the fucking gods, she betrayed me. My most loyal pupil.* The one to whom he had entrusted this entire venture. *Betrayed me. The whore, Chanel de Montrichard.*

No, what was her actual name? Before he had taken her. He shrugged. *It matters not; the vile woman was nothing more than a peasant. I gave her a life of power. A life of authority. And this is how she repays me?* He would enjoy torturing the armless whore until she breathed her last breath.

"Alpha Passeriform, an explanation please—"

Cygne choked on his words as Ebras raised a hand, gripping Theta's throat with his metaphysical ability. Ebras moved and screamed in the old man's face, "Silence, you damned fool!"

The Theta grasped at his throat, his feet dangling in the air.

Ebras released the grip and let the man crumple to the ground. "Now, immediately stop her bleeding. Keep her alive."

The woman was now near losing consciousness and mumbling aimlessly.

The Theta Passeriform crawled over to the woman bleeding to death on the cobblestone path. He reached out and put his hands over the hemorrhaging holes where her arms had once been. Cygne's face darkened with strained intention.

Ebras Corb watched as the Proctor spasmed frantically. He felt the veins in his forehead pulsing. *Dying is too good for her. She will not have the easy way out.*

She gasped, eyes bulging. Then she was still.

"I've stopped the bleeding, Alpha," Cygne Caladrius sighed heavily. "But she requires further care and bandages. She needs rest and time. I will stay with her."

"No. I will see to the bitch from myself. Now, begone."

"Alpha, I beg you to reconsider—"

Ebras simultaneously opened a portal and hurled the old man through it swiftly. The white-haired old man yelped as he disappeared through the bright light of the portal. Ebras was the only one among the council who could use teleportation at will. *That I know of.* The Council did not give information about their powers freely, even with other members. They had to use Epsilon's enchantment stones infused with Ebras's spells if they wanted to travel quickly.

The little fledgling cardinal has flown the coop. Where did the teleportation stone take her? It had to be configured to a pylon. He would get the information out of his former Proctor, one way or another.

He sneered down at the unconscious woman. He surveyed the carnage. *Where are my orderlies?* His eye glanced over the exploded corpse of the man who had pushed the cardinal through the portal. *There must be more around here.* He strolled toward the silo-shaped building where the women were kept.

"Ah, there they are," he muttered as his eyes adjusted to the interior darkness of the chamber. He surveyed the bodies sprawled about: his two questionably-contracted thugs and the other regular orderly of the Convent Enclosure.

There was one more body, naked and quivering.

"Ah ha, the fat little magpie still breathes." He slinked over to her.

She was chained to the cage's bars, lying on her back. Ravaged.

I could use this. Ebras flicked a gloved finger, and the chains around the bars shattered, then wrapped a sheet around the woman while propping her up, cradling her in his arms. *Disgusting wretch.* He pulled off a glove with his teeth and put two fingers on the girl's forehead. He penetrated her thoughts, entangling her mind, playing with her memories.

The red-haired girl has escaped without you and left you to die. She betrayed the trust of the Alpha. And what's more, she mutilated the Proctor. You hate her. You will strike back at the red-haired girl. This—Hata. This—Sunstone.

Ebras grimaced. Sunstone? What was this? And how did this magpie know the girl's actual name? She should have lost all her memory. *This must be what provoked this incident.* He focused back on the magpie's mind.

The Alpha will help you. The Alpha is your friend. Your caring sweetheart. He cares for you, and you love him. He was nearly ready to wake her. He would mold her to his will. This time, she would not have an inkling of her own understanding.

You are my Proctor anew, Joanna Ohleoc.

The magpie gasped as her eyes shot open. Her sky-blue irises darted wildly with shock. As her gaze found him, she calmed immediately. The woman shakily reached up a hand, gently caressing his cheek. "Oh, my love—"

Ebras faltered. *When was the last time someone showed me such affection? Even if it is forced.* He composed himself swiftly, disguising his small blunder by aiding her to her feet. *No, she is a disgusting woman. I will use her.* "Come, my," he paused, nearly calling her a *fat magpie.* "My *raven.*" The words clung to his lips. "We have much work to do. We have been betrayed."

The girl's face contorted in a fury. "Skrull take the whore! Qav bestow her with misfortune! Hettra, turn your mercy away! Hata Vasara! The Primus curse you for eternity!" The Proctor of the Convent Enclosure, Joanna Ohleoc, threw the words to the heavens. "You will pay for what you did! I *will* find you."

Chapter Twenty-Three

STORM

Do it!

Anora sat up with a gasp, sweating profusely. The pain burned in her side as she looked down at her waist wrapped in bandages, a slight red stain where she had been stabbed. *The last thing I remember was that the other Shepherd's Eye soldier was in trouble. Where am I?* She was in a large room with many beds, shelves, and carts full of medical supplies.

"Good afternoon," a man said.

The sergeant, Dermont, who had fought to defend her life, lay in a bed beside her. Looking much worse, Kanti lay on his opposite side, wrapped from head to toe in blood-soaked bandages.

"Dermont!" Anora exclaimed. "You survived. Kanti, too?"

"Nearly didn't. Kanti hasn't awoken yet," he sighed remorsefully. "She is gravely wounded; I fear for her life."

"I'm sorry, Sergeant, this is my fault. I got you pulled into this mess."

"Your mess?"

"Never mind, I don't want anyone else further involved."

He grunted.

"What happened to the last cutthroat?"

"Made a suicidal attack on the both of us. I took a dagger in the shoulder, and Kanti took his sword. Not to mention a score of other cuts before I got to her. But we managed to finish him off."

"Hettra's mercy to her. My thanks again, Sergeant Dermont."

"Simply doing my job, ma'am."

Anora threw her legs off the bed and stood. "Well, I best be getting back to the Company."

"You think that wise, going off alone after what happened?"

"You'll need to catch up," another voice said. "Company Kafilah departed this morning."

Captain Blake strode through the doorway to the infirmary. "I have worse news, Lady Kafilah," he said with a dark expression on his scarred face. "One Company Kafilah guard was found dead in the streets last night."

Anora's eyes widened. Her mind immediately went to Ovella, leaving the tavern for a piss. "Who is it?!"

"One stout Vouri woman. We have the body in the middle barrack yard. If you think you can identify it."

"Yes, please, take me there."

He nodded.

Anora followed Captain Blake from the room. She put her thumb to her lips in thanks toward Dermont as she departed.

Ovella's dead eyes stared back at her. Throat slit. *Fuck that man. Gaddaar, Armand, and anyone else in league with the traitors.* Anora closed the dead woman's eyes and whispered, "Teras guide you up the mountain."

"I'm sorry, Anora," Blake said. "If you ride swiftly, I'm sure you could catch up with your Company." He paused and arched his brow, eyeing her. "Strange they did not wait or investigate that you two had gone missing."

"For they are the culprits behind the attacks, as you have guessed." *What will I do alone against them? Ovella was my strongest supporter.*

"What reason for this?"

"It's a long story. You need not concern yourself."

"Two women were just attacked in my town, one fatally!" he barked irritably. "It is now *my* business."

"What can you do? They are already gone. What are you going to do? Arrest them? For what?"

"Murder and attempted murder by way of assassination. By the King's judgment, I can execute them on the spot. Though some proof would aid us."

Do it. Gaddaar's words echoed in her mind.

"I have only the words out of Lord Kafilah's mouth, ordering to have me killed."

"Lord Kafilah?! Your own husband is behind this? By the Primus."

She nodded.

"What did you do to him? Why does he wish you dead?"

Of course, it is somehow my fault that he wants me dead. Skrull-damned men. She sneered in disgust. "My only sin is bearing him a daughter instead of a son."

Captain Blake tilted his head inquisitively. "Is that all? It is the luck of Qav's coins, as they say. Pardon my forthrightness, but you did not wish to try for another?"

"He started beating me after our daughter came. He never loved me. We were wed in an arrangement. I put much effort into avoiding bearing him another child."

"Understandable." Blake nodded. "None of my business as it is. At any rate, our horses are ready. We'll catch them in no time."

"Our horses?"

"How am I to arrest him otherwise?"

Anora smiled. *At least there are some honorable men left in this Lân.*

It was nearly dark when the two riders galloped through the foothills east of Dagad. They would make better time with no wagons in tow. Even so, the Company was almost a day ahead of them.

I will need to persuade those loyal to me to aid in this. Blake and I alone are not enough.

"Let's make camp!" Blake called. "We will rise early and surprise them at dawn."

"If we sneak in at night and catch them unaware—"

"You are wounded, Anora. We need to rest. We can take our time; let you recover." Blake slowed his horse to a stop.

Anora did likewise.

"Even so," Blake continued. "They may be too far as it is. The Burning Sea takes over a month to travel. I swear on my life we will find them."

My Skrull-forsaken husband, he will not escape. "I suppose you are correct; we have the time, and we are faster," she exhaled heavily and touched her wounded side tenderly. *I do need rest.*

That night, Anora slept fitfully by a small fire. The words kept echoing in her head.

Do it.

My own husband tried to kill me.

Do it.

The coward could not wield the blade himself.

Do it!

Louder and louder, the voice boomed.

DO IT!

Anora leaped to her feet, panting and sweating profusely in terror. Her sword gripped in her white knuckles. The sun was peaking over the vast sea of dunes to the east. A slight gust of wind blew grains of sand before her feet.

"Let's move on," Captain Blake said as he packed and saddled his horse.

Hours went by as they rode. The wind began to pick up.

"When we arrive, Captain, a man will be in a luxurious-looking carriage. He is a grit dealer and owns a slave. I will confront my husband. You find this man and drag him out as proof of Lord Kafilah's dishonor."

"Aye, are you planning on fighting your husband?"

"If it comes to that, yes. I will first persuade as many Kafilah guardsmen to side with me."

"Aye, Lady, as sound plan as any."

They rode on. The wind gathered further, and they had to wrap their faces as the sand started to bite.

It's not quite a whole-blown sandstorm yet, thank Hettra.

"They will have to stop in this wind!" Blake yelled through the din. "Their animals won't be able to take much more!"

Finally, through the dust, they caught sight of the bulky wagons of the caravan ahead. The Company was setting up the wagons to shelter from the east-blowing wind. Creating a wall of sorts with the wagons. Then, moving the pack animals behind the makeshift barricade.

Anora spotted her husband directing the operation, his back toward her. *You can't get rid of me that easily, dear husband.* She spurred her horse into a gallop, praying the wind and dust would mask her approach. She got within ten paces when Gaddaar turned and cried out. Her foot planted on his chest, the force of the horse's gallop throwing him back into the sand. She swung from her mount and drew her sword in the same instant. "Company Kafilah!" Anora shouted.

Those nearby turned to see.

"Lord Kafilah has betrayed his own house!"

The Company soldiers began to gather around, hands readying on weapons.

"Ha! My wife has gone mad!" Gaddaar bellowed, picking himself up. "Where was she yesterday morning when we were readying to depart? Leaving us to do all the hard work."

"Gaddaar hired assassins to kill me!" Anora leveled her sword at her husband. "Ovella died alone. Her throat was slit in some back street of Dagad. Simply to get her out of your way."

"He killed one of our own?!" a company guard questioned.

"She had it coming!" Another man retorted.

The wind roared menacingly. Sand bit at Anora's eyes.

"My wife, I had nothing to do with any assassinations. That would blemish House Kafilah's good name. How can you accuse me of this?"

"Blake!" Anora shouted.

The captain dragged Armand from his carriage into the circle formed around Anora and Gaddaar. He pushed the spluttering man to his knees. Two young boys followed behind, *bruised and beaten.*

"This man is a slaver and grit dealer! Lord Kafilah has dishonored his house by going into business with the likes of him."

A murmur of discontent rippled through the guard.

"About time we made some real gold!" she heard Vasil shout.

Others rallied in agreement.

"Hettra's Mercy! Please!" Armand pleaded.. "I am only traveling to visit my dear sister."

Anora nodded to Blake.

The captain grabbed Armand by the hair and put his blade on his quivering throat.

"Now, my *love*. Surely this is a misunderstanding?" Gaddaar urged. "You have just met this man at the gates of Nidhaut."

"No, it is not my first time acquainted with him." Anora glided up to her husband. *He has never called me his "love" until this day.* She stood a few paces from him, staring into his dark eyes.

He held her gaze.

"I was there," she whispered. "*At the Paon.*"

His brow furrowed. "No...it is not possible."

She held his gaze. Just like she had while pleasuring him that night at the whore house.

His eyes widened in realization. His face changed, resignation darkening it. "Fine. Then you will die here." Gaddaar stepped away, drew his sword, and bellowed, "Company! Kill them both!"

Just then, a massive wall of sand crashed into the caravan. The storm had come.

Chapter Twenty-Four

HUSBAND

Blinded by the massive wall of the sandstorm, Anora pushed through the wind and silt as Company Kafilah soldiers turned against one another. She threw herself against the side of a wagon, the squall defused somewhat. She drove toward where her husband had been standing as the storm hit. *Where did he go?* She faintly heard the clash of blades through an eerie howl upon the wind. *A bestial howl.*

"DIE!" Gaddaar lunged for her from behind.

Anora spun off the wagon wall, catching his blade with her own and arching it upward. Swords locked, they pushed against one another, face to face.

"You fucking cunt," Gaddaar seethed. "Why my family picked you out of the countless whores who would have obeyed my every wish is a Skrull-damned wonder."

"Bastard! How I wish mine could have found me a *true* man," she spat back. "One who would not leave me wanting."

He roared in a fury, pushing her back toward the wagon.

Anora backtracked, kicking her feet against the wall and launching her head into his face.

He reeled, blood dripping from his nose.

Anora *danced*. She danced into his guard, scoring a gash along his arm before he had recovered.

He regained his composure and retaliated with rage-induced blows bombarding her.

She continued the dance, deflecting his blows and scoring minor, merciless cuts back unto him. *He is weaker than I.* She cut his thigh. *I can win.* His chest. *I'm not afraid of him.* His cheek. *I've spent years training while he sluggishly enjoyed himself. How many years of whoring and grit has he indulged in?*

He hissed in frustration as each wound bled him, and his aggression was slow and projected.

The howling of the wind became distinct. *It sounds like the howling of wolves! That is not the wind alone.*

A dark shadow leaped over the wagon, sailing through the sand and dust above Anora and Gaddaar. Anora tried to track it with her eyes, catching a glimpse of it bounding on all fours toward another pair of Company guards locked in combat.

Gaddaar, seemingly unaware, continued to strike at her.

Then she heard the screams.

"That is the sound of my loyal men finishing off your handful of followers." Gaddar laughed in triumph.

"*No,*" she whispered. "*It is not.*"

The *wolf* landed on Gaddaar's back.

Another bit into Anora's leg. Her reflex carried her sword through its neck. Its head and jaws still clamped to her thigh. *An oddly human head? No, it was canine.*

Gaddaar screamed, trying to dislodge the animal gnawing on his shoulder. He finally caught it in the eye with the tip of his blade, causing it to release him with a yelp and race away.

"What in Skrull's fucking hell was that?!" Gaddaar cried.

Anora took a moment to glance around; some of the beasts were humanoid, standing on two legs with fur and claws. Others were purely brown-beige or grey wolves. She could faintly see her and Gaddaar's soldiers overwhelmed by this new enemy. They were being swarmed, outnumbered, and torn apart.

She saw Blake push Armand toward a group of beasts, the man screaming as he died, all for naught. Captain Blake was attacked from behind. Falling under a pile of bloodthirsty wolves.

"Our people need help!" Anora cried, turning back to Gaddaar. She saw his silhouette disappear behind the wagon. *Skrull-forsaken bastard.* She looked toward her screaming, dying people and then at where Gaddaar had fled. *I can't let him escape, or this will never end.* Anora followed after her husband.

He was a shadow through the sandstorm. His feet dragged, leaving large trenches in his wake.

Anora followed him deeper into the storm for what seemed like an eternity. Minutes. *Hours.* The storm dispersed as she followed him, and the sun returned to cast its blaze upon them.

"Leave me be!" Gaddaar turned and shrieked at her. "Curse you! Cunt woman!" Then, he would turn and jog a bit before slowing to a slog once again.

This continued for far too long. Anora kept his pace, never losing sight of him.

Darkness had fallen when he finally stopped to face her. "So, this is it!" his voice was coarse, *desperate.* "We will both die in this desert because of you!"

"So be it," she stepped toward him. "For you will never hurt our daughter again. Never scream at her again. Never *control* her. Even if it costs my life!"

"She will be alone. Parentless."

"SHE ALREADY IS!" Anora summoned her strength and charged.

Gaddaar kicked sand up in her face, blinding her momentarily. Taking the opportunity to strike, his stab caught her waistline, piercing flesh, glancing against the outside edge of her pelvic bone. Blinking the sand from her eyes, Anora saw Gaddaar standing, mouth gaping, her sword through his belly. She stepped in, sinking it deeper. Again, face to face with the man she had wed. The man who had given her a beautiful daughter. The man who beat and abused her. Dominated her with fear. *He gave me Saudett, the one good thing to come of all this.*

"Fucking—" Blood gurgled from his mouth, and his eyes burned with *hate.* Then they glassed over.

"Farewell, *Lord Kafilah.*"

They both collapsed to the ground, lying clutched together as if still lovers. The scorching sands of the Burning Sea, their bedding...

...Anora awoke sometime later to a splash of water on her face. The appearance of a man looking down at her.

His violet-irised eyes studied her intently.

"And that is how I met Rojas," Anora finished. "He saved my life. I then took to the creed of the First Otsoa and vowed never to leave Hasiera again. Even if it meant leaving you, Saudett."

"Marvelous!" Simon exclaimed. "What a tale! You must remember to tell the ole grand babies such a tale."

"Simon," Saudett elbowed him gently. "The story is a bit *mature* for a baby, no?"

"Of course not!" He gasped playfully. "It is a tale of love and abandonment! Of sex and drugs! Of family and revenge!"

"Oh, get off it!" Saudett pushed him over, then sighed. "Still, I searched this desert to find you, Mother. Things could have been different. I could have joined you here."

"I know, Saudett," Anora's face was sullen. "There are many regrets of the past, but many good things came of it, too, that I love." She looked toward Kiana.

"Mother," Kiana's eyes watered. "I just wish you had told me this before. This past that made you so hard on me; now I understand *why*. It was all so no *man* could ever have such power over me as Gaddaar Kafilah did to you."

Anora nodded with tears in her own eyes. "Yes, Kiana. That *is* why. And I'm sorry for how I treated you. I love you, Kiana, with every ounce of my being."

Kiana stifled a sob as she entered her mother's arms and whispered, "I love you, too."

CHAPTER TWENTY-FIVE

SURVIVE

The wind had lessened outside the stone shelter, and Hata wrapped herself in the skinned pelt of the mountain bear. She was still *intensely* cold. *I need a string to tie the makeshift moccasins tight and better close the hide around me.* The bear was massive, and its fur was enough to fashion a cloak and smock around her waist, covering her legs. Some long dry grass or young saplings perhaps could help. *But that means I will have to go outside.*

The Proctor's medallion hung around her neck, strangely warm against her skin. Almost humming. She fiddled with it, pondering what else it was capable of. She shook her head. *I must focus. I need the warmth of a fire and better shelter.* She had food, but she needed to be able to cook the bear meat. After butchering the animal, she wrapped the raw flesh in small bundles of left-over fur and placed it outside the craggy shelter to freeze and not begin to rot.

Where am I? I am definitely in the North Iron Belt, but the vast mountain range stretches across half the continent. Focusing on the rock dome before her, it creaked and groaned as a crack widened. She stepped out into the wilderness of the North Iron Belt. The blizzard had ended, but light snow was still falling. The clouded skies obscured the peaks, so she could not determine if she recognized them as landmarks to home.

First things first, she thought. *Fire, food, and something to hold my pelts together.* She gathered the bundles of meat in her arms and began walking. She was surrounded by shaggy pine trees and leafless mountain birch. The latter being small and twiggy, more bush-like than the birch trees of the forests further down the mountain. She did spy a few of the taller white birch trunks here and there. That meant she was relatively high up in elevation. She chopped at the branches, and as she broke one away, she saw that the wood was green and malleable. She would carve long strips off it to use as twine.

She nodded to herself. *That's one problem solved.* Her arms were full of twigs and bundles of bear meat; she could not go much further. Squinting through the snowfall, she spied the greying stone of a cliffside, jutting skyward. She stumbled to the base of it, picking a spot with as many pines and bushes as possible. She dropped her spoils and moved to the wall, placing both hands against it. *I will make a cave.* She envisioned it in her head, straining as dust and rock discharged around her. She was exhausted after finally digging a few feet into the rock face. *That will have to do for now. The next step is warmth.* This would be the most challenging task. Hata wished Joanna had come with her. *Escaped with me.* Jo could start a fire quickly; they could have huddled together for warmth. *Held each other.*

Hata was grateful for finally leaving that hellhole and that man. *The Alpha.* The man who had killed Chanel and Luftan. *This is just like Taryn all over again.* She had done nothing, and people had died once more. *If I had just helped, maybe I could have saved them.*

"Teras, grant me strength," she whispered aloud. *I must distract myself from the despair.*

She gathered more branches and placed them in a pile just before the small hole she had carved out of the mountain. Her father had shown her how to light a fire with a tinderbox. Even if she had one, she needed more than green twigs to catch the flame. Her father had shown her that birch, even when frozen, would still burn well because of the natural oils it contained. Also, the birch bark was an amazing kindle to catch the flames once she had created them, as well as dead, dried pine needles or leaves.

Exhausted, she gathered her supplies. A pile of bark kindle, another bundle of smaller dried twigs, another pile of oversized sticks to feed the flame, and so forth. She took a long branch about the width of three fingers and carved a notch deep along the twig using her stone knife. Her hands shook with the cold as she strained, taking another smaller branch and cutting the end into an edge to fit into the notch. Finally, she piled some birch bark, dead pine needles, and the driest leaves she could find under the end of the incision. Using her body weight to apply pressure, she rubbed the edge of the smaller stick back and forth in the notch as fast as she could. It felt like an eternity, her arms burning in agony and her hands blistering. There was not even a puff of smoke.

"Skrull-forsaken horseshit!" Hata screamed in frustration and let the stick fall from her hands. She rocked back and forth on her knees in despair, the medallion dangling about her neck. Tears welled in her eyes as Hata ripped the jewelry from her neck, pulling her arm back to throw it away. She halted mid-swing; the medallion was *warm* in her hand. Inspecting it closer, the item was a multitude of different-colored marbles embedded in the metal of the pendant. She felt the warmth emanating from the black opal in the center, yet the heat seemingly pointed toward a reddish-orange marble, *like a flame.*

Her eyes widened as she picked at the red marble with her sharpened rock. It popped free. *I need blood.* She pressed her thumb hard against the point of her makeshift knife, and blood welled out of the prick. She rolled the marble between her thumb and forefinger. Then, Hata dropped the marble into the pile of sticks. She sat staring at the would-be fire. *Nothing is happening.* Then suddenly, the sun broke through the cloud cover and caught her eyes. She looked up and, in horrific realization, saw the massive ball of flame hurtling toward her. Using as much power as she could muster, she created a diagonal pillar of rock directly underneath her and launched herself backward. The explosion stole her breath away. That or the impact of landing on her back against a boulder, her neck lurching backward painfully. A flash of heat buffeted her.

"Hettra's mercy," she moaned as she slid to a seated position against the boulder. Dazed and confused, she could make out the small grove of pines burning intensely. *That's one way to do it, I suppose.* She coughed and crawled toward the burning woods. There was a blackened patch of ground where the spell had impacted. Hata gathered some of the smaller flaming branches and logs she could and piled them before her cave entrance. Soon, she had a good fire going. *I need to rest for a bit.* Her stomach grumbled. Some of her bear meat had been charred by the blast. She took a few bites of the nearly raw meat and swallowed laboriously. Finally, inside the cave, she curled into a ball under her pelts. *The fire should last.*

Chapter Twenty-Six
MOREAS

The Daanav did not know what hit them as Simon and Gaelin stepped through the portal into the marshy world known as the Moreas Lân. A handful of hounds and a few more enormous hulks idled around the muddy grounds before the Wayfarers' Gate.

Kogs, mounted on Gaelin's shoulders, shrieked as he saw the Daanav, "The masters are here! They will kill us!"

"Bael cnytells," Simon and Gaelin said in unison.

Cords of white-boiling fire screeched from their fingertips, disintegrating holes through the black flesh of the Daanav. Some squealed and died, and others turned to defend the gate.

"KYAA!" Kogs cried, shaking his mane. "DIE! Stupid masters!"

The monsters charged the trio. A hound, different from the ones seen in the Burning Sea, back bristling with sharp quills, shook on its haunches and released the deadly projectiles toward Simon.

Lind. Afléotan. The shield of warm light deflected the missiles, and Simon took to the air as he shouted, "Windan!" A razorblade of pressurized air cut through the spiked hound.

The Daanav attacked.

Hasieran warriors charged through the portal, their offensive meeting the creatures of the Skaad Lân in a fury. Simon saw Saudett leading the charge. An ululating war cry carried across the din.

He watched as his wife deftly skewered a hound on her spear into a gigantic tree trunk. Then, she immediately ducked the swing of a hulking arm, spinning free and slicing with the spear tip along the massive creature's leg.

Skrull's hell, that woman must get hold of herself, or I will lose her and our unborn child!

He glided down toward her and muttered, "*Maegen.*"

The hulk she combated was crushed to the ground like the weight of a mountain had just crashed upon its shoulders. It wailed under the intense pressure.

"I had that one," Saudett said, a playful frown on her brow. She smiled as she stabbed and twisted her spear into the pinned beast to finish it off.

"Dear wife, please, you need not exert yourself. Think of the baby!"

"I can determine how to use my own body, *Simon.*"

In most species, physical exercise at this point in gestation has little effect on a fetus of this age. It actually aids in the birthing. Even when the fetus is nearing the end of the bearing, the mother should move about as much as possible.

"Skrull's balls, Gaelin," Simon moaned. "Speak aloud so everyone can hear your overly descriptive facts of nature!"

"Ah yes, of course," Gaelin coughed. "I forget you can hear my thoughts if I am not careful."

"What did he say?" Saudett queried, brow arched.

"Oh, you know," Simon grimaced. Saudett was the victor *this time.* "He said that it is actually healthy for *animals,* the keyword here, to exercise themselves while pregnant. Makes birth easier for them."

"Indeed; all mammalian creatures, really," Gaelin added.

Simon shot Gaelin a glare.

Saudett smiled. "My thoughts exactly! Thank you, Gaelin."

Simon felt *stimulation* momentarily from Gaelin. The three-armed being stood smiling back at his wife. *Just staring at her.* Simon stepped in front of Saudett. "At least rest now. Have some wine."

"This battle was far too swift. I'm left wanting," she grinned as her hand brushed Simon's groin.

The skirmish *was* short-lived. The nomads had overwhelmed the few Daanav that had not succumbed to the powerful magic of the Iban'mael. Hasierans and Simon's work crew had already begun carrying construction supplies through the portal to fortify this side of the Gate.

He shook his head, realizing what his wife had just said and done. *Wait, what am I thinking? My wife is in the mood!* He looked around to see massive, gnarled trees twisting high above his head and the bog lands stretching about them until a fog clouded the distance. Insects buzzed around them. The wet earth seeped through his sandals. *This is not an ideal environment, but could we hide behind a tree for a quick romp?*

Saudett arched a brow as she watched him, likewise observing the surroundings. "Those tree trunks are quite *wide*."

"Ahem," Simon cleared his throat. "Now is not the time nor the place, but by Hettra's tits, you are a tease!"

She stepped in close, pressing up against him. "Just push me up against that *thick* trunk and—"

I can hear your thoughts as well, Simon. Gaelin slid into his mind.

"Oh!" Simon yelped. "Fucking gods, man!"

Saudett sprung back. "Skrull's hell, Simon! What?"

"I'm sorry, it's Gaelin; he's not letting up...oh, never mind. Shall we continue this later?"

She shrugged, then turned away to help with the supplies.

Skrull-forsaken son of a goat fu—

Yes, yes, curse me to your heart's content. Enough of your lusting. Gaelin thought at him. *Let us be on with this. The sooner we liberate the Kadal from the Daanav, the sooner we can shut off their access to other Wayfarer Gates.*

Firstly, it appears, Gaelin, I am not the only one lusting after my wife. "Secondly," Simon continued aloud, "what are you talking about? Other Gates?"

"When the Daanav destroyed my home, the Heil Lân, they gained access to many other worlds. We had many Gates set up to traverse to many Lâns. Your wife is the least of my concerns."

"Gaelin, I agreed to help with Sir Kogs' homeland and secure Hasiera a water source. After that, my wife and I will go after Baal and company to ensure their daughter is safe."

Kogs looked up from where he had been kicking a Daanav corpse that was beginning to melt.

"Well, more important things are at stake than finding a young girl," Gaelin blustered, his three hands clenching. "The fate of all Lâns is in our hands, Simon! We are the last of the Wayfarers, the last of the enlightened. It falls to you and me to protect them."

"No! *You* are the last of the Wayfarers. I never asked for this. You decided a random human child would have to help you save the world. I do not care about any other Lân. I care about my wife and child and our life together, growing old and dying happy."

"Not just any human child. A well-educated, *intelligent* human child."

"I was a babe. You could not know my worth."

"I saw it in your past, through your parents' lifeblood. I investigated the history of your family."

"Well, there must be an uneducated individual or two in my family tree!"

"No, Simon, there is not."

He is telling the truth, and I can feel it. Somehow, he knows. "Fine. We will figure it all out. One thing at a time, we need to find the river and revert a large channel toward this gate."

"Indeed. Little Kogs?" Gaelin called to the lizard man.

Kogs scurried over to him. "Three arms?"

"Do you know the way to the *big* river from here?"

"Oh yes, Kogs knows his home. Much easy to find the big river." He leaned his head back and sucked some breaths through his mouth with a hiss. "This way!"

The child-sized lizard scampered away through the grey atmosphere of the bog.

"Uhm, shouldn't he be more careful?" Simon asked cautiously. "There may be other Daanav out there."

"Perhaps." Gaelin shrugged. "Though he is probably the least noticeable thing about our company in this Lân."

They did not come across any more Daanav as they walked through the thick swampland. Muck bubbles popped around them in pools, puffs of foul-smelling clouds wafting upward.

Perhaps we could connect these pools along the way to the river, Simon thought as they continued.

The massive tree top canopy dampened the sun's rays, creating an ever-grey and dim light. The sound of many insects, amphibians, and other animals carried about them.

"Sir Kogs?" Simon called out to the Kadal lizard leading the way. "Is there anything other than Daanav we should be worried about in your homeland?"

"Oh no, not much," he said, hopping along. "Maybe *quraanjo* swarm. Maybe giant *caaro* web. Or hunting *bisad*. Is a big cat and likes to drop down from the tree cover onto prey. But not much, no, not much."

"Not much, indeed," Simon muttered. *Skrull's balls, what have we gotten ourselves into?*

Nearly half an hour from the Wayfarers Gate, Kogs found the river. It was massively wide across, the water slow-moving. Tall cat-tail reeds created a wall along the river's border, and lily pads dotted out from the banks.

"Yes, yes. Kogs finds big river, simple as that!" he said triumphantly, shaking his mane. "Now we follow it this way to Rawa and save my Gaks."

"Soon, Sir Kogs, mighty member of the Kadal," Simon praised. "We must gather our forces and scout the area before we strike."

I need my men to mark the path and begin digging a channel to this river, not to mention building some defenses around the Gate.

"Certainly, little Kogs and I will venture to the town of Rawa and see what there is to see," Gaelin stated.

"Just the two of you?" Simon frowned.

"Indeed, they cannot hurt what they cannot see." Gaelin placed two hands together, fingers entwined in a strange pattern. "*Dunnian.*"

Gaelin and Kogs vanished.

Simon blinked. "Alright then, good luck. I'll just head back through the dangerous, deadly swamp all *alone*. Strength in solitude, as they say."

No one answered.

Skrull take you to hell, Gaelin. Simon turned and began following the muddy trail they had created in their wake.

Saudett watched as her husband, Gaelin, and Kogs disappeared into the mire.

"The boss goes off on another pursuit, eh, ma'am?" Naurr's voice said behind her.

"I thought once I found him again," she muttered, turning to the workman. "I thought everything would return to how it was."

"Aye, ma'am. I am feeling the same most days."

"You miss your son and wife, I imagine."

"Deeply so."

"It seems we have been caught up in more unbelievable things about the Lân."

"As the Primus be willing it. After what I've seen, I think it is all part of His plan."

"I never took you as a religious man, Naurr."

"Oh aye, never been a practicing man, except under me old mam's sandal." He grinned. "But, as of recent happenings, my faith is renewing."

Saudett nodded. *There is something more significant to all this. An influence? Simon's dream. The Daanav. Her long-lost mother and sister. Is it fate?*

"Well, ma'am. Back to work, says I." Naurr smiled and trotted off, shouting orders to the other workmen. Already, a barricade was being established around the Wayfarers Gate.

"Lady Builder," a new voice said.

Saudett turned to see a Volkinn crouched low, feminine, with long limbs and tufts of fur peaking through linen and leather wraps. "Just Saudett if you will. I am no *builder*."

"Of course, Lady Saudett."

Saudett rolled her eyes. "Alright. What is your name then?"

"Darkclaw Marah."

"Marah, what can I help you with?"

"Some of the Daanav have escaped."

"What? How do you know this?"

"We can smell their scent. It is fresh and ran off when we emerged through the Gate."

"By Skrull's unholy hell! They will warn the other Daanav!" Saudett cursed. "Think you can track them?"

"Yes, but we must hurry to catch up to them."

"Alright, let's go."

Darkclaw Marah took a hissing breath and then sprinted on all fours.

Saudett dashed after them, spear in hand, hard-pressed to keep up.

The Volkinn twisted around trees and leaped over fallen logs ahead of them.

Saudett pole vaulted with her spear shaft over the fallen wood. Marah did not look back to ensure Saudett was still following, and at times, Marah would disappear behind a massive trunk or bush, and Saudett would summon a burst of speed to catch up.

By the Primus, I will be exhausted when we finally reach the Daanav.

As the thought came to her, she nearly crashed into Marah, who crouched behind some foliage, peering between the branches. Marah made a shushing gesture and pointed, holding a branch aside for Saudett to see.

Three Daanav lumbered along slowly. There was a spiked hound and one of the lanky molten-rock creatures. The third was another new one to Saudett, similar to a hulk and hound, but standing on its hind legs and hunched over, powerful-looking jaws and thick-muscled arms hanging nearly to the ground. Whereas hulks and hounds had matted black hair across their bodies, this beast was hairless and sickly grey.

Saudett readied her spear, desperately trying to catch her breath after the full-on sprint. "We need to stop them." She whispered through gasps of air. "Shall we attack?"

Darkclaw Marah flinched.

The hound turned its head and yowled.

"Fucks. I guess that answers the question," Saudett grunted and hurtled through the bush, branches scraping at her. To her surprise, the grey beast burst into motion.

Using its long arms to propel itself forward, in two leaps, it was upon her. Six yellow eyes glowed in two lines along the sides of its head, focused intensely on her.

She raised her spear haft to block the incoming claw.

It latched on and *pushed* against her.

Skrull-forsaken thing is fucking strong. She spun on one foot and used the creature's weight against it to make it stumble past her. In the same instant, she brought her spear around to stab it in the back. The spear thudded into something solid.

The creature roared and spun, ripping free of the spear tip and clawing at Saudett. She backstepped, countering each swing with a jab of her spear, finding flesh each time, yet consistently unable to pierce deeply into it. She ground her teeth. *Does it have bones everywhere within? I'll just have to slice it into ribbons!* She scored cut after cut on its arms, torso, and legs.

The grey beast did not stop. It launched a powerful strike, knocking her back against a tree, the air blowing out of her lungs. She gulped at the air.

The beast came in, jaws open to finish her off.

With a howl, Darkclaw Marah landed on the grey Daanav's back. The thick arms of the Daanav could not reach up and throw their attacker off. Marah's hands wrapped under the beast's chin and pulled as their feet pushed into the grey beast's back. Marah pulled, growling and hissing, but the Daanav's neck would not break.

Saudett put all her strength into the two-handed thrust into the Daanav's exposed neck. The spear collided with unnaturally hard bone but glanced and slid further *upward*. The gray beast went limp as the weapon reached the creature's brain.

"By the Primus," Saudett panted. "That was close."

Darkclaw Marah cracked their neck back and forth, then pulled some sharp spines from their shoulder with their teeth.

"The hound got you?"

"As it died beneath me, all its barbs burst outward," Marah said, licking at the wounds. "Nearly took a lot more than this."

"I'm glad you're alright," Saudett pulled a clean cloth wrap from her pouch and began wrapping Marah's shoulder. They smelt of wet fur and sweat and something feral. "What of the other one?" Saudett asked, finding a hint of curiosity, allure. *Marah is stunning. In their own way.* "I was too focused on this one to see what was happening."

"Dived into the mud," Marah grunted, crouching lower for Saudett. Fur and muscles glistened with blood and muck. "Escaped."

"Fucks."

"I cannot track it when it travels beneath the ground."

Saudett nodded. "We'd best get back and ready for an attack on the Wayfarers Gate."

Marah threw back their head and let out an ear-splitting howl.

Beautiful. Saudett thought, then shook off the feeling. *By the Primus's will, I only need Simon from now on.*

Chapter Twenty-Seven

KNOWLEDGE

Kiana Ahmadi beheld in amazement the different shades of color about her. *It is beautiful.* The leaves of the trees were changing from greens to shades of crimson and gold. Dark pines contrasted with the colors of the leafy trees. The sounds of the forest echoed about Kiana and her small party as creatures and birds skittered through the canopy, rays of sun piercing through.

Baal sucked in a deep breath and laughed aloud, "Joo! Good to be out of hot desert air!"

"Indeed," Brena agreed. "Autumn is well on its way; the mountains will be covered in snow this time of year."

"I've never seen anything as gorgeous," Kiana said. "The oasis valley of Hasiera is stunning in its own right, and it's all I have ever known. But this is just so *natural.*"

"The Earste Lân is vast and home to many fascinating environments, my dear daughter," Anora said, her eyes meeting Kiana's. "I am happy you can now witness some of them."

Is she trying to be a good mother after all this time? I suppose it's better late than never.

"It does have a peacefulness to it," Kaplan agreed. "Perhaps one day we can visit a man-made wonder, the golden and silver teardrops of the Dhan Ka Mahal of The Jewel of the East."

"I thought your life there was not," Kiana paused, regarding Kaplan Mir sympathetically, "not pleasant."

She remembered the tale he told them one night in the desert as they made their way to Hasiera while trying to avoid the Daanav. How he had grown up as an orphan, stealing and begging for food. Then, he found himself indentured to a grotesque *Sultana* of the orphans.

"Oh, Sultana Nishulk, the Orphan Queen, made my childhood wretched. She did, by second hand, teach me how to read. But still, the Jewel is a sight to behold, framed by the cerulean Sea of Xamid. Lush isles in the distance."

"Oh, for Skrull's sake," Zalias Ershya's reedy voice cut through the sounds of nature. "Can we get a move on? The sooner we get this over with, the better."

"Cut out grit-man's tongue?" Baal growled expectantly.

"*Unfortunately*," Anora said. "He still needs it."

Baal growled again but left it at that, and they listened to the sounds of flora and fauna as they walked through the woods.

The Gate had teleported them to a heavily wooded area of rolling hills. The Gate had been tucked between massive boulders and shaped to look like fallen stone, much more subtle than the Hasiera Gate. *Once we were all through, the blinding light blinked out of existence, and I could barely tell there was a Gate at all. Skrull-forsaken witchcraft!* Kiana contemplated. *Reminds me of Kaplan's story about Nishulk, how she had touched him and read his thoughts.*

She moved closer to Kaplan's side as they walked. "Nishulk taught you to read. No bewitchment involved?"

Kaplan smiled. "I knew you wanted to hear the rest of my story."

"Well," she nudged him playfully. "You did leave off at the most exciting part, as it were."

"Yes, Nishulk took credit for me learning to read. She may be the cause of where I ended up, but she did not teach me herself nor use her mind manipulation to do so. Finally, after years of sulking on the streets of Al'Jalif, stealing and spying for her, and recruiting other homeless children to her cause, she granted my wish. Though she always played favorites with us children. Whoever brought her the finest gift was rewarded with extra food and having to tend to her needs. The latter was no prize."

He was silent for a long moment; Kiana saw the agony on his face. "We need not uncover what abuse you suffered under her, Kaplan. I can see it brings you no joy." She wrapped an arm behind his back and gave him a gentle embrace.

Baal whistled from behind them.

Kiana blushed and let go of Kaplan.

"Thank you, Kiana," Kaplan said with a chuckle and gave a half grin. "You are kind." He gathered himself and began again, "Nonetheless, after three years, Nishulk finally called me to her chambers. 'Kaplan boy! You have grown so big after all these years,' she said. 'I have one final task before I grant you your wish.' 'Yes, Sultana,' I answered. 'You must sneak into the palace and find the greatest gift you have ever given me. A scholarly advisor named Tarvinder Locha has a vast library of scrolls, tombs, and books that would greatly enrich you and me, Kaplan boy.' I thought of rejecting her, telling her it was too dangerous, but I nodded in agreement. Sultana Nishulk *always* got what she wanted."

"Did you do it?" Kiana asked, genuinely intrigued. "Did you get into the palace?"

"It took a long time, and I did not sneak in. It took me so long to get into the palace because I needed to save every copper I could to buy a clean tunic and get myself washed up. It took months to be admitted to the Dhan Ka Mahal as a servant. I applied at the Office of the Ministry of Royal Labor when I no longer looked like a beggar. Unsurprisingly, the Dhan Ka Mahal is always in need of servants. Part of the workforce consisted of unpaid slaves, but most slaves were used as objects in the noble's bedrooms. The Sultan is said to have hundreds just waiting on standby for him to select and do with as he pleases. That, along with his horde of wives. The man has hundreds of children scurrying about the palace and the gardens, or so it is said."

"Would you not have witnessed these children when you entered?"

"The Dhan Ka Mahal is massive on a scale beyond dreams. The royal wing is an isolated domed citadel with gates, walls, gardens, and beaches. Very rarely are new servants allowed into that part of the palace."

"Hettra's mercy," Kiana tried to imagine the magnificent teardrops reaching skyward. "It must be a wonderful sight to see."

"It is. There are good and bad things about every country; pride in knowledge, education, science, and architecture is prominent in Xamid. I think Simon's father, Yakeb, studied in Al'Jalif, if I remember correctly, from what he told me."

And passed on his knowledge to Simon. "Thank the gods he taught it to his son, or Hasiera would have been devastated even further than it was." Kiana recalled Simon's anguish when the First Otsoa had murdered his father.

"A needless loss," Kaplan said, reading her emotions. "I never knew the man well, but he would try to get to know *you*. Everyone in Dagad knew of Yakeb. He visited the Shepherd's Eye barracks weekly and chatted with whoever was about. We got into talking about Xamid and the Jewel one day." He nodded, a warm expression on his face. "He was a good man."

"That's your brother-in-law, my dear daughter." Anora, who had been leading the way, turned her head and added. "I want to hear more about your man, Kaplan Mir. The story has been somewhat sidetracked."

Kiana saw the grin on her mother's lips and sighed, "Mother, mind your business."

"Joo, book man!" Baal's large hand landed on Kaplan's back. "I like story too! Go on." Brena giggled like a child.

"Ahem," Kaplan cleared his throat. "It seems I have grown an audience. Perhaps we should make a stop and take some vittles?"

"By Skrull's scrotum, yes, my feet are killing me," Zalias wheezed and sat on an overly large tree root at the base of an oak.

The others did likewise; flatbread and boiled yams wrapped in young palm leaves were passed around. They ate.

Kaplan continued. "It is not very exciting; I worked in the palace, beginning with small tasks such as running errands, cleaning, and emptying chamber pots. Learning servant etiquette. After just one week, I was paid more than I could make in a month on the streets. Eventually, I was assigned to a lower lord as a personal servant. He was an older man, Daksh was his name, a distant uncle of one of Sultan Muzumdar's wives. Qav's luck, I was assigned to him.

"He did not demand much of me, *but* he always had a book or scroll on hand, spending days in bed or in the gardens reading. Only having me bring his food, help him dress, and tidy up his chambers. He was slow and sore; he would send me to the library for him to acquire new reading materials. One day, he says, 'Son, you need not stand at attention as I read to my heart's content all day. You should pick up one of these books and see how interesting and exciting they can be.'

"'Thank you, Lord, but I know not how to understand the letters.'

"'Pah! Then, go to the Grand Library and find the *Xamidian Alphabet and Phonics* textbook. What? Did you grow up in the gutters?' I avoided the question and hurried on to the library.

"Not until I found myself walking into a magnificent room with shelves of books, scrolls, and parchments lining the walls and aisles did I realize my predicament. I could not find the book *Xamidian Alphabet and Phonics* because I could not *read* the title. I wandered about the corridors of shelving aimlessly, looking at the spines of thick-leathered books. Eventually, I walked past a dimly lit corner, and a voice, in a not-so-quiet whisper, said to me, 'You look lost, boy.'

"I turned to see a man sitting lengthwise on a bench, feet up, curly-toed slippers on his crossed feet as he stretched out. I remember his fine jacket of navy blue and silver diamond shapes covering warm beige robes. A dark mustache curled on his cheeks, along with a neatly pointed beard. 'You hearing me? Are you looking for something?' he said, throwing his legs from the bench, a soft grey turban upon his head.

"'Uh, sorry, my Lord, I was sent to find a book. *Xamidian Alphabet and Phonics.*'

"'Ah, is some Aurulan princeling arrived needing to learn our language?' the man said with a grin. 'This way, boy.'

I held my tongue and followed. He led us to an aisle near the entrance to the library and stopped, nodding toward a particular shelf. I began to sweat as I leaned in, scanning the spines helplessly. 'Ah, I see. This is for *you* then,' he said as he pulled a book from the shelf I was staring at. As he handed me the textbook, he looked upward at the sunlight beaming through a magnificent circular window of multi-colors in the ceiling. 'I suppose I can spare an hour. Come, boy, all peoples of Xamid should at least be able to read and write.'

"He led me to a corner of the Grand Library, where a few desks were lined up. 'Sir, you need not waste your efforts on me, a simple servant,' I pleaded.

"'Nonsense, boy. Knowledge is *potential*. It lets us analyze the world around us. It tells us to question everything and learn the facts before judgment. To become aware of new skills or how things work. You can use knowledge to better yourself and to become greater than you are,' he paused and grinned. 'To start, I'm confident that a scribe's assistant is paid tenfold than that of what you make now.'

"I remember choking on air at those words. 'Tenfold?' The possibilities of all that coin were endless. I would never need to look upon Nishulk again.

"'Indeed,' he answered. 'Have a seat; we don't have all day.' With that, I began to learn. Hours flew past, and I suddenly remembered old man Daksh.

"'Oh gods,' I stood abruptly. 'I need to get back to my master! He has been waiting.'

"'Who is your master, boy?'

"'Lord Daksh.'

"'Ha! Tell him Tarvinder is commandeering your services in the afternoons indefinitely. If I remember correctly, the old daredevil won't mind; he is nose-deep in that epic romance saga of the adventurous swashbucklers. What was it called again? Ah, yes, *Tales of the First Land.* It is quite the page-turner. Who ever heard of attractive pirates?' He laughed and sent me on my way.

"From then on, *daily*, Tarvinder taught me primarily to read and write, but also developed my knowledge of many other topics. A particular interest to him was religion. Or for him, rather the lack of it. He would get visibly heated when speaking of people's blind faith in imaginary beings. Or of being born and indoctrinated into said faith.

"'If I had been born a few hundred years ago, would I not be worshipping the old gods of Xamid? Before the Auru brought their pilgrims of the Primus to our door. Or if I was of the Vouri, would I not bow down to Teras, God of the mountains? It is all circumstance, and I did not get to choose. The good things about religion are community and the stories that tell us to be good people. Stories! That is what it is, *fiction* written by men to control other men!' He would go on about this, repeating himself every other day. But his overly passionate, critical thinking and arguments began to make sense to me, and I now share his point of view."

"You do not believe in the Gods?" Anora gasped dramatically. "That is depraved news for us."

"Mother, you never taught me about the gods unless you cursed their names," Kiana retorted. "That is the only thing I ever learned about them from you."

"Teras is forever," Baal said with a grunt. "Like the mountain, he was before me and is here when I am gone."

Brena nodded her agreement.

"I'm with Mir on this one. What have the Gods ever done for us?" Zalias said skeptically.

"You are Xamidian," Kaplan said to Zalias. "I would like to say our education has enlightened our country somewhat, but Anora, also of Xamid, stands to differ. So, it is up to us to make our own choices."

There was silent regard to Kaplan's words.

"So, you learned to read and write and question the universe," Zalias answered. "Is that the end of the tale?"

"Nearly, I stayed in service of Daksh and Tarvinder for a few years. I was now an educated young man. But I had left something in Nishulk's keeping, a book I had found in the back lane of a manor that I had treasured as a child and always dreamed of reading one day. I took my leave of my lords and found myself at the Sultana's door." Kaplan stopped and took a deep drink from his waterskin. "I think the conclusion of this story will have to wait; we spoke for too long of theology. We have a few more hours of daylight. Let's go find the Sunstone."

Murmurs of agreement followed as they gathered themselves and began the march toward Nidhaut again.

Chapter Twenty-Eight

DOUBT

Hata awoke to the shrill call of a silver-beaked hawk far above. That distinct cry reminded her of her old home, Oitilla, the mountain village where she had grown up. *That is where I need to be.*

She stood and stretched, the embers of her fire burning low in the morning light. She had roused herself throughout the night and added wood to the fire. The birch burned slowly, and her small cave and thick mountain bear hide kept the warmth. *It is surprisingly cozy.* She added another branch to the flames, unwrapped some bear meat, and skewered the meat over the fire.

"Thank Teras for the gifts of the mountain," she praised aloud and tucked in heartily.

She surveyed the rising peaks around her; the snowstorm had now cleared, and she could make out her surroundings. *Which way is home?* After a moment, she saw it. *There it is, the Anvil of Teras.* The largest mountain of the North Iron Belt. Its odd shape, nearly anvil-like in itself. Oitilla was located in a neighboring peak to the southeast of the Anvil. Looking at the sun's location in the sky, she figured she was roughly northeast of the Anvil. *If I head directly south, I should come across Oitilla.*

She hesitated to leave her fire. *I don't think I will be able to start a new one. The flaming sphere was responsible for this. But I cannot just stay here! Moreover, I have too much bear meat, extra fur, and wood kindling to bring. What would my father do?* She breathed, listening to the sounds of the peaks.

The thought of her father drawing his wood lacquer sled with the entire weight of the slain bear upon it came to her. *A sled, how can I make a sled?* Her eyes came to rest on the rough mountain stone rising around and above her cave. She shaped the rock with her mind into a flat disc and hewn it from the cliffside. It fell into the snow and promptly began to slide away from her.

Oh, Teras! Hata dashed after the disc and leaped atop it. She used her hands and feet to bring it to a halt, resulting in a face full of powdery snow. Hata sat up, spitting and grasping the edge of the flat piece of stone. It was heavier than she expected from the look of it. *Now, how am I to fasten this behind me?* Slowly, laboriously, she pulled the makeshift sled back to her fire. Her hand brushed dry yellow grass as she pulled herself through the deep snow. *More kindling? Or could I make a rope out of this?*

Hata remembered the hours combing and then plaiting her mother's long blonde hair. She nodded to herself. *Teras' fortitude is inherited from my family. I hope they are doing alright. Father must have gone into a rage when I was taken; Mother too. What would they do because of that? Undoubtedly, they would come after me. But how would they know where to look?*

Hata pondered her parent's actions as she dug in the snow and yanked long grass stalks out of it. Once a sufficient pile had been gathered, she divided the grass into three strands and tied them into an oversized knot. Then, crossing one strand over another, began to braid. When she reached the end of the strands, she would gather three more small bundles of grass and weave them into the bottom of her completed one, creating a link. It took some time, but she was glad to be busying her hands in the cold mountain air while keeping warm near her fire.

Her mind wandered, thinking about how her earthen powers had awakened and how things had gone to Skrull's hell ever since then. *Perhaps I would have met Saudett on better terms instead of during her overwhelming grief and loss of her husband and father-in-law. But then, I do not think we would have had the same connection. We could be back in Dagad, living a peaceful life without so much death. Taryn would be with the living. Many of the nomads would still be alive. The Daanav...the Daanav would still be scourging the Burning Sea, killing far more innocent people.*

She let it sink in. *It is almost as if I was meant to discover my ability and meet Saudett. To help her find Simon and vanquish the Daanav. And we did; we saved Hasiera!* Hata felt pride swell within. *Then I was taken; someone invisible to the eye grabbed me from behind and pulled me through a portal. The next thing I knew, the Alpha was leaning over me, and my life turned into constant pain ever since. And now I am alone. But at least I am free.*

Hata judged she had fashioned a long enough rope out of the strands of dry grass. Before tying the knot at the end of the braid, she needed some way to fashion the rope to the stone disc. Hata closed her eyes and imagined two holes a couple feet apart at the edge of the disc, large enough to thread the grass cord through. Then, she would make a large knot at the rope's end to stop it from being back-pulled through. As she opened her eyes, the holes were there.

It is becoming simpler to control my abilities. I suppose the Proctor's training had worn off on her. The image of Chanel's arms being torn off buffeted in her mind. *Hettra's mercy, I'm so sorry, Chanel, Luftan, Tomas! They are dead because I am weak. Dying to save me! Why me?!*

Guilt swept through her as she began to tremble, not from the chills of the mountains, but with fear and disgust in herself. *Could I have done anything to save them?* Try as she might, she could not turn her thoughts from the misery. She sat in the snow, staring ahead, trembling. The rope was loose in her hands.

Her tremors changed to shivers as she realized darkness was approaching and her fire was naught but cooling embers. *How long have I been sitting here wallowing in my self-pity? Hours?* Hata shook her head and began kindling her fire again. Luckily, she managed to catch new flames by blowing on the embers. Next, she finished attaching the rope to the sled.

I will spend another night here and head out for Oitilla in the morning. Walking down the mountain in the dark of night was far from a swell idea. Nodding to herself in decisiveness, she cooked more fatty bear meat and ate it unrestrainedly. Then, Hata cooked some extra for tomorrow's journey. A thought came, and she formed a small stone bowl out of the rock face. Hata filled the bowl with snow and placed it over the fire. Until now, she had been eating snow to keep herself hydrated, which also caused her body temperature to fall. Once the snow melted, Hata added more until the bowl bubbled with boiling water. She crushed some pine needles with stone upon stone to release their extracts and dropped them into the hot water. The bowl was scalding, so Hata used some extra bear fur to pull it from the flames and let it cool. Subsequently, she took a sip. *Gods, that is good.*

Her belly was filled, her fire emanating, and her body warmed. Hata curled up in her furs under the shelter of her cave and slept.

Hata awoke before the sun had even begun to peak over the ranges. She piled the meat bundles upon the sled and extra furs packed with kindling. Then, she placed as many branches as possible around the packages. Finally ready to depart, Hata lifted the rope around her waist and began to trudge south on a slight decline down the mountain, the stone sled sliding along in her wake.

Once I reach the bottom, I must ascend and skirt the base of another crag with this heavy sled. Hata dreaded the thought of it but resolved herself to keep moving.

Hours dragged by as she walked. Her feet and hands began to feel numb. *I pray to Teras that I can start a new fire tonight.* She looked down at the pendant necklace Chanel had given her. There was the empty socket where the crimson marble had once been before using it to summon the flaming sphere.

There were other colored stones within. A milky yellow, a snowy white, cerulean blue, and the large midnight centerpiece, black as death itself. *What does each spell do?* She fiddled with them, trying unsuccessfully to divine their nature. *I can't very well test them; they only work once, as far as I know.*

She remembered a lesson Chanel had taught in the Convent, a study of enchantment. Those enchantments were one of the other Council members' specialties. *Epsilon, was it? Yes, the Epsilon did not have powers such as my earth, Joanna's fire, Chanel's wind, or even the mental manipulations and telekinesis of the Alpha. What was the extent of Ebras Corb's power? The man could also create portals, but according to Chanel's lesson, he needed pylons, which could only be built through Epsilon's enchantments.*

Hata sighed heavily; she had used the portal stone to escape the Convent. It dawned on her that a pylon must have been back at the broken-down hunter's shack where she had appeared. *Probably buried under the snow. Skrull's hell, I should have looked for it.* Even then, what could she have done if she found it? *Nothing.*

The way ahead began to ascend. Her legs burned with exertion as she pushed her feet through knee-deep snow and pulled the stone disc behind her with as much might as she could muster. Finally, she stopped to catch her breath and eat some frigidly cold bear meat, which was challenging to chew.

Hata pushed on.

Teras, grant me the stability of your stone and the perception of your highest peaks. Darkness began to fall as Hata made her way up and up. Nearing exhaustion, she halted her journey and settled under a grove of pines.

"How am I to make a fire?" Hata pondered aloud as she began stacking some sticks and birch bark together. *How am I to start it?*

Chanel's voice echoed in her mind, *perhaps even causing it to rotate, even create your own heat.*

Hata remembered the spinning sand projectiles she had often used against the Daanav. *Of course; why did I not think of this before?* She selected a small stone, placed it against one of her thicker branches, and then put a bit of bark and smaller twigs near the rock. She focused on the stone, moving her hands as if to twirl a child's spinning top. It began to rotate faster and faster against the wood. A tiny tendril of smoke curled up. *Joo! Faster!* The stone created an unpleasant squeal against wood as the smoke began to billow. She moved the bark over, and it caught the flame.

"Voitoon! I did it!" she exclaimed, adding more kindling and branches, tending her fire like a newborn babe. She cooked and ate and slumped down in the warm nest of pine needles overhanging her. Exhausted, she slept.

CHAPTER TWENTY-NINE

CHARM

Skrull's unholy hell. Fat flies, as large as a coin, buzzed about Simon, biting at any exposed flesh. His nomadic-fashion cloth-wrapped feet and sandals were soaked through. *By Hettra's sagging tits, can this get any worse?* He thought as he squinted and swatted at the flies. He then walked face-first into a massive cobweb. Stumbling into more webbing, he suddenly lurched to a stop as he realized his torso could not move.

Then, a low clicking noise derived from above.

Oh, gods. Simon craned his neck to see an *enormous* arachnid's mandibles clacking together as it crept down its thick webs, interconnected between two massive marshland trees.

He tried to raise his arms in defense, only entangling them further.

"Bael cnytells!" he shouted. White fire shot into the ground from his fingers, and flaming moss began warming his squelchy footwear.

Oh gods, oh gods.

The spider skulked ever so slowly, seemingly sizing Simon up.

Gauging if it should proceed to eat me! "Stay back! I'm more than you can chew!" Simon yelled at the creature while trying to stamp out the flames at his feet. "Your eyes are bigger than your stomach, as they say!"

The spider paused, head tilting, forelegs rubbing together desirously. Then, in a sudden burst, it *surged* forward.

"*Bael cnytells!*" Simon screamed as he curled his fingers up in the repeated incantation. This time, the white flames shot up, nearly scorching his face, but managed to burn through the web and impact the thick arachnid legs. Two of its limbs were seared off as the boiling fire drilled upward. As the spider reared back in pain, the legs came free and dangled in the webs where they had been.

Squealing, the creature's globular body retreated into the tree's canopy and vanished.

"That was too close," Simon sighed in relief. He had managed to stamp out the rest of the flames at his feet, the soggy ground aiding in that. *Now, to get out of these webs.* He created the barrier of magic, but it did not affect the webbing attached to him. Next, he tried to float, but that only caused him to rise further into the trap.

"*Windan abrecan,*" Simon said finally. *Windan* was usually a sharp blast of air from his hand. This time, the air wrapped around him as a spinning vortex and sheared through his constraints.

"Ah ha, freedom at long last! Now to get back to the Wayfarers Gate." Thoroughly disoriented, it took him some time to find the muddy footprints of their maiden track to the river. Simon cast the windstorm about him a second time to clear the buzzing flies, then immediately brought up the shield of light to protect himself from the pests. He found he could keep it dim, less powerful. Yet strong enough to keep the large flies at bay. *Not to mention that the barrier will protect me if anything should surprise me again.*

He soon found himself back at the portal to the Earste Lân. It was abuzz with Hasierans and Simon's crew. Weapons and supplies were still being brought in from the valley, and a short palisade was just beginning construction. Already, a massive tree had been felled and was being sawed into beams and planks. Simon sought out his foreman, Naurr, and found the man directing the work on the massive tree.

"My good man," Simon greeted. "You have been busy."

"Well, the boss went and disappeared when the work started," Naurr countered.

"Ah, um, my apologies, but I managed to find the river and need to get a crew out that way on the double."

"Steady now, boss. Trouble is brewing. That wife of yours went hunting after some Daanav, but one did escape her wrath."

"Oh, Skrull's scrotum, where is she? Is she alright?"

"*I'm fine,* dear husband," Saudett scorned as she joined them.

A lanky Volkinn crouched low, shadowing her.

"Thank Hettra!" Simon embraced Saudett.

She grunted in response but leaned into his arms. "Perhaps next time, inform us of your intentions before you run off alone."

"I could say the same of you! Chasing after the enemy like that by yourself."

"Not alone," Saudett nodded to the Volkinn. "Darkclaw Marah was with me."

"Lady Saudett hunts well," Marah growled.

"As do you, my friend," Saudett smiled, eyes darting up and down Marah's body. "At any rate, one of the Daanav escaped, and we can expect them to retaliate soon."

I thought you wanted us to be exclusive, my dear wife? Simon pondered at his wife's blatant attraction to Marah. But he turned his focus on the conversation. "Gods," he exhaled. "If their forces are as large as those in the Burning Sea, this will not be simple."

"Yes," Marah hissed. "Hasiera is most formidable in mounted combat. This Lân will not let us ride. More of my kin are needed, but Howler Thien has taken them to explore the southland jungles."

Simon closed his eyes. *I wish I had some way to help our soldiers and protect them.* A memory came to him, the image of four pale hands tinkering with wood and metal. The hands etching symbols into the grain of the wood. *Windan.* Simon could read the strange runes. He clapped his hands triumphantly. "Naurr, I need two pieces of lumber, no bigger than two or three feet long."

Naurr nodded and sauntered to the crewmen who sawed the tree into lumber. He promptly returned with a few pieces for Simon to select from.

Simon laid two pieces in a t-shape, the top plank substantially shorter. He slowly notched out a hovel to fit the smaller board into the longer one. Then, he began to chisel a small divot along the ridge of the longer board. It looked like a child's toy crossbow at this point.

Now for the fun part. Simon began to etch the runes in carefully along the small trench. He connected the runes with another spell. *Croda,* which simply meant *"trigger."* He cut out a handhold on the base of the longer board and closed the rune there. The charm was complete.

"Finished!" he exclaimed and handed the contraption to his wife. "My dear, if you would be so kind as to steady your aim upon that log and fire at will."

Unfortunately, as she took the makeshift weapon, her hand grasped the *trigger* rune. The symbol glowed bright, and a blast of razor-sharp air shot skyward.

Branches and leaves crashed about them.

"By the gods, Simon!" Saudett exclaimed as she flung the weapon away.

Nomads and workers alike stopped what they were doing and gathered around to observe.

"Oh my, perhaps I need to work out the activation better," Simon muttered. "Right now, it will simply go off at the touch of a hand."

"You are working with the unholy there, boss," Naurr cautioned. "Primus's wrath be coming our way before we know it."

"Bah, superstition, my good man." Simon picked up the weapon and went to an unassumed part of the felled tree. He rested its cross beam upon the log, aimed at a tree, and gently touched the rune *Croda* with his free hand. Once again, the etching glowed bright, and the burst of air shot and exploded into the base of the thick trunk, wood splintering with force.

"See," he smiled.

The others stared at him. People's mouths hung open in awe.

"My people!" Simon addressed the gatherers. "We have a new weapon to aid us in our fight against the Daanav!" He raised the silly-looking crossbow above his head.

A cheer elevated about him.

"The First Otsoa!"

"The Builder!"

"Get me more wood!" Simon called in answer. "I will create more of these."

The hours moved swiftly as Simon worked tirelessly.

At some point, Saudett interrupted him to suggest, "Husband, we should use these trees to our advantage. Can we make some ladders to climb into the canopies and defend with the new weapons from there?"

"A brilliant proposal, my dear," Simon agreed, waving to Naurr. "My good man, can we nail some simple handholds to these trees to get a better vantage point on the Wayfarers Gate and surrounding area?"

"Aye, boss," Naurr answered, "A simple task, we'll make it so." He bustled off to relay the message to the other crew members.

"Ha, so you're not just a pretty face," Simon said amusingly, grinning at his wife.

"Simon Meridio!" Saudett smacked him playfully. "I'll have you know I have spent many hours watching a young engineer toil on endlessly for hours. Some things have *rubbed* off on me."

"Oh?" Simon smirked. "You are in the highest form today, my star."

"Watching you create that new weapon caused me to remember why I fell in love with you. You get so impassioned by a project that your mind is upon nothing else." Saudett leaned close and whispered, "Take me."

Her aroma suffused Simon with desire. "Gods, woman," he groaned, pulling her in and kissing her.

Saudett moaned with desire as their lips departed.

Simon looked about frantically. "We may have to retreat through the portal unless you want swamp muck stuck in your fanny tonight."

Saudett's face became serious. "We should not leave; should the Daanav come in the night, the people will need us. Especially since Gaelin is nowhere to be found."

Just then, thunder cracked, muted by the canopy above. Rain began to drizzle, then streamed through the foliage. It was a warm rain.

"Skrull's scrotum! Nature seems to dispute our tantalizing thoughts, my dear," Simon griped, surveying Saudett's now-soaked linen wraps. Her wet, jet-black hair was flat as water dripped down her ringed nose. Her lips. Her nipples showed faintly through her soaked garments. *It's as if she has cast an appealing charm on me.*

She gazed back at him, biting her lip. Then, with a nod to herself, she took his hand and led him away.

They found a *wide* tree some distance away and worked their appetites out of each other with great fervor. Abounding tensions unfettering in spousal passion. Bronze and pale skin glistened against each other, naked in the warm rain.

On the positive side, the rain kept the insects away.

That was...stimulating, Gaelin noted after they had concluded.

"Oh, fuck off, Gaelin!"

CHAPTER THIRTY

NIDHAUT

Kiana looked on in wonder at the massive city of Nidhaut, the capital city of Aurulan. Immense stone walls snaked about the sprawling municipal as Kiana and the others waited in a long line of people waiting to enter through the gates. There were eight strangely constructed towers rose from behind the walls. A smooth pitch-black spire with a rounded peak centered in the city. "How can men build such things?" Kiana pondered aloud.

"Those keeps are not built by traditional means such as your brother-in-law would employ," her mother answered.

Kiana flinched, still unused to how her mother had readily welcomed Simon and Saudett. Referring to Simon as a brother-in-law felt so odd.

"Yes, yes, fascinating city," Zalias whined. "Can the line move any slower?"

Baal's massive hand fell on the wiry merchant's shoulder. "Quiet, or something on the grit-man break by chance."

Zalias laughed uneasily and squirmed, trying to pull away, but Baal held him fast and continued holding him as they made their way forward slowly.

Brena shadowed her husband, her hand resting readily on her sword hilt.

Kaplan moved close and whispered to Kiana, "The Vasara duo is keen to watch the grit dealer. He could try something now that we have arrived."

"Indeed, let us keep an eye on the surrounding people as well," Kiana nodded. "If anyone recognizes him and reacts, we should take action."

"How so? Confront them in the streets?"

"Perhaps, but if they react and flee, we should have one of us follow."

Kaplan nodded and left it at that.

At long last, they were next in line to enter Nidhaut.

"Good day, state your business in Nidhaut," a gate guard greeted them gruffly, his black and white padded surcoat depicting an eagle with wings spread wide upon his chest. Wanted posters lined the wall of the inner gate behind the man.

"We are mercenaries seeking employment with the local caravan guards," Anora answered curtly.

The guard measured them up, hovering on Baal and Brena. "You are Vouri?"

"We are," Brena answered.

"All Vouri refugees will be escorted to the Delta's citadel for questioning."

"We are not refugees," Brena specified. "We have lived among the Auru for some time, not been back to the North Iron Belt for some years."

"Oh," the guard paused. He studied Baal for an even more extended moment.

Baal answered with his signature toothy smile.

The guard turned to survey the wanted posters as if to find an excuse to apprehend their group. He finally shrugged and nodded at Baal. "Mercenaries seems about right, judging by this fellow. Move along, then." He waved them through.

The gates opened to a large square with plenty of space for wagons and carriages to pull into the city. People bustled about hectically, unloading wagons into smaller carts to be delivered to the city shops and markets. The townsfolk hurried briskly about their day-to-day business.

Anxiety teemed within Kiana as so many people surrounded her. She itched to run away, back to the forest, and breathe deeply. There was scarcely room to walk, and people naturally brushed into each other as Anora led them through the crowd.

Her mother waved them to a side street, and they gathered in the alley.

"Alright, *merchant*," Anora addressed Zalias. "Where are these contacts who would know where to find the Magnus Huntsman?"

"Of course," Zalias said, wringing his hands together nervously. "I have a few sources scattered about the city I can aim to treat with. But any information in this town is not free of charge."

"We have no payment to offer," Kaplan stated flatly.

"Kaplan is right," Kiana agreed. *I adore his matter-of-fact, no-nonsense take on things,* she mused inwardly. "What can we give in exchange for such information?"

"Well," Zalias smirked. "Young slaves are the prime currency in the company we seek to agree with."

Zalias yelped as Baal's hand squeezed his shoulder tightly. "Skrull's hell, it was a joke!" the sleazy merchant whined.

"Why not sell our friendly merchant himself?" Brena asked.

All eyes turned to Zalias Ershya, and he shrunk into himself.

"No, no, no, it will not work. First, I am much too old to be a sellable specimen. Secondly, one needs a reputation. Repute among my acquaintances is necessary should you even dream of being allowed an audience."

Anora grasped Zalias's collar in her fists, pulling him from Baal's grasp, hissing in his face, "Alright, you shameless son of a whore. Don't waste time with anyone else. Take us to the one who will know what we need to know. And *you* will figure out our payment. I'm sure you have a hoard or account with a bank in Nidhaut?"

"I have nothing; my home is Al'Jalif; you confiscated my caravan goods and brought me here with nothing but rags. I am penniless."

"Figure it out! Now show us the way!" Anora pushed him into the busy street to lead them on.

Zalias stumbled forward erratically. Then, he grabbed a passing woman, shoved her into the surprised group, and ran. His now faded, filthy red turban bobbed through the throng of people.

"That's why I no take hand off," Baal grumbled as they sprinted after him.

"Out of the way!" Kiana yelled as people ignored the group's commotion and continued to mind their business but congested their progress.

Baal let out an ear-deafening bellow of a roar, and people stopped in their tracks to look and see the massive Vouri man charging through. The crowd parted rapidly before him, bodies scrambling out of the way.

Kiana followed closely, scanning ahead to locate Zalias's crimson turban in the crowd. *There's a yellow one and a blue one there!* There weren't that many of the particular headdress in the turmoil.

A blur of red disappeared around a corner.

"There!" Kiana pointed and called out. "That way!"

They made it to the corner, and Baal collided with a patrol of black and white-clad soldiers. Men flew back onto the cobblestones at the impact. Others immediately readied their arms to apprehend the party.

Baal kept his momentum and did not look back.

"Halt!" one of the soldiers ordered.

"Sergeant! I need to report to my king," Kaplan called as he saluted the soldier to distract him, at the same time nodding to Kiana to follow Baal. "Kaplan Mir, Shepherd's Eye Ranger out of Dagad, we bring grave tidings."

Kiana slipped away into a gathering mob and found Baal's large back pushing on up ahead. She peered at the throng of people's heads, trying vainly to find that hint of crimson fabric. *I can't see it! It's gone.*

Baal slowed to a trot and bent to the ground. Knuckles whitening in rage around a long red piece of fabric.

Kiana approached slowly, gently resting a hand on his back, "Friend Baal?"

He tore the fabric in half and roared, "I WILL KILL YOU, GRIT MAN!"

The multitude froze like a wave centering on Baal, and an eerie silence washed over the onlookers.

He shook like a bull readying to stampede once again, then turned to regard Kiana, his eyes bloodshot and watering.

"I'm sorry, Baal," Kiana consoled.

He grumbled and moved past her back toward the others.

When Kiana joined them, she looked about, surprised that Kaplan was not among them. The soldiers who had stopped them were also nowhere to be seen.

"He was escorted to a town barracks to report to a Captain," Anora answered Kiana's unasked question. "We agreed to meet at an inn called *Vider Son Verre.*"

Brena moved to her husband's side. "My mountain, by Teras' guidance, we *will* find the grit dealer."

Baal slumped dejectedly and did not answer his spouse.

"Baal, that was my fault," Anora tested cautiously. "I did not think him so quick-witted to act in such a way."

Again, they were only met with silence.

"Well," Kiana sighed. "We'd best do what we can. Where is this inn?"

"Come," her mother gestured. "Let us acquire a map of the town and some supplies at the market."

Anora led them through the busy streets, white stuccoed homesteads with thatched roofing hiding under the shadows of the Aerie towers as they went. They entered a bustling *Marché de la Ville*, with shops and market stands everywhere. Anora would stop at intervals to purchase food and chat with the townsfolk, casually questioning them about news around town.

It comes so naturally to her, Kiana thought. *She is a different person than the one who raised me.*

They learned that a significant military force had gone to the North Iron Belt, and a few Aerie council members, acolytes, and the King himself accompanied the army. Yet, nobody seemed to know what the military was fighting. Vouri refugees were being detained.

At long last, as dusk approached, they found themselves at the inn, *Vider Son Verre*. An elongated building of blue-tinted plaster. It looked to have many rooms; three stories high. The establishment's title was written finely in white paint below the image of two crystal goblets clanging together in celebration over the entrance.

Even more people, Kiana thought anxiously as they entered.

A rosy-cheeked elderly woman greeted them warmly, a round monocle glinting in one eye, standing behind a lectern. "Welcome to *Vider Son Verre!* A few drinks in the tavern, or will you require room and board?"

"The latter, if you will," Anora answered. "Also, a note to a companion who is to join us later."

"Of course, Lady..." The old woman squinted, taking her monocle and peering through it at Anora. "You look awfully familiar, young lassie."

"Well, it has been nearly twenty years since Caravan House Kafilah made use of your fine services, Cloudia."

"Lady Kafilah?" the woman hobbled from behind the counter. Her eyes widened in amazement. "Anora!"

"Cloudia Maria!" Anora announced with arms extended.

The two embraced sincerely.

Kiana clenched her jaw. *Hettra's mercy, mother, who are you? So jubilant and outgoing. Where is the desert-hardened warrior who beat me into one myself?* Irritation and jealousy of her own mother simmered within. *She has hidden this side from me for all these years. Yet another reason for me to hate her.*

"Where have you been all these years?" Cloudia exclaimed. "Last I heard, you and Lord Kafilah vanished, and a daughter was managing the Caravan House, but she retired it to settle down."

"That was one of my daughters," Anora smiled. "It is a long story for another time. We have traveled far and required rest."

"Of course, of course; where are my manners," Cloudia shuffled back behind the desk. "Premium suites for you and all your companions!"

"Hettra's blessing upon you," Anora answered appreciatively.

They were assigned three large rooms. The Vasaras took one, her mother another, and Kiana and Kaplan, when he returned, took the last. Kiana fell onto the massive bed of a comfortable feathery down mattress. *I've never lain on something so soft before.*

Kiana awoke sometime later as Kaplan touched her gently on the shoulder.

He leaned in with a whispering breath, "My Otsoa."

"You're back?" Kiana moaned sleepily. "What happened?"

"I informed the local Captain of the Guard of our plight against the Daanav. Though I left out the details of your home, Hasiera."

"Thank you, Kaplan. How did they take it?"

"In stride; they are too preoccupied with the North to care. Every spare soldier has been marched off. They also wanted to poach me, but I insisted I report back to my Captain in Dagad. At any rate, I did my duty and got us out of a peculiar situation."

"Well, I am glad you are back," she said, reaching out to him. "Come to bed; you must be exhausted."

He nodded; eyes red with fatigue. He lay beside Kiana, kissed her, closed his eyes, and began to snore faintly.

Kiana traced his weary bearded face tenderly, then soon drifted back to sleep.

Anora drank the warm mulled wine deeply, sitting comfortably before a hearth, fire crackling. The wine soothed her throat after relaying where she had been all these years to Cloudia Maria. She did leave out most of the details, such as everything that happened between her and her *deceased* husband.

Cloudia sat in a cushioned rocking chair across from Anora, a woolen blanket over her shoulders.

"Twenty years in the desert," Cloudia said in astonishment. "By the Primus, why not come back to society?"

"It was not so simple. I gave up all this, my life before."

"Yet now you are back."

"Desperate times," Anora sighed. "Speaking of which, there is a favor I would ask of you."

"Ask away, my friend."

"Have you heard of the Magnus Huntsman?"

Cloudia's brows raised slightly. "Everyone has heard of them, though most believe they are fictional. A folk tale. Spread to scare anyone with even an inkling of dabbling with sorcery."

"So, no more details on them?"

"Folk tales indeed!" Cloudia removed her monocle to clean it on her smock. "I would agree with the stories if I had not seen one such Huntsman at work in this establishment."

"Primus tell?" Anora leaned closer.

"Some years ago, a man presented a black iron feather after apprehending a young man in my tavern."

"What did he look like?"

"It is challenging to recall," Cloudia paused, polishing her monocle while pondering. "He was hooded and dressed in dark clothing. That is all I can remember."

Skrull's hell, Anora thought. *It could have been him, Jude Nelon. But again, how many Huntsmen were there?*

"Anyways, one of my regulars, a lad who worked as a courier in town, was the one he took. The lad would come to have a few drinks with his friends after work every day. I remember the boy could throw his voice across the room, sometimes *deafeningly* loud, usually after drinking. Unnatural loud. If you catch my meaning. Honestly," Cloudia sighed in relief. "The boy was likely to hurt someone sooner or later if left unchecked."

Best not to mention Hata. She sympathizes with the Council's view of magic. "Do go on."

"Where was I?" the elder tilted her head. "Ah yes, after hearing one such outburst, the Magnus Huntsman slyly befriended the boy and his crew, and the next thing I knew, the boy and all his companions were passed out on my floor and tables. The huntsman carried the boy on his shoulder, showing me the black iron feather and stating, 'Aerie business.' Then he was gone."

"Unfortunately, that doesn't help me much, but I thank you for the information, Cloudia."

"Why are you seeking a Magnus Huntsman? Is there a mage wreaking havoc somewhere in the Earste Lân? If so, you can report it to the Alpha's tower in the town center, and he will deal with it."

"Oh no, he just took a personal object of one of my companions and forgot to return it. I traveled with him for a while as he made his way through the Burning Sea."

"Ah, so they *are* human! So mysterious! Well, I can keep an eye out, and who knows, perhaps I will sight him for you."

"My thanks again, Cloudia. You are a true friend." Anora stretched sleepily. "But alas, I must retire."

"Of course, lovely chatting with you, Anora. My best regards to Lord Kafilah."

Anora winced as she departed. *I had failed to mention the part where I killed him and found a new love.* As she readied to turn in for the night, she could not help but think about her blunder of letting Zalias Ershya escape. *Baal and Brena must be loathing me. We have no leads on the Magnus Huntsman, barring knocking on the Alpha's front door.*

Anora slept fitfully, thoughts of regret keeping the slumber away.

CHAPTER THIRTY-ONE

QUELL

Ebras probed the armless woman's mind. *I need a clue as to where that pylon was located!*

Wave upon wave of *hate* crashed toward him. Hate for him, *Ebras goat-fucker*, bubbled within the former Proctor's mind. That, and a smug little inkling of victory. *She escaped, you bastard.*

Even though the woman was unconscious, it still emanated at him.

I will strip everything from you! He tore memories from her mind, ripping them from her being. Her body convulsed each time he gripped and pulled. Love for the boy Luftan. *Gone.* Care and remembrance for her students, *all* of them over the years. *Away with it!* A necklace of spell stones...revealed under the sheet of a newly-delivered bathtub. *Epsilon, that Skull-damned meddler!*

Ebras churned with rage as he broke the link to her thoughts, panting with exertion from raking the woman's mind for hours. He remembered the Epsilon Passeriform had offered Chanel de Montrichard the bathtub as a gift. Ebras had not thought of inspecting the thing all those years ago. *I should kill that fool Hornero for this insolence!*

Pacing, he tempered his anger and assessed. *At least I have finally found a clue about this pendant. It is time I paid Rofous Hornero a visit.* He rushed to the intersection of the *Convent Enclosure* and opened the teleportation spell to Epsilon's tower in Nidhaut. Ebras had pylons set up in each of the seven other council member's citadels. He would not be seen walking amongst the peasants of Nidhaut, and rarely did he show himself to the general populace. If he did, it was only to incite fear.

Stepping through the portal, he found himself in a disgustingly colorful chamber. The terrace was riddled with jade plants and variegated flowers, decorating the railings and parapets. Balcony doors stood open on all five chamber walls, letting in the warm sun of the day. Stained glass windows reflected all the rainbow colors cast down upon the Epsilon, Rofous Hornero, who languished in a sea of purple, teal, and auburn pillows and beddings.

Rofous lay on their side, propped up on an elbow, a shirtless young man repeatedly fanning the Epsilon with a large palm. Rofous's bright body tattoos glimmered against the rays of sunlight. They brushed their blonde-violet-streaked hair from their face and gently rested their hand on a man in bed at their side.

Cygne Caladrius's eyes widened at the sight of Ebras, and he hustled to the bedside to grasp his white robes that lay aside.

Ebras noted the two's company. *Primus Inquisitors will enjoy knowing this bit of information.* It was against the Prime teaching for those of the same gender to fornicate—even if the Epsilon considered themselves to be of neither gender. *Yes, I can use this.* Ebras had suspicions over the years, but generally left the other council members to their own devices. As they did unto him. He could not care less about the Primus or any fictional god's doctrines. *For I am nearly a God myself.*

"Alpha!" old man Cygne wheezed. "What brings—"

"SILENCE!" Ebras bellowed over the reedy voice. "You!" He pointed a black-gloved finger at Rofous. His had re-formed into a fist, and he pulled the Epsilon forcefully through the air and held the Epsilon aloft before him as the rage took over.

Rofous flailed wildly in the air, a look of shock and fear upon their cosmetically-colored face.

Ebras grinned wickedly. *Yes, fear me, you little maggot!* "Where did the teleportation stone in your gift to the Proctor lead!?"

"I don't know!" Rofous's voice croaked in their throat.

"DO NOT TAKE ME FOR A FOOL!" Ebras screamed again, squeezing his fist tighter.

Pain shot through Rofous's expression, "Gods! The mountains! It led to the mountains."

Ebras lessened his grip slightly. "*Where* in the mountains?"

"An old hunting shack," the Epsilon gasped. "About a day or two from the Vouri village, Oitilla."

"Alpha, please, release—" Cygne began.

He was cut off as Ebras raised his other hand and pulled the old man in, slamming him against Rofous.

They both cried in agony as Ebras forcefully held them together. "If either of you defies me again, it will be the last thing you ever do." The Alpha dropped the two struggling people to the floor, opened his portal, and vanished.

Aerie Proctor Joanna Ohleoc was delighted to see the Alpha approaching the gates of her dome.

He walked briskly toward her, a deep, thoughtful frown on his handsome brow, his dark eyes brooding with intent. As he looked up to see her welcoming him, his brow twitched; then a closed-mouth smile curled his goateed lips.

By the Primus, he has such an air of power and authority about him! It is desirable, Joanna thought. "My Lord Alpha," Joanna said with a curtsy. "You have returned!"

"Obviously," the Alpha started, then cleared his throat. "Ah yes, my elegant raven. I have come back to you now." He brought a gloved hand to her cheek. "I am deeply frustrated with your little friend, the cardinal."

"Do not think of her, my love," Joanna answered, pushing her breasts against him. "Let me distract you. Let me comfort you, for I am yours."

His hand traced down her chin to her neck. "I *do* need to release some pent-up sentiments." His grip tightened around her throat.

Heat bloomed within Joanna as she gasped and moaned in pleasure. He pushed her through the doors into the former Proctor's bed.

"Yes! Alpha!" Joanna choked. *Take me!*

He slapped her face with his other hand while holding her by the throat. "Shut your mouth and please me!" He spat in her face.

The pain and ridicule mixed within her. A combination of revulsion, devotion, and enchantment. *I love him,* she told herself. The voluptuous hunger for the man overpowered an underthought of hatred.

The Alpha tore her new black dress from her body and, using unnecessary force, bent her onto the bed. He pulled at her hair, neck craning back *painfully* far.

I love him! I want him! The need for him was engraved into her mind, but the pain was causing underlying detestation to bubble through the seal.

Then, he was finished.

Joanna lay, unsure what to feel, wanting to scream with hatred. *But I love this man!*

"Get up, my raven; I have a job for you."

"Yes, Alpha," Joanna murmured, sitting upright. Her ambition suddenly fortified her resolve. "I'm ready to serve."

"The bitch cardinal has returned to her home in the Vouri mountains. *You* will find her."

"Of course, my Lord." She paused and tilted her head. "How will I get there, and will I be provisioned? The traitor, Hata, is powerful. Is it wise for me to face off against her alone?"

"Do not question me!" Ebras Corb's fists repeatedly clenched in a fury. "Do not use her name in my presence!"

Joanna's head bowed, closing her eyes, expecting a blow to come.

"Ah, my fair raven," the Alpha sighed, putting a hand gently on her head. "Fear not. You are in my care."

She opened her eyes and found his dark gaze piercing her.

He had removed the glove from his hand and touched her face gently.

Something tugged at her mind, and the overflowing affection and need to please Ebras came to her once more.

"You will not go alone." He grinned wickedly.

CHAPTER THIRTY-TWO

ANGUISH

The days expired, and then the *weeks* as Kiana and her small group desperately searched the city of Nidhaut. They awoke each day and divided up, leaving the tavern inn of *Vider Son Verre* to scour the city streets. Inquiring about the Magnus Huntsman as well as Zalias Ershya's whereabouts. The hours were spent visiting merchants and other taverns while speaking with many of the town's folk. The weeks turned into months.

Kiana was utterly exasperated. *Everyone we ask about the Huntsman directs us to the Alpha's tower. But what would this magi do to us if we came to his door seeking Hata?*

As time passed, Baal became increasingly dejected.

There were stretches of days when Kiana would not see the man.

Brena informed the group that Baal would not get out of bed or feed himself. When he rarely emerged, he would drink in *Vider Son Verre's* tavern until they had to carry him back to his room. The man's strength gradually dwindled, his body becoming gaunt after two months of despair at not knowing Hata's whereabouts.

Gods! It was not despair that grew within Kiana but frustration and rage. *Baal will die of a broken heart if we don't find anything soon!*

Brena had become accustomed to joining Kiana's mother on their excursions into town. Brena found support through Anora when her husband would not speak to her most days. Even so, she cared for Baal, bringing him food and water, trying as she may to get him to eat or wash up for the day and join them in the search.

He would only moan and roll over in bed.

All except Baal gathered in the tavern after a long day of finding nothing in their search.

"We are low on coins," Anora stated as Kiana found her seat among them.

They had brought a fair amount of coin that the Hasiera had gathered through banditry over the years, but it would not last forever.

"You are correct, Mother," Kiana answered. "Perhaps we should find work if we are to stay at this inn any longer."

"Could we find cheaper lodgings?" Brena asked. "Purchase our own food? I haven't cooked in ages."

"We could indeed," Kaplan agreed. "Though we won't be able to afford a lavish homestead."

"*Ville de Voleurs*," Anora said. "There are many run-down or abandoned buildings for sale in those criminal-infested slums. We could even discreetly take up residence in an abandoned one."

"Not a bad idea," Kaplan nodded. "Though it may govern unwanted attention by said criminals."

"True, but it will be cheaper than the luxury we live in now," Kiana sighed woefully. *I enjoy this life here; going out with Kaplan daily, then returning to drink and spend the night with him in our incredibly soft bedding. It's such a stark difference from back home in Hasiera.*

"We will still need coin if we are to survive," Brena said, taking a long draught from her tankard.

"I have a few thoughts on that," Anora deliberated. "There is one place we have not looked at regarding our quarries."

"And you're just now bringing it up?" Kiana snorted.

"It is a last resort," Anora answered gravely. She regarded the group readily and continued as they leaned in, awaiting her response. "*La Maison du Paon.*"

"The brothel from your story?" Kiana questioned.

"Indeed," Anora said. "If Zalias is anywhere in this town, I wager it is there."

"Then what are we waiting for!" Brena stood, face slightly flushed with alcohol.

"Peace, friend." Kiana steadied Brena by the elbow, guiding her back to her chair. "We cannot simply storm the place."

"What is your plan?" Kaplan directed to Anora.

"We work...as Personnes."

Personne, the name of all workers at this brothel house. From the bouncers to the servants and the harlots themselves. No one gave their real names.

"You would have us sell our bodies?" Kiana glared. "For what gain, Mother?"

"Not all of us. Brena and I are a bit old for it, but the owners may let it pass. You, dear daughter, on the other hand, are our ticket in, for you are young and gorgeous."

Kiana's eyes rushed to Kaplan's.

He gazed steadily toward Anora, pondering her words. He gave the slightest of nods, agreeing internally.

He knows it is a good plan. No, it's a brilliant plan. But my mother would sell her own daughter's flesh to accomplish this goal? Kiana erupted in fury, "Fucking hells, Mother! You will use me any way you see fit!"

"What is the issue?" Anora rebuked with a smirk. "Not a few months have passed since you spent your nights in the long tent. Is it not the same thing? At least with this, we can gain information and perhaps even save Hata Vasara."

Everyone murmured in agreement.

All except Kiana.

"I will do this," Brena stood once more, slamming her tankard to the table. "For my daughter!"

"It's the best idea we've had in weeks," Kaplan agreed.

Kiana glared at the man. *Does he not care that I will be used and abused as a whore?*

"It's settled, then; we will present ourselves to the owner of *La Maison du Paon* the day after tomorrow. First, we will find a new home." Anora raised her mug of mulled wine. "To Personne!"

"Personne!" Anora, Brena, and Kaplan Mir clanged their mugs together.

Later that day, Anora led the party in exploring the slum streets of the district of *Ville de Voleurs*. Muddy roads, no cobblestones in sight. Buildings of greying wood, looking near to collapse. Rough-looking denizens clustered at the entrances of dark alleyways, eyeing the newcomers as they walked. The Delta's dark, crooked tower loomed ominously above the district. The party soon spotted the colorful building in the dinge of muted greys that was *La Maison du Paon*.

Anora gazed at the brothel for a moment before continuing. *All those years ago, when I followed Gaddaar, my life changed forever in that whorehouse.*

They continued their search for a place to stay. It did not take long to find a sizeable shack near the southeast walls of the city. The front door had fallen in, and the thatched roof was nonexistent. Only bare boards were left overhead, allowing the weather to seep through. This caused the interior dirt floor to be a constant sludge, unable to dry before more rain seeped in again. A stone hearth was in surprisingly good shape in the corner of the two-chamber abode. Along with broken cupboards near the chimney corner and a table tilted on its side, missing two legs.

"Joo, this is quaint," Brena said, her finger coming away with a layer of dust from the hearth. "Larger than our home in Dagad. Unfortunately, your son-in-law is not here to aid us in the repairs, Anora."

"Terribly unfortunate," Anora smiled proudly. *Saudett chose well in Simon. Imagine what he could do with such a home: make it a special place.* "But we will have to make do," she breathed. "At least we have enough coins to purchase supplies to repair the roof."

"We will need some extra straw to dry up the muck," Kaplan added.

"I was just getting used to sleeping on that down bedding at the inn," Kiana groaned and stretched.

"Reality is calling, my dear daughter," Anora answered incredulously. "Dare I say we were quite spoiled these last few months."

"Skrull's hell, Mother, let me enjoy these small new things."

Anora opened her mouth to retort but held her tongue. *I need to think before scolding her. She is not a child anymore. She is a grown woman.*

"Let me talk to Baal. I think he and I could handle fixing up this place," Kaplan suggested as he righted a fallen shelf on the wall.

"He will have to leave the inn either way, but I wish you luck," Brena said doubtfully. "He will not even listen to me."

"I'll get him up and busy," Kaplan said, scratching his black beard. "You all handle the brothel."

Kiana snorted disdainfully, "Of course you would leave it to the women."

Lovers' spat? Anora though.

Kaplan avoided Kiana's glare.

Young love... Anora broke the awkward silence, "Yes, the women. We have a better chance of finding Zalias this way. Are you all ready? Let us present ourselves at the *Paon,* then. The day is still young."

The three women departed, leaving Kaplan to tend to the homestead. Not a score of steps from their new home, they were confronted by a motley crew of six greedy-looking scroungers. Knives and cudgels bared threateningly.

"Now then, loves," a wiry man with a patchy blonde beard and scraggly hair sneered. "Be ladylike and drop your weapons." He paused and grinned wickedly.. "Then," he squealed in delight, "be dropping your loins and let the boys have a go at ya!"

Brena rushed in like an avalanche, fist cracking into the buck tooth man's nose and upper lip.

Unconscious, he fell to the dirt road.

Brena drew her broadsword.

The other hoodlums reacted too slowly as Anora and Kiana danced into their midst, twirling about, blades flashing and *cutting.* Anora removed the hand of one, then the ear of another. *I'll try not to kill them...*

They tried to outnumber Kiana, three of them rushing to mob her, but her daughter dashed out of Anora's peripheral with incredible speed and grace. Head inching back as a cudgel swiped and missed a hair's breadth from her face. Kiana's blade returned the favor with a slash up the man's chin and mouth. Then, with a duck and spin, Kiana's agile movement was unmatched as her sword twisted behind her back, slicing through another man's thighs.

Brena crashed into the third thug menacing Kiana, her broad sword slicing the criminal's chest. She completed the slash and kicked him down, and he lay dying in the muck.

So much for not killing them; the Vouri do not hold back, Anora thought, wiping her curved blade clean with a rag as the muggers retreated, screaming as they ran back into the dark, murky alleyways of *Ville de Voleurs.*

"Voitoon!" Brena shouted after them, rolling her shoulders and cracking her neck back and forth. Her thick blonde plait swung down her back. "I feel refreshed. My mate would have enjoyed this."

"I agree," Kiana laughed aloud. "It felt proper to be in the thick of it again. Those sleazy bastards didn't know who they were messing with!"

"Indeed, they did not," Anora said with a wide smile. She put a hand on Kiana's shoulder. "You are a skilled warrior, my daughter. I have nothing left to teach you."

Kiana opened her mouth to retort but stopped suddenly. Finally, she sighed and said, "Thank you, Mother. And yes, you still have much to teach me." Kiana waved a hand around her. "Teach me about this world outside of our little valley of Hasiera."

Anora smiled warmly, nodded, and whispered, "I can do that."

At long last, they found themselves before *La Maison du Paon*. Two prominent men dressed in fine violet uniforms, contrasting the dark greys and browns of the district, greeted them at the entrance.

"You have coins?"

Anora jingled a small pouch with a few coins. Kaplan had taken most to purchase supplies for their house.

The man arched a brow suspiciously. "Your purse sounds light."

"Well," Anora nudged her daughter forward as if to display her. "We are actually seeking employment at this fine establishment."

Kiana did an extravagant spin to show off.

"Ah," the bouncer grunted, gesturing with his thumb. "Round back, pull the bell string outside the door."

They thanked the bouncer and rounded the building to find a heavy iron door in the back corner of the structure. There was a rope hanging from a hole just above the door.

Brena reached up and pulled the string. A few moments passed, and Brena pulled it again. Then again.

"ENOUGH! We heard you the first time!" A metal plate slid open with a clank, and a weary eye peered at them.

"We are seeking employment," Anora said.

The bulgy eye studied each of them in turn. "Two old ladies and a young wench, eh? Alright, come in; we'll have a good look."

The sound of many locks and latches was heard from the other side, and finally, the door opened. A hunched, greying man with an eye patch beckoned them in, a candle in one hand. "Come now, we don't have all day. Up the stairs, the lot of you."

Upon immediate entry, stairs began to rise. The stairs were dark; only the faint candlelight behind them gave any vision.

This doesn't bode well. Anora led, hand ready on the hilt of her sword.

They came to a corner, and a second flight of stairs ascended further. Up they went, and at last, another door appeared.

"Go on, open it," the man grumbled from below.

Light shined in as Anora pushed against the door, momentarily blinding her. As her sight adjusted, she saw a beautiful, sprawling rooftop garden. Tall walls on all sides hid the sanctuary from the outside world, violet clematis vines winding up them. There was a steaming pool in the center of the garden.

A stunning, golden-tan woman sat with her lower body in the pool, arms outstretched on the tiled edges. She was naked of all but a cobalt mask that covered her nose and cheeks in a V-shape, leaving her mouth and chin free. It then crested the woman's head, covering her ears and hair in a helm. Only her hazel eyes peered from behind the mask. Odd oval discs protruded from the helm where her ears would be.

Two young women sat behind her, one with a bowl of fruit, the other with towels ready.

"Dame Personne," the eye-patched man said, ushering them to stand before the pool. "These women are looking for humble employment."

Dame Personne tilted her head for one of the young ladies to feed her a fig. She slowly regarded them as she chewed slowly, not speaking.

"Greeting Dame Personne, I am Ano—"

Dame Personne held up a finger in silence. A whisper came to their ears, nearly imperceptible, "No names."

"Of course," Anora answered. "We are new to Nidhaut and anxious to get our feet steady under us."

"You would serve our customers with the use of your bodies?" the masked woman asked drearily.

Anora nodded and turned her head to look at Kiana and Brena.

Brena repeated the nod.

"Yes." Kiana's mumbled through a clenched jaw.

"Remove your clothing and wade into the pool," Dame Personne said indifferently.

Anora flinched internally.

Kiana glared daggers at Anora.

Brena immediately undressed and walked down the two steps into the pool before Anora and Kiana started removing their nomadic linen wraps and robes.

A smile played on Dame Personne's lips. "I like this one," she said as she stood and moved toward Brena. "A straightforward heart. I see a true woman's constitution." She circled Brena, surveying her, waves sloshing about in Dame's wake.

Brena flexed with a smile. Her muscles constricted into chiseled lines. Brena was nearly a head taller than Dame, her powerful arms and legs glistening in the steam of the bath. There were black lightning bolt tattoos etched across her body, contrasting her fair white skin. That thick golden braid dangled nearly into the water.

"Now," Dame said, coming to Brena's forefront. "I ask you a question, and the provided answer will determine the outcome of your employment."

Brena grunted in agreement.

Anora and Kiana stood bare, just inside the pool's edge, awaiting their turn.

"I will touch you now?" Dame Personne asked.

Brena paused for a moment, milling it over. Finally, she spoke, "By the will of Teras, do it."

Dame Personne smiled and glided in, embracing Brena warmly. "Welcome, Personne." Dame turned and nodded to the women with towels. "Get dried up." She guided Brena out of the pool, a hand on her back.

I do not want to be touched, Anora realized. *Even in such a calming embrace as that.* The thought of Gaddaar grasping at her came like a hurricane. It took her years to warm up to Rojas's touch. *What would my husband think of me for doing this?*

Kiana stepped forward and said, "Yes, you may place your hands on me however you see fit."

"Patience now, young one. A flaming heart may burn too bright for the work done here." Dame flowed back through the pool, again examining Kiana slowly.

Their Xamidian heritage of tan tones nearly matched the Dame's, though she was a few shades darker from days up in this sunlit pool.

Dame Personne turned to Anora momentarily. "You are kin? Identical except for her stunning eyes and the age marks upon you."

Anora flinched again. "We are."

Dame nodded and returned to Kiana's forefront. "I will touch you now?"

"Yes," Kiana said, head held high.

Dame moved closer and rested her hands on Kiana's shoulders. "Welcome, Personne." She then let Kiana go to the waiting towels.

Panic set in. *By the Primus! Not me!*

Skrull-damned bitch! I will have you! Gaddaar screamed in her mind.

Anora began to quiver.

Dame looked at her calmly. *Gently.* "I think I need not ask the question here."

"I'm sorry I cannot do this," Anora wailed as she fell to her knees with a splash. "Kiana, I'm sorry!"

"NO NAMES!" Dame's voice resounded suddenly and painfully in Anora's ears.

Anora cowered, her body shaking as she repeated, "I'm sorry, I'm sorry."

"No," Dame sighed measuredly. "I apologize for the outburst; I can see that darkness has haunted your past. Get dried up and dressed. Your companions will be in good hands here. I will not let anything happen to them that would go beyond comfort. They will see you soon."

Anora dressed, avoiding Kiana's scowl.

The eye-patched man ushered her back to the door.

Anora glimpsed them one last time, speaking quietly with Dame Personne as the door shut her out.

Chapter Thirty-Three

TEA

"By all the fucking gods, this is the life," Jude Nelon sighed in contentment as he sipped his concocted herbal tea of chamomile, rosehip, and ginger. He wiped at a sweat with a handkerchief the warm brew had caused on his glistening bald head. Wrapped in a silk sleeping robe, he sat in a cushioned rocking chair beneath a trellis in his estate garden. Jude's housekeeper, Bertrand Rochefort, busied himself with some shrubbery near the back gates.

Ebras Corb emerged after barging through his home and into the gardens, followed by a short, stout, black-haired, black-clad young woman.

"Oh, for fucks' creek," Jude moaned; he did not stand from his seat. "Couldn't you just send a messenger like usual?"

"The ginger bitch you caught has escaped me!" Ebras flicked his fingers up, and Jude was magically forced to his feet.

Tea splashed to the ground before him. *Oh, he is grumpier than usual.* Jude smiled sardonically, answering, "Fucking hells, that is a first. I've never had to capture one twice in all these years on the hunt."

"Well, you will now!" Ebras shrieked, stamping back and forth through Jude's garden in a fit. "And you are taking this one with you!"

Jude tilted his head. "I work alone. It is the sole reason I'm good at this."

"Instruct her, then! She will be the first fully functional magi to hunt her own kind. I am running low on reliable Huntsman as it is."

"Aerie Proctor and Magnus Huntress Joanna Ohleoc," the girl whispered.

"Silence!" Ebras turned, raising the back of his hand, but then stopped himself with a heavy exhale. "Yes, my dear," he soothed. "A mighty title for my greatest paramour."

Fucks. Jude Nelon gagged. *That is disturbing.*

"Oitilla in the North Iron Belt." The Alpha refocused on Jude. "The mountain peasant has fled back to her home."

"But the Vouri have abandoned that place," Jude answered.

"It matters not. The battle will be over by the time you get there."

"The battle?"

"It does not concern you. Just find the girl! I don't care if she is alive this time." Ebras fumbled a pouch off his belt and flung it to Jude's feet. Gold coins scattered about the flagstones.

"Well fucks, isn't that kind of you," Jude muttered as he bent to pick up the mess. Then his eyes widened. *This is triple my regular price!*

"Satisfied?" Ebras asked with a disgusted sneer.

Jude nodded.

Ebras turned and tramped away.

The young woman moved to follow.

"Stay!" Ebras ordered, and then he was gone.

How do I get myself into these messes? Jude pondered as he returned to his seat. "Bertrand! Fetch me the pot, if you will."

"Yes, Master Nelon, sir," an older, smartly dressed Tulu man said as he appeared from behind a bush.

The girl's eyes extended. "How long has he been here?"

"Joanna, was it? Or Proctor Huntress, or whatever the fucks," Jude griped, then heaved an ill-fated lament. "Do not heed the harmless servant. Come sit. Would you care for a cup?"

The woman relaxed visibly. "Yes, my name is Joanna. And yes, please, to the tea." She sat on a bench across from him and slumped wearily.

Jude could see faint bruises on her pale skin. *Gods, she looks dreadful. Skrull's hell, what has that bastard been doing to her?*

Bertrand returned with a platter with a steaming pot and two fresh cups, accompanied by cranberry biscuits and an assortment of cheeses.

Joanna looked longingly at the tray.

Bertrand poured her a steaming cup, which she took and sipped gently.

"Go ahead then, girl," Jude urged.

She put the tea beside her on the bench and grabbed a handful of biscuits and cheese, filling her mouth hungrily.

Does he not feed these girls?

As if to answer his question, after gulping down a mouthful with a sip of tea, the girl said, "Since the former Proctor's demise, no one told me how to use the room which supplied us with food each day." Tears welled in her eyes. "I looked inside door after door and could not find it! I was so hungry, but I dared not tell the Alpha, lest he beat me again."

Poor sod, Jude thought. *Should I really be helping that bastard?* He looked around his quaint garden and decent-sized home. He jiggled the pouch of coins in his hand. *Fucks, it does pay off, though. I should at least hear this girl out, at any rate.* He cleared his throat dramatically, "I don't know what you are talking about. What is a Proctor?"

The young woman sobbed out her story. How she and the ginger were drugged, tortured, and abused. Beaten and trained into magi. Schooled by the Proctor. When finally, the Proctor snapped and killed some of Ebras's thugs. How Hata had escaped. How she had betrayed Joanna by leaving her behind.

"Yet, for some reason," Joanna wailed, "I love Ebras! I love that vile man and know he is a sick, disgusting bastard. I want him. I want power. And I want nothing more than to *kill* Hata Vasara!"

"Fucks woman," Jude said, astonished. "You really laid it all bare there."

"Primus, I'm sorry. You are the first person I've talked to in ages, and it just came out of me."

"Not a problem." *Kind of a problem.* "Anyways, there are some ground rules if we do this together." *Fucks, what a headache.*

She nodded, stuffing more cheese into her mouth.

"Rule number one," Jude stated, lifting a finger. "Do everything I tell you."

She nodded again.

"Rule number two." He lifted two fingers. "Refer to rule number one."

"That's it?" she mumbled through a mouthful.

"That's it." Jude smiled.

She shrugged and continued eating.

Well fucks, at least she listens.

Chapter Thirty-Four

FIRST

Two days after arriving in the Moreas Lân, the Daanav retaliated.

Two days of preparing their fortifications. Two semi-circular, four-foot-high barricades had been constructed before the portal. Platforms had been placed in the overhead tree canopy, and many Hasieran archers, nearly two dozen with the new *Windan* crossbows, were perched above. Warriors with long pikes were stationed along the barriers, readying to hold back an assault.

Now we wait. Simon sat on the edge of a high platform, surveying the gloom below.

In the darkness of night, the Daanav skulked into range to attack the Gate.

An eerie howl reverberated through the air.

That's Darkclaw Marah's signal that we are under attack. "*Leoma!*" Simon shouted. A sphere of light appeared above Simon, floating near the tree cover, blinding all briefly and lighting up the ground below.

A throng of Daanav screeched and wailed, stunned for only a fleeting moment.

"Now!" Simon called out his order.

The humming pulses of the *Windan* crossbows thrummed and loosed. Ripping through the air. Pieces of flesh exploded from the Daanav's bodies. Arrows whistled down upon the chaos.

An undulating wail rose from the back ranks of the Daanav, and the monsters suddenly turned and charged the barricades. Hulks and hounds surged forward.

Simon hovered down as the Daanav crashed against the first barricade, spewing white strings of fire from his fingers as he did so. He saw Saudett beside Naurr, her spear piercing a hound as it leaped at the barricade.

Naurr's iron banded lumber cudgel smashed into the side of a hulk, crushing bones. Simon descended further.

Rapidly, a handful of grey-skinned, thick-limbed, ape-like Daanav bound up the lower branches of the thick trees. They began climbing up to the archers above.

Lind. Simon formed the barrier nearly too late as one grey beast leaped and barreled into him.

It wrapped its dense arms around him, jaws gashing at his head as they fell to the earth.

His light barrier cracked and hissed under the massive strain against it. His shield protected his flesh, but his arms were trapped at his sides as they hit the ground. *I can't do anything!*

Still, it held him, bending the barrier through sheer strength, its jaws gnawing against the protective shield.

He thought back to how he got out of the spider webs. *"Windan abrecan!"* Simon cried. The wind battered them suddenly, cutting and tearing around them, lifting him and the Daanav from the ground.

Still, it did not let go as its grey flesh was ripped away. Six milky yellow eyes glowered as its skull became exposed. The bone glistened with a metallic sheen. *I'm going to die,* Simon thought as the wind receded.

"Get off my fucking husband!" Saudett's spear pierced the neck of the creature. Once. Twice. Her blade deflected.

Still, it would not let go.

"Skrull-forsaken hell," Saudett panted. "These things do not die!"

Naurr ran over and began hammering the exposed skull of the creature with his iron-clad lumber. Over and over and over. The last blow rattled something within it. It shuddered and released Simon, head lolling from side to side.

The two slowly extracted Simon from the creature. He sat up with a groan and asked skeptically, "Is it dead?"

"I think so," Saudett said as she jabbed it a few dozen times more.

Looking about, Simon saw that the Daanav were in retreat.

"First Otsoa!" a man called as he hustled up to Simon. "Heavy casualties on one of the tree platforms. Two of those grey beasts got up and wreaked havoc. But the *Windan* crossbows from another platform were effective in tearing them down eventually. The first barricade was held. I do not think the Daanav expected such a defense."

Simon blinked. *It is strange to be treated like a king or general.* He clasped the man's shoulder. "Thank you for the report. Well done. Have them start bringing me the wounded."

Gehae, the healing word. Simon diligently tended to each wounded person, resting his hand on the wounds and muttering the word. Warm green-yellow light pulsed from his hands.

"Thank you, Lord First," the last wounded Hasieran woman said as he finished tending to the cut on her arm. It fizzed with steam as it sealed up miraculously.

Sweat beaded down Simon's brow.

"Not a problem; off you go then." He smiled and stretched. *Gods, I'm hungry.*

At the thought, Saudett arrived with two wooden bowls of yam curry. She handed him one and sat next to him. "Eat, husband. You need it."

"You are simply wonderful, my dear wife," he expressed, eagerly spooning a mouthful of the fragrant spiced curry.

Saudett nudged him and leaned against him as they ate silently.

Simon sighed in contentment as he slurped up the last of the gravy. "Ah, delicious."

"What is next, oh First Otsoa," Saudett asked, hand waving and gesturing to the people before him.

He stood. He realized in awe that the people of Hasiera had gathered, facing him as they ate. Waiting for him to speak. *What in Skrull's name is next? I wish Gaelin would contact me and tell me what he's up to.*

Indeed, I am on my way back, Gaelin answered instantly. *We surveyed the city of Rawa and managed to locate our little Kogs mate.*

By Hettra's tits! That is good tidings, Gaelin.

A few dozen Daanav patrol the city, but it seems most departed to attack the Gate. From what I saw within your mind, you took care of them.

They retreated with about half their forces.

Very good. That is manageable. Had I been there, we could have slaughtered every last one of the foul creatures. At any rate, I think there is one in charge of the Moreas Lân we must be wary of.

Simon nodded. Then blinked. He had been standing before everyone, gawking like a dolt. Clearing his throat, cheeks red with embarrassment, he addressed the crowd. "Hasiera! The Daanav flee from us with their tails in their arses!"

"Hasiera! Ah-lai!" A swelling cry lifted from the people.

"They do not have the number we faced in our valley home," Simon called out. "We have cut off any reinforcements they could send by taking the Wayfarers Gate. We will finish what's left of them and free the Kadal. And we shall once again bring water back to Hasiera!"

"Hasiera!" They answered again, echoing his words.

Simon even saw Naurr and the workmen take up the cry.

"Now, we send a crew to begin digging the trench to the river, with a detachment of warriors for protection. Watch out for the horrendously large spiders." He spread his hands to show them how giant the spider was.

Laughter rippled through the crowd.

"Skrull's hell, people, I'm serious!" Simon cried. "One almost ate me! Who knows what other dangers this swamp is home to."

There was more laughter but also an abundance of head nods and mutters of agreement.

"Right," Simon continued, "we will leave another group to guard the Gate. Those left of us will head to the Kadal city of Rawa after the Iban'mael Wayfarer, Gaelin, returns."

"First Otsoa! First Otsoa!" A repeating cry carried through the bog lands.

Simon stood taller. Passion for these people simmered within his chest. *Hettra's mercy, I feel...important.* He gripped the magical bone dagger in his hand. *I feel powerful!*

CHAPTER THIRTY-FIVE

MORTIFICATION

Hata peered up the peaks at a ring of dark navy clouds surrounding the mountain where she had grown up. *I have seen this darkness before.* Fear began to grip her as, step by step, she pulled her sled up the snow-covered ascent. At long last, she came to a ridge at a slightly higher elevation, looking down at the village. The village of Oitilla.

The cloud, *no, the smoke,* was moving, twisting southward, following the mountain road that led to Aurulan. The dark smoke billowed from the cave town of Oitilla, snaking out around the massive frozen waterfall in the town's center.

Hata saw the hint of blue flames dotting the path, and a throng of shadowed movement, from Oitilla, ushering forth from the mountain. *No, it cannot be!* Her horror transformed into realization. *It is the Daanav!* She sat in the snow, watching for hours as the column of beasts did not stop emerging from the inner cave of Oitilla and marching down the pass. Two of the massive vulture-like birds, *Kahytul,* circled thousands of feet above the army of Daanav, their circling slowly drifting southward.

"By the Primus," Hata murmured aloud. "What am I to do?"

How can they be here? I wish Saudett were here; she would know what to do. Saudett, Kiana or even Chanel. Isä and Äiti. Anybody! She shook her head and stood. *No, I can't keep only relying on others. Saudett saved me in the desert. Chanel helped me escape the Alpha. I will figure this out myself!*

She started her descent once more. The sled bumped into the backs of her legs with each step. Thoroughly annoyed, she crouched behind the sled, gripping the sides. With a bit of a dashing start, she hopped on. It picked up speed faster than expected, zipping past trees and boulders. The freezing wind whipped and slashed at her face. Leaning from side to side, she barreled down the slope, holding on for dear life. Even as she *willed* the disc to go where she wanted.

A rise in the snow came before her, and she crested it. *Oh, Teras!* Suddenly, in mid-air, she was plummeting straight down a drop-off. The cliff angled at nearly ninety degrees. Hata leaned forward, slamming the base of her sled into the immensely steep slant. Craggy stones jutted up at the bottom of the cliff far below.

"By Skrull's hell! I will not die!" she screamed into the chilling wind and leaned left, simultaneously calling the stone from the cliffside to her will. The rock splintered and grew, creating a smooth, curved slide before her. Left and then right, she willed it, twisting it in wide bends. It slithered ahead of her as she held on. The sound of the stone crackling and rumbling echoed down the mountainside.

At long last, the terrain leveled, and the twisting rockslide brought her to a slow stop. Panting with exhilaration, she rolled off the sled and lay in the soft snow, looking up at the sky. Smiling, Hata thanked Teras for her life. The smile faded as the dark smoke covered nearly half the clear blue sky. *It is expanding further and further from the mountain.* The adrenaline fled from her as the thoughts of infiltrating the Daanav-infested town constricted in her gut. *What am I to do? I wish I could be invisible.* Her fingers instinctively brushed the brooch around her neck. *Perhaps one of these gems could help me?*

As she looked more closely, a few colored marbles were left in their sockets. A pure white marble, a creamy beige, and a greenish-blue one. Two sockets were empty: the red fire spell Hata had used and the one Luftan had used to help her escape through the portal away from the Convent Enclosure. The large obsidian opal in its center glimmered oddly, almost as if there were faint stars deep within.

Or was it a shining eye? Hata thought. *Whatever it is, it is beautiful.* She lifted it, gazing into its depths.

Indeed, it truly is beautiful, is it not?

"Who said that!?" Hata exclaimed as she nearly flew out of her skin. The pendant fumbled into the snow as she looked about desperately.

There was no answer.

Am I going insane? Hata paused and asked again, "Is anyone there? Come out where I can see you." Only snow, sparse pines, stunted birches, and the odd stone outcropping stretched around the mountainside. She shook her head, bent to pick up the pendant, and then hung it around her neck.

A warm voice came again as she tucked it under her furs against her skin. Both masculine and feminine, it was like two people speaking at once.

It's a beautiful gemstone for one of my beautiful creatures.

Hata closed her eyes. *Is this one of the Alpha's tricks?*

No. That man has fallen away from the Primus, from my teachings. He is forsaken as one of my children.

"Your children?" Hata asked aloud.

All people of the Earste Lân are a part of me, and I am of them. For I am—

"The Primus!" Hata finished the words.

Yes, my child. And I am with you. I have been with you.

Hata mused in disbelief. *This can't be happening! I didn't believe all that Aurulan dogma... but the Primus is speaking directly to me?*

It is true, my child. All my teachings are just and absolute. You, Hata Vasara, are a sinner. That you would lay with another woman is a grave immorality.

Shame. Shame stabbed into Hata's heart. All the teachings from the Proctor's lessons. The condemnation to Skrull's hell should you commit such a despicable evil. Commandments she had previously ignored and hated. *It is all true!* "I am sorry! Primus," she prayed aloud as she fell to her knees, looking up at the smoke-filled sky. "Please grant me your forgiveness and mercy."

I forgive you.

"Oh, thank you, Primus!" she lamented.

It is finished now, my child. Let us focus on the task at hand.

"The task at hand? You will help me against the Daanav. Why?"

The people of Skaad are also a part of me. They are simply misunderstood by humans.

"But they have killed so many, and they march to war against humanity?"

Far more of them died to the genocidal campaign of the Iban'mael. The Children of Skaad were hunted nearly to extinction before being exiled.

"Iban'mael?"

A race of people who seek knowledge and power over all others. A race that ignores the gods and strives to ascend in their place.

"Yes, alright. But why have the Daanav not come in peace to us, seeking refuge?"

It is simple. My children are afraid. The Iban'mael have their influence in all Lâns. They have been converting the Earste Lân for centuries. They travel, planting seeds to rule over all creation. To rule over my design. Humanity is already nearly lost.

"Teras strengthen us," Hata breathed.

You would take the name of a false god in my presence?! The voice boomed and reverberated, rattling within her mind.

"No! No!" Hata cried, prostrating her head into the snow. "Never again! Primus!"

My child. The voice calmed. *Pray to me.*

She sat, knees sunk into the snow, bent over, head against the cold for an eternity, pleading repeatedly for the Primus's mercy and forgiveness.

Finally, the voice in Hata's mind spoke.

Again, my child, you are forgiven.

"Thank you! Praise you, Primus," Hata exhaled, depleted. "But what will we do about the Daan—the Children of Skaad?"

Have faith. You need simply walk, tor you are under my guidance. I will take care of you.

Hata did just that. She walked up the mountain toward the malevolent smoke-ringed peak, toward her old enemy, the creatures of the night. The Children of Skaad.

CHAPTER THIRTY-SIX

TENACITY

Baal's fist thudded into Kaplan's gut.

Kaplan crumpled over the massive forearm in pain.

"You think you funny, bookman?" Baal growled.

"Let me repeat myself," Kaplan spat, gasping for air. "You can't save your daughter!"

"RAAAH!" Baal roared as his arm surged, launching Kaplan across the room.

He crashed and rolled over one of the inn beds, thumping to the floor behind it. *Gods, I will be hurting for days after this,* Kaplan thought as he slowly pushed himself to his feet. *This had better be worth it.*

Baal stepped toward him.

Kaplan held out a hand haltingly. "You can't save her if you sit on your *fat* arse all day!"

Baal exhaled like a bull and rolled his shoulders. Then, he charged.

In a quick burst of speed, Kaplan crested the bed and leaped. Both feet planted on Baal's chest as the giant's arms began to close on him.

The impact rocked Baal back, teetering on the brink of collapse.

Kaplan quickly capitalized on the large man's loss of balance and swept at Baal's legs with his own. Pain shot through Kaplan's shin. *It's like kicking a damned tree!*

Luckily, it was enough to send Baal back and to the side, crashing into another bed. It crunched and split in the center, Baal's total weight busting through the flimsy wooden frame.

Both men lay, groaning and panting with exertion and pain.

Baal began to chuckle slightly, and his laugh grew in volume and heartiness.

Kaplan could not help but smile and laugh as well.

"My thanks, bookman," Baal said, still lying between the broken bed. "Did you learn that jumping kick in one of your books?"

Kaplan grinned. "Indeed, I did. A long time ago, I read a book on Tal'tulu martial arts techniques."

"Ha! Stinking books!" Baal slowly came to a seated position. Cracking his neck back and forth. "So, what needs doing?"

"Let's grab something to eat below, then make for the market to acquire supplies for our new lodging. I'll explain what is happening over a full stomach."

Baal's stomach audibly groaned at Kaplan's words.

Kiana imagined she was back in Hasiera in the long tent as she *serviced* patrons of *La Maison du Paon*. On the main floor was a large communal area hosting group activity, similar to the long tent revels back home. One could come and go as they pleased and partake in the staff assigned to be there. All new prostitutes started in the *celebration* pit until further patrons began to take notice of them. Said patrons paid a flat rate to join the orgy, and all employees on the bacchanalia floor would take home a cut. Once promoted to personal companion, she would make tips on top of her flat rate. The higher-paying customers made use of the private rooms on the floor above. *That is where Zalias Ershya will be.*

Kiana was not surprised that she immensely enjoyed the physical pleasures of her new job with *some* patrons; for others, she was indifferent but acted the part. Intercourse was how she unwind in Hasiera, releasing tension after her mother's challenging training sessions.

And Kaplan does not seem to care that I use my body this way. Kiana pondered Kaplan as she pleasured a middle-aged woman. *I had hoped he would at least make an objection,* Kiana thought as the woman's legs quivered, wrapping around Kiana's head, a hand gripping her hair. The woman's enthusiasm pulled Kiana into the experience, arousal within herself bubbling up; clearing her thoughts, she focused on the woman...

....The woman sighed in relief and beckoned Kiana into her arms; for a long while, they just lay together, not speaking, only enjoying their bodies pressed together as the glow slowly faded.

As Kiana lay there, her thoughts returned to why she was doing any of this. *It is to find Zalias and rescue Hata. I will show them, my mother and Kaplan, that I am capable. I will gratify every fat old man who needs it if it helps us find Hata.*

Kiana noticed Brena on the opposite side of the common area with a grim expression on her pale face. One such fat old man was groaning, trying to get into a position over top of Brena.

He was flopping about, sweating, panting, and wheezing.

Brena grimaced as the man's weight fell atop her. She pushed him off and onto his back, then mounted him. Kiana could not tell if the man groaned in enjoyment or pain as Brena milled roughly against him. Brena's eyes met Kiana's, and she gave a gritted nod and a sidelong look of disgust toward the man beneath her.

Brena is having similar thoughts. She would be unfaithful to Baal, the love of her life, as long as it let her save their daughter.

The woman stirred beside Kiana and said gently, "Thank you, my dear Personne, you were most pleasant. Perhaps upon my next visit, we can attain a more intimate private room for the both of us?"

"That would be wonderful, my Lady," Kiana answered genuinely.

The woman leaned over and kissed Kiana tenderly on the neck, then stood and dressed. Before leaving, she palmed a silver coin into Kiana's hand.

Kiana sighed and took the coin to the communal jar in the front entryway of *La Maison du Paon.*

With makeup caking his middle-aged face, the slightly greying blonde-haired man sat behind a desk and tilted his head as the coin clinked into the glass jar. "Another gratuity earned this evening, Personne? That is your fourth today. Are you trying to prove yourself to the Dame early?"

"I simply enjoy my new occupation, Personne," Kiana answered brashly. "Far less boring than minding a desk all day."

"Ha," he snorted. "I've seen our clientele. Most I would not touch with a ten-foot pike."

Kiana shrugged, "All people can be beautiful in their own ways. Some just take better care of themselves than others."

"Suit yourself. At any rate, keep this up, and the Dame will be made aware of your... enthusiasm."

That is what I want! Kiana gave a gentle bow, saying, "Very well." *Perhaps I can take that geezer off Brena's hands.* She turned and hurried back to the floor of indulgence. She heard the old man's angry complaint before she saw him waddle past her on his way out.

"Despicable vixen!" he cried, face pink and perspiring with rage and discomfort. "You are supposed to please me! Not the other way around!"

Brena met her on her way, a Baal-like grin on her face. "I heard something crack, and then he went soft. Not that he had much going for him in that manner."

"Careful, Brena," Kiana cautioned. "You may lose your station if things keep going like this."

Brena grunted, then sighed, "I do not think I have what it takes. During the act, I can only think of my mountain, my Baal, and am bursting with immense guilt. This is more difficult than I imagined it would be."

"Perhaps we could speak with Dame? This place requires security as well. I would also be more confident if you had access to your sword should Zalias show his smug face, and I need to call upon you."

"Do you think she would allow it?"

"Only one way to find out," Kiana put a hand on Brena's shoulder. "Shall we?"

Brena nodded, and they marched off through the Personne lounge. Many Personnes watched them go, sitting around on their intermissions. They exited the building and found themselves around the back, ringing the bell to access the rooftop gardens.

The eye-patched man soon answered and ushered them up, his candle flickering.

"Come to me, my Personnes," Dame beckoned them into the pool. "What brings you to me this day?"

They waded in, Dame Personne gliding over and embracing each in turn.

"Thank you, Dame," Kiana whispered with a blush as their skin pressed against one another. *Gods, she is magnificent. Tender, kind, and stunning.*

"So, tell me, *warriors*," Dame said, a smile playing on her lips below her white mask. "Why, genuinely, are you employed at *La Maison du Paon?*"

Kiana blinked in surprise.

Brena laughed aloud. "We are looking for an elusive criminal."

Dame slid to the pool's edge and waved a young man over. "Bring a carafe of wine, my dear."

The man promptly presented a decanter of wine and three goblets. He poured the chilled, vibrant liquid and handed one to each woman in the pool.

Kiana sipped and sighed as the cool golden drink quenched her throat.

"A criminal, you say?" Dame sighed, sitting on the pool's edge, taking a sip of her own goblet. "It is unfortunate to say that many such individuals frequent *La Maison du Paon.*"

"He's Xamidian," Brena stated. "Usually dressed in fine green robes and a bright red turban."

Dame tilted her head. "It does not ring a bell, I'm afraid, but let me put out a missive to the rest of my Personnes. They will know if he has been here."

"No!" Kiana cried, then cleared her throat. "I apologize, Dame. We fear someone might warn him. They may be in league with him."

Dame's head tilted the other direction. "What did this man do to gain the wrath of such powerful women as yourselves?"

"Firstly, he drugged my daughter and nearly kidnapped her," Brena growled, reminiscing. "Secondly, he aided a Magnus Huntsmen in his mission to capture that daughter. They succeeded."

Dame stood abruptly. "I do not get involved in the Alpha's business. Go! Go back to work and speak nothing of this again." She waved, and two brawny sword-baring men appeared from where they had been hidden behind a vine-covered trellis.

"Dame—" Kiana started.

"GO!" The voice felt like it rattled the walls around them.

Were the plants and flowers shaking? Kiana turned and began to leave.

"I will save my daughter!" Brena roared in answer. The two men stopped at that. "If this *Alpha* is behind it all, he will die on my sword."

Dame's head lulled back, and a wicked laugh echoed from her gaping mouth. "Ha! Ha! Ha! The Alpha is *invincible!* He is literally a god amongst men. Untouchable. Mourn your loss and move on with your lives."

"All men bleed the same blood," Brena declared, then turned to leave.

"Wait!" Dame called after her. "Very well, I will not hinder you. You may continue your employment at *La Maison du Paon.*" Dame pointed at Brena. "You, my dear warrior woman, may work as a ground floor bouncer as you wish."

Kiana frowned. *How did she know that?*

Brena grunted and walked away.

Kiana hurried after her, following her down the dark stairway.

Anora stumbled into the barmaid as she fumbled her way to the latrine.

"Steady on," the barmaid said.

Anora leaned against the woman, the bar spinning about her. "I—I need to—"

The barmaid reacted swiftly, ushering Anora toward the end of the bar, a much shorter distance than to the latrine out back. A bucket and mop were tucked just behind the bar, and Anora lurched over the bucket, dirty water sloshing about as she grasped the edges and vomited. The muck splashed about her face, and the acid burned in her mouth and throat, blistering in her sinuses. Heaving, another spew of dark wine-colored bile poured into the pail.

The next thing Anora knew, she was squinting her eyes in wakefulness. Head pounding, mouth dry, stomach lurching. *Where am I?* Agonizingly, she sat up. She was on a small cot in the back corner of a large kitchen. A massive pot was bubbling on a large charcoal grill in the center of the room next to a wide oiled butcher's block. Thick cuts of pork sizzled beside the pot. The delicious smell floated over Anora, and her stomach grumbled.

By the gods, I do not think I can keep any food down right now.

As the thought came to Anora, Cloudia Marie pushed into the room through a swinging half door, carrying a tray of dirty dishes.

"Dear me," the woman exclaimed. "You are finally awake."

Cloudia's voice rattled Anora's headache. "I am," she answered with a groan.

"Quickly now, lass," the woman ladled a spoonful of stew into a wooden bowl. "Eat up. It will do you well after such a ceaseless binge."

"I do not think—" Anora started.

The woman forced the bowl into her hands. "Oh, Anora, what's become of you? I know my way around a drunk patron or two. Food will help."

Anora sighed and slowly sipped at the thick medley. *Delicious.* She soon cleaned the bowl, and her stomach settled.

"My thanks, Cloudia," Anora said contently. "Though I am slightly shocked I was not laid out in the alley. I cannot pay for a room anymore."

"If you were a man, without a second thought, I'd have you kicked to your face out back." Cloudia chuckled, adjusting her monocle. "But I wouldn't leave any woman to such a fate. Some thug may find you unconscious and take you away to do the unspeakable."

Anora shuddered.

The image and words of Gaddard echoed in her mind. *You are my property! I'll have you as often as needed until I have a son!* His body weight was heavy upon her. The guttural helplessness washed through her.

"Anora?"

Anora returned to reality. "I apologize. What were you saying?"

"Your little crew found a place to stay?" Cloudia asked.

"Yes, my thanks again. For the food and the safety," Anora answered but closed her eyes. *I am a horrible human being. I subject my daughter to abuse but will not offer myself in her place. I am despicable.*

Cursing herself, Anora exited the kitchen and then the tavern proper, setting out for the shack they now called home. *I will tell Kiana she no longer needs to work at the whorehouse. I just need one more drink before that.* Anora changed her course.

CHAPTER THIRTY-SEVEN

LABOR

The smell of charred meat in the morning made Saudett's stomach turn. *If you could even call it meat.* The few Volkinn in their company had hunted one of the giant spiders Simon had encountered and were now roasting it on a spit. She watched Marah tear off one of the spider's curled legs and promptly chomp into it.

Hettra's mercy, I can't take it. Saudett stumbled away from the camp to vomit. Every morning, she awoke with a headache and nausea. She was also exhausted; her body was sore and weary, even after a night's rest. Blood vessels under her eyes had popped from regular vomiting and given a violet sheen to her brown complexion. *I wish this to be over. I want to go home and have our baby in peace.* The last thing she should do was trek through a swampland, readying to assault a settlement full of demons in some unknown Lân.

As she returned to the encampment, she saw Simon standing on a felled stump, watching as the Hasierans broke camp. As people bustled past him, they would bow and say, "First Otsoa." He would nod in answer, and they would continue on their way.

He sure is starting to take this leadership thing seriously, Saudett thought. "Husband," she said as she approached him.

His stern expression softened as he turned to look at her, then smiled brightly. "Good morning, my dear; the early worm gets the dirt, as they say!"

"I do not know who *they* are and why *they* say all these strange things," she answered, tilting her head questioningly. "Did you read a book of silly sayings or some such?"

"Nonsense, it is all through word of mouth. Everyone is saying these things!"

"I have yet to hear another person utter such absurdity."

"Pah!" he exclaimed, hopping down from the stump and embracing her. "Anyways, how is my pregnant wife? Having another bout of vertigo?"

"Your daughter is taking the piss out of me every morning."

"Daughter?" Simon arched a brow incredulously. "How do you know we will not have a charming little boy?"

"I've heard sons are easier to carry, and the symptoms are less overpowering."

"You've heard? Have you spoken to a physician? Or is this just some nonsense *they* made up?"

"You are winning my argument about your own little proverbs."

"I..." he trailed off, then blinked. "Hmm. I suppose you are correct."

"When am I not?" she smiled triumphantly and pinched his buttocks with a hint of force.

"Ouch!" he yelped, then pulled her close and kissed her.

Saudett felt the sudden need to vomit again as their lips touched and felt a heave rising within. Eyes wide, she pushed Simon away, and he toppled backward over the log. She fell to the ground and threw up what little was left.

They groaned in unison as they picked themselves off the damp, swampland floor, blinking at each other in a daze.

Simon let out a barking laugh, and Saudett could not help but join in.

"By the gods," Simon said, catching his breath. "I love you."

Saudett smiled even broader, if possible, her cheeks aching. "No, you," she whispered.

"Well," Simon stretched and nodded to himself. "Best get to work; we will reach Rawa by nightfall."

Simon strode off toward Gaelin, and Saudett packed their wool blankets into a bundle from where they had slept. The fabric was damp from the marshland and needed to be set out to dry near a fire. *Will we sleep tonight? Will we attack the town as soon as we arrive?* She shrugged and scanned about for Darkclaw Marah as the company began to move. She caught sight of the Volkinn moving swiftly to the head of the group.

Saudett jogged to catch up with them. "Marah," Saudett called out. "Hold up."

The Volkinn stopped and turned their head, crouching on all fours. "Lady Saudett?"

"Are you scouting ahead?"

"Aye."

"May I join you?"

"Ha," Marah snorted. "If you can keep up." The Volkinn immediately bounded ahead.

Saudett rushed after them. As they distanced themselves from the more considerable troop, Marah slowed and let Saudett catch up.

"One should not be jostling unborn cubs within them, Lady Saudett." Marah said as Saudett arrived, gesturing for her to walk and talk at the same time.

"Skrull's unholy balls." Saudett rolled her eyes. "You too? Everyone has an opinion. Who is carrying this child?"

"I am sure you know your body's limits, but it does not hurt to be careful. I smell the fatigue on you. And I see you retch in the mornings."

"I know. Everyone *wants* me to be careful."

"Yes," Marah nodded. "The pack cares for cub bearers; we bring food and let them rest instead of hunt."

Saudett raised her brow; she knew so little of the Volkinn. "You have females and males of your kind?" she questioned curiously.

"Of a sort," Marah gave a fang-toothed smile. "All Volkinn have male and female genitalia."

"Really?" Saudett answered, envisioning what that must look like. A tingle of voluptuous excitement prickled at her nerves.

"Your scent has changed, Lady Saudett." Marah leaned close to Saudett's neck and sniffed.

Marah's own warm aroma and proximity increased the sensation. *Fucks, I thought I was over this sort of thing. I only want Simon. But it is new and exhilarating. Maybe just one more time?*

"You smell nice too," Saudett tested.

Marah's head tilted questionably. "You are like the pack? You may have many mates?"

Saudett simply nodded in answer.

"This is good," Marah stood up from crouched, towering over Saudett. "I have scented your curiosity, which has piqued my own."

The Volkinn's waist was at Saudett's head height. *Oh, by Hettra's sweet tits, look at that.* She lifted a hand to gently touch.

Marah grabbed Saudett's wrists and pulled her off the ground. "We are still human enough to do this first." Darkclaw Marah's fur-covered lips pressed into Saudett's tenderly as Marah held Saudett up.

Saudett dangled like a doll on wires and returned Marah's caress, her yearning blazing within.

Marah gently released her as they heard the sounds of people catching up to them through the swamplands. With a grunt, Darkclaw Marah turned and continued.

Saudett was slightly taken aback. "What? You are just going to leave it at that?"

Marah's head turned with a mischievous grin as they stalked away. "I will continue tantalizing you as we travel and work you into a great frustration. Only when you can no longer bear it will we join together."

Saudett squirmed with anticipation. *By all the gods! Yes!*

Simon, your constant inappropriate thoughts toward your wife are beginning to grate on me. Gaelin's voice echoed in Simon's mind as he sought the Wayfarer from within the force of Hasierans readying to march.

Can you not simply get out of my head? Simon retorted.

"Certainly," Gaelin said aloud as Simon approached him. "If you give me the dagger."

Fury flamed within. "You were the one who bound this power to me! You wish for me to give it all up now?"

"Of course not. I need your help. I was objectively telling you the only way to get me out of your head is to return it to me."

"Hence ridding me of my power?"

Gaelin shrugged.

Simon felt a hint that the man was holding something back. He could sense and hear Gaelin's thoughts as well, but it was very random and far less than the constant intrusion by Gaelin into Simon's mind. "Fine, let us focus on the task at hand. What is the plan once we reach Rawa?"

"Ah yes, a plan; there is no such need. We merely terminate all of the Daanav. We cannot let a single one of those abominations escape."

That seems overly aggressive, Simon thought, then said, "Can we not just drive the Daanav out of Rawa?

"Drive them out?" Gaelin stood, three arms stiffening with clenched fists. "Can you imagine being the last of your kind? While the rest of your people are slaughtered by fiends? Or while your homeland was conquered and destroyed? Can you imagine if everyone you ever knew was dead? The Daanav ravaged the entire Heil Lân. They will do the same elsewhere."

"I—" Simon started, then stopped himself with a breath. "I suppose I cannot."

"No, you cannot." Gaelin stepped up to Simon. "They are evil incarnate; they will stop at nothing to root out and destroy all other worlds besides their own."

"Alright, I get the painting, as they say," Simon muttered, gazing about. *This Lân, the Moreas Lân, does not seem all that ravaged. Though it is already a very hostile environment, I imagine there is little to loot and plunder.*

They have enslaved the population of this Lân! Is that not warrant enough? Gaelin answered.

Hettra's tits, man, Simon rebuked. *Let me have my own thoughts.*

They were silent for a time.

Gaelin finally said after a sigh, "Ah yes, those weapons you created, they will be a mighty boon for our soldiers in this war. A godsend for the humans of the Earste Lân."

"A wonder you never shared such knowledge with us before?"

"The Wayfarers were sent to observe and study each Lân, to gain knowledge and learn the history of all peoples. We were not to interfere in the natural progression."

"Well, critical times call for critical actions."

"Correct," Gaelin nodded. "I suppose you could create the same type of weapon using our fire cantrip, could you not?"

Skrull's hell, why didn't I think of that?! Simon cleared his throat nonchalantly and muttered, "Of course, I was about to suggest that."

Gaelin gave him a stare, his pitch-black sclera around his grey iris and white pupils unsettling.

Simon gave a half-bow and went on to find the materials for such a thing. *It will be difficult to create while we march, but I'll remember to try it once we camp. If we make camp...*

It was dark when they caught sight of the Kadal village of Rawa. It was not a sprawling village, yet it included hundreds of treehouses stretching vertically along the wide tree trunks and throughout the canopy. Wood and rope bridges crisscrossed the spans between trees. Saudett crouched beside Darkclaw Marah as they peered through the bushes toward the town. A few faint glowing lights glimmered low here and there.

"The Daanav are difficult to see in the darkness," Marah whispered. "But I can smell them. This place reeks of them."

Saudett scanned the ground level of the town. It was hard to see in the blackness, but she thought it was rough with mossy mounds and divots of muck. She tried desperately to catch a glimpse of movement but saw nothing. "Hmm," she pondered aloud. "It is too quiet."

They heard Simon coming, crunching through a thicket of brambles.

"By Skrull's hairy balls, this swamp will be the death of me—"

"Quiet!" Marah and Saudett hissed at him simultaneously.

"Oh," Simon clamped a hand over his mouth. Then, he whispered through them, "My apologies. We are at Rawa, then?"

"Yes, Lord Builder," Marah replied.

"We cannot see any of the Daanav," Saudett added. "What should we do?"

"Good question," Simon muttered, then tilted his head as if to listen. "Gaelin suggests we move the troops in carefully. Creep up on them."

"It is doubtful we can take them by surprise," Marah snorted.

"Should battle ensue," Simon reassured. "I will shed some light on the situation."

"Better to act than to sit on our arses all night," Saudett nodded. "Let's spread the word to the line." She turned and crept off, finding Hasierans huddled along the tree line waiting for orders. She touched men's and women's shoulders along the line, gently ushering them toward Rawa. "Move up as quietly as you can. If the fighting starts ahead of you, join the charge."

As she reached the end of the line, she joined the last group and slid out of the safety of the tree line. The dark snake of Hasieran warriors skulked through the shadows to her right. Then, there was shouting from the center point of the line.

Immediately, a black-clawed hand burst from the murky ground, grasping around her ankle.

A blinding light exploded into existence above.

Daanav leaped and tore out of the mud all around them.

Pain shot through her leg as the clawed fingers dug into her and wrenched downward. A head and another arm appeared.

Saudett spun her spear to aim the tip down, pounding it in a two-handed thrust into the eye socket of the emerging Daanav.

The creature did not let go as it died.

Fucks.

A spiked hound pulled itself from the earth and yowled at her.

Fucks!

The hound raised its haunches and began to quiver.

Saudett pulled and hacked with her spear at the hand, death gripping her leg.

Ffft!

The needles sailed toward Saudett.

Darkclaw Marah appeared before her, the Volkinn's back toward the incoming missiles, shielding Saudett with their body. The Volkinn hissed in pain as the barbs buried into them. Marah smirked, trying to cover their agony, and tore the arm away from Saudett's ankle. Then the Volkinn sunk down and lay still.

"Marah!" Saudett screamed but had no time as more Daanav moved in on her.

A hulk lumbered toward her, flailing its greasy, oversized arm.

Saudett reeled back, the claws inches from her chest. Stabbing out with her spear as the attack slashed through the air before her. Her spear tip scored flesh in the beast's lower gut.

A hound rushed in to join the fray.

Barely twisting around the bulk of the hulk, Saudett brought the spear in a wide arch and caught the hound in the head with the shaft, stunning it for a breath. *Not long enough!*

The hulk turned with a massive backhand.

Saudett raised the spear shaft in defense, but the densely muscled arm snapped the spear in two and struck full force directly into her gut.

NO! THE BABY!

Saudett flew ten feet through the air and thudded into the muck, mud caking her face as she tried to breathe, the air driven from her lungs. Gasping, the darkness encroached on her vision.

Suddenly, the sound of razor-sharp air exploded above her. A handful of Hasierans came rushing to her aid, discharging the *Windan* crossbows at the creatures advancing to finish Saudett off.

She clutched at her stomach and lay still, unable to move.

Chapter Thirty-Eight

CONVERT

Hata looked about nervously as she walked through a never-ending horde of the creatures called the Children of Skaad, what she used to know as the Daanav. When Hata had climbed onto the road leading to the village of Oitilla, the beasts cried out as if to attack her, but she felt a pulse emanate from the obsidian gemstone. The Children of Skaad were immediately silent.

Excellent, my child. Trust in me. Trust in my will.

"Yes, Primus," Hata answered and wearily walked the winding mountain road through the column of creatures staring at her hungrily. Only paces away from ripping her apart. Yellow glowing eyes regarding her, all heads following her. Thousands of the black, greasy-haired hulks and hounds with bones jutting from their joints. There were grey hairless ape-like creatures, which she had never seen before. More rarely, there was the blood-red glow of the molten, almost stone-like humanoids, crackling and sanguine. She could smell all of their foul stenches and hear their ragged breathing.

Come to me.

"Yes, Primus," Hata murmured again as she straightened her back and walked ahead with resolution. *The God of creation is speaking to me. I will follow his plan.* She kept her eyes forward, away from the ravenous stares of the Children of Skaad.

Smoke billowed from the cave carved out of the mountain where the village of Oitilla resided. The unnatural smoke was not from the warm chimneys of the many homesteads filling the cavern or the smithies working blistering hot iron. It was from those massive, blue-flamed arthropods that spewed navy smoke into the air. Hata had to move aside as one lumbered up the road toward her, the creature extending its legs so it walked taller to fit along the narrow mountain pass. The humanoid torso was steering the larger bulbous body with its four arms and scythe-like upper limbs.

It snapped its head toward her as it caught sight of her, suddenly rearing up as if to attack her.

There was another vibrating pulse from the pendant around Hata's neck, and the creature froze. After a pause, it lumbered as fast as its unwieldy body could away from her and down the road.

Hata sighed in relief. *Thank you, Primus,* she prayed.

No need to fear, my child. I am with you.

She entered the town that she once called home. The frigid log homes were desolate and idle. It did not feel like home as the creatures huddled in the dark streets and inside the homesteads. Their milky yellow eyes glowed through windows at her. Hata strode past the massive longhouse where the village chief, Ota Vastaan, once lived and ruled the town. *This is where my father was defeated by Ota. Right here.*

She stopped before the longhouse, the gravel stone crunching under her hide-covered feet. Figures of warriors brandishing swords, spears, and axes looked down upon her from beside the massive doors and atop the eaves and rafters of the long house. The skull and spine of a person long dead hung from a rope above the doorway.

Agony flooded into Hata as the memories of that time returned. *Silja! Ota Vastaan had hanged his own mate by the neck on the rafters of his home.* Hata's first true love. She thrust the thought away. The *pain* of losing Silja, her childhood friend, turned beloved. *It hurts too much. It's why I never told Saudett about her. Go away! Get out of my head!*

Her mind went blank, and she found herself staring at the carved symbol of a hammer set before a mountain backdrop that was fashioned above the entrance to the massive building. *This is the depiction of Teras.* Her pride for her people bolstered within her. *I am Vouri, one of the people of Teras. I am of the mountain.*

AND WHO CREATED THE MOUNTAINS?!

Hata froze in fear as she atoned aloud, "You did, Lord Primus! You did!"

Do not forget it. As the voice echoed in Hata's mind, another tremor pulsated from her pendant. The creatures began moving toward her.

"Please, I'm sorry..."

The vibration lessened, and the Children of Skaad halted.

This god of the mountain is a false divinity, a conjuration of an archaic people.

"Primus, oh creator of all Lâns, you tell me my upbringing is false? That the strength and unity of the Vouri is nothing but a fairy tale?" Hata asked uncertainly. "Everything my parents taught me was a lie?"

Yes, my child. Remove your thoughts of any other god, and follow me.

Hata hesitated.

Again, the jewel pulsed, and again, the creatures advanced toward her.

"I will follow you!" she screamed, terror twisting in her gut. *What other choice do I have?*

The Children of Skaad stopped once again.

Hata fearfully continued through Oitilla toward the mines at the back of the cave town. Darkness engulfed her as she entered the tunnels, following the glowing yellow eyes of the Children of Skaad deeper into the earth. As she descended, she pushed away all thoughts of Teras and even her family from her mind. *There is only the Primus, and I will follow Him.*

CHAPTER THIRTY-NINE

TREPIDATION

Fucking hells. Jude looked out over the battlefield from atop a hill. *Why do I always find myself in these situations?* The same creatures he had fought against alongside the nomadic tribe were here. *The Daanav are here. Only a few days' ride from Nidhaut and from my little paradise. Skrull take us.*

"What are they?" Joanna Ohleoc asked, mounted on a creamy white mare with splotches of black all across it.

"Demons from Skrull's own hell," Jude answered flatly.

Two massive armies stretched out across what used to be farmers' fields. Waves of arrows and thundering catapults launched missiles into the sea of Daanav. The shining silver armor and heavily shielded soldiers glimmered as they held a battle line for leagues across. Blue-black smoke billowed over the forces of the Daanav. Hundreds of those giant, flaming insectoid-like creatures dotted the army of Daanav. Jude had slain one such beast with the help of his magic stones in the battle amid the Burning Sea. The darkness engulfed the horizon, and Jude saw a long line of creatures waiting to reinforce the front line. The column spiraled and disappeared into the woods beyond toward the northern mountains.

"What are we going to do?" Joanna question. "Go around?"

"That would add days to our journey," Jude sighed. "And it looks like these things are coming from exactly where we need to go." The dark clouds shrouded the distant mountain peaks.

"The bitch is as good as dead, then," Joanna smiled eerily. "The Alpha will understand."

"He is not a man who would be satisfied with lack of proof in completing this task."

"Well, what do you propose—"

Speaking of... Jude watched as a wave of Daanav exploded in gore on the front line. A single dark figure was moving out into the midst of the creatures. As the Daanav rushed toward him, wave upon wave of invisible force burst into them or ripped them in two.

A cavalry formation charged out behind him to engage the creatures.

The Alpha, Ebras Corb, massacred all enemies before him.

All along the line, other explosions of magic caught their sight. Lightning rained down and crackled out from a person flying above the din. A pool of water suddenly appeared and sucked in Daanav further down the line. Violet flame leaped and arched into the masses of Daanav.

"It appears the council and their acolytes have taken to the battle as well," Jude mumbled.

"Other council members have acolytes?" Joanna blurted in surprise.

"Indeed, though all of them have been through the Convent or Seminary Enclosures beforehand. Ebras takes anyone who displays their magic and shapes them to be pawns of the council."

"Truly?!" Joanna exclaimed.

"Of course," Jude said bluntly. *Many of the young people I have taken to Ebras now fight for the glory of Aurulan. I suppose it is not all terrible. Though I can't imagine what they've been through.*

"I am simply surprised he lets them go," Joanna exhaled disbelievingly. "I guess he is a better person than I thought. This must be why I love him so."

"No, girl," Jude rebuked. "He is a despicable human being, as am I. At any rate, we need to break through this and make haste to the mountains beyond."

"How?"

"By following the Alpha," Jude stated. "We trail close in his wake and pray to Qav he breaches the line. We ride for the safety of the forest beyond." He nodded to himself and decided. He spurred his horse into a full gallop down the hill without waiting for Joanna's reply. He heard her muffled cry of surprise, then her mares' hooves pounding down the knoll behind him.

Joanna gripped her reins, terrified. *I barely know how to ride a horse, let alone gallop through a battlefield!* Her buttocks painfully thumped against the hard saddle as she descended the hill. She managed then to fall in behind other armored soldiers on horseback. The Huntsman, Jude, was pulling ahead as he merged with the column.

"Wait for me!" she called, but it was drowned out by the thundering of hooves. Gritting her teeth, she focused on staying in the saddle and not losing sight of the Magnus Huntsman. Bumping and jostling into other riders, she was horrified to find that she had slowly been pushed out to the side of the cavalry charge, within reach of the abominations.

Sinewy, disproportionate limbs swung out at her. Long claws and fangs gnashed at her. She dared not relinquish the reins as she leaned her horse away from the attacks.

A horse and rider fell before her to one such assault, and her horse leaped over the fallen body.

Her head jolted, and she landed excruciatingly on the neck of the mare, grasping at the mane for dear life. As she righted herself, two massive beasts, blue flames burning along their backs, surged perpendicular to the cavalry. The first crashed into the column. Joanna caught a glimpse of Jude disappearing behind the destruction.

The other blue-flamed goliath was on a collision course directly at her.

"I will not die like this!" Joanna screamed and summoned a spear of spinning red flames. She hurled the spell into the bulk of the beast. An odd humanoid torso took the drilling flames to the chest with a screech. It pierced through and dug deep, and fire burst from the creature's opposite side as it crashed to the ground with a gaping, blistering hole bored through it.

A cheer erupted among the riders about her.

Joanna caught her breath; now riding with one hand, she continued casting javelins of flame and arching blades of white-hot molten at any creatures that came too close for comfort. Searing through black muscle and bone. For what felt like an eternity, she fought and rode. And suddenly, there were no more of the creatures before her. The cavalry had breached the line and turned in a wide arch to attack the flanks. Jude sat, looking relaxed, on his plain tan horse near the edge of the woods.

The Alpha hovered a foot off the ground, hands clasped behind his back, waiting impatiently.

Joanna trotted toward them, hands white-knuckling her reins, sweating and panting with magical exertion.

"You took far too long to get here," the Alpha snorted as she joined them. "You two should have been long into the mountains by now looking for that ginger bitch."

"Are you daft, man?" Jude grunted in return. "Have you looked around? The Daanav would have halted our progress or killed us, for that matter."

"The Daanav?" Ebras turned his gaze on the Huntsman inquisitively.

"I fought them in the desert when I first chased the ginger. Did I fail to mention that?"

"Indeed, you did," Ebras hissed, his face reddened. "You'd better tell me everything you know about them now!"

Joanna listened in awe as Jude made a brief report, unperturbed by Ebras's rising agitations.

"I learned the girl had gone out into the Burning Sea. She was trying to rescue someone captured by raiding nomadic bandits. Little did I know there was a war in the Burning Sea. I lured the nomads in and joined their ranks to find the girl. When we came to their little oasis in the desert, it was under siege by these same creatures." He waved a hand nonchalantly toward the multitude of Daanav. "I aided in the battle, for there was nothing else I could do. Luckily, the creatures went into disarray and were routed. After the clash, I pursued the girl and brought her directly to you," Jude exhaled. "Alpha, I'm surprised. You usually do not care for the details of my work."

"Except when an army of abominations threatens the entire Lân! All my work is threatened because you failed to mention this *small* detail." Ebras hissed cynically. "Even I can put my ambition aside when confronted with a greater threat."

Joanna kept silent, still wondering why this man, the Magnus Huntsman, addressed the Alpha so readily. *Does he not fear him?*

"At any rate, I need to return to the front," Ebras's stern glare turned to Joanna and softened...*unnaturally*. "You find that traitorous cardinal, my sweet, sweet raven. When you do, you will be handsomely rewarded. Now go!" Ebras launched into the air and backed out over the battle, raining down destruction as he did so.

"Thank the Primus, that's over," Joanna exhaled heavily.

"You did well out there," Jude nodded. "By Skrull's hairy balls, there is nothing like a quick riding lesson in the middle of battle, eh?" He stifled a laugh. "Come, we linger here far too long. Into the woods." He turned his horse and picked his way into the forest, away from the din of battle.

Joanna followed resignedly, then remembered what Jude had just said about a riding lesson. "What!?" she cried. "You knew I was a green rider and still galloped into that mess without me?!"

The bald-headed man turned his head and smiled, brushing his shining skull with a hand. "If you wish to be a Magnus Huntsman, it is best to learn by doing. Fucks, it is the only way to learn anything, in my opinion."

"I suppose it is better than sitting at a desk listening to the Proctor drone on about some herb or another," she said as she spurred her horse up alongside him.

"Are you not the Proctor now? You will be the one droning on."

Joanna blinked. *He is right.*

"Well, by Hettra's tits, don't get your head in a knot thinking about everything. Relax while you have a chance, empty your mind, and think of something you enjoy."

"Something I enjoy?" she asked hesitantly. *What is this man talking about? Meditation?*

"Yes, anything," Jude nodded, and his stare became distant. She barely heard him muttering something about his garden and his tea.

Something I enjoy? What do I find pleasure in?

The Alpha's face flashed in her mind.

I need to love him! I need to make him happy!

The memory of his fists beating against her exposed flesh as his face peered down at her in disgust.

How can I love him? What was I before all this?

They crept along under the cover of the woods. Surprisingly, no Daanav came across their path. All the while, Joanna thought and strived to find *something* she enjoyed. She came up with nothing. A tight knot formed in her chest and stomach. Her heart began to beat faster and faster. *What do I enjoy?!* She began to tremble, helplessness washing through her, a sickening feeling of impending doom.

"Girl?"

Joanna startled.

"You alright, girl?" Jude repeated.

The trembling and anxiety ceased. *When was the last time someone cared to ask me if I was alright?* "I'm alright, thank you."

He nodded and continued.

Joanna regarded him as she followed. This Huntsman had an air of irritability about him. It seemed he honestly detested the world and his occupation, yet he showed hints of kindness toward her. *He looked so pleased while we were having tea in his garden. Yet this is the man who captures innocent people and brings them to the abuse of the Alpha.*

Finally, Jude halted when darkness began to fall. "No fires tonight, no need to draw attention to ourselves," he said, swinging down from his saddle. "We will continue tomorrow, taking a wide berth of the road to the North Iron Belt. The creatures seem to be staying on that route." To her surprise, he offered her a hand to help her dismount.

Joanna felt her face flush as her eyes met his. *Hazel with a touch of jade.*

His own face reddened slightly, and he cleared his throat.

She quickly grasped the still outstretched hand, "My thanks, Huntsman."

"Call me Jude," he murmured, then turned and began unpacking some provisions and bed rolls.

"My thanks...Jude."

CHAPTER FORTY

BLOOD

Saudett was bleeding. *I've lost the baby.* She felt the blood between her legs. *I've killed our child.* Pain coursed through her gut in waves. *I did this.* Cramps twisted her abdominal muscles into knots. *I should not have been fighting.* She lay on her side in the mud, the sounds of battle distant. *What will Simon think? He will hate me for this. Resent me.* She slowly, *agonizingly*, began to crawl away from Rawa. *I can't let him know...*

Leoma. The orb of floating light shined over the battlefield.

Gebod. The spell caused Simon's voice to carry and echo out over his troops from the sky, where he floated, commanding a view of the battle.

Pandemonium ensued as the Daanav leaped from the murky ground in ambush. Many Hasierans were caught off guard and were cut down by the initial onslaught.

"Form up behind the Windan crossbows!" Simon shouted over the murk. At the same time, he launched strings of white-hot fire at the enemies below.

The Hasierans retreated, diving into the mud for cover as other men and women leveled and discharged the thrumming magical weapons at the assaulting Daanav.

Gaelin! The warriors need aid on the far-right side! Simon ordered in his mind.

Indeed, Gaelin answered dully.

Simon watched as the three-armed man flew to where Simon had indicated. Kogs's red mane swayed as he road Gaelin's shoulders into battle, shrieking and pointing down at the Daanav. As the lizard man pointed out, each Daanav, Gaelin, would unleash devastating destruction upon them.

Simon squinted at the explosive onslaught. Were those Hasierans stumbling from the smoke? He began to fly in that direction to discern better when he was suddenly hit with a dark wave of shadow. His vision went white as he slammed into a massive tree trunk, the wood indenting around him where his protective barrier held. Cracks spiderwebbed across the magical shield. Blinking in shock, he looked about, trying to perceive his attacker. He floated cautiously away from the tree.

It came from above this time.

The impact propelled Simon straight to the ground with an explosion of muddy earth and roots. The barrier crackled, then dimmed and fell apart. Simon lay on his back, the wind knocked out of him, gasping for air as he looked skyward.

A winged humanoid creature hovered above in a dark cloak and black studded armor. Violet-black energy fumed from its hands and the bat-like wings upon its back, obscuring it in a dark, eerie haze. It tilted its cloaked head and then rapidly dived toward him. Blistering energy crackled from an outstretched hand as it came.

Simon aimed two fingers. *"Bael cnytells!"* he screamed. The white fire streaked upward.

The wings of the flying person closed about it as it twirled deftly in the air, the flames narrowly sizzling past by inches.

"Oh fucks," Simon breathed as his mind reached for what to do. Then it came to him. *Dunnian!* He vanished and rolled.

The creature exploded into the ground where Simon had been a split second earlier. Violet-black fumes blasted in a shock wave about the person.

Simon got a good close look at it. *It is nearly human!* Silvery skin was barely visible on a smooth chin not concealed by the hood's shadow. This close, it was definitely a man.

It turned to where Simon was crouched.

He stayed as still as possible as his invisibility held.

The *man* spread his wings and smiled at Simon.

"Strangung!" Simon cried and rushed forward. His own speed startled him, the spell *Strangung* empowering his physical body. Still, the man heard or sensed him coming and put an arm up to block Simon's incoming hook.

Black teeth grimaced as the blow caused the winged man to stumble to the side.

"Windan!" Simon incanted.

The air sliced at the enemy, but he took a mighty leap, using a thundering flap of his wings to launch himself into the air.

"You use the egotistical Iban'mael sorcery well, *human*."

"So, it speaks," Simon answered derisively, letting his invisibility fade as the flying man seemed to stare directly at him.

"I have never witnessed one not of the Iban'mael themselves to wield those powers. The covetous beings are not known to share their knowledge with such lesser peoples."

"Well, after *you* destroyed the Heil Lân, they had little other option."

"The Heil Lân was our vengeance!"

"You think I believe a word you say?" Simon grunted incredulously. "Go back to Skaad and take these abominations with you."

"Are those your words or his?" The man nodded toward the right flank of the battle.

Simon's eyes widened in horror. *It burned.* The massive trees. The town. It was all ablaze. *No! Gaelin! What are you doing?!*

Gaelin's cackling laugh emanated in Simon's mind. *Yes! Yes! All of them must die!*

"Stop!" *Afléotan!* Simon began to ascend, but the winged man cut him off.

"This is where your power comes from, human. The wanton insatiability of the Iban'mael and their goals to dominate all Lâns."

"Get out of my way!" Simon brandished his dagger. *Byrnsweord,* he thought as he hurled through the air at the winged man.

"Hear me, human! The Children of Skaad and I, Trije-fan Skaad, will never submit!"

Simon's dagger grew with crimson flame as he met Trije-fan Skaad.

The man caught Simon's wrist in a violet-empowered hand.

The agony caused Simon to release the flaming bone dagger. It plummeted to the earth.

Trije-fan's other hand, palm flat, thudded into Simon's chest. The violet-black energy ate through Simon's shirt with a hiss and began melting his skin.

"Save the First!"

"Fire! Fire at will!"

A score of Windan blasts ripped through the air at Trije-fan Skaad. He immediately released Simon and retreated through the canopy above.

Pain engulfed Simon as he fell, limp and. lifeless, back to the blood-covered swamp of the Moreas Lân. Simon's own blood pooled around him. Simon heard one last word from Gaelin's contemptuous voice within as he fell into darkness.

Pitiful.

Chapter Forty-One

SLAVER

He is here! Kiana was astounded to see Zalias Ershya in a booth on the upper level of *La Maison du Paon. The fucking bastard is here!* Kiana peered through the private room's curtains; Zalias and two other men sat lounging on cushioned couches and chairs.

Zalias took a long swig of wine. "It has been months since those fools let me escape," he said with satisfaction. "I'm sure they have given up hope and returned to that god-forsaken desert."

"Your tale is far too fetched, good sir. I hardly deem it true," answered another man, Auru, slim, well-dressed, and well-groomed; wearing a fine cobalt suit. An ornate, jeweled hilt of a rapier sat on his belt. He sipped at his own wine and grimaced. "By the Primus, they must refine their beverage selection in this place."

"We don't come here for the wine, gah ha!" the last man bellowed. The man took up nearly half the room. Sinewy, hairy arms and chest near burst from a leather vest with a black beard and long black hair.

"I suppose not," the finely-dressed man said with a smirk.

"Speaking of which, where is our Personne?"

Kiana turned to leave just as someone came up behind her.

"Come now, Personne," the young male Personne said, placing a hand on her back to guide her toward the room. "First day on the second floor and having second thoughts? Are you afraid to serve three at once? Fear not. I am assigned to this room as well."

"I, uh..." Too late, she found herself gently guided through the curtains and into the room.

Skrull's hell, I need to call Brena to get this bastard. Kiana had gone overboard donning the makeup supplied by the *Paon,* so her face would not be easily recognized. *Qav's bad luck that these violet eyes may give me away!* She kept her head and gaze down, eyes nearly to slits as the men leered at her naked body eagerly.

"Ah yes, my favorite Personne!" the man in the cobalt blue suit greeted them, standing and taking the hand of her counterpart.

"Xamidian lass, too," the more enormous brute panted. "I have a thing for Xamidians! Gah ha!"

Kiana shivered but resolved herself. *I will hide myself by attending to this man's needs.* She sauntered toward him, legs crossing seductively, hips swaying. She put a finger to his chest and ran it down slowly toward his groin.

His eyes widened with lust. "Gah ha! Sorry, boss! This one's mine!"

"Skrull's hell," Zalias cursed. "Remy, you are supposed to be *my* bodyguard. Are you daft? What if I were to be attacked at this very moment?"

"Gah ha! Then I'll pry this little one off my cock and hurl her at the would-be attackers."

"Gods," the blue-clad man moaned, his fine trousers around his ankles as Personne kneeled. "You said so yourself. The seekers have given up the chase."

"This is my first day out of hiding. I am merely being cautious."

Remy turned Kiana and propped her on all fours on the couch he had been sitting on. Thankfully, away from Zalias. Kiana strained to listen as Remy used her. She heard Zalias muttering about finding new slaves to sell and the finely-dressed man responding through groans.

As suddenly and enthusiastically as he started, Remy finished.

Done already? Kiana withheld a snort. *What if I must service Zalias now?*

As if to answer the question, Remy said, "Gah ha! This one is Skrull-damned beautiful. I could not control myself." He promptly pushed her toward Zalias. "Have a go, boss, then I'll be ready for another!"

Kiana stumbled and turned to the entrance, "Pardon, sirs, I will use the latrine and be back with a friend. Another Xamidian woman, perhaps?"

"Yes, do it, woman." Remy nodded enthusiastically. "I will have you both! Gah ha ha!"

She began to leave.

"Wait," Zalias's voice stopped her in her tracks.

She turned back, head bowed, eyes nearly closed.

"You seem...familiar," Zalias studied her for a long moment. Just as his eyes widened in realization, Kiana bolted through the curtains.

"BRENA! HE IS HERE!" she yelled, stretching over the balcony and looking down on the communal floor.

Brena did not hesitate; she unsheathed her sword from where she stood on guard along the chamber wall and dashed for the stairs.

A hand gripped Kiana's shoulder painfully and twisted her around.

Remy lurched over her, an iron-studded cudgel raised to dash her brains out.

Kiana counter-pivoted his grip with a quick back bend, forcefully thudding a knee between his legs. Her hands gripped the balcony spindles as the cudgel shattered the banister above her head. She would have liked to vault him over the balcony to fall below, but he was too heavy.

"Kill her, you fool!" Zalias shrieked and came out of the curtained room. His eyes widened in horror as Brena crested the top of the stairs. "Never mind her; she is unarmed! Stop that one!" he squealed at Remy, pointing at Brena.

With a groan and one hand on his crotch, Remy moved to intercept Brena.

Brena's sword drove through the large man's gut. Even so, he managed to wrap his arms around the Vouri woman.

"G—ah ha!" he gurgled, pulling them both over the balcony railing.

"Brena!" Kiana called as the two plummeted into the crowd below.

The people stared up at the commotion. Some desperately scrambled out of the way as the bodies landed with a crash.

"Hells!" Kiana whirled about to see Zalias and the finely dressed man retreating along the balcony away from her. *I don't have time to check on Brena! He will escape!* Pain glanced at her bare foot as she kicked a partially broken spindle from the rail and wrenched it free. Then, she gave chase. *They make for the back stairway.*

As Zalias disappeared through the door leading down, the blue-clad man turned to greet her, rapier flicking into the air before him.

"You see," he sighed regretfully. "He pays me to protect him as well. I'm afraid you die here." He swiftly lunged forward with a stab.

Kiana turned the jab with her wooden spindle in a right-handed grip, simultaneously spinning her body along his sword arm as if to be dipped by a gentleman in an exquisite dance. Only in this dance her elbow collided with the side of his head.

He toppled to the ground.

"He doesn't pay you enough," Kiana grunted, picking up the dropped rapier and running down the stairs. She caught sight of Zalias's red turban just as it disappeared around a bend in the alley behind *La Maison du Paon*. Sprinting after him, she saw him again. *By the gods, he is surprisingly quick.* Luckily, he was running in the right direction. *I can force him toward our shack.* As Zalias retreated into another alley, Kiana took a turn, aiming to head him off and usher him toward their dwelling. She turned another corner.

At the exact moment, Zalias exited the alley in the street ahead of her. His eyes bulged as he saw her and spun about to flee in the opposite direction.

Perfect, she thought. *Not far now.* As she slowly gained on the man, her endurance outlasting the idle merchant, she angled her run so he would flee to the right.

Saliva dripped from Zalias's mouth as he turned his head to look back at her.

They turned another corner.

"BAAL!" Kiana screamed.

Baal was tossing a bundle of straw thatch to Kaplan, who waited on the roof of the small homestead. He turned at Kiana's shout and saw Zalias approaching him. With a roar, Baal thundered toward the slaver.

Kaplan leaped from the roof and rolled as he landed, sprinting after Baal.

Zalias shrieked in horror, halting in his tracks and looking about in a panic, trying to discern a new course.

Too late. Kiana careened her shoulder square into Zalias's back, and his neck jerked back as he crashed forward to the ground. She kicked him onto his back and pointed the razor-sharp rapier at his throat.

Baal came, reached down, and shook Zalias violently. "You die now!"

"Wait!" Kiana started.

"Jude Nelon!" Zalias babbled. "I know where he lives!"

Baal stopped rattling the man and held him up until Zalias's feet dangled in the air.

"Why would you help us now?" Kiana asked doubtfully. *He investigated the Huntsman even when he was in hiding from us.* "Why should we trust you this time?"

"I did it," Zalias panted, trying desperately to catch his breath. "I did it in case of this very scenario. In case you found me again."

"You will take us there immediately," Kiana commanded. "After that, we will figure out what to do with you. Kaplan, get a sturdy rope."

Kaplan nodded and quickly procured a rope from his construction materials. He then bound Zalias's hands behind his back and let a length of rope trail to hold on to the prisoner should he try and flee once again.

Kiana entered their little house to put on some clothes.

Anora lay on some straw bedding in the corner and groaned when Kiana cluttered about.

"Saudett, is that you?" her mother mumbled.

Of course, Saudett, your favored daughter. She's drunk again... Kiana ground her teeth, saying nothing, quietly dressing in a spare linen robe, and tied a maroon sash about her waist. Then, she returned to the others outside.

"We must stop by *La Maison du Paon* and gather Brena and my gear," Kiana said.

"Right, let's be off," Kaplan said. Then, he turned to Kiana. "Your mother will not be joining us?"

"She is...indisposed," Kiana murmured.

"Go. Now," Baal growled, shoving the Zalias forward.

Zalias stumbled, but the rope went taut. He hissed as his arms were pulled back painfully and muttered hateful comments as they returned to *La Maison du Paon.*

To Kiana's surprise, Brena met them on the way. Her sword arm dangled limply at her side. Under her other arm, she carried a bundle.

"Here are your things, Kiana," Brena said as she met them. "Dame was none too pleased, and we are no longer welcome at the establishment, as we are apparently *bad* for business."

"Vaimoni, you are wounded?" Baal asked in concern, handing Kaplan the reins of Zalias. Baal then went to his wife and gently inspected her arm.

Brena winced as he moved it slightly.

Baal gently undid her belt, loosening her chainmail; he managed to slip it down and off the tender arm. Their attention was brought to a massive swelling and redness on her upper arm.

"Bone is nearly through," Baal said.

"I'm fine," Brena grumbled, even as sweat beaded on her face.

Kaplan leaned in and studied it closer. "We need to set the bone and sling the arm. I can take her back to the house. I have some rudimentary supplies and have read a few medical tomes."

"We are going to be going up against a Magnus Huntsman," Kiana urged. "We need all the help we can get."

"We do not even know if he is home. Brena needs care now. You two could survey the place and report back. Then we can make a plan to act."

Skrull's hell, we don't have time for that! Kiana breathed deeply, composing herself, and finally exhaled, agreeing, "I suppose you are correct."

Kaplan nodded, returned the rope to Baal, and promptly led Brena away.

"Lead on," Kiana urged Baal.

With his signature toothy grin, Baal grunted and pushed Zalias into the streets of Nidhaut to search for the Magnus Huntsman.

CHAPTER FORTY-TWO

SKAAD

Nearly there, my child.

The Primus's voice led Hata deeper into the mines of Oitilla, even as scores of the beasts, the Children of Skaad, filed out of them. Their glowing eyes watched her fervently as she walked in their midst.

These mines were dark and unused. Hata's people, the Vouri, had long fled from them. Yet she could feel the earth, the shape of the tunnels in her mind. The dismal, cold lanterns sconced on the stone surface of the walls. Carts were full of lonely rubble and ores covered in dust. Pickaxes, shovels, and other tools were discarded hastily on the earth bed. As she walked, she desperately clung to the Primus's presence. *He can read my thoughts. I must have faith in His will. Everything up to this point is part of His plan.* Hata's faith held...until she saw the corpses. Bones were all that was left of them. Notches of gnawing teeth marks riddled the cartilage as they were piled high along the walls.

It was a feast.

"Is *this* your mercy, Primus?" Hata asked aloud.

The creature's heads turned at the sound of her voice.

She ignored them and trod on away from the piles of bones.

Had they surrendered peacefully, all such strife could have been avoided.

"Were they not fleeing from your Children in terror? Were they not cut down as they ran?"

No. My Children tried to negotiate peacefully. It is those fools, the Iban'mael Wayfarers, who murder before speaking.

"I don't know what an Iban'mael is, but *your* Children have murdered these people. My people!"

The pendant pulsated about her neck, and the trudging Children of Skaad halted and turned toward her.

You are testing my patience, my naive little child.

Hata bit back a retort as a storm conflicted within. *If the Primus is the creator and God of all things. Why, then, is He warring with other planes? And why yet has so much misery been wrought by His Children?*

ENOUGH!

The pendant trembled furiously, and the Children behind her moved in, taking up shrieks and yowls.

Hata moved away, and they continued closing.

The ones in front parted before her as she was forced through the tunnels. She was ushered down and down, deeper into the earth, by the growing horde of creatures falling in behind. They began to push her faster.

Fearing to look over her shoulder, Hata ran ever deeper.

Gnashing at her heels, the Children of Skaad screamed and wailed in her wake.

She turned a corner and tripped on a pile of bones. *No. Please stop, Primus!*

He did not answer.

Hata leaped to her feet and continued to flee as her earth sense guided her through the darkness. She could see the twisting tunnels in her mind's eye. *I have never been so far into the mines before, not even to visit Isä while he worked.* Suddenly, a red light appeared before her as the tunnel opened into a massive chamber. A black and green marbled archway, a hundred feet high and half as vast, shone with crimson radiance. Silhouettes appeared through the light. One of the blue-flamed creatures, accompanied by a throng of hounds, hulks, and grey beasts, emerged from the cloudy red portal. A slow trickle of water at their feet.

The Children stopped to regard her.

The pendant pulsed, and the creatures plodded away in another direction through an oversized tunnel.

Come to me.

The pendant seemed to pull under Hata's bear skin tunic toward the archway. She stopped just before the massive crimson clouds that rolled over the surface of the light. Water soaked through her hide-covered feet. She looked down to see the pendant necklace protruding against her furs. She removed the obsidian jeweled pendant and held it up, inspecting it. There was a faint violet, yet black aura about it. A flash of white moved within the obsidian darkness of the stone, like the shadow of a man. *How long had the Proctor worn this and not felt anything?*

It was difficult to reach her through that man's cage. She was to be my loyal follower and come into my service, as you are to do now in her stead, my sweet child. Simply step into my Lân.

Hata closed her eyes. *This is the Primus, the true God, and I must have faith!* She stepped through the red wall of mist before her. A twilight glow surrounded her as she stepped into knee-high water as far as the eye could see. A starry sky encompassed everything, reflecting off the rippling water. The archway loomed behind her, and five other massive gates formed a circle around an enormous hole. Water poured over the sides into blackness. *What is this place?*

There was a sudden *thunk* and a groaning screech, and then the air was filled with a constant sound of metal grinding against metal. To her astonishment, a massive, rusted iron platform slowly ascended from the hole before her. It came to a squealing halt as water flowed over it, hiding it beneath.

A man in pure white clothing stood at the center.

"Welcome to my Lân." Four arms opened in a hospitable gesture. "Welcome to the Skaad Lân."

"Where is the Primus?"

The man's fair face of light grey and perfectly smooth skin smiled, blackened teeth glistening. He lifted one hand. **You are looking at Him.**

The pendant tore from Hata's grip and soared into his outstretched hand. She felt the presence leave her. The gem emanated violet-black light around the man as he nonchalantly hung it about his neck.

"No, no, this cannot be!" Hata cried in disbelief. "You are just a man!"

"And a far more powerful one, now that you have brought me one of my shadow stones." The violet-black light grew around him, causing his lengthy white hair to glow. "Long have I hunted for these, strewn about the Lâns by those ingrates of the Heil Lân."

Fury began to boil within Hata. "If you are not the Primus, then I have no reason to be here!"

"Like I said." He casually raised another hand. "You are to serve me, Lord Hear-fan Skaad."

"I will not!" *There is still earth beneath this water!* She punched her fists together, then slammed both into the ground. An explosion of water and stone burst forth toward the man. The upward wave of rockslide engulfed him. A spear that had lain hidden in the water shot up into the air and landed point-down in front of one of the gates.

I need to escape and destroy this gate so no more of these creatures can come through. Hata glanced at the other five gates towering about her. *Could I destroy them all and seal this false god in his Lân?* Hata turned around and touched the cold black and green of the marble archway. She felt *nothing*. Her power could not see the gate. It was nonexistent to her earthen sense. She tried to push and pull against it with magic to no avail.

"These gates are warded against such futile efforts," the man's voice came to her from above.

She turned to see him floating above the rubble of her attack. "What would you have me do? You plan to conquer the Earste Lân! My home! Why would I ever serve you?"

"For vengeance, perhaps?" he idly rubbed his chin. "Vengeance upon that vile man who abused you. We can cleanse your world together and create it anew."

The platform behind began to creak and groan as it descended beneath the water again.

"But why? Why would you do this?"

"Utter boredom!" he boomed, followed by a malevolent laugh. "No, no, of course, I have genuine *reasons*. To prove that I can achieve what those ignorant fools of the Heil Lân squabbled about for millennia. To conquer all Lâns. Just as I did when I started with theirs."

I must do something! Hata's mind raced. *Keep him talking.* "I would be your equal?" she asked curiously as she took a step backward toward the portal.

"My Children await you on the other side should you walk through that door, girl."

The platform began to rise again, clunking and squealing. Accompanied by the monstrous cries of more of the Children of Skaad.

He keeps them down below; there must be a vast cavern there!

"No, you would not be my equal. And, of course, you would require some...*alterati ons.*"

The rusted platform stopped, and hundreds of Daanav ambled toward the gate Hata stood before.

"I'd move if I were you," the man said, a wicked grin on his face.

"I will not!" Hata spun about and stretched her hands above her. *If I cannot destroy the gate, I will close it for good! Teras aid me!* Hata sensed the mountain beyond the gate. *The entire mountain. Isä, lend me your strength!* She began to pull. She began to scream.

"Scua bael cnytells!" the man shouted behind her.

A black string of flame struck her in the right shoulder. It pierced through her and sizzled into the water at her knees. Pain like none she had ever felt spread through her entire body.

Äiti, lend me your heart!

The ground began to quake.

Dust and debris began to spew from the gate around her, obscuring her vision. Hata formed a dome of protective earth about her as she pulled and strained against the mountain. The earthquake rumbled and echoed into the Skaad Lân, and the ground shook violently.

"I AM...THE SUNSTONE!" Hata Vasara *ripped* the mountain down.

CHAPTER FORTY-THREE

NEVER

Simon awoke to the face of a crocodile looming over him, its stubby scaled arms smothering brown muck on his chest.

"Skrull's boiling balls," he exclaimed. "What are you doing?!"

Its maw opened a gap, its neck bulged and vibrated; then a cavernous croak emerged. It continued to scoop the feces-like mixture out of a clay bowl and onto his chest. A stench wafted over him.

"Hettra's tits!" he gagged. "Is this made out of shit?"

"Quraanjo defecates. We gather and mix with geed tree sap and chewed Carro web." Kogs's face came into view. "Make monkey-warlock all better!"

There *was* a relieving feeling to the skin where the flying man's magic had burned Simon's chest.

The crocodile lizard croaked and purred, rubbing its head against Kogs.

"There now, my Gaks," Kogs hummed affectionately. "I am home now."

Gaks stood double the size of Kogs, yet still shorter than a man, with a large head and broad shoulders on thick reptilian limbs. Clothed in the same leafy garments as Kogs.

"By all the gods," Simon sighed. "Sir Kogs, please tell me what happened. The flying man? Gaelin?!"

"Three-arms chases the winged man. He killed all the masters."

"He was burning the village!"

"Yes, yes, but can be rebuilt. Kogs and his Gaks go home to farm anyway."

"What about my people and the rest of the Kadal," Simon urged. He strained to sit up, realizing he was inside the trunk of a massive tree.

Gaks croaked and pushed him back down, shaking his broad head.

"I do not know about the humans," Kogs answered. "But most of the Kadal were saved from the fires. Rest now, warlock friend. We go now." With that, Kogs mounted Gaks's shoulders, and they disappeared through a vine-covered entrance.

Simon lay for a long while, tingling itchiness beneath the Kadal medicine on his chest. *Gaelin is unhinged. Where did that fanatic get off to?* He half expected Gaelin's reply, but nothing came. A sinking feeling suddenly turned in Simon's stomach. *Where is the dagger?* He pushed himself up, the drying mixture on his chest cracking as he did so. "The dagger! Where is it?"

A Hasieran rushed into the room at Simon's commotion. "First Otsoa, what's wrong?"

"My dagger. Where is it? Did I lose it on the battlefield?"

"You had no weapons when we came to your aid," the man answered.

"*Fucks!*" Simon hissed and got to his feet.

"First Otsoa, you need rest—"

"Shut up and help me. Bring me to where you found me immediately."

The nomadic man reluctantly put an arm under Simon's shoulder and led him out of the tree trunk. Smoke dwindled in the air as heavy rain battled against the swampland canopy far above. The black muck that was the corpses of the Daanav mixed with the swamp's mud seamlessly. The charred corpses, on the other hand, did not. Most of the burnt bodies were human, riddling the area.

"Hettra's mercy," Simon breathed. "How many died because of him?"

"The Wayfarer did this," the man aiding him said. "He cared not for friend or foe, only that the Daanav died at his hand."

"I am responsible for this. I let Gaelin join us and let him take matters into his own hands."

"Nay, First," the man whispered. "You did not hold the blade that cut us."

The blade! Simon urged the man onward.

"Here we are," the man said. "This is where we came to you after the winged man retreated."

"Quickly, help me look for my white dagger around here. I must have dropped it."

"A white dagger?"

"Yes, yes, a white one. Come now—"

"The Wayfarer took it."

Simon clenched his teeth. "Gaelin."

The man nodded.

Simon's fists whitened as he held back a scream. He closed his eyes and took a deep breath. *I suppose it's all over, then.* He let himself come to a seat, leaning against a scorched, crooked log. *I can't do anything about it. Fucks to Gaelin and that flying bastard. What did he call them again, the Children of Skaad? I never wanted to be a part of all this in the first place. Perhaps, now...Saudett and I can return home and raise our child.* Exhaustion overwhelmed him, and he could not open his eyes. "Where is that wife of mine?" he murmured as he fell asleep.

Saudett crawled into a thicket to rest. Bone-weary, she slowly began pulling out the large thorns stuck into her shoulders from pushing through the bushes. It had been a few days since the battle, and she had wandered aimlessly away, praying to the Primus she would find the way back home. The bleeding had stopped, but there was still pain. She had discharged a lot of blood and tissue. There was no doubt in her mind that the child was gone.

I can't bear the thought of Simon's face if I tell him I have lost our child. That it's all my fault. She *never* wanted to see him again. *I will find my mother, and we will run away and hide from the world.*

Her stomach groaned in hunger. She plucked some wet leaves from the bush above her and began to chew them. *Naurr and the men will be at the river. They can lead me home. I will rest and then find the river...* Saudett's thoughts trailed as she closed her eyes. *I never want to see him again...*

Kiana watched as Baal gave the door a mighty kick, and it crashed inward.

A well-dressed Tulu man stood awaiting them, a refined jeweled cane in one hand. Grey curly hair peeking out from a tilted beret. He smiled welcomingly. "Guests of Mister

Nelon must make an appointment!" He sprung over the door toward them, and the cane cracked against Baal's skull.

Baal laughed, grabbed the well-dressed man by the arms, and lurched him into the air. "Where is Hunter Man?"

The man's eyes widened in terror. "I don't know what you speak of. This is the home of Mister Nelon, a humble herbalist."

Kiana pushed Zalias through the opening of the fine home. They had seen a walled fence surrounding the sides and back of the large homestead, and many plants could be spotted growing up the sharp pickets along the top of the wall.

"You mean Magnus Huntsman Jude Nelon?" Kiana retorted. "Cut to the chase and tell us where he is."

"His business is private. He does not confide in his humble steward and gardener."

"His humble steward who is ready to protect his master's home by attacking a man like this?" Kiana slapped Baal's massive bicep. "Only the Vouri make men like this."

Baal turned his toothy grin at her.

"Now, tell us where Jude Nelon is."

"The North Iron Belt!" the man sputtered.

Baal dropped the man suddenly and muttered, "She went home. My tytär went home."

"Well, that was far simpler than expected," Zalias rasped. "Now you can let me go. As was our deal."

"Hmm," Kiana purred, putting a finger to her lips. "Did I not hear you say you were coming out of retirement back at the *Paon?*"

"Of course not! I am finished with such nasty business. I swear on the Primus!"

Baal growled and moved closer to Zalias.

"Wait, friend Baal," Kiana said. She got within inches of the merchant's face and hissed her hatred to him. "You will *never* again rape and enslave anyone." She gripped the man by the head and dragged his throat across her blade.

"By all the fucking gods," Jude Nelon muttered in astonishment. "There should be a mountain right there."

"I've never seen anything like it!" Joanna babbled in disbelief. "How is this possible?"

The air was finally clearing from the dust, and all that was left of the mountain village of the Vouri was a crater of rubble.

EPILOGUE

Hata emerged from beneath the rubble, digging with her mind. She looked about, observing for signs of the being, Hear-fan Skaad. He was nowhere to be seen. The Children of Skaad had been crushed under the explosion of earth along with him. Hata then crept through the dust and stone spewing from the archway to the Earste Lân.

Hata circled the depthless hole, heading for the nearest glowing portal. She grasped the spear jutting out of the water, and without a second glance back, she plunged through the closest doorway and into another Lân...

FREE NOVELLA

Greetings,

Thank you for reading. I hope you enjoyed this story and hope you wish to follow the Sunstone Saga of Hata, Saudett, Simon, and their companions on their journey into new Lân's. If so, please sign up for my reader group newsletter. I send out a monthly update on my progress on upcoming books in the series and any special offers or events I may be attending.

If you sign up for my newsletter, you will receive a **digital** copy of my novella *Caste of the Mountain*. A prequel story following Baal, Brena, and Hata before the events of *The Shepherds of the Sunstone*.

Click HERE to sign up and receive your FREE copy! Or go to www.nicolinodel.com

THE SUNSTONE SAGA

Book One - The Shepherds of the Sunstone

Book Two – The Children of Skaad

Book Three - The Wayfarers War

PREQUELS

Prequel One – Caste of the Mountain

REVIEWS

As an independent or self-published author, marketing and promoting my business is ultimately out of my pocket. One of the most incredible things a reader can do to help with this is to leave a review. This will help other readers interested in buying my book and give me more visibility in the marketplace.

If you liked The Children of Skaad, please leave me a review on the store where you purchased the book.

Thank you for your support!

EARLY ACCESS

If you wish to support me further and are interested in reading the next book in the series before anyone else, consider subscribing to me at ReamStories. You can read the first chapter of the next book for FREE by following me on REAM or subscribe for access to the entire book or weekly release.

Thank you for your support,

Nicolin Odel

About the Author

Nicolin lives in the Greater Toronto Area with his wife and two daughters, writing books, gardening, or shoveling snow.

For more information:

www.nicolinodel.com